THE

BEAST LORD

BOOK TWO

OF THE GOD-SLAYER
CHRONICLES

THE BEAST LORD

Book Two
of the God-Slayer Chronicles

ACKNOWLEDGEMENTS

To F. J. G. for putting up with me these many years. Thank you.

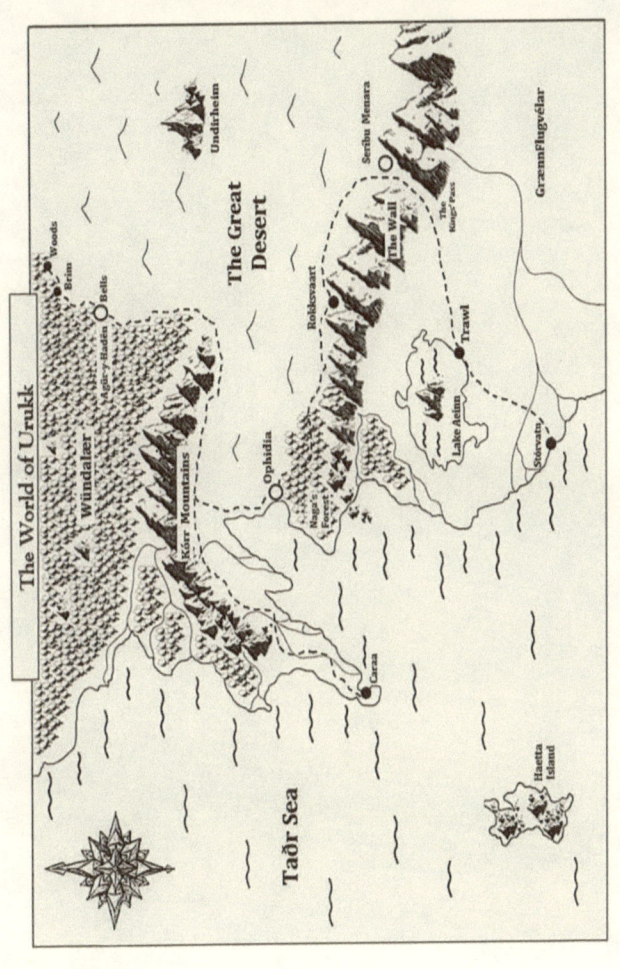

The World of Urulk

Taðr Sea

Wündaler

Kärr Mountains

The Great
Desert

The Wall

Woods
Brim
Belu
Agley-Raðdin

Undirheim

Ophidia

Naga's
Forest

Carsa

Haetta
Island

Robkvart

Seiðu Menra

The
Sluga Pass

Trawl

Lake Aeim

Sölevam

Grænnflugvélar

Prologue

Life had been hard for the people living in the human dwellings north of the Great Desert for as long as they could remember. Trapped between the ever-encroaching golden sands and the darkness within Wündalær, the few, small villages at the edge of the realm struggled for survival. Summers, blistering-hot, and winters, long and cold, repeatedly tried to break the will of those few thousand souls who called this place their home. But despite the constant threat of famine or the danger of Beasts prowling within their walls, the few humans clung to life. Such was their existence, relentlessly challenged, but also filled with the happiness of their simple life. The latter always seemed to thrive in hardship-riddled places, like specks of light born out of pure darkness, like those bright flowers of the sands.

Isolated within strong walls of stone and stronger even fear, the humans witnessed the desert grow outside their gates. They watched the foulest creatures known to man descend from deep within the forest and prayed their walls would hold so that no sands, nor Beasts could find their way inside their strongholds.

Yet, many found their end starved to death or frozen, while others were swallowed by the desert's sands. But some got dragged inside their graves by fangs and paws. Aerö was one of them.

Taken by the dreaded Hounds, Aerö awoke inside a cave terrified and hurt, only to find himself saved by the Healer Velas. But despite the old man's promises of help, Aerö soon realised that he could not go back to Bells.

He was the son of Eldur, an Elemental, and as much as he wished he was like him, filled with knowledge and power, when his powers flared and levelled the village of Woods, Aerö understood the curse that came with them. He could not go home until he could control his father's flame.

Together with Velas, his father's crimson pendulum, and a tattered map, Aerö began his long journey to the City of Sands where the Healer promised that the King will teach him how to control his gifts.

While the two travelled south, no stone was left unturned in Bells by its leader Petra. And once word of the destruction of Woods reached Bells, the one solution was agreed by all. They would abandon their homes, shed their former lives, and join with the survivors of Brim and Woods. They would call themselves Turmenn, travellers, and seek their much-desired safety further south, away from Beasts and Sorcerers alike.

But unbeknown to them, death awaited both Aerö and the Turmenn in their perilous journeys they had embarked on.

Torn between returning to his home or learning to command his skills, Aerö is persuaded by Velas to ask for help the only one who had the strength to offer it. The Sorcerers' King. Naively, Aerö puts his trust in Velas, not knowing that the Healer had a plan of his own for him.

When Aerö saw the gory remnants left behind from a fight involving the Turmenn, and learns from Velas that the Beasts were to blame, he starts on a journey of revenge, not self-discovery. But Velas had lied to him. No Beasts had harmed his friends, but the King and Queen's High Counsellor under their command.

Misguided, Aerö is taken to the Sorcerers 'capital city, not for his salvation, but to meet his end. The King and Queen plan to use him as their weapon in Urukk's cleansing of all Beasts and humans. Blinded by hatred and poisoned by Velas's venomous words, Aerö walks willingly into a trap set before him since his foretold birth millennia ago.

But plans that old work rarely as expected.

Underestimated by the King and Queen, Aerö escapes their trap and heads for Undirheim, the Beasts' Lair, to avenge his friends. There, spurred by the recent finding of their long-sought "weapon", the King and Queen had sent their armies to exterminate them all.

Trapped deep within Undirheim's tunnels, Aerö learns the truth about his foretold birth, about his origin, and most of all about the parents he had never known. Now, Aerö must choose: to fight and find certain death or flee and live on the run. The King and Queen will not so easily be frightened, let alone defeated.

The Doing and Undoing of a King

Time ruled for an eternity in Urukk and the lands beyond; ruled by a savage, merciless tyrant whose only aim was to remain in power. Untold seasons came and went, and still, no soul dared challenge its aeons-long control over all that breathed beneath its tired eye.

Time had ruled too long, too many moons had passed, too many lives had come to be and vanished, and still time swayed both life and death as it saw fit. But as generations popped into existence and then turned to dust, only to fuel time's endless cycle, some turned their faces to their Gods, demanding to be left to rule themselves.

Such were the times before the Order, before the magic blood ran through human veins, before the First Three.

They sprung from nowhere, as no records spoke of things like those they wielded; some deemed them demons, some gifts to men from the Gods, while others saw them Gods themselves. The three that raised their heads above all others were much more than human, more than Beast, more than anything and anyone who dared stand tall before time's ever-present sight. They commanded flames and flesh and Beasts. They called themselves sorcerers.

The first of them was Arnleaf Uriel, a young man shunned by his own village because he summoned and controlled the fiercest flames. The tongues of fire leapt and licked at his command, obeyed his every order. His own family feared him for what he could do, they hated him for what he was.

The second one was Valdis Ezelle, a girl whose touch mended both flesh and bones, sealed gaping wounds and broken hearts. She, like Arnleaf, had inherited the purest complexion. Like graceful ghosts, they moved about, white-skinned, white-haired, imbued with the Gods' power. Shunned by the hatred harboured by their own kind, they found each other and found love. Two perfect beings, two halves of the same whole.

And then was Skeggor Skalidur, the last of the First Three. A monster of a man. If the first two were pure and noble, Skeggor had the appearance of a beast from the distant lands. Broad and tall he loomed over Valdis and Arnleaf's frail frames, dark-haired and bearded. His body was muscled; his arms like tree trunks. He was strong-willed to match the rest of him. His skills, however, were not seen as having been sent by the Gods, but rather by the Demons. Skeggor could shed his human form and take that of a bear. He was a Beast himself. He hunted, preyed, and killed as he saw fit.

So it was for them to meet. Had it been Narrử, had it been fate or chance, what started as a need to defend themselves against the very ones that birthed them, Arnleaf, Valdis, and Skeggor began to build what would be known throughout the realm as the Order.

Years passed, yet time seemed unable to turn their bodies useless as it had their fathers', powerless to touch them, change them, kill them. Narrư had indeed granted their wish to have no master. But as humans came to be, loud and purple, and then die quiet and white; their whole existence but a shift of state, a change in colour, more humans awakened with skills like those of the First Three. They were few, they were the future. They were Sorcerers.

And as the First Three sought to forge their own family, others sought them too. Sorcerers like them; scared and spurned by their loved ones, searched to find a place where they belonged.

It was then, when ever-growing numbers of sorcerers travelled from the corners of the realm to meet the legendary Arnleaf Uriel, Valdis Ezelle, and Skeggor Skalidur that the three understood their purpose, the mission bestowed upon them by the very Gods. They were to unite and reign above all the sorcerers as humans in Urukk. The future of the realm was theirs to shape.

Deep in the Wall, they chose a place to gather and ignite the birth of the world's new Order, guarded by sky-high naked cliffs and Wündalær. There, in the heart of the Wall, the three began to build a new home for themselves and all those who now followed them. Out of rock and ash, Seribu Menara rose its many pointy roofs, a forest of towers, a marvel to behold, a new Capital for all those who lived in Urukk to be proud of.

At first, the humans wished no contact with the rising new power, but with ever-growing numbers of sorcerers awakening amongst them, they simply had no choice. They could no longer hope their ignorance would save them. Their fear of losing rulership of Urukk came to be, and there was nothing they could do about it. Since the elder times when men crossed the Wall from the plains

7

beyond and wove paths through Wündalær, no one dared challenge their rule over the land. Until now. Angry and frightened, the many humans who populated Urukk saw with their own eyes the end of their age. But despite their fear and hatred towards the sorcerers, they bore boys and girls through which the Gods' blood ran.

Whole generations turned from wish, to flesh, to matter while the sorcerers lived on. Their gifted sons and daughters tried in vain to give their human parents breaths as many as their own, but in the end, all they could do was offer them a better life, though short. With their fleeting existence no longer troubled by disease and war, by hunger and pain, the humans accepted their generous brothers as their rulers, some even as their Gods.

The First Three knew that the humans' hearts had been easily won. They wielded the greatest weapon against them; stronger than their spells, more potent than their potions; they had the power of time. The sorcerers had plenty of it and put it to great use while waiting for the humans' hatred and distrust to die with them.

However, Skeggor Skalidur had greater plans for Urukk. He not only wished for all the sorcerers and humans to thrive in peace, but also the Beasts that roamed the realm. He could have the power to reason with them and wanted to unite them under his own banner.

But Arnleaf Uriel and Valdis Ezelle did not agree with him. They saw themselves as the Gods' true children and believed only their kind deserved to rule in Urukk. What started as an unbreakable bond between the First three, an unbridgeable schism began to tear them apart.

The divide soon spread throughout the Order and the followers the First Three each commanded. Arnleaf called his Elementals, sorcerers who wielded crippling spells. They used rings and gems to store their might. They were white-haired; they were all flawless.

Just as pure as the Elementals, Valdis'Healers bore their white heads proudly. However, their persistent search for the most compelling potions made them mark their perfect skin with runes of power. They bore their marks with pride as proof of their vast knowledge and the sacrifice of its pursuit.

Unlike Arnleaf and Valdis, unlike all the Elementals and the Healers, the Beasts and Skeggor followers, the Beast Lords, did not share their perfect complexion nor their silver hair. In the eyes of the First Two, that made them lesser.

With the Order governed by the First Two, Skeggor travelled far and wide in search of Beasts and Beast Lords. But when he returned to Seribu Menara to take his place among Arnleaf and Valdis, an army of creatures such the world had never seen arrived with him.

The Capital opened its gates before them, welcoming them in its heart; the streets and bridges cluttered with the many sorcerers waiting to greet them. Many golden towers rose from the paved roads, tall and slender, pointing at heavens only birds dared touch. Many more than Skeggor Skalidur remembered, the giant spears of rock hugged the monstrous pit that yawned hungrily from their midst. A bottomless crater, a patch of darkness, a blemish of disease which not even the sorcerers managed to close or heal.

9

Creatures large and small returned with Skeggor Skalidur from his years-long endeavour, some fierce and bloodthirsty brutes while others, conscious entities that time forgot. Among them were the Feonds, giant creatures from beyond the edges of the realm.

Gifts and riches fit for Gods the Beasts, they brought with them; things of power, things of gold to offer to the many who had welcomed them in their new home. But no gift compared with what the Feonds wished to give.

They gathered deep in the heart of Seribu Menara; hundreds of monstrous bodies surrounding the bottomless pit that scarred the city. What would have taken sorcerers and humans decades to create, the Feonds built the highest tower known to man, a home fit for their new rulers. From deep within the gaping hole, the Ivory Tower stretched upwards for what looked like leagues, a pale, stupendous construction that defied the very rules of the world. A wall encircled the pit and the Ivory Tower, a barrier for the three who now commanded the entity of Urukk to rest behind; while radiating bridges fixed in place the spire and wall as one. A throne room from which the three could see the corners of the realm was adorned at the very top of the tower, a room fit for Kings and Queens. Those were their gifts, the most prodigious of presents.

The last to present their offering to their new lords, were the magnificent Oaks. Three ancient beings made of purest gold yet breathing and alive who shed away their millennia-old existence to guard the imposing spire and the three who occupied its highest chamber.

But not all were impressed by Skeggor's grandiose return. Many feared the countless Beasts that prowled the streets at night, or the Beast Lords and their fanged familiars who lived among them. Of them all, Arnleaf and Valdis were the most displeased with how their perfect Order now provided sanctuary for the creatures they did not trust, nor wanted to take part in their absolute creation.

But the sorcerers had spoken, and the Beasts bowed low before their King. Despite not having the other two's perfection, Skeggor Skalidur had the respect of all three clans and that of the humans; something Arnleaf and Valdis never wished nor had.

As years passed, each of the three houses enlarged, the Elementals, the Healers, and the Beast Lords; each of the First Three commanding thousands under their own banner. But envy seeded deep within Arnleaf and Valdis's heart of hearts and spread throughout their bodies like a vine, turning them weary of humans and Skeggor's impure kind.

The whole Capital gathered before the three golden Oaks at the entrance to the Inner City to celebrate their new King. Skeggor Skalidur walked before his suite of a thousand Beasts, threading slowly, carefully on the paved road that lead to his throne. Spells burned the clear welkin, multicoloured and bright. Tongues of fire, ice crystals, and mineral dust bonded together to create a spectacle of light and colour for the newly chosen ruler. Fists and daggers, swords and flowers flung in the air as Skeggor walked, spreading like a glade in bloom between the forest of pale towers.

Feonds, stags, Hounds, and bears bowed before he who had brought them together. Humans, sorcerers, and creatures, the kind no one had seen before, paved the way to the Ivory Tower. It was magnificent to see all that breathed in Urukk come together to honour their King.

Arnleaf, Valdis, and Skeggor had created the Order to help those few who, spurned by their own parents, were in need of a new home; a place to learn. But many more than they expected awakened powers like their own.

It was then that Arnleaf and Valdis suggested that each of them should build a city of their own, for their own kind. Elementals to live with Elementals, Healers with Healers and Beast Lords with their Beasts. This was to be the beginning of the end of peaceful prosperity between sorcerers, humans and Beasts. That was precisely what Arnleaf and Valdis had planned since Skeggor's return.

Jealous of Skeggor's tower and throne, Arnleaf chose Seribu Menara as the Elementals' home. The spot that had once been his village, his home, now marked the place where the Capital rose to the heavens. There, under the many spires, roads and bridges, lay the graves of his bloodline. It was also there, in the heart of the Wall where the mountain's rare, black rock was being chiselled in their coloured gems. Arnleaf Uriel had finally taken his fair city back. He was now the King.

Valdis also took her kind to the place of her own birth. On the shores of the Taðr Sea, from the ashes of her village, Ophidia greeted all those who called themselves Healers. She, like her much-beloved Arnleaf, had become a Queen among her people.

For *Skeggor Skalidur*, the choice had also been a simple one. Deep within *Wündalær*, far away from where *Arnleaf* and *Valdis* gathered and trained their clans, he chose the place to be his home. A city just as magnificent and breathtaking as the Capital itself, *Agür-y-Hadën* provided shelter to humans, Beast Lords, and their Beasts alike.

If the Feonds had raised the Capital's' Ivory Tower as a gift to their new rulers, in *Agür-y-Hadën*, they built halls and palaces, homes and walls for them all to enjoy. The humans called it Eden and believed it to be of greater beauty than *Seribu Menara* itself; a city *Narrǔ* himself would call home if he were to ever return in *Urukk* in a mortal's form.

Giant halls, big enough for Feonds to walk through, rose above the ancient trees' bright canopy; their round, protruding, domes glistening like multicoloured, gem-encrusted hills. Fluid spires wound organically as if they had grown not had been built, the skill with which the Feonds shaped *Wündalær* to make the Beast Lords' home, outmatched that of even the most gifted of sorcerers. Just as they did in *Seribu Menara*, the Feonds placed in the centre of the newly constructed city a tower like no other. Much smaller than the Ivory Tower, but just as striking, a golden spire rose towards the skies. At the top, however, instead of a throne room filled with riches for the King to revel in, twelve black bells swayed tickled by the winds; their enchanting music to drift throughout the busy city and delight them all.

A thousand years passed since the First Three had built the Order, ten centuries in which all humans, sorcerers, and Beasts prospered in peace. It was then that *Arnleaf Uriel* and *Valdis*

13

Ezelle decided to celebrate the strong relationship between all races. Large festivities were thrown throughout Urukk, both Ophidia and Agür-y-Hadën honouring their founding fathers days on end.

But nothing compared with the celebrations taking place in the Capital. Seribu Menara lay adorned with the coloured banners of the three houses; crests of golden dragons, silver serpents, and burnt-black bears flapping from the highest towers, while the streets and bridges awaited patiently covered in flowers. Masses gathered from the Capital's high gates all the way to the Inner City; the roads packed with the many who awaited Skeggor Skalidur's return. Many years had passed since the First Beast Lord had been seen roaming the streets of the Capital and every soul clustered together to witness it.

When the colossal gates of Seribu Menara opened to let in their crowned King, the cheers of those gathered could be heard through the realm.

Slowly, Skeggor walked, followed by Beasts and Beast Lords between the neatly ranked Elementals and Healers on either side of the straight road that cut the city in two, until he reached the golden Oaks at the entrance to the Inner City. There, dressed in their finest robes, and looking just as young as when they had last seen each other, Valdis Ezelle and Arnleaf Uriel waited to greet their long-gone brother and friend.

But what Valdis, Arnleaf and their gathered armies had in mind was as far from celebrating Skeggor as the sun above was from the city teeming with sorcerers below.

For a thousand years, Valdis and Arnleaf had hated Skeggor for what he was and for his affection for humans. They despised him greatly for what he had done to their beautiful Order; allowing both humans and Beasts to live among them in their home.

So when Skeggor reached the Inner City's gates, and the three great Oaks chanted their greeting, Valdis and Arnleaf revealed their hand.

All Elementals and Healers closed on Skeggor and his followers at their Masters' command, trapping Urukk's chosen King in their midst.

Beasts growled, frightened, as Skeggor, and his kind readied themselves for battle. No matter how hard Skeggor tried to make the other two see sense, they no longer saw him or the Beasts as part of their home and Order. They wanted them gone; slaughtered and burned.

The three golden Oaks wept from their rooted spot, begging Valdis and Arnleaf to spare he who had brought them there, and banish them instead. But the two knew that as long as Skeggor lived, his rage would live and that his kind would not find rest until their betrayal was avenged. At Arnleaf's and Valdis's command, the Elementals and Healers began their attack against the Third as did their mindless followers sent to Agür-y-Hadën. The two had planned this well. After the day was gone, so would be all the Beasts and Beast Lords.

Brave as the Beast Lords fought, they were greatly outnumbered, and their defeat was inevitable. With the very few of his kind still standing, Skeggor rammed into the ranks of sorcerers no longer loyal to him and ran towards the distant gates.

When Wündalær's full shade welcomed them and guided them to safety, Skeggor gave his last advice to those he thought of as his brothers, then vanished with the few who had survived their treacherous trap. His prophecy would stain Valdis and Arnleaf's mind for millennia to come.

It took Valdis Ezelle and Arnleaf Uriel ten centuries of careful planning, of growing their skill and numbers, to grasp what they sought all along. But they desired not only control over the realm, to be King and Queen, but much, much more. They made themselves true Gods above all Urukk.

Unwritten Letters - Volume XXVII

Greindur Gamall

Unknown Knowns

*When Gods battle, do they consider all the lives they crush beneath
their feet?*

Anonymous Author

Aerö read the writings he now knew to have belonged
to the great sorcerer Greindur Gamall. He read them a
few times before he put away the thin book he had been
pouring over for days. Disbelief resonated through his
body as he'd devoured page after page of ancient script,
unsure if they were real or just embellished stories for the
young.

Almost a month had passed since Aerö found himself
underneath Undirheim, in the Beasts 'throne room, and
learned the truth about his so-called friend and saviour -
Velastrum.

Almost four weeks flew by since he'd repelled Valdis
Ezelle and Arnleaf Uriel's vast armies and killed the one
who had murdered his father.

Aerö had learned so much about his father since his arrival in the Beasts' underground city, much more than he ever believed he would. He felt closer to his long-dead parent, yet so impossibly far away. Eldur had been the most powerful of sorcerers; his skill matching that of King Arnleaf himself. The decades of search for the knowledge time itself had hidden from the eyes of mortals, made Eldur known not only among his brother Elementals but throughout Urukk. Sorcerers and ancient Beasts had known his name and might.

Bells unfolded like an old painted cloth before his mind's eye, as it often did deep in the bowels of the world where Aerö spent his days and nights and all the moments in between. His former home unravelled like the ancient tapestries that dressed the walls of Agür-y-Hadën's mighty Hall. Ugly holes burnt through its coloured face; cuts and gashes where memories once made it whole. Aerö was already starting to forget his tiny village and its streets; the many faces that never seemed to mind him. Voices and shadows were what his mind conjured to fill the empty space in that once, so detailed tapestry. His mind focused on Petra, Robin and his friends whose faces shone coloured, bright, and branded in his mind, as did the things he would rather not remember.

Funny how the mind worked, thought Aerö, *how it would sooner undo the memories of those he loved, but would hold with all its might to those of pain, fear, or regret.* Aerö could not remember, for the life of him, the faces of half the villagers that lived in Bells, but saw all those who chased him, harmed him, or those who came and begged for food, half-starved, as if they were with him in the Beasts ' home. Every winter, fathers and sons hit Bells 'gates with the little strength they had, for someone to allow them in and spare some scraps to feast on. The spent bodies of the fathers ploughed through the hip-high snow, animated only by their will alone to see their sons survive. But they were poor and starving inside Bells as well, so the sons died like their fathers, as did many villagers during the long winters.

Tears rushed down Aer'ös face, as they always did when he remembered them. Their playful chase across his cheeks tried in vain to keep those thoughts at bay. Fathers and sons.

He had never felt so different from his father as he did now, learning of his strength and fairness, of his life. Too many times, Aerö had wished he was like him, a powerful, respected Elemental. The many nights spent reading from his journal about far distant lands and sorcery, about the Order; had only made him realise just how unlike him he really was. Weak and feared, a total contradiction of his bloodline. Aerö had heard his new-found mother say he looked just like him, a mirror image of Eldur; and he somehow saw it too. Like the upside-down reflection of the clouds onto the silver lake he saw so many weeks before, or the inverted self beneath its polished surface. He was a negation of the original; the mirrored antithesis of he who gave his life so that Aerö could live his. Eldur, his father, had been not only the strongest Elemental of his time, but was also loved among the Beast Lords. Aerö learned as much from his mother and the many books she had buried beneath Undirheim. He had been everything Aerö ever hoped he was. But the eagerness and pride of hearing Estrelle and her Beast Lords speak of him so greatly, quickly turned to shame. Aerö felt like an outsider, rejected by them, feared even by the fiercest Beasts. Just like the sons who managed to escape the winter's deadly jaws and live to see Bells 'green rebirth, only to find themselves rejected, chucked beyond the closing gates; so did Aerö find himself so close to everything he once yearned for, yet further than he had ever been.

Embarrassed, angry, and riddled with doubt, he lay in the corner of a room piled with knowledge, away from all those yellow eyes that never ceased to follow him. Beasts and Beast Lords stared at him incessantly from within the darkness of their home. They were terrified of him, afraid of the flames that claimed so many; afraid he could read their minds. Alone, Aerö spent his days in total solitude, buried deep within the Beasts' Lair. Undirheim was now his hiding place, his tomb. No one dared, nor wished to talk to him apart from Estrelle - his mother and Queen of the Beast Lords, and Nóór, one of the very few youngsters to roam the giant halls beneath the desert.

Four weeks had passed since Velastrum died in a casket of his own, the flaming coffin Aerö conjured to seal his friend for good. Aerö still thought of Velas as his friend, despite his betrayal, and blamed the King and Queen for what he did and what he had become. He missed him, he missed talking to him.

Books and tomes and parchments older than the world were now his friends; knowledge Skeggor and Eldur, millennia later, had saved from Valdis and Arnleaf's relentless purge. Aerö now understood why he had never heard of Beast Lords. The Betrayers spent millennia undoing everything that Skeggor did, erasing his kind's existence. But crumbs were left, and friends were still out there awaiting his return. Aerö was the prophecy, he had a destiny more perilous than any soul in the realm; Aerö would have to face the Gods and their uncountable armies, while he commanded none.

The grinding sound of the large door opening pulled Aerö from his thoughts and exposed him to whatever lay beyond. Instinctively, he cupped the single candle that provided warmth and light and smothered it. He did not want to be found; he did not want to see them look at him as if he were their prey.

But through the darkness, still weak from the battle with Velastrum, Estrelle walked gingerly towards her son. The lack of light almost unnoticeable to her senses. She was a Beast; she had lived her whole life in the blackness of the deep.

"Aerö, you cannot hide in here forever, my son." She spoke tenderly. And although Aerö knew she came in human form as she preferred to show herself to him, he could still hear the White Wolf's growl behind her tongue.

Bare feet slapped the stone floor closer and closer until they were beside him. An invisible hand, then another pulled him in a tight embrace. He allowed himself to sink into Estrelle's fur mantle. She did not bother to bring a candle for she could easily see him. Aerö had extinguished his, for he did not wish to be seen. Tears wet their faces as they always did. They were so happy to have found each other, yet so pained for what was yet to come. The darkness helped both forget.

Everything was at extremes, in constant conflict. Aerö saw this clearly; happiness and dread, love and hate, found and lost; father and son.

"They do not want me here among them. They hate me …they fear me …"

"Of course they're frightened, my sweet, sweet boy. You have the power to control them all, Beast and Beast Lord. But they do not hate you. We have lived in secrecy for millennia, and now we can no longer hide, that scares all of us."

"But I didn't do this! I didn't know…," he sobbed, although but muffled sounds emerged. His face pressed hard against his mother's shoulder.

"I know. But as we lost our way of living, so have you lost your blissful innocence. You can no longer hide from your fate, my son. You are to learn, to practice, for we are all going to war."

"I don't want to be the prophecy!" he moaned, afraid, showing his young age.

But Estrelle said nothing. She tightened her arms around her son and sobbed in silence.

"I want to see Petra; I want to see my friends!" He shook in her arms like a leaf.

"You know you cannot leave this place, dark and scary as it is. They will hunt you down, Arnleaf and Valdis will have you killed before you can get stronger. Your grandmother and the remaining villagers are safe for now. We are keeping a close eye on them. I cannot let you leave, not until you are ready."

"I am ready! I killed the High Counsellor and his Draugur!"

"We were lucky, my son. If Valdis and Arnleaf had led their armies themselves, we would be dead. That was a mistake they will not repeat. Next time you meet them, they will show you what true power is! We cannot win without you, nor can we survive. Accept your powers, and we might stand a chance."

With that, Estrelle let go of Aerö and walked towards the door. She knew how hard it must be for him, and hated herself for asking so much. But they no longer had the privilege of living separate from the world they once belonged to. They could not make everybody, sorcerer or human, unlearn of their existence.

Aerö sat down and lit the candle he had choked to death moments before, watching the orb of orange light expand and fill the room. The many shelves cut deep into the walls themselves, packed with books awaiting him to stir them from their age-long slumber.

Books upon books lay open on the floor around him, their time-tinted pages staring back at him, but Aerö no longer had the desire to extract their knowledge trapped within. His mind drifted again to Bells, to the crooked house he'd hated and now missed so much; to his friends and mostly to his Petra.

He had believed them all to be dead, as Velas had tried to convince him. He had even seen the battlefield where so many had lost their lives, some friends, others from Brim and Woods. Now they were all part of the same family. They called themselves Turmenn, Aerö knew this from his mother, and he should have been one of them. His friends Trevor, Sam, Daniel, Taro, and Grov had fought valiantly to defend their family and friends while he turned his back on them and chose to run with Velas. He felt ashamed by his decisions; guilty that he chose to see the Order he dreamt so much about, while his own family fought for their lives and almost lost. They needed him, and he needed them more.

More shame poured into his body as he realised how selfish he had been and worse, still was. It was not about him, yet so many died for him, and worse, because of him. Woods crumbled at his feet as he unleashed his father's flames upon it. So many innocent lives lost because of him. The Turmenn chased and slaughtered like cattle because of him. Hundreds of Beasts and sorcerers dead because of him. His own father dead because of him. Aerö's mind spiralled down the rabbit hole of guilt.

They had all sacrificed themselves so he could live a life he did not want. He was no longer the young boy from Bells, spoiled and loved. He was now Gudmaour, the prophesied child; he was the enemy of the realm, the nemesis of the Gods themselves.

Apprehension, guilt and fear swirled inside him like a storm, fighting for control; the vast unknown beyond those shelved walls waiting to be conquered, terrifying Aerö more than anything. The more he learned about the self-proclaimed Gods and their world, the more he feared them. Skeggor had foreseen his actions millennia ago, yet Aerö could not see it, nor believe it. He was expected to bring an end to the Gods 'rule of Urukk. He, a mere boy.

Could he have the skill and strength to do it? Or had Skeggor been so wrong to even think what everybody deemed impossible?

Again the grinding noise of the stone door forced Aer'ös thoughts to flee and hide in the shadows of his mind. Aerö considered extinguishing the sole flame once again, but did not move. In a place where all but him could see within the darkness, such actions only proved his childishness.

A face peered through the pitch-black gap looking for him.

"Psssttt! Aerö! Aerö!" whispered Nóór from within the darkness. His lit face floating eerily above the ground. "Aerö!"

"I'm in here," Aerö answered half-heartedly, not wanting to be disturbed.

"I've got something to show you! Come! Now!" the young Beast Lord urged him impatiently.

Aerö suspected Estrelle was behind it, but he had been alone with his dark thoughts for too long.

"Nóór wait! I'm coming!"

Down Under

The tall walls with their carved in, piled shelves vanished in a moment as Aerö extinguished his candle. The room vanished as if swallowed by some giant mouth.

"Come! Quick!" Nóór hissed again from somewhere nearby.

Aerö moved as fast as he could through the invisible room, guided by his friend's hushed voice. But the darkness of these depths was absolute. Aerö feared he would walk straight into Nóór, or worse, head-on into the large stone door. That would not be a first. Aerö touched tenderly, with the tip of one finger, the egg-shaped lump on his forehead he'd got from running into the same door the night before.

Having been a child in Bells, among the many others, Aerö had gathered an impressive collection of scars and marks time could not erase. But no matter how many times he had scraped his knees or bruised his hands playing amid the crumbling ruins of the ancient city, no pain matched that of brushing against the sharp-edged walls of Undirheim. Far worse, was running blindly into one.

A hand extended through the void and grabbed Aerö by his forearm, pulling him with unexpected force through the narrow gap and into the hallway. The outline of the long passage formed before Aerö as his eyes adjusted to the infinitesimal amount of light that escaped another set of giant, solid doors, some many feet ahead. That was the way out, past Estrelle's personal quarters and the stationed guards. Further ahead and up, past too many living quarters for how many Beast Lords dwelt in Undirheim; through pantries, storage and gathering rooms; a labyrinth of tunnels branched like the hollow roots of a swamp-tree. In their hundreds, the passageways dug upwards and sideways, branching and joining others. None but the Beasts could navigate through them, and Aerö knew that, even though this was his home, he was as trapped as he and been inside the Ivory Tower by the deceiving King and Queen. He could not run away, he could not find his way back to the surface. So he did the only thing he could. He lay hidden day and night on his own in Estrelle's library or in his room.

The wonderful outside, thought Aerö as he stared down the hallway into the orange aura that escaped his mother's chambers. So many colours, scents and textures, he could not even fathom to name them all. The reds and greens and blues he missed the most, the strong, bold colours of the outside world he always took for granted much like everything else. His family, his friends, his home — his simple, happy life, were all but distant memories, bright thoughts that kept his insides lit and warm.

The world Aerö now lived in was drowned in blacks and greys and mossy greens as if the vast underground system of rooms and tunnels had been built beneath the sea. And he could feel it. The suffocating weight of all the rock above his head; the walls that seemed to close on him. Aerö lived at the very bottom of the Lair, the furthest place from everything he loved and missed.

He took two steps towards the golden halo that radiated through the massive doors before Nóór grabbed Aer'ös arm again and pulled him backwards.

"Where are you going? This way!"

"OH! Are you sure?"

"Be quiet! They're going to hear us coming! I know a shortcut."

Aerö did not know what to think. He had explored those rooms and tunnels for weeks, and there was nothing else so far beneath the Lair but some wells and rooms no one had touched in centuries. Not even Estrelle remembered what most of the rooms down there had been used for or by whom. They had always been empty for as far as she could remember.

"Come quickly! We can't miss it!" Nóór pulled on Aer'ös hand stronger. The two were almost running down forgotten hallways. The little glow that seeped outside his mother's chambers vanished in a heartbeat. Nóór was taking Aerö away from the known, away from light.

"Where are you taking me? There's nothing—"

"Shhhh!" Nóór slapped his hand across Aer'ös mouth to make him quiet. "Follow me," he whispered.

Nóór must have been able to see in that absolute darkness for he knew exactly where to turn. Not once did he brush against the walls, nor stumbled. *That must be a gift of being a Beast Lord, extraordinary sight*, thought Aerö as he fumbled through the black. Even a young Beast-less Beast Lord was stronger, more adapted and more courageous than he was. Someone, somewhere had made a mistake. Had it been Skeggor, had it been his father or had it been himself, Aerö seemed to have swapped places with a saviour, a warrior; he was none of those.

Ahead of him, Nóór stopped, and Aerö realised that he lost track of where his friend had taken him. Again his mind had wandered off and left his body to get lost.

"Now we go down. Hold the rope!" And Aerö felt the braided cord replace his friend's warm hand. "Quickly!" Nóór's whispers emerged, hollow sounding.

Utterly blind, Aerö felt for the hole Nóór had vanished into. His hand found a circular stonework, and he realised his friend was descending into a well. Afraid, not sure how deep it was, fearful that he might slip off the rope and fall, Aerö followed the young Beast Lord deeper under the Lair.

"Where are we going?" asked Aerö, barely making any sound. No answer came. "Nóór! Nóór!"

"Come down! It's not that deep!" came his friend's hushed words, bouncing off the walls around him.

With a loud splash, Aerö reached the bottom of the well; his fleet, ankle-deep, in water.

"Come! We can't be late!" Nóór urged.

"Where are you taking me?" demanded Aerö as fright made its way into his heart. He was so far beneath Undirheim, so deep into the blackened bowels of the world that he was afraid he might never go back. Nóór had taken him far deeper than he knew was possible. Doubt, fright, and the feeling of being utterly vulnerable without his sense of sight riddled Aerö as he waited for Nóór to answer.

"Not far, I promise!"

Again, Nóór's hand grabbed Aer'ös and pulled him along.

Wet hallways welcomed the two, long straight lines dug beneath the mountain by unknown hands. Estrelle had told him that the Lair had been like that long before Skeggor had brought his kind and hid from those who wished him dead. Arnleaf Uriel and Valdis Ezelle spent millennia to find it and destroy it, but they did not expect him to be there. By magic, and Estrelle was right, by luck alone, Aerö had managed to repel their armies and secure at least a few more days to live for Skeggor's kind.

Air, hot and musty; humid, hit the two as they advanced through the dark tunnels; ever descending towards whatever Nóór wanted so much to show Aerö. A smell of burning oil, subtle at first, now powerful enough to make Aerö lightheaded, drifted from wherever they were headed.

A cough tickled the back of Aer'ös throat as it struggled to escape his hold. Convulsions soon followed, and Aerö was forced to let them go. Their yells of freedom multiplied tenfold as they echoed down the endless passage.

"Shhhh!"

"I can't breathe in here! It's like inside old Alistair's smithy!"

"What?"

But Aerö did not answer. His mind had fled again, his flesh and bone container. The heat and moisture of the air that hung inside those tunnels transported Aerö back in time and back to Bells. So many times, he sat and watched Alistair work. The old man making knives ploughs, and horseshoes for the villagers to work the earth. It was so hot in there and humid too, that the burning ambers and the steam tightening around his neck like gauntlets. That is what these tunnels reminded Aerö of. Sweating and choking.

Light, or something glowing far ahead, brought Aerö back. Nóór still led the way down hallways that never seemed to level. It was hot, yet no fires burned in sight, but as his mind rejoined his body, Aerö noticed something else. The walls around him shed their cloak, the orange glow ahead revealing them to him. Aerö and Nóór were rushing down rough tunnels that looked as if they had been dug before the ones above used by the Beast Lords. They were also smaller, narrower, barely tall enough for Aerö to walk through, so he wondered what their use had been.

The glow ahead grew brighter, as did the infernal heat. There must be great fires roaring deep within those unknown halls so far beneath Undirheim to generate such warmth. Aerö mused, intrigued.

Before the two could reach the opening through which the orange light flooded the narrow tunnel, Nóór stopped abruptly. The look on the young Beast Lord's face of utter excitement, but also something that resembled fear, burned in his eyes.

He pressed a finger on his lips, and Aerö understood he needed to stay quiet.

"If someone sees us, do not run!" Nóór muttered barely making any sound.

If until now he had been curious to see what lay buried so deep beneath his feet, Aerö was now afraid. He should not have followed Nóór. He was not supposed to know of these hidden places, least see them with his eyes. He was terrified of whoever lived down there and whom they were not to be seen by. Even the bewitching orange glow in all that darkness changed in Aer'ös apprehensive eyes which he perceived now as an ill omen. That flameless fire and the wall of heat pressing against their faces was a clear sign that they should not trespass.

The light dimmed and flickered as Nóór turned and entered the room. His body cast a great shadow on the opposite wall; another omen. Aerö contemplated turning back, but he had no idea how to get back up to the library or to his room. He had come so far, he wanted to know who lived within the glow. Aerö only needed to take a few more steps.

Hot and humid, the heat barrier tried to stop Aerö from entering the room and learn its secrets. Another step and the orange glow surrounded him, pulling him inwards. Aerö felt a pang of panic as he imagined being consumed by some great fire inside the unknown chamber. He saw how similar he was to the moths who flew straight into flames, attracted by their warmth and light.

An underground emptiness opened before him, long and wide; a cavernous space the size of Estrelle's throne room so far above his head. Tunnels and caves opened their black mouths in their tens, no, hundreds from the cavern's walls; rooms and galleries spread like a maze from this central, hollow space.

Aerö marvelled at the size of the place and wondered who had made, or rather unmade, Undirheim's insides. The more he thought about it, the more the Lair resembled a hornet's nest like the ones he liked to poke and run from so long ago in Bells. Thick floors and giant empty spaces layered on top of each other. Whenever Aerö thought he reached the bottom of the Beasts 'Lair, he found tunnels that took him even deeper under the black mountain.

Gems encrusted the cave's vaulted ceiling; the coloured stars pinned into the black rock allowing Aerö to comprehend the impossibly vast empty space before him. No columns held the dome in place, no shoulders for its massive weight to rest on.

It took Aerö a few moments to gather himself and realise what wonder-of-a-place revealed itself to him.

There were lights within the darkness, flameless fires, gems and sparkling metals set inside the stone. There were waves of humid heat coming at him, pulsating from deep within the emptiness. And there were sounds. Rushing, splattering, sizzling noises echoed a dozen times before finally dying; a confusing racket that made Aerö lightheaded.

Aerö walked towards the heart of the giant hole; his eyes glued to the distant vault and walls when heavy drops of water rained on him. At first, he was startled; how could there be rain so deep beneath the surface and the clouds. But then he thought of all the water trapped in wells and walls and roots. Water washed through sands and seeped through stone and miles down it rained inside the hollowed mountain. It was wet, and it was hot. And that's when Aerö saw them. Giant cracks of amber set within the walls pulsated with light. They looked like veins beneath the blackened skin of some dying organ, trying to deliver their nourishment, fighting to keep it alive. The colossal carcass 'clean insides made Aerö think how many chisels had been needed to make it so smooth, so polished.

Drops of water hissed and turned to steam as they came in contact with the glowing threads; the walls around the cavernous cavity spawned billowing clouds of steam.

Aerö had never seen nor read about anything like them and burned with curiosity to know their secret.

Things seemed to move inside the dome, cloaked and crouching figures coming in and out of the many galleries and tunnels that opened all around. They were not alone. He needed to hide.

Out of the corner of his eye, Aerö caught a glimpse of Nóór crouched down behind a pile of grey rocks. Instantly, memories of the cave he found himself in Wündalær washed over him as he realised that next to Nóór was no mound of stones, but skulls, bleached by tongues and time.

Aerö almost lost himself, and it was Nóór who pressed his hand onto his mouth and almost smothered him to make him still.

Skulls of lesser beasts grew in heaps all around the two young boys, signs of a used habitat, indications of a thirst for blood, traces of a fleshy feast.

"What is this place?" Aerö begged for an answer, although he knew too well where Nóór had taken him.

Here lived the Beasts that served the Beast Lords; hundreds of Hounds and Feonds. Creatures Aerö knew from age-old books, while others he simply could not place, moved about within the shadows.

Beings with six legs walked like giant spiders; their clumsy, skinny limbs treading on top of other smaller creatures. Some resembled caterpillars, only the size of carts, crawling up and down the walls of the vast cavern, unafraid of falling. But the Beasts that most intrigued Aerö were the ones that seemed to float above it all. Transparent and delicate-looking, these bell-shaped, tentacled demons looked just like the monsters of the sea Aerö had read about in Estrelle's books. Blind murderers of the deep. But instead of water they floated lazily through the air, their long tentacles swooshing and swaying ten feet beneath them.

It must be the steam, thought Aerö as he watched a billowing cloud roll down towards him from a burning crack above his head. Maybe it was the heat, or perhaps they weighed less than the air around them. Speculate he may, but in his heart Aerö knew he could not even grasp their existence so deep beneath the surface, least understand how they worked.

Before Aerö, unfolded a realm not seen by other eyes than those of Beasts and Beast Lords. He should have felt excitement and pride. Instead, he felt nothing but terror.

Miracle

"You need to stop, sister. You've gone too far."

"We both know that there is no such a thing...sister."

"Both Father and Mother grow weary of your cruel games."

"HA! If my games are cruel, then what about yours, Goddess
of Death?"

"Oh, Sumnäę, leave them to their own devices..."

"Are you the one to speak, Izanami? Had you not gifted them
with immortality? Have you not done enough?"

"Father will not be pleased..."

"He is a fool!"

"Sumnäę!"

Even the Gods Quibble

Mirë the Unwise

Nóór took hold of Aer'ös hand and pulled him close to him behind the mound of whitened skulls and bones.

"We need to get past them and down that tunnel," he whispered, pointing towards the Hounds and Feonds and the other creatures Aerö stared transfixed at.

"Are you mad?! They're everywhere! We cannot pass unseen!"

"If we are quick and move from pile to pile…" Nóór pointed, and Aerö followed his finger, "…we can do it! But we do not have much time!"

Aerö felt sick with fear. He tried so hard to stay away from those cold yellow eyes for weeks, and now he was about to walk straight into their midst. What was he thinking? They hated and feared him for what he was and Aerö hated them for that.

Aerö could already see hundreds of eyes focus on him as the Beasts felt his fear, smelled his sweat. But as his mind kept busy spawning nightmares and entrapped him in a body he no longer ordered, Nóór grabbed him by the arm and ran. Moments later Aerö found himself pinned down behind a smaller mound of bones barely large enough to hide but one of them.

Another jerking of his arm against his will and the mound stretched and vanished in a blur, replaced by rock debris that must have fallen in a different age. Nóór had chosen to take Aerö closer to the wall instead of running straight towards the tunnel. There in the shadow of the looming dome, the two stopped to catch their breath.

One of those orange cracks pulsated at them excitedly, the heat coming from it unbearable and dry. It was hotter than the sands above the Lair, fiercer than the furnaces that smelted metal back in Bells. Aerö felt an urge to touch it, to feel its moving contents, but even getting an arm's length from it made Aerö back away in pain. Two moments that close to it and he could tell his skin felt thinner, tighter.

But moving so close to those great veins revealed something else about them. They did not carry through them some kind of liquid fire as Aerö initially thought, instead their bodies seemed to reflect great fires down below. The veins, as Aerö saw them, that fed the whole dome and maybe the entire Lair, were cracks within the smooth black stone Undirheim was made of. The same material the sorcerers mined in the Wall and used to make their swords and gems, was here used to transport warmth and light.

Everything about the place felt alien to Aerö. Its creatures, its secrecy; even the way it had been built.

Nóór was about to run along the wall of the great cavern when Aerö noticed something substantial moving towards them from above. At first, all he could see was a shadow moving in the darkness, but as his eyes adjusted and the thing came closer, Aerö could see his own reflection in the creature's large and many eyes.

This was one of the creatures Aerö had seen from afar. Large, smooth-skinned and slow, the Beast crawled up and down the dome, its body vast and puffy.

Aerö fumbled to grab Nóór, who was waiting for his chance to run towards another pile of bones and had not noticed the monster preying on them.

"Don't move," was all that Nóór said and Aerö obeyed; the intensity with which the Beast looked at him made him reluctant to even breathe. Glassy, black eyes glared at Aerö without blinking. The creature's pale skin undulated as its insides tensed and inched a little closer to the two young boys. Aerö stared at the caterpillar of sorts and wondered what it was. The way it moved stuck to the wall above them, gently tensing and releasing rings of muscles, reminded him of slugs, but that was not what this Beast was. A thin transparent skin covered the thing, and through it, Aerö saw its innards work lazily but with clear purpose.

A few more inches disappeared under the creatures bulbous body, a few more inches still and it would be upon them. Both Aerö and Nóór strained their necks to see the thing descend the vertical wall to meet them. When the creature tensed and stopped so close that Aerö could have touched it with an outstretched hand, he knew they had been found.

Lazily the thing's head stretched and lifted off the wall, peeling back towards its grotesque body. Its bulging, spherical eyes levelled for one moment with Aer'ös; then like a slug whose body has no inner structure, it doubled back on itself, revealing its underside. Aerö shook with terror.

A terrible mouth gaped at Nóór and Aerö from beneath the brute. Pink and round this hole that could easily swallow both, was lined with teeth, small and sharp, but in their thousands. Ring upon ring of tiny daggers covered the inside of the lipless mouth.

Aerö easily imagined their horrifying purpose. Like the hooks he used in spring when streams rushed out of Wündalær, bringing with them delicious fish, those teeth were there to keep things in. Aerö felt a chill run up his spine as he imagined being chewed by the Beast's circular jaws; once caught by them the only way was in.

Aerö jumped as something brushed against his back, and for one moment thought another creature had crept up on them. Instead, Nóór's hand, pulled on his shirt.

"Calm down," his lips moved, but no sound came. "CALM DOWN!" he repeated mutely.

Afraid to make the faintest sound, Aerö grabbed his father's pendulum through the rough shirt the Beast Lords wore and squeezed it. The gem quivered gently at his touch, as it often did, then fell still. Since the terrible battle that almost wiped out Estrelle's kind for good, the scarlet rock refused to lend its flames. Or maybe they had all been claimed to decimate Arnleaf's and Valdis 'armies and seal Velas in his burning coffin of flames. Aerö simply did not know if the pendulum was being stubborn or just spent.

The Beast's neck-less head peeled further back as it stretched towards the ceiling and revealed yet more of its grotesque underside. Its lipless mouth chewed at the few inches of air that stood between it and the boys, sucking it in, gaping at their faces.

"Go away! Eat someone else!" thought Aerö as he stared into the creatures bottomless maw. He must have also flinched for Nóór yanked yet again at the hem of his shirt.

Then when the thing seemed close enough to almost gobble the boys whole, the giant Beast twisted around its boneless body and began a laboured ascent towards the dome's high vault.

It must have heard his thoughts, thought Aerö as the bloated thing crossed one of those giant orange veins and vanished into the darkness up above. Maybe his powers were not gone.

"I did it again."

"Did what?" Nóór looked puzzled.

"I did it again! I talked to that Beast!" answered Aerö in a smothered voice, but his excitement beamed through him like a lantern.

"What are you talking about?"

"I told the Beast to leave, I ordered it to spare us!"

Aerö had told Nóór how weak he felt, how his own powers seemed ashamed of him and hid too deep within his soul for him to find them. Nóór was his only friend, and he expected him to share his excitement. Instead, Nóór clasped two hands around his mouth and burst out laughing. His face turned a dark shade of purple quickly. They did not want to be noticed, they did not want to be heard, but Nóór found his friend's words of rare amusement.

"You saved us, alright!" Nóór gasped for air between chuckles. "That cave cow almost got us!" He had to cover his mouth again so as not to give away their presence.

"Cave what?"

"They may be big, but they are brainless. They eat the algae that thrive on these walls. They keep the caves clean, they are no flesh-eaters!"

Aerö felt his face go warm and knew Nóór saw his colour change in unadulterated embarrassment.

It took Aerö and Nóór three more runs to reach the far end of the cavern where the mouth of a large tunnel opened to them. They stooped every so often behind mounds of bones or rocks so as not to be discovered. At but a few feet away from the large opening, Aerö could now see in great detail the strange creatures he had observed from afar. Six thin legs held at ten feet above the ground a hairy little body. The Beast that seemed to be a crossbreed between a spider and a monkey walked gingerly as if unsure on its own legs. Hounds and bears chewed on bleached bones between the many fragile-looking legs, while above them all the translucent bodies of the weirdest creatures Aerö had ever seen, floated weightlessly. Their many, ribbon-like tentacles swayed beneath them, tangling and untangling with a mind of their own. Aerö could not help but stare and wonder what they were.

"What are they?" He whispered without taking his eyes off the levitating transparent bodies.

"They are our Verndari; Guardians."

"Why would there be Vern…guardians so far beneath the Throne room?"

"You'll see. Now, even though they're blind, they see you better than any other Beast." And as if expecting Aer'ös question, Nóór added with a smirk in the quietest of voices, "They feel your intent. Try not to think of killing anyone."

Aerö froze in place. All he could now imagine were the battles he had witnessed; all the dead, all the suffering. As if Nóór had jinxed his mind, he simply could not think of things other than death.

At once, the many tentacles that drooped entangled from the Verndari 'bell-shaped bodies turned rigid and spread out towards the two. Like a hundred joint-less limbs, they stretched and felt the air above Aerö and Nóór, reaching towards them drawn by Aer'ös darkened thoughts. Reacting to their guardians, all other Beasts stood up and moved towards the tunnel Nóór and Aerö tried to reach and disappeared in it. Even the giant spider-like monkeys folded their legs and lowered their bodies, scattering away from the awakened Verndari.

"Stop doing that!" groaned Nóór watching the many tentacles descend upon them.

It took Aerö all the willpower he had to break the spell that ensnared his mind. He thought of Petra and his friends, of Robin and their games and the Verndari lost their interest in him.

They were left alone in the vaulted chamber with only the ghostly bodies of the Verndari looming over them. The two moved slowly, Nóór leading the way, while Aerö craned his neck and watched the swaying guardians, half expecting them to swoosh upon them any moment or fall down.

A tunnel yawned at them, larger and longer than the one they came in at the other side of the cave, and this one, too, descended even further into the heart of the mountain.

A pained growl reverberated through the suffocating mixture of air and steam that filled these lower parts of the Beasts' Lair. Nóór seemed to quicken his pace as the noise repeated itself over and over again. Something terrible was happening ahead.

"When we reach the room, we must stay hidden. They will be really angry if they find we came down here."

"We should go back," Aerö muttered as fear worked its way into his heart. Chills walked up and down his spine like tiny spiders.

"Too late for that."

Crouching, one behind the other, the two emerged into a wide and long, but very shallow, chamber not even tall enough for them to stand in. Thick pillars joined the ceiling and the floor. A maze of sorts took form between the black rock structures.

Aerö shook with apprehension at the gathering before him deep in the very bowels of Undirheim. Beasts of all kind poured into the shallow room; pushing and cramming; determined to occupy all available space. Aerö even saw a few Hounds climb on top of others just to reach whatever they had come there for. To his bewilderment, Aerö also spotted cloaked Beast Lords gathering around a small alcove in a wall a few dozen feet before him. It took him a few moments to realise that every pillar seemed to have round holes dug at their base.

Chaos ruled the depths of Undirheim, Aerö concluded as he watched both Beasts and Beast Lords try to get in front of that one hollow.

They sat there at the mouth of the tunnel, stooped down and waiting like everybody else; two young boys before a billowing sea of Beasts and Masters, unsure of what was about to happen. Or at least Aerö did not know.

The growls they had heard inside the tunnel now rang loud and close, howls and grunts echoing grotesquely from inside the hollowed pillar.

There were so many Beasts amassed before his eyes that Aerö scanned the chamber for the only one he knew, his mother in the White Wolf form. Every Beast in Undirheim must have answered the pained call. However, all he saw were Hounds and bears and those six-legged creatures crawling, inching ever closer to the ring of Beast Lords that stood waiting, facing the black column.

Aerö felt his body spasm with fear as he saw the Hounds 'long tails whip the heated air excitedly within the chamber. Memories of his last night in Bells took hold of him. The Hounds frightened him then, and they still frightened him now even though he knew they would not harm him. Nóór, however, beamed in front of him; his face brightened with every excruciating growl.

A piercing cry cut the air before them as it travelled through the shallow labyrinth and through the gathered masses. In its wake answered a deadly silence.

Aerö thought he might have lost his hearing. He could no longer hear the terrible growls that lured them and the Beasts so deep into the Lair, nor the shuffling of bodies or the swishing of excited tails. Everything was still.

The group of ten or so Beast Lords that stood arms-crossed at the entrance of the burrow shifted their weight nervously. They too, like Nóór, seemed to be waiting breathlessly for something to happen. One in particular caught Aer'ös eye. Tall and broad, clearly respected by the others, he stood before the opening with his right hand petting gently the gruesome head of a monstrous Hound. He looked wild, untamed, and above all, anxious.

A low cry finally emerged from the den that for a few long moments seemed to have absorbed all sounds. An uproar broke within the chamber as the little cry echoed around the room. All Beasts and Beast Lords howled as if mad. Nóór almost burst out shouting with the others. Even Aerö felt like clapping with the Beast Lords at the front of the commotion. Within moments, their celebration spread infectiously.

"I see you two have found the primal chambers," came a voice from behind, at which both boys jumped to their feet then stumbled backwards. Neither of them needed to see the person that had found them for they knew that voice too well.

Standing tall, Estrelle, in human form, loomed over them, her fair complexions somehow amplified by the diffuse glow of Undirheim's orange veins.

"You almost managed to get here unseen — almost." Estrelle smiled at the boys. Two faces drained of all colour stared back at her.

"Mo…Mother,"

"My Queen!" Nóór yelped.

"Why are you still down there on the floor and not in that nest?" came another voice, rough and cold, this time from within the overcrowded chamber. The tall Beast Lord that seemed, earlier, to be in charge stood behind the two. A curious look painted his face. The muscular Hound at his side growled softly as if to punctuate its Master's words.

"Congratulations, Hildúúr! Your line is strong," added Estrelle grinning. Fangs, reminiscent of the Beast within, sparkled in the orange light.

"Thank you. We are few now, but we shall be many once again, my Queen!"

"That, I dare hope as well."

"Father…" squeaked Nóór in a voice Aerö had never heard coming from him.

Could he be Nóór's father? Aerö questioned his own ears. The two looked nothing alike. Where the father bore himself strong and strict and clearly a rule maker, his son had made a name for himself as a rule breaker. Maybe Aerö had failed to see why Nóór and he had become good friends, perhaps it had nothing to do with who he was, but rather who he was not. They were both expected to walk in their fathers' footprints while they both yearned to make a path of their own.

"Go, Nóór! Your Beast is waiting," Hïldúúr raised his voice which made his dreadful Hound release a growl that shook the two boys'I innards.

" Y…yes, father!" Nóór stammered almost incomprehensibly.

"You are now a Beast Lord, son! Behave like one!"

"Go," Estrelle spoke softly, waving a pale arm towards the burrow where Nóór's own Beast cried restlessly for its young Master. "Go." Aerö watched half scared, half curious as his only friend under the mountain kneeled before the burrow. But now, a new question burst into his mind, what would the Beast Lords do to him for being there?

Black Sands

A black blemish marked the face of the Great Desert for as far as one could see. Its once golden sands now looked burnt as if by some great disease. Animals refused to cross the ill-fated dunes and birds flew high above it, never to descend and rest or feast upon the many rotting dead. It looked to all who laid their eyes upon it, like a sea that turned to stone and trapped within its solid waves the bodies of a thousand men.

Away from the sickness that ate the sands, a few dozen black ash-covered tents raised their pointy tops above the Barren Lands. Their dried skin faces flapped noisily in the winds chasing across of the Great Desert. Fires in their tens roared and spat columns of smoke and sparks around a sleeping camp.

Here were all who survived; here was all that remained of the Turmenn.

Few escaped the gruesome battle of the Kórr Mountains unharmed and even less could sleep, so most of them gathered around the lashing tongues of fire. No one spoke, no one moved; they stared in silence, not knowing what would become of them.

The battle they had survived against the High Counsellor and his faceless Draugur stripped them of the little hope they had had to find safe refuge in Ophidia, the city of the Healers; after all, they were the very sorcerers they sought help from.

Coughs cut the mourning silence of the night. The black ash cloud Vondur Blöö created upon his death poisoned them all. Smudged faces, blackened clothes, and death was what was left behind after the ash had settled. No one even tried to unearth the dead from beneath the thick blanket of cinders for they were far too many. Only those of children to have been put to rest beneath tall mounds of stone and sand; a poor sendoff for their guiltless souls to meet the Gods.

Summer had arrived in Urukk from the eastern lands and brought with it, like every year, life-smothering heat and dryness. Year after year, the summers grew in strength, their sand-carrying winds pushing away all living things further and further towards the edges of the realm. There had been times, although no human tales remembered, when greenery and life spread throughout Urukk; from the Wall to the Kórr Mountains to the sea; times when Wündalær was genuinely endless.

Hot and heavy, the desert's winds had plagued the human villagers for centuries, yet now they seemed far worse. Their breath now carried death.

A fetid stench of putrid bodies hung over the blackened dunes like a poisonous blanket. If, at night, crisp winds descended from the sky-high summits of the mountains, during the day, swarms of thumb-size flies plagued the Turmenn's makeshift camp; hauling on their hairy bodies the decomposing corpses of their very relatives and friends. This was, for the remaining humans who once inhabited the northern parts of Urukk, the place priests often harangued about. This was Hell.

Away from their abandoned villages, the Turmenn camped at the base of the Kórr Mountains, lost of hope and wounded; afraid to even voice the questions that tortured all of them." *What will they do? What could they do?"* They were not only afraid of the Beasts that chased them from their homes, but now faced something far more terrifying. The thought of being at war with the Order's sorcerers broke even the bravest. They were wounded, they were defenceless, and they were trapped between the mountains, the desert and Ophidia. One of them would surely claim their lives.

A tight circular camp had been quickly established a few miles north of the infected scar that marked the battlefield which claimed so many. The blighted sands still chewed, weeks after their fall, at those who lost their lives so far from home. The dunes that had reddened as they drank the Turmenn's blood, now bathed in decomposing matter.

Fires hissed and belched columns of sparks; their orange tongues tasting the air as they ruthlessly tried to feast upon their own luminous spores. In a place where nothing ruled but death, no one was safe; not even those too innocent to know it.

Tents dotted this island of life, this last refuge for those few humans who stubbornly survived the hunger, the sands, and the battle that tried so hard to claim them. Rocks and rags were used to cobble together the Turmenn's temporary housing. And though they never knew of wealth nor comfort, the Turmenn's new circumstances made their far abandoned homes gleam in memories like palaces of gold. They were too hot during the day, freezing at night, hungry, and always frightened.

At the centre of the encampment, a larger structure rose above the rest. A tent whose dead-grey skin lay stretched over the few large carts the Turmenn took with them from Bells. Like the carcass of a gigantic beast, the tent's hide expanded and contracted as if still alive. If every single other tent lay drowned in darkness, their position only given away by lashing flames and sparks from fires nearby, the central tent glowed brightly from within. Black silhouettes danced onto its skin in a performance most hallucinating. Like the mythical Nymphs that enslaved the minds of men, so did the shadows to all who traced their contoured curves spin and sway. It was the dead of the night and all those who could close their eyes fought gruesome battles in their sleep, while all the rest stared mindlessly into the many fires or towards the central tent. Few could sleep, so the Turmenn huddled around the blazing fires and listened to them hiss. None spoke, none cried; they no longer had the power nor the fluids to waste on such frivolous things.

* * *

"This silence is nerve-racking. Do you remember, brother, when we used to climb the South wall in Bells?"

"We used to hide there every day instead of helping father with the forge. We ran and slept up there like cats, baking in the sun. No carts, no hooves, no shrieks or voices; utter silence. But I no longer have a taste for it. Whenever night descends, and nothing makes a sound, it feels like Death walks right among us, her frozen lips feasting on our hopes and dreams."

"We tried so hard to anger father, we were so stupid…" spoke Daniel, this time much lower; his voice began to fail him. "…We lost mother, and now we lost him too."

"He died because of us," muttered Sam, the words clawing at his throat as he released them.

"He died because of her!" corrected Daniel looking at his brother through glossy eyes. "Hadn't it been for her, he would be here with us, brother."

"Daniel! You know that's not true."

"He died protecting her—"

"Too many have died under our watch too, brother!"

Daniel clenched his jaws, ready to retaliate, but this was not the time to have such conversation, nor the place. The two young men stood guard at the entrance of the central tent. Inside, Petra and Sara tended to the wounded and the dying, day and night. Weeks had passed since the battle that killed or maimed so many, yet there were wounds to heal still. Not only that, but the Turmenn were becoming desperate; desperately hungry and desperately anxious; thus, they tried to take their own pained lives. Many tried, a few actually succeeded. Within the largest tent's grey skin, Petra and Sara made miracles away from prying eyes. Of course, it was all Petra's skill in mending flesh and bones; after all, she was a Sorceress, a Healer.

Cold and windy, the night assaulted the small encampment the Turmenn had made north of the graveyard that now slowly ate so many of their relatives and friends. Fires hissed and sent their millions of seeds up into the endless sky.

"I'm really worried about him," muttered Daniel under his breath, turning his eyes upon a distant fire where Trevor stood by himself. "Since Syll took that nasty blow for him, he hasn't been the same."

"You know how much he loves her!"

"He's an idiot! He played with her for years and only when he lost all hope of living he told her so."

"Not all is lost. He will be fine, he has to be for we need him now more than ever." Sam said, shifting his weight. They had been on guard for hours, with a few more to go before they could finally sleep.

"I hope so, brother. I really do."

* * *

Inside the central tent, mats and blankets hugged the many wounded. About a dozen oil lamps sizzled and smoked as they filled its inside with bright light. Sara and Petra moved from makeshift bed to makeshift bed, dressing the Turmenn's wounds, washing them, changing them. Their bodies cast the dazzling contours the others followed from afar.

"She's burning up again," called Sara as she brushed away a clump of wet, red hair off a woman's face. "It's been four weeks…"

"She swapped her life for Trevor's, and for that, she must pay. The Goddess of Death does not appreciate such trade."

"Will she ever be the way she was?"

"That I do not doubt. Her wounds are fine…" added Petra lifting off Syll's naked shoulder a pink-spotted cloth, "…but she has been away for long and not even my skills can mend what Death and time have done. All we can do is make her body whole and pray that Izanami will release her soul. Narrū knows that all my thoughts are with her."

"He will die if we can't bring her back."

"Trevor lost so much that day, his father, his love, but maybe most damaging, he lost himself. But he will have to find his way back, like the rest of us, for we cannot survive like this much longer."

"But surely we cannot—" Sara's voice rose then drowned in a clamour coming from outside the tent. Someone was trying to get past Daniel and Sam. The sound of clashing steel reverberated through the night as, beyond the flap of the large shelter, people fought full-heartedly.

"I said MOVE out of my way!" came a woman's voice as more clashes tore the heavy silence of the night.

"You cannot go in!" bellowed Sam as he tried to force the attacker to back away.

"I have business with her, and you shall not stay in my way, boy!"

"Not at this hour you don't! It'll have to wait 'till the morning." Daniel put all his strength behind his sword and pushed. With no support nor balance, the woman dropped her sword and grabbed both boys by the hem of their shirts and pulled them down with her. With a tremendous crash, the three hit the hard ground outside the tent. Swords clattered, fists clenched, grunts echoed in the dead of night.

"What, in Yalla's name, is the meaning of this?" came Petra's voice through the peeled-back flap of the tent. Her long shadow obscured the ball of tangled limbs from view. More angry shouts rose from the ground to meet her.

"She tried to…force…herself…inside!" came Daniel's muffled words as the woman's forearm strangled him from behind. Her other hand, held Sam pinned by his hair. They squashed her body while she held them down. None could breathe, none could move.

"Get off me!" the woman barked.

"Adriana! Why are you trying to kill my guards?" Petra asked calmly. Although she could not see through the entangled mass of flesh and clothes, she recognised Woods late leader's daughter.

"Let me go!" Sam growled squirming like an eel.

"Stop this right now! All three of you!"

But neither the boys nor Adriana were willing to see sense. They had been sparring over the ownership of the Turmenn's safety ever since they met weeks before, before even the battle.

"I will not be humiliated by some boys who grew up on a farm!"

"Smithy!" snarled Sam and Daniel, now both wiggling as if possessed.

"Enough!"

Yet the three kept fighting and shouting at each other, ignoring their leader altogether.

I tried… Petra mused as she grabbed the bucket of grimy water in which Sara had just washed the wounded's soiled clothes, and threw it onto them.

A cold and foul waterfall hit the three straight in their faces, and since their hands were busy throwing punches, the repugnant liquid went straight into their mouths and nostrils. Coughs and retches emerged from the sodden ball of limbs, now so entwined they could not separate.

"What is this?" Sam gagged on his words, his hands no longer trying to restrict Adriana's movements, but trying to wipe the sick-making substance off his face.

"That was unnecessary!" muttered Adriana releasing Daniel then standing up. She was covered head to toe in dirt and something else, something none of the three wished to know what. "I was almost done with them."

"Yeah, right!" growled Daniel as he moved next to Sam to face Petra and Sara.

"As I was saying…" Petra went on, ignoring the three who threw each other angry looks, "…what is the meaning of this, Adriana? You two…" she added, pointing a white finger at Sam and Daniel, "…go clean yourselves and come back to your posts!"

"But Petra—!" they moaned at unison.

"Now! As for you, young lady, come inside. These awful flies will eat us all alive if we let all of them inside the tent."

The Protectors' Pact

Adriana was shocked at the sight of the many
wounded sprawled inside the makeshift tent. Tens of
hemp sacks filled with hay and clothes had been arranged
and used as mattresses. And although rough at the touch
and itchy, they provided some amount of comfort to the
gravely wounded and protected them from the night's
chills. When the sun blazed high up in the heavens, the
camp felt like an oven, but at night, cold winds battered
at the broken Turmenn. Dead on the inside, dead-cold on
the outside.

Adriana stopped but feet into the central tent and
stared, unable to resist, at the pale faces around her. Will-
less and tearless eyes blinked at her in their dozens; and
whilst still alive, their owners, looked as if they had long
given up all hope. The heavily lit inside of the tent made
it too easy to notice the depth of their despair.

Her unusual olive skin and long raven-black hair
glistened wet under the many lamps; the metallic shine
upon her skin made Adriana look much like a statue cast
of bronze and compulsively polished.

"Things are going on in this camp that I do not like.
Secrets and odd behaviour and now this! I agreed to take

my people on this journey of yours because you seemed to know more than we did. It's now time you come clean!" She pointed at the twenty or so Turmenn sprawled on the tent's floor. "What happened to them?" She was clearly surprised by the sheer number of wounded. "There should not be so many still wounded from the battle. That was four weeks ago!"

"Adriana—" Sara spoke softly, but Petra stopped her.

Petra looked up at Adriana from across the room, where she was dressing the wounds of an infant. "Most were not injured in the battle," she said slowly.

"What?"

"Come closer." Petra waited, then, finally, after a few moments of awkward silence in which she seemed to weigh the benefits of honesty. "This is Mara," she added once Adriana reached her and the cot.

Adriana looked down over the young girl's body and gasped at the pink bandages that shrouded her whole body head to toe. Instantly she clasped her hands onto her mouth and nose, not in repulsion, but as if afraid to catch whatever Mara had, herself.

"What did this to this poor girl is not infectious," Petra whispered without lifting her gaze from the cot.

"What did this to her?" asked Adriana through barely parted fingers, clearly afraid to even breathe the air within the tent.

"Her mother," answered Petra matter-of-factly, her green eyes scrutinising Adriana for her reaction.

"That cannot be…" the words came out with none of the determination Adriana had shown but moments before. "Why would anyone do that to a child, least their own?"

"Her mother wrapped a cloth around her mouth and walked straight into a pyre three nights ago. Luckily, Erlend who was patrolling the camp that night, spotted the blazing, shrieking ball of flames, and rescued her from her mother's charred limbs. Her mother, luckily I might say, did not survive the burns for if she had, I would have tied her to a horse and sent her to Ophidia. Though scarred for life, this little one will live."

Adriana could not muster a sound, both her and Sara cried in silence at the cruelty of their own people.

"You want to know the truth, daughter of Tarn and rightful leader of your people? Then here it is!" added Petra in a voice clear like a bell, her hands waving around her.

"Petra, don't," pleaded Sara taken aback by the old woman's words.

"It's alright, child! Adriana, much like Erlend, yourself and Alistair - Narrū watch over his soul - has the right to know the unspoiled truth."

"I will answer all your questions, but you cannot repeat any of it outside this tent. Give me your word!" Petra demanded, stretching an open hand to Adriana.

"I cannot do that! My people's safety will come first!"

"That I can accept. You will understand why sacrifices have been made and why, more will be asked from us the coming weeks and months."

Without waiting for Adriana to ask her first question, Petra pulled a stool next to Mara's cot and sat down, clearly strained from the many hours of tending to the wounded. Then after pointing at another one, she slumped her shoulders and began to speak.

Sara did not need to listen to the two for she knew well Petra's old secrets, so she tended to the pained, the mad with fear, and the soon to be dead.

"These are the people many have given their lives to save, since we abandoned our villages. They are no warriors, they are no heroes. And I can't blame them. Generations lived their lives believing in the safety of the walls, trusting them to keep at bay the Beasts they feared so. However, they were never safe. Not from the Beasts, who never really meant them harm, nor from the real enemy, the Order, and its sorcerers.

With all their beliefs taken away, they simply cannot function. I've seen lovers feed each other poison, mothers kill their babies, husbands kill their wives, children kill their elders. And you know why? Because they've lost all hope. That is, of course, my blame to have for I believed that the Healers in Ophidia will help us, but many things seem to have changed in fifty years.

Trapped deep in this desert, far from their imagined safety and with an enemy they simply cannot hope to slay, they've given up. That's why there are so many wounded in this tent a month after the battle. They are afraid of the things to come that they would rather take their own lives here and now."

"How do you know the Beasts are not our enemy? They destroyed my village! They burned it to the ground!" Adriana yelled angrily. Petra's calm and unwavering demeanour did not help.

"They are not now because they have never been," Petra answered calmly. She looked ancient; wrinkled and round-shouldered on that stool, her hair so white it shone.

"You are wrong, old woman! So wrong!"

"Please do not waste my time with such remarks for I have work to do. This is merely for your entertainment, not mine."

"Then tell me how do you know such things?" Adriana demanded, moving on the edge of her seat like a feline ready to jump. "People are talking, you know, of how you knew danger was coming even before Woods burned; of how you asked them all to trust you and follow you in this blasted journey through the sands! HOW DID YOU KNOW?"

"People are talking about you too, child. About who you are and, the far more interestingly for their simple minds, what you are." Petra said vaguely. "Alas, I have no interest in such gossip."

"Please keep your voice down!" Sara intervened. "These people are sick and in need of rest!"

Adriana glared at the two. Her old skeletons seemed to have followed her all the way from Brim.

"Firstly, no Beasts, no matter how large or many, have the skill to burn down villages. That, my dear, is a talent wielded only by particular sorcerers called Elementals.

As for how I know the Beasts are not your enemy or how I knew that Bells was in grave danger, there's no simple answer."

"Petra don't," Sara pleaded once more from behind. The last the Turmenn needed now was more to fear, or worse, focus all their hatred onto her.

"We need everybody's help, and for that, I need her to trust me. It's alright!"

Adriana sat cross-legged and watched the two, one young, one old, women talk; their trust in the other absolute. These were two women that had no secrets from each other, realised Adriana. *Will she be able to trust Petra? Will she even believe her answers?* This could all be part of some sick game played by this ancient-looking woman. A thing many Turmenn thought to be true. She would have to wait and decide for herself, she concluded.

"You see…" Petra continued seemingly undisturbed, "…I know so much about the Beasts, the sorcerers and their damned Order because I was once part of it myself. I am a sorceress, a Healer."

The words hit Adriana like a well-aimed blow below the ribs. All air went from her lungs, and she felt her chest collapse in pain as it tried to suck in fresh one. She could not speak. She had forgotten even how to breathe.

Could this be true? Could Petra really be a sorceress? Or is this yet again one of her tricks?

"Breathe, dear" spoke Petra softly noticing Adriana's change in colour. Even though she was the colour of rosewood, shiny and dark, she now looked about to faint.

"Sara, child, please pour some of that hot water into mugs and come sit down with us. I think it's high time we had some tea. Bring the rest of it as it is, so Adriana can wash that stink off her skin."

Moments later, Sara came with three dented metal mugs which steamed angrily in one hand and a bucket in the other. A square of cloth rested on her forearm, ready to be used. Petra immediately produced, out of the many folds of her dress, a metal box small enough to lay concealed inside her fist. A purplish powder spilt slightly as she opened it, at which Adriana moved slightly backwards on her stool.

Three pinches, one in each mug and the box was gone, lost again within Petra's many folds. When the mug was presented to Adriana, she could not force herself to take it even if she wanted to. She was shocked by Petra's words, worse, she was terrified.

Both Sara and Petra pushed their faces into the billowing steam and inhaled deeply, the scents rising from their mugs impossible to resist.

"Go on, drink your tea," invited Petra, "It is my own concoction!" She grinned. She allowed herself to enjoy the shock on Adriana's face. "There's nothing harmful in it, that I promise!" and took a loud gulp of it. Both Sara and Petra drank their tea in silence.

Reluctantly, Adriana accepted her mug and barely touched the liquid, still not sure if it was safe to drink. And while Petra spoke of who she really was, or better, what, she wiped herself clean.

"For more than two centuries, I was part of the Order, and I was truly happy. I had everything a sorceress could ever wish for: power, friends, a husband, and a son. But for whatever reason, fate, Narrū, chance, call it what you wish, took it all away." Petra gestured with a dismissing wave of her arm, but then stood up only to return short moments later with a bundle in her hands. "This is the only thing I brought with me, an heirloom, a treasure of sorts, but it turned out to be more of a curse." She handed the dark leather object to Adriana. Her voice sounded far and empty.

"So, because of that…" Petra pointed at the bundle Adriana was turning on all sides, not certain how to hold it, "…or better, because of the knowledge it contains, I could no longer be part of the Order I would have once given my life for. You see, Adriana, the thing you hold is called the Unreadable Book, and it contains all knowledge. It knows the past, the present, and the future, or of realms far beyond our own. Within those pages lies knowledge of both the living and the dead. It knows all."

"This book contains all that?" asked Adriana almost mockingly as she sized the leather-bound book. "Then why don't we just read our future and see if we survive this damned journey right now?"

"Its size means nothing to what is trapped within," Petra replied sternly, although she found the interruptions rather amusing. "As for reading from it, no one can pry open its secrets. Even if you were to cut it, its pages would be blank as your knowledge of the powers trapped within. However, at times it does decide to open, and when it does, it only shows the answers you most desperately search for. It has opened for me four times,…" she added neutrally, "…albeit in almost three hundred years."

Adriana could simply not wrap her mind around it. How could this woman, old as she was, be three centuries old? It seemed impossible that anyone could live that long, human or sorcerer.

"It is that very book that told me of the Beast Masters' existence, sorcerers themselves yet persecuted for their gifts. Of how my love would turn against us all and side with the wicked King and Queen. Of my own son giving his life to protect that of his love; and last time, during the battle when it answered, why is Aerö in the midst of this all? I know how this sounds, but the Unreadable Book's truth is absolute." Petra looked spent. She closed her eyes and seemed to sleep. It must have been but hours before dawn.

"You still did not answer my question. How did you know the villages were in grave danger?" demanded Adriana. She had the body, the attitude, and the skill to rule men. Young she may have been, but also a force to be reckoned with.

"Can we do this some other time? Please, Petra," whispered Sara caressing Petra's right hand lovingly. "You need to rest!"

"Rest, I shall, but not quite yet. I only have a few more things to say, and then we can all go and try to sleep. Most of us seemed to have lost that ability anyway," she sighed longingly.

"But you are right Adriana, I have not quite explained myself. What I am about to tell you, no one knows, not even you, my dear," she added, putting her other hand on top of Sara's. Sara's expression changed from one of passive listener to keen curiosity.

"I have kept secret the knowledge of Aer'ös birth for fourteen years. I have always known who his mother is. Many years before I left the Order, Eldur, my son, a sorcerer himself, found out about the Beast Master's existence. Together with his father, his Master, and a small army, they went into their lair to slaughter them, for the King and Queen deemed them unclean. They fought hard, but lost, and we all thought the Beasts' Queen had taken my son's life. It turns out, she only took his heart." Both Sara and Adriana gasped.

"Years passed, and she gave birth to Aerö Gudmaour Skalidur, a son that age-old prophecies foretold. But when the traitor King and Queen wish someone dead, there is no safe haven against their wrath. So Eldur brought him to me, to raise him in anonymity in Bells. So now you understand that when a Beast took Aerö in the dead of night with no blood-trail to follow, I knew that something terrible was on our way. Under no circumstance, would the Queen of the Beasts have allowed her only son to be harmed by her own, nor would she have negated his safety by taking him back. She knew that we were all in danger and hoped that her own Lair would give him a better chance to live. And right as rain, she was!"

No one spoke. Sara stared at Petra, her face frozen in an expression of bewilderment. Adriana however seemed deep in thought. Had she been Petra back in Bells, would she have done the same thing? Probably so.

The first to speak was Sara. Her melodious voice now somehow heavy, monotone.

"Did Aerö know any of this?"

"He knew of Eldur and me, yes, but nothing of his mother. He thought she was dead. I swore to protect him, I did not want him to go looking for her, not yet."

"If all you say is true, what now? What can we do? The Beasts might not harm us, but the sorcerers will,"

Adriana asked calmly, her anger gone, the questions and doubt that clouded her thoughts, all gone.

"We cannot stay here much longer, that is obvious, for they will come for us. The King and Queen and by extent, the Order, will hunt us down for what we did."

"You mean killing those sorcerers?"

"They were no brothers of mine, but soulless monsters. But she knows they're dead. The Queen knows we did it, and she will seek revenge."

"Then what?"

"We must make it to Caraa and from there to Stórvatn if I am to see you children old like me. There, beyond the Wall, humans still live in great cities of their own, built by themselves. Only there, reunited with your ancestors, will you be safe."

"Caraa…" repeated Adriana thoughtfully. "Are you sure?"

"There is no other way."

"Then we should make a Pact!" repeated Adriana, her voice confident. "We are not to lie or hide things from each other. We shall travel as Turmenn, and you will be in charge, while I will be given command of our guards."

Petra seemed to consider Adriana's offer, but then stood up and, moving noiselessly, she peeled back the tent's entrance only to see both Sam and Daniel stumble at her feet.

"I know a few places where eavesdropping is punished by leeching, boys!" she bellowed. "Stand up, you fools!"

"We are sorry, P…P…Petra!" they stammered, terrified, a reaction she had never seen from them. They had been listening for quite a while.

"So what do you say?" she demanded matter-of-factly. The boys looked from Petra to Sara to a half-naked Adriana, puzzled. Sam's eyes lingered just a moment longer on Adriana's bronze-like skin.

"You have been listening to us, you know of our Pact. Are you with us? Or will I need to think of ways to dispose of your bodies before dawn?" she added swallowing the grin that threatened to break her stern demeanour.

"We are in!" both boys stammered at once.

The Alliance of the Accursed

Petra felt no guilt over terrifying the two boys to which she owed her life.

Sara, however, crossed her arms in disapproval. She thought it was a mean thing to do. They were mere boys after all.

Adriana laughed from her stool as she fastened her shirt.

"They'll be fine!" She chuckled. "They may seem young, but after all they've seen and done, they're no less men than any other in this camp."

"Still! That was mean!" Sara pouted disapprovingly; her beautiful face contorted like a child's trying to mimic an adult's angry expression.

"Can we trust them?" asked Adriana, serious again.

"They're good boys. We can," answered Petra, somewhat distracted. Tiredness was catching up with all of them.

*　*　*

At the southernmost edge of the encampment, closest to the blackened dunes, few fires crackled. Their orange glow appeared like nothing more than tiny specks against a pitch-black sea. Here, at the brim of the death-marked battlefield, the stench of putrid corpses and the flies were at their worst. Only a few would choose to camp in such a place, so far away from Petra and her guards, from food and medicine.

"It's all her fault!" growled Elfredda like a wounded animal, "They're dead because of her! My beloved husband…"

"We will revenge them, sister!" hissed Bathilda menacingly. "Petra will pay with her life for this."

The two Greed wives mourned their slaughtered husbands around a dying fire away from the rest of the camp, their wet faces glistening in the amber light.

"She must die!" whimpered Elfredda between sobs.

"Soon. She might be guarded day and night, but we have a plan!" At this, Elfredda lifted her head from between her palms to see Bathilda grinning coldly.

Behind her, a group of a few dozen villagers from Woods, Brim, and Bells nodded approvingly.

"Good" she croaked shedding her pained demeanour. Murder and loathing painted her shrivelled face.

* * *

The colours of the night began to soften. Blues and pinks slowly replaced the blacks with which night painted the skies and everything beneath them. A new day was about to come upon the Turmenn and their makeshift camp, a new chance for the sorcerers to find them, for the sands to eat their flesh, or for madness to devour their last strands of sanity.

These were the few hours when most slept or simply rested. When the night was giving way to daylight, but the sun had not yet claimed the sky, the Turmenn closed their eyes and tried to dream of better things and places.

"You two should get some rest," came Grov's high-pitched voice as he walked around the corner of the central tent. Taro walked beside him, silent and sick-looking as usual, his complexion even more so since the battle at the foot of the Kórr Mountains. "We'll keep watch here while you sleep."

"We thought you're going to sleep 'till noon!"

"For once there were no fights or shrieking children to keep us up all night," answered Grov patting Taro on the back. "We are well-rested! How was your night?"

Sam and Daniel did not know how to respond. They wanted to tell their friends about the Pact, about Petra and her plan, but this was not the place, as Turmenn started waking up and could easily eavesdrop on them; much like they did on Petra.

"All good!" they stuttered somewhat overexcited. "Although we had a little brawl with *her* again!" finished Daniel rolling his eyes.

"You two are always looking for trouble, especially with her!" Grov chuckled loudly. "Asking her out would be more effective. Not to mention safer for everyone around you!" he shrieked.

"Shut up!" moaned Sam and walked towards the tent he shared with Daniel and Trevor; although their older brother much preferred to spend his nights on his own, away from them and the restless Turmenn.

Places were swapped, and Sam and Daniel retreated to their modest shelter while Grov and Taro guarded Petra and the tent in which she had been tending to the wounded.

"We'll make it through! I know we will Taro!" Grov tried to comfort himself more than his friend. Taro nodded solemnly.

* * *

A couple of tents north of where Taro and Grov stood guard, Erlend watched Sara sleep. She had been up all night with Petra.

Much as he did not want his wife to work so much, he understood how crucial their work was. They were not only caring for the ill, but also blessing all the food and water for the Turmenn. That was how they called Petra's indispensable gift. And Erlend knew that without all the spells and potions Petra put into their food, many more would die from cold or heat or flesh-eating infections.

"I'll be back in a few hours, my love," he whispered in her ear. A soft kiss upon her lips and he was gone. There were too many fights, and men that took from those who had already lost too much. Erlend, Trevor and his group, Adriana and her men worked day and night to stop the Turmenn from killing each other over the smallest of scraps. It was as if they had all lost their minds during that fated battle. Erlend sighed as he pulled back the flap of his tent and emerged into bright sunlight.

* * *

"I don't know who started that fight down south," muttered Trevor from his usual spot at the northern edge of the encampment. He did not need to turn around and face his friend. Erlend seemed to have made a habit of checking up on him each morning.

"That's not why I'm here!" Erlend's voice came, as expected . "But for someone who seems to have no interest in the welfare of these people, you know an awful lot about what happens every night."

"I can't help it! In the dead of night, you can hear old Murg fart from the other side of the camp!" Erlend chuckled, and Trevor seemed to laugh as well at his unintended joke. They had been friends for far too long to not talk to each other. Yet what plagued Trevor now, was something Erlend struggled to accept. Trevor had lost all faith in Petra and her plan, worse, he blamed her for his losses, for his father and his love.

"She is not dead, you know," Erlend said, lowering himself next to Trevor. "You should go talk to her, not waste yourself out here."

"She has been like that for weeks—you never wake up from such wounds. It should have been me. It should have been Petra and not my father!"

"You know that isn't true. We all swore to protect them. It could have been me, just as easily, that day instead of Alistair. You think I don't think of that? You think I do not miss him too?"

"He wasn't your father!" Trevor barked, breaking a twig with his hands.

"No, he wasn't, not by blood, but I thought he was just as much as I think of you as my own brother!"

"Well, that's not true either then! No brother of mine would be her dog!"

"You might not trust our leader, Trevor, you may think she should be dead, but hear me, brother. If any of us are to survive this war, we need her just as we need you!" and with that Erlend patted Trevor on his back ready to leave. "Stop acting like a spoiled brat, Trevor. Syll needs you, your younger brothers need you. This is not the time to sit and watch the Turmenn crumble, only to spite Petra." With that, he turned and walked away before Trevor could say another word. Despite the many years of friendship, of brotherhood, their exchanges of late were always full of anger.

* * *

The newborn sun gathered its strength just as the night's bright guardians let go of their last flames.

"How long until we have it?" growled Elfredda impatiently.

"Not long, sister, not long. Martens said she will have it done by nightfall. We're lucky to have Woods 'old apothecary on our side."

"Good! Good!" Elfredda sneered rummaging through a leather sack.

"Found anything of value?"

"All worthless! Wooden toys and clothes!" Elfredda growled, throwing the bundle in the cracking fire she kept alive with the many things her gang had stolen the night before, but which were of no use to her.

"That was the last they took, dumb monkeys, and almost got themselves caught for it. I had to ask big Burt to go and tell the woman, we'll take her damned kid next time if she doesn't shut up," she said displeased.

"It's good that Burt knows how to make the fools keep secrets!" Bathilda sniggered slapping some imaginary face. "Luckily, Petra's goons believe those drunkards fought again! Ha!"

"Too bad there was nothing of worth in there."

"Yeah, still, there are plenty of tents the boys have not yet visited." And both laughed sickly as someone's stolen toys turned to ash before them.

* * *

Hundreds of miles south, hugged by cliffs so vast they pierced the very heavens, Seribu Menara glistened golden in the new born light. Its many slender towers rose like spears from the ground, rings upon rings of walls and towers, streets and bridges built to guard the Capital's most inner part, its very heart. There in the middle of it all, passed magic-infused stone and gateways watched by ancient beings, the stolen, colossal home of Arnleaf Uriel and Valdis Ezelle rose higher than anything that ever dared to stand upright.

It was said that the Ivory Tower had been built so tall, so that the King who lived up there could see his entire kingdom; from the Taðr Sea to the vast Wündalær to Stórvatn.

At the top of the Ivory Tower, inside the hexagonal throne room, a nervous Valdis paced in circles under the scrutinising, painted eyes of many fairer, younger selves. Her naked feet threading onto the polished floor sent clamorous echoes through the quiet room.

"Why?" she grumbled as she stopped before the painting she had cut weeks before in anger. The young Queen's depicted face looked in pain at the real Valdis. A hideous gash split its once fair face in half.

She stood there and stared at her own ruined face and wondered what she should have done differently, where she had gone wrong.

Just like the painting before her, something had severed inside her with Vondur Blöö's second, and final, failure to undo the Beasts and their Masters. She had lost her beloved Draugur, she had lost her faithful, although completely useless, servant, and she had lost her youth.

"I should have sent more shadows after HER!" she growled to herself, scratching so hard at her folded arms she drew blood.

"My love," came Arnleaf's measured voice from behind. "We underestimated her once more. We will not make the same mistake again."

"He killed them all! That damned son of hers killed them all! We had him! We had him right here in this room, and still, he managed to find her! My much-loved Draugur!" Valdis cried at the top of her lungs. "LOOK AT ME!" She wept hysterically.

But although Arnleaf kept his composure, his insides sizzled with anger just as his Queen. They, Gods among sorcerers, had not only been fooled by a mere boy, but also deprived of the very souls that made them young. The moment Aerö burned to nothing Valdis' army of Draugur and their white translucent bodies were consumed by Aerö's roaring flames, their souls — which she and Arnleaf feasted on— returned, just like their bodies, to their true creator.

Arnleaf moved towards his Queen and held her in his arms; her trembling body aged and shrivelled by a thousand years.

"Look at me!" she repeated, disgusted.

"You will have your youth again, my love!" he whispered. His old complexion mirrored hers, two ancient beings stared into each other's eyes with love and something else. Determination.

"Then find me souls!" she hissed.

"Be patient, and you will have your souls, my Queen!" Arnleaf said softly. "But first we need to teach those Oaks their lesson," he added, seething with anger. "Those damned guardians still hold their faith to Skeggor! How dare they defy us, Gods?!"

But then Valdis spoke, her voice no longer carrying the signs of pain or madness.

"I have a plan," she said flatly, relinquishing her overly-dramatic mien. "I know how we can get our souls and get that boy before he's strong enough."

"Yes?" the King looked most curiously at his Queen.

"We'll kill his friends, kidnap that traitor Petra and rat him out like the vermin his kind is!"

"But we could never leave the tower without the damned Oaks knowledge—"

"Oh! But my sisters have been begging for years for a chance to test their skills!" Valdis teeth flashed behind two cracked, dead-looking lips.

"Yes….yes!" Arnleaf considered. "That might just work! But if I may, my love, I would also like to send my Seraphs too. They will be our eyes and ears and weapons if we need them."

"Send your assassins. We mustn't fail!"

"We won't, my love. Not again!"

* * *

Night was brewing behind the rugged cliffs of the Kórr Mountains. All the Turmenn scurried between the many tents in preparation for the night to come. Fires roared in their tens like luminous oases around which the Turmenn sought refuge from the encroaching cold. Mothers grabbed their babies, husbands wrapped their arms around their loved ones as the day's last rays of light began to fail.

"Is it ready?" Bathilda asked anxiously.

"As promised," Martens replied, and from behind her, a dozen faces grinned at the news. A small leather flask wobbled in her hand as the poison within it splashed against its walls excitedly.

"Good! Very good!" exclaimed Elfredda pleased.

"And are you sure it will work?" came Bathilda's spiteful voice.

"Of course!" Martens snapped insulted.

"And if it doesn't?"

"It will! A mouthful and she'll be as dead as a snared rabbit!"

"See, sister…" Bathilda turned to Elfredda, her hand holding the death-carrying flask, "…I told you we will have our revenge! Petra shall be dead before morning!"

Fright Always Thrives in Darkness

Before the time itself began

The magic blood started to run

In some it dwelt, in some did not

And they were born out of the lot.

There were just a few under the sun

And soon the three of them were done

Three families that age forgot

Roaming the lands and watch them rot.

And so together they have grown

To be the greatest ever known

With powers that were vast and bold

They built a city and behold!

Deep in the mountains lies the place

Where out of rock and sand with grace

Arises tall as made of gold

Seribu Menara as it is called.

A thousand towers stand upright

With pointy roofs of blinding-white

A thousand bridges intersect

Trying all towers to connect.

It was the place where all began

All sorcerers gathered as one

They lived and worked and studied too

It's here where the Order grew.

The first of them were skilful lords

That bent the elements with words

With silver hair and neck-chained gems

They fought the evil from the lands.

The Light of God he was so-called

For to the World he wisdom showed

The name of Arnleaf Uriel remained

Forever praised, in all hearts chained.

The second place was taken by those

Who mended souls and flesh and bones

With silver hair and tattooed skins,

They eased the pain from the beginnings

The kindest heart she had it' true

And powers that were soon taboo

For she performed the one unsaid

Valdis Ezelle could raise the Dead.

The third and final ones were those

Who could control the Beasts they chose

Black hair they had and no tattoos

No gems or chains or words they used.

They were the strongest, fiercest ones

Too deep in them a Beast's blood runs

But skills as Skeggor Skalidur's were rare

For he was also a bear, beware.

Five thousand years later still,

The Order grows in men and skill

For if the right blood flows within

The Order will be next of kin.

Unwritten Letters - Volume XII

Greindur Gamall

Aerö read the verse out loud a few times before closing the old tome Estrelle had given him to read. He had read it many times before, in his father's journal back in Bells; although he now realised, it had not been complete, nor truthful. Unlike the poem in his father's journal, the one before him mentioned the Beast Lords as equal members of the Order they helped build as well as Skeggor Skalidur and his surprising gift.

It all seemed incredible to Aerö, Arnleaf Uriel and Valdis Ezelle's effort to erase his grandfather's existence. The many centuries they hunted Skeggor's kind and burned all writings mentioning his name. *All that for what? Had they hated him? Or had they been so frightened by his strength and skills that the countless centuries of purging him from memory seemed needed?* But that was what had happened, and Aerö read enough in Greindur Gamall's writings to comprehend the traitor King and Queen's tremendous efforts to have all Beasts, and Beast Lords killed.

Yet they had failed time and time again. Despite their power, their knowledge, and control over vast armies, Arnleaf Uriel and Valdis Ezelle had failed to obliterate Skeggor's kind. They had revelled in their god-like powers for too long and underestimated Skeggor's determination for survival. The one chance they had to have him slain along his kind within the Capital's high walls fell through their desperate fingers; an opportunity that would never present itself again.

Once safe inside the rocky fortress of Undirheim, the Beast Lords and their Beasts survived in complete concealment from the outside world, hidden and separated from their very brothers and sisters with whom they had built a kingdom for all. Urukk, a realm of godly power, a place that sorcerers, humans and ancient beasts once called their home. Now all that Urukk was, was a broken land, a carcass, a shadow. Where once was order now thrived tyranny; where once was green, seas of sand and death now formed; where once was unity, now was but war.

Deep within the dark room where Aerö spent most of his days, the hours flew unnoticed. The many books that had been saved from Valdis and Arnleaf's purge, waited, collecting dust and little creatures somewhat resembling snails in the room's shelves.

Outside, above the deadly dunes that assailed Undirheim from all directions, it must have been night time. The weeks Aerö had spent away from the sun's reigning light, skewed his senses. He now lived in perpetual darkness, in a never-ending night.

The sound of footsteps and something else; scratching, lashing noises; came from outside the room in which Aerö devoured millennia-old books. The pitter-patter of bare feet and the other sounds Aerö could not quite place stopped behind the heavy door that stood between him and whatever prowled the deep hallways of Undirheim. A last barrier of sorts meant to make Aerö feel safe. Sniffing, panting sounds seeped through the smooth-black walls, as did the lashing, and Aerö knew exactly what waited for him in the dark corridor beyond.

Memories of the night the Beasts took him from Bells came back to him with the force of a thunderstorm. The darkness of the cellar, the fetid smell of the Hound's breath, the panting, and clearer than any, the lashing sounds of its tail whipping at the air. Aerö felt his blood freeze in his veins as he remembered the night of his abduction and salvation. On the other side of the door, a Hound was waiting for him, Aerö was sure of it.

But then the door began to move, slow and laboured, grinding as it moved inwards to allow the Beast to enter. Terrified, Aerö pushed himself backwards from where he sat on the bare floor, until his back hit the sculptured shelves at the opposite side of the room. He was trapped in there with nothing more than the large book he was reading to protect him from the Hound. Aerö raised it to his face and peered over its top edge as if it were a shield.

"What are you doing?" came Nóór's voice as his head appeared disembodied through the pitch-black opening. Aerö felt relieved to see his friend. They had not seen each other since their adventure to the Beasts' forbidden chambers three days before. But as Nóór entered the room, between his legs, a frightened pup showed its head; the small creature hiding behind its Master.

"Is that your Hound?" asked Aerö in a loud and high-pitched voice putting his makeshift shield aside.

"Shhhtttt! Not so loud! I am not supposed to take him out of the nursery yet. Dad would hang me by my toes if he knew!"

"He would what?" asked Aerö incredulously.

"Oh, nothing! This is Ári!" Nóór grabbed the little pup and lifted him in front of him for Aerö to see. The young Hound growled and writhed, most unhappily for the way Nóór handled it.

"I don't think it likes it."

"Ári is a he, not it, Aerö!" Nóór corrected his friend coldly. The Hound wriggled in Nóór's hands until he put him back onto the floor.

Aerö stared at his friend's Beast, unsure how to react. The thing before him looked so scared and innocent, even endearing, but Aerö knew that was only a temporary state. The creature would eventually turn from scared to scary, into a flesh-eater. A monster.

The Hound sniffed and panted in Aer'ös direction just as unsure as he was.

"Go Ári. It's alright, he's a friend!"

Tentatively, the pup moved closer to Aerö, clearly frightened, but curious nonetheless. Ári's tail lashed as he anxiously approached the boy of whom the prophecy spoke as his future King. A chill ran up Aer'ös spine as the Beast's wet snout touched his arm in friendship. Or maybe he was tasting him, thought Aerö, flinching.

Startled, Ári moved backwards from Aer'ös arm, then waited there for him to touch him.

"He likes you!" said Nóór smiling, checking the hallway to make sure that no one saw him and Ári come inside.

"I don't think he does," muttered Aerö as the young Beast growled at him.

"If you would really listen, you would know his heart. Ári wants you to play with him." And the pup produced a yap so loud, Nóór rushed to pick him up, then stuffed him in his shirt. They might have been heard.

"Right! Time to go!" Nóór added, checking once more the hallway. "Come down with us, there are many galleries we haven't yet explored!"

Aerö shuddered at the thought. The mere mention of the gigantic underchambers, as Nóór and Aerö called them, seemed to have turned his bones to mush. Although Aerö was seated on the floor, he knew his legs would never carry him again passed the Verndari and the spider-monkeys. Aerö tried to mumble something back to Nóór, but no words came.

"But if you'd rather stay in here and read, at least pick something other than children's stories!" And as if reading Aer'ös mind, Nóór added, "My dad used to read them to me when I was very young."

"Hmmm let me see…oh here…" Nóór rushed to the far end of the room, Ári squirming in his shirt, and produced a tattered book from the top-most self. "…I think you'll find this much more interesting!" he added brushing off a dozen shelled creatures that slumbered on its covers. Then, without stopping, he rushed out of the room. "I'll come back tomorrow." Nóór's voice drifted lazily through the darkness-leaden air.

Aerö was once again alone in the room he spent more time in than any other. The slapping echoes of Nóór's naked feet vanished within moments; he was becoming good at moving without being noticed. His friend, now a true Beast Lord, was getting stronger by the day, while he spent all his time drowning in books he did not understand half of.

Even Ári had sensed his fear, Aerö was sure of it; a Beast not more than days old, yet he could not muster the strength to touch the pup. He was pathetic. He was a coward. Aerö had the liberty to walk freely throughout the buried prison Undirheim turned out to be, yet he lay hidden, day and night, behind thick doors and walls impossible to breach. He was afraid of the place and its many secrets; he was afraid of the Beasts and their Masters; he was terrified of his own powers.

It must have been quite late at night, for Aerö felt his strength seep through the rock beneath him. The tattered tome Nóór picked for him from the tall shelves, slowly gained in weight, pushing against his hands, forcing him to lower them and rest. Aerö soon fell into a restless sleep of nightmares both too real and too terrifying.

Bells burning, houses crumbling under the weight of his conjured fire, his father's pendulum belching new flames without a moment's rest. His friends and Petra waving at him from amid the raging inferno, their smiles melting off their blistering faces as their limbs stiffened and stopped petrified — charred. The King and Queen, each with a hand resting on his shoulders, laughing madly at the blackened world before them; patting his back, congratulating him. Aerö watching himself in the Beasts' throne room, black blade in hand, decapitating Estrelle in her White Wolf form.

The floor and the shelves 'rough edges cut deep into Aer'ös flesh until the pain woke him. He was soaked in sweat and tears, his hands bone-white from clutching at his father's pendulum beneath his shirt.

Gasping and coughing, as if his lungs neither could breathe in, nor trap fresh air within them, Aerö found himself in a tight ball on the cold floor.

Since the Hound took him from Bells many weeks before, Aerö found it increasingly difficult to close his eyes and rest. If at first, it was the Hounds who preyed on him in every dream; it then became his flames, the King and Queen, and his deceiving old friend, Velas. Now it seemed that everything he ever feared came to haunt his dreams.

Aer'ös life of late seemed to have gotten stuck between the daily gut-knotting fear of living with the Beasts and the night terrors that turned him useless. Every day he tried to break the cycle, he tried to be courageous, but utter fear was something he did not understand. Until now.

Aerö knew now that once a seed of fear was let into one's soul, no matter how courageous, how valiant and good that person was, they will one day succumb to it.

The tiny seed would slowly feast onto the person's darkening thoughts until a vine would grow from it and fill them on the inside. A body filled with fear the mind no longer has control of.

Aerö now understood the permanence of his terrors.

Unrest

It was not yet morning outside Undirheim, Aerö realised as he pulled his thoughts together and got up. The stillness of the mountain told him as much. Although neither the sun nor the moon was visible from anywhere within the Beasts' underground Lair, the creatures and their Masters had a system of their own to track the unstoppable passing of time. If at night, no sound was made and everybody rested, or at least tried to, during the outside-day, various noises reverberated through the mountain's galleries, telling the time.

At dawn, noon, and sundown, high-pitched cries announced them, letting the Beasts and Beast Lords know a new day had arrived or ended; while for the small hours in between, a deeper call travelled through rock and air.

Aerö thought about the scary sounds the first few days since his defeat of Arnleaf's and Valdis' forces, but then he learned that this was yet another task the Feonds had within the Lair. They were not the vicious brutes Aerö believed them to be, but rather the workers of this colony of sorts; their sheer size and strength allowing them to carry out their labouring tasks like none other.

No shrill cry had yet travelled from the depths of Undirheim to announce the cracking of dawn outside their fortress. Aerö still had a few hours of sleep, so he moved slowly from the room filled with old books, down the narrow hallway, and retreated to his simple room to rest. He wanted to sleep. No, he needed to sleep. But he knew the never-changing dreams would take over his mind, and he would melt the world once again. And as predicted, the burning, killing, melting nightmares came once more and haunted Aer'ös sleep. The terrifying ones, but some new too; but all of death and solitude.

"Wake up little one," came Estrelle's voice from where she sat on the edge of Aer'ös bed. Her pale hand brushed Aer'ös damp hair off his face as she called him to awake most lovingly. "You've been having those bad dreams again, haven't you?" she asked when Aerö finally opened his eyes, relieved. He was happy to have escaped his own mind's destruction of the world; at least until nightfall.

Slowly, the images of where he was replaced the ones his head had conjured. And although Estrelle sat with her back to him, half-turned to face him, Aerö could see her other hand gingerly touching the place where Velas stabbed her. It had been weeks, yet she still had the injury his poisoned blade had made.

"Does it still hurt?" he asked, moving his eyes to where her hand pressed on her wound as if she tried to link some parts that had been cut by the old Healer's blade and stubbornly refused to mend together.

"It's nothing, son," she said, failing to mask the pain that still burned through her flesh as it had done the day the wound was made. "I'm here because I worry for you, Aerö! You lock yourself away from me and everybody else. I never see you in the halls, we never see you in the training grounds. And all those nightmares. You're wet from crying in your sleep. Please let me help you!" Estrelle pleaded.

"I hate it here!" came Aer'ös words as he pushed himself into a sitting position. "I miss my friends, I miss Petra. I want to go outside!"

"You know I cannot allow that, son."

"But I can't live down here like a Beast! I can't be day and night trapped under a whole mountain with them around! They look at me, mother, with their yellow eyes and I don't need any powers to know they mean me harm! I'm scared!"

"Valdis and Arnleaf would like nothing more than you to leave this tomb only so they can kill you. And I can't let that happen, Aerö. We are few and weak, you are so young. We need to grow in strength, and you need to also, for if we fail, everything you know is lost." She patted his arm, then pressing the other hand onto her wound, she stood up to leave.

"We cannot have this conversation every time we talk, son. You cannot leave the mountain, none of us can."

∗ ∗ ∗

"Are you sure this is going to work?" asked Elfredda, scrutinising a basket in the orange light of the fire.

"Yes! Yes! It will, I am sure of it!" said Martens inspecting, herself, the bundle the Greed sisters carried in their hands like an offering to the Gods.

"It smells so good!"

"There's nothing nicer than fresh bread for breakfast!" smirked Elfredda; her tongue licking at her lips like a serpent's.

"We don't have much time, sister. Dawn is almost here, and we still don't know who will take these to receive her blessings!"

"We can't, they'll be suspicious! But Burt's sprog can!"

"I'm not sure he's ready…"

"He is." Burt said in his deep, thoughtful way from behind the three women who had not seen him watching them. The darkness of the night was just about to fail. "Elijah will take those to her at dawn."

"Good! Then it's settled!"

* * *

Aerö sat back in his cot after Estrelle's departure, his anger quickly draining from his heart. He was too tired to hold a grudge against the mother he had always thought as dead, but found under a mountain.

His life could one day fill one of those weighty tomes inside the other room, he thought. A series of fantastic stories and events that, although true, would seem impossible to those who, years later, would read them.

The story of the boy without a mother and abandoned by his father but weeks after his birth. A child who would grow deprived of their much-needed love into a place where those around him would abhor him if they knew the truth about his parentage. But loved he was, and friends he had, until one night a Beast with claws and fangs abducted him.

Prophecies and Beasts both mythical and ancient appear to the young boy and speak of war and death. Through flames and wars, he travelled throughout Urukk, getting to know sorcerers, Kings, Queens, and Beast Lords. Until one day he found her. Under a mountain in the middle of a sea of sand, the mother he thought he never had, welcomed him into her home…

A cry so loud, hearing it hurt, travelled through Undirheim's entwined tunnels for every soul to hear. Dawn had come. Instantly, Aer'ös thoughts returned to where his body lay — in his simple cot, in his simple room, alone and tired after another night of restless sleep.

Breakfast, as usual, was waiting for him on a tray inside his room, his mother, or maybe someone else, had brought it in, while his mind wandered. Mushrooms and fruit looked at him sadly from the wooden bowl between his hands, the same food he had every morning since his arrival. Oh! How he missed Petra's hearty meals and freshly baked rye bread.

With his breakfast spooned, fast, down his throat, Aerö dressed and headed for the door. Like every morning, he tried to reach the room filled with old books before the other Beasts, and Beast Lords began to prowl the hallways of the Lair. Not two steps into the long and ill-lit corridor that a lean Beast Lord and her Beast, that looked much like a stag, almost collided into him. Aerö had to glue himself to the wall so that the two would not run over him.

"How dares she!" the Beast Lord growled furiously; her white Beast's antlers grinding with an unbearable screech the tunnel's walls. "Move, boy!" she boomed.

Aerö ducked so the two could pass without the Beast's great horns tearing him to shreds. Taken aback, Aerö turned after the female Beast Lord, but she vanished out of sight in the dim-lit hallway.

What was that all about? Wondered Aerö staring into solid blackness. More yells travelled through Undirheim's tunnels from the direction of his mother's chambers; cries and angry calls rippling through and amplifying as they advanced. Without even thinking, Aerö broke into a run.

The long hallway came to an end. On the left, Estrelle's beautiful rooms glowed orange from the ornate lamps that hung from its walls; all still and quiet; on the right, the stairs that wound up to the throne room. Suddenly another Beast Lord came rushing through the staircase as Aerö peered into his mother's chambers. A man with a hard look on his face, determined and angry, rushed passed him down the same hallway the other Beast Lord and her Beast had gone; he too vanished after a few purposeful strides.

"The throne room!" exclaimed Aerö, realising where the angry shouts came from. Now, from where he stood, at the bottom of the stairs, Aerö could hear Estrelle's voice too, booming over those of many.

Not knowing what to expect, Aerö burst into the vast throne room ready for battle. Although he had not used his powers since the battle that destroyed, but also saved so many, Aerö was prepared to unleash his flames upon whoever threatened his still injured mother.

"We cannot stay idle while our enemies prepare for war!" bellowed a tall Beast Lord as the slimy-looking serpent around his neck, uncoiled itself ever-so-slowly.

"We cannot hope to defeat the Betrayers and their armies with this!" another cried, pointing his fingers around the room. No more than three dozen Beast Lords and as many Beasts surrounded the throne in which Estrelle sat in her human form. Apart from the young ones and the two Beast Lords that Aerö saw leaving the room, these were all of them.

"We must train! All of us!" yelled Nóór's father, Hïldúúr, whom Aerö recognised. As always his right hand patted the huge head of the largest Hound Aerö had ever seen.

"We stand no chance, Hïldúúr! Open your eyes!" a female Beast Lord snarled. "We need to ask for help!"

If until then, the throne room shook with the echoes of the many angry voices, the woman's words drowned all of them in deadly silence. Had it been her disrespectful command to Hïldúúr or her call for help, Aerö did not know, but the effects of her utterance were most compelling.

No one spoke, even their Beasts lowered their gaze as if afraid. A taboo had been spoken.

"May I remind you, Finndôra, that we have no friends!" said Hïldúúr finally, in a disapproving tone.

"We may not have friends, but every other Beast in Urukk is in danger if they are not stopped! Even the damn Skrímsli!"

"Do not mention their name, woman!" snapped Hïldúúr as every other Beast Lord in the throne room gasped and murmured. "They would sooner eat us than aid us! Even our son knows that!"

"They could let us move unnoticed! Gather forces! Even save those humans we keep watch on!" She glared at him, not in anger, but in disobedience. Behind her, something large moved closer through the shadow cast by one of the colossal pillars that held on their shoulders the whole Undirheim. Aerö almost turned and ran back down the winding staircase and into his room as a Feond stepped into the green light raining from above. That must have been the very Beast he had spoken to so many weeks before, before Vondur and his army reached this very room. Aerö could recognise its scars as well as its master. Finndôra had been there before he charred the place.

Could this Beast Lord be Nóór's mother? Aerö wondered from where he stood at the entrance of the Throne room. No one had yet discovered him.

"That's enough!" growled Estrelle from her fear-inducing throne. She looked sallow and pitted. And although she was surrounded by her people, Aerö could see how she cradled her wound in one hand while the other tapped impatiently on the side of her seat. "Hildúúr is right! My father forced them once, but they will not help us again!"

"Then we should walk out of this tomb and face our end, my Queen!" muttered another Beast Lord. "We are so few it will take us decades, centuries to build our numbers enough to stand a chance against their armies."

Aerö waited for Estrelle to put the man before her in his place and share her cunning plan to kill Arnleaf and Valdis.

"That, unfortunately, I believe as well. We need to all work together, we need to train, and we will need to ask to join the war the only ones who owe us anything — the humans."

Aerö felt all strength he had, scurry to the bottom of his being. His mother's words, his Queen's words, left him empty. Fear, anxiety, desperation quickly filled that void and made him tremble, made him want to run and hide despite his limbs' refusal to even budge. A gasp escaped him, and his covertness was broken as if the brightest light was now illuminating were he stood.

Heads turned, maws gaped, tongues flickered in the thick-with-tension air as all the Beasts, and Beast Lords faced him. Still paralysed by fear, Aerö could do nothing but look at his stupid feet and cry. He could have long been in his refuge-room, read through books and parchments, sleep and daydream as he pleased; if only they would have agreed to carry him.

"Why are you here, boy?" asked Hïldúúr coldly, watching Aerö so intently, even his thoughts would be disclosed. Estrelle sat quietly on her throne, unsure how to react. She looked troubled by the finding of her own son listening to their not-so-private debate.

"I…d….nothing"

"How long have you been spying on us?"

"I didn't…" Aerö tried to explain himself, but simply could not find the words he needed. Then, as if his body suddenly came back to life, Aerö was in control of his own limbs. Quick as a fox, he turned around and sprinted towards the tunnel that would take him back to safety. One step before he could descend the spiralling staircase and escape the Beast Lords 'questioning, a giant hand extended through the air and grabbed him by his feet.

He tripped, he fell, he smacked his hands onto the floor before the air went out of him as the Feond's hand lifted him upwards. Aerö dangled breathless ten feet above the gathered Beast Lords, with no option of escape.

"Put me down!" he pleaded; his tears raining down onto the angry Beast Lords below. "Please!" And still, his mother sat and watched, one hand still pressed onto her wound, the other tapping one elongated skull that protruded from her throne, impatiently.

"Speak!" hissed the tall Beast Lord with his snake around his neck.

"Put him down, Finndôra!" said Estrelle finally although no mercy painted her face, only disappointment.

"Not until he answers in truth!"

"Please let me down!"

"Speak!" she growled, and the Feond shook Aerö by his feet as if he was nothing more than a cloth hanging on a wire.

"I said, let him go, Finndôra!" But Nóór's mother would torture Aerö until she had her answers, even if that meant ignoring her Queen's direct command.

But then a deep growl echoed through the vast throne room, pained and angry. And Finndôra knew that she would not be allowed to continue.

"PUT HIM DOWN!" barked Estrelle, this time in her White Wolf form; her enormous jaws snapping at the female Beast Lord. "NOW!"

"He should spend his time training, learning to control his skills; not spying on others!"

"That's enough." Hïldúúr tried to rein in his life partner.

"We all work day and night to come up with a plan to outlive this war, while all he does is hides inside his room and eats and sleeps!"

"I said enough! As long as I am your Queen, you will do as I say, Finndôra!" The White Wolf spoke descending from the bone throne. Estrelle's scared head but inches away from her. But Aerö was already on the floor, shaking stupidly with fear. Finndôra knew, just as every other Beast Lord, that Estrelle would not have hesitated to tear her to shreds. She was not a Beast Lord that could turn into a Beast, but rather, a most vicious Beast that could take the shape of a woman.

"Everybody, leave!" she commanded, and they all obeyed, even her scared-witless son. "Not you, Aerö!" And the Queen of the Beasts returned to her white seat.

"You've run out of time, son. And I've run out of patience!"

The Bringer of Death

"It's almost light," mumbled Grov between loud yawns. He and Taro had been keeping watch over the central tent all night. "Sam and Daniel will be here any moment, and we can get some rest, Taro!"

Taro nodded, forcing a weak smile.

The two young men stretched and yawned in the morning's fresh pink light. They were tired, hungry, and wanted nothing other than to climb into their cots and sleep. The camp was still asleep and quiet, only the seldom coughs of people waking up and the flapping of tents to break the eerie silence. Grov and Taro appreciated the lack of noises; for once the Turmenn were awake, the encampment buzzed with their chatter and movement, their squabbles and sobs.

* * *

"This is getting tiresome!" said Trevor morosely, as footsteps approached from the direction of Petra's large tent.

"And you are still wasting your time watching that fire burn and die, day and night," came Erlend's voice as he stopped behind Trevor. "You've let that fire eat your mind enough, brother!" he added, dropping next to him.

"Brothers, you still claim that after all I've said. You come here every day trying to change my mind, and every day you leave just as you came, empty-handed. Your help is neither needed nor wanted."

"Of course I still think of you as my brother, Trevor," chuckled Erlend light-heartedly. "How could I go to sleep at night knowing that I turned my back on you. Like it or not, Trevor, I will come to this gloomy place of yours until you feel the sun again shine on your face!"

"Has she been teaching you how to speak inside that tent too? You sound just like her!"

"Ha! You think so?" Erlend asked, grinning boyishly. Both men watched, in silence, the fireplace before them, and despite their differences, their thoughts wandered just the same to Petra's tent and Syll.

"This is the time you tell me what I need to do and then you leave," muttered Trevor rudely.

Erlend patted Trevor's back, considering what he should tell his friend. Trevor might have tried to sting him with his words, yet Erlend felt helplessness in his inability to help his dearest friend.

"You know very well what you need to do, Trevor. She's waiting for you. Petra thinks you could really help her come back."

"She knows nothing! Syll has been dead, just as my father has, and it's all her fault! I could never kill a friend and act like nothing happened!"

"The hatred you bear for her comes from the darkness within your own heart, Trevor. You cannot blame others for your own guilt!" And with that, Erlend stood up and left Trevor to his sullen thoughts, a pang of guilt troubling his own heart for saying such rough words. Trevor needed to wake up and accept the facts that Alistair would never be coming back; and that Syll lay in a dead-like slumber from which she might never come from.

* * *

The night was slowly shedding its dark cloak as newborn light gnawed at its eastern edges. A new day was about to come and with it all the pains, the cries and fears of the Turmenn. Like Grov and Taro, Erlend much preferred the stillness of the night. Weeks had passed since the sorcerers attacked the marching villagers at the foot of the Kórr Mountains and killed so many. Weeks since the Beasts had helped them slay those who determinedly wanted to kill them instead. But although many days had passed since then, without a single Beast to harm the Turmenn despite their unbroken presence outside their makeshift camp; the humans feared the unwelcome guests, and even tried to kill them. However, no swords or fires, no matter how deadly, managed to scare the creatures who, at every dawn, placed food and water at the northern edges of their camp. Not only had they saved the Turmenn from certain death, now they fed them too. Erlend felt embarrassed that he too was afraid of them. They needed the Beasts for, without them, they simply could not survive the desert's harsh conditions. But he also felt uneasy with them waiting just beyond the encampment; watching them.

Erlend's feet took him between the many tents without him thinking about what he was supposed to do, or where he was going. Ambers dressed in ashes puffed and hissed at him from lone fireplaces; their light and warmth long gone. And, as it seemed to happen often recently, as if his thoughts found it too difficult to focus on his tasks at hand, his mind wandered to the friends he lost, to his parents, to the many he would never see again.

* * *

Trevor, too, gazed at the cracks of pale pink light that spread at the horizon. Beyond the camp of Turmenn, he had fought to bring together, lay the blackened sands the High Counsellor conjured upon his death. Somewhere within those waves of ash and dust was his father's body separated from his head. Trevor had spent a fortnight trying to locate Alistair's remains, only to find no trace of them. In one day he had lost the two people he loved most.

His father lay dead and lost within the blackened sea of ash and corpses, south of the Turmenn's camp; while Syll awaited death, lost in a sleep she could not wake up from.

How things have changed, thought Trevor, as his wandering mind settled on Erlend and their, once deemed unbreakable, friendship. How he used to trust whatever he or Petra said or asked of him. Now, when everything had seemed lost, Trevor remembered his youngest brother's words. Too many weeks had passed since then, yet Daniel's questioning words and distrust in Petra came back to him as if it had happened but days before. He should have listened; and then maybe they would still be alive.

A lump of coal hissed as it gave its final heated breath, pulling Trevor's thoughts back to the fireplace before him. His face was wet, his hands were shaking, and realised he had been crying. Could he have been wrong about Erlend? About Syll? Maybe his oldest friend was right. Perhaps he did need to see Syll, but not to save her, which he knew he had no power to do, but rather to save himself. He needed to say goodbye before she truly left this world and joined his father in the other.

It was still early, the day had just begun. If he could sneak now into the central tent, he could say his goodbyes and leave before Petra would even notice. He could not forgive her, he would not. The blame he put on Petra for losing his father burned through his flesh, impossible to drown.

Finally, making up his mind, Trevor stood up and started the long walk between the still sleeping small tents towards the centre of the encampment. There, rising six feet above the flapping, ash-covered shelters of the Turmenn, Petra's makeshift hospital stood quiet; only the seldom arid gusts to disturb its stillness.

Yawns roared from within the many tents as the Turmenn stretched and sighed. Few could sleep at night, but even fewer wished to spend them in the open. Only those who had lost everything they had and loved, wasted away in solitude around small fires. Trevor had been one of them.

Trevor quickened his pace as more rustling of bodies drifted through the morning air. His eyes scanned the pitiful camp the Turmenn had erected, focusing on the scattered figures that had survived the battle, stripped of their lives, wives, and children, yet left them breathing. Living corpses. They all had families of their own before Petra dragged them into this cursed journey of hers. Watching them, Trevor could not help but think of his own loses, but also at what he still had; friends and family; two brothers and a few close friends, any of whom would give their lives for him. Sam, Daniel, Grov, Taro, and Erlend were all he had, and for the first time in weeks, he felt lucky, blessed for that.

Something was warming up deep inside his being, a spark of hope, a flicker of happiness that kept at bay the chilling guilt and regrets.

Trevor's thoughts returned once again to his body as in the distance, before the central tent, he noticed the vague outlines of two people. He knew the shelter was guarded day and night, and probably by his own friends and brothers. If the silhouettes belonged to them, they would allow him entry.

The morning haze began to lift; the grey amorphous blanket that covered everything in sight dissipated before the sun's widening eye. The closer Trevor got to Petra's shelter, the more he saw of the camp as well as of the two who stood guard at its entrance. The sight of one rather large, and the other slim and tall, made Trevor breathe with relief. He could recognise the outlines of his friends from across the camp now that the low cloud that had obscured his sight, melted away.

* * *

Erlend walked between the modest shelters of the Turmenn in the growing light. Every day, he checked each tent, each of the wounded and the orphaned. Every day, he made sure they had something to eat and drink, and that they were safe. Too many troubles plagued the camp at night when guards were few, and those who still held to their wits preyed on the hopeless. Tens got robbed, Turmenn got wounded, some even got killed with no one to be caught. The encampment was slowly sinking into lawlessness, and Erlend knew that if they did not leave soon, there would not be much left to fight for.

The worst area was at the south of the camp, closest to the black scar that marked the battlefield they had barely escaped. There, almost all who refused to acknowledge Petra as their leader gathered; a community of thieves and thugs. Erlend made his way towards the southern edges of the camp, the area he least preferred to visit. Not because of the many who defied his leadership, but rather because of the clouds of flies that swarmed in from the rotting corpses in the sand. Still he did, day and night, fruitlessly trying to enforce the law upon the unruly.

The smell of freshly baked goods reached Erlend's senses the further south his legs took him. Hunger stirred in his belly as he remembered his last meal, the stale bread he had before he left his tent in the dead of night.

"I thought you said you had no food," Erlend said at the sight of the Greed sisters gnawing at a fresh loaf of bread.

"We said we have none to share," answered Bathilda sniggering. "We don't eat yours! Why would we give ours to you?"

"People are dying of hunger. People from Bells! People you know!"

"We don't have any to spare," said Elfredda flatly as she tore a whole loaf in half and stuffed her face with it. *People would throw punches for the crumbs alone*, thought Erlend, watching, disgusted. But he had no power over them, for he knew there were a few good dozens following the Greeds. Men from Bells and Brim and Woods, men just like them, wicked and pitiless.

Erlend looked around for any signs of loot. The Greeds' followers were known for having sticky hands, but he could not see anything. Only the bread which steamed fresh in the women's hands, reminding him of their true cruelty. They had no goods to make the bread, but others did, and most got robbed. He had seen enough of the despicable gang the sisters led and turned around to leave. But from behind a set of tents, two figures rose, advancing towards him.

Burt's large frame moved slowly in his direction, at his side, a woman walked briskly to keep up with his long strides. Burt was a mountain of a man from Bells with a temper to match. But despite his size, Erlend's eyes focused on the little woman that accompanied him. She was not from Bells, he was sure of it, but what drew Erlend's attention was the bundle she carried in her arms.

Bathilda and Elfredda's eyes narrowed at the sight of the two, their cold eyes set upon the blanket Martens cradled.

"We made enough. You should give these to your men. Gods help us if we are to be attacked again with only hungry children to defend us," came Burt's rumbling voice as he gently pushed the woman to deliver her bundle to Erlend.

Erlend looked suspiciously at the blanket the woman was carrying as did the Greed sisters. But there was too little food for him to refuse such an offer, so he stretched out his hands, took the steaming bread, and left.

Some moments later, from afar, Erlend heard Bathilda's angry voice whipping at the two who dared to give away their food. "Fools!"

Erlend's hands sweated, carrying the bundle of warm bread, his mouth hard at work salivating. The smell that drifted from them only aggravated his own hunger. Erlend wished to stop and tear one bread, then and there, and feast upon it, but others needed them much more than he did. Petra was to have them, she was strict about it, for with the food and water she distributed around the camp, she also healed the masses through the potions she infused them with.

* * *

"Have you brought it?" asked Valdis Ezelle, eagerly jumping off her throne at the top of the Ivory Tower. Arnleaf Uriel watched his Queen rush to the middle of the room where a young woman waited with her hands wrapped around something dark and small.

"Of course my Queen!" the woman who must have barely reached adulthood answered. She was wearing a tight, hooded cloak and was strikingly beautiful. Long black hair flowed free over her shoulders; an air of carelessness but also confidence radiated from her. As Valdis approached her, her clasped hands trembled, struggling to keep pinned down whatever she held in them that wanted to get free.

"Let me see it!" demanded Valdis stretching her ringed hands like an animal to snatch its prey. The young woman had no choice but to pull her hands and move a few steps backwards. Valdis beamed at the living thing that struggled to set itself free from her iron grip.

"Thank you!" said Arnleaf to the black-haired woman before him. "You have done exactly as I asked of you."

Hearing her King's words, the young woman's lips curved in a sly smile; her attractiveness suddenly accentuated.

"You and your sister must prepare, my dear Seraphs! The importance of your next assignment is absolute. You two must make sure your Queen's plan works. But if it does not…" Arnleaf added, lowering his voice, "…you will do whatever needs to be done to kill the boy and all those human apes!"

"As promised, my good King!"

"Leave as soon as you are ready! If the Queen succeeds tonight and her Priestesses receive their long-awaited message, the Gudmaour will be drawn to them like a mindless moth."

"We will be waiting for him, Master!" And with that, she moved away from the silver lamps above and stepped into the darkness of the hallways beyond.

No sooner had the young woman left the hexagonal throne room, that the Queen was already pacing the floor of melted gold; her cracked, brown lips moving incomprehensibly as she conjured her impressive spells.

Minutes passed before Valdis stopped before her seated King and put down, at his feet, the black creature she held.

A raven squawked from where it lay paralysed on the floor. Valdis had taken its ability to walk or fly, and that was only the beginning of what she had planned for the poor creature. A jewelled dagger seemed to materialise in Valdis's right hand as she knelt by the bird.

"Although I have seen you perform this spell a thousand times, my love, it still excites me just as much as when I saw you do it your first time on that old fool Gamal so many lives ago!"

The Queen said nothing but lifted her gaze upon Arnleaf, her eyes as empty and dark as the night outside. Black veins throbbed beneath them, visible through old, paper-thin skin, her complexion poles apart from the beauty she once commanded. Darkness and cold seemed to encroach from the corners of the room despite the many lamps that overflowed with light. Like a vine that grew in the rhythm of Valdis's chants, the gloom spread and conquered the throne room; swallowing the two and the paralysed raven between them.

Valdis's voice rose and fell quicker and quicker in anticipation of the spell that she would soon release, as did Arnleaf's breathing. The ritual ensnared his thoughts like a drug.

The dagger gleamed despite the lack of light, before it came down upon the frightened creature, unmercifully. The Queen gasped as her spell took place and inhaled the bird's last breath; its soul was hers to have. The darkness broke as soon as it had formed, dissipating through the walls that seemed to have become permeable to it, returning the throne room to its prior state. Lit and warm, the room exposed once more the King on his stolen throne and his Queen crouched before a bird of purest white. The once black raven screeched at her as it unfurled its wings and stared at its own bleached van.

"Good," she murmured as she observed her creation, her eyes having their colour once again, her face, less old. Arnleaf looked at Valdis just as pleased, his own appearance somewhat younger.

The bird screeched once more, then, fluttering its puffed up wings, it flew around the room in swooping circles only to settle onto Valdis' seat. There it waited for its new master's orders.

"Fly you will to my good sisters in Ophidia and them you will then tell to go and take care of their old friend, Petra! She is closest to their walls. The boy will come for her, and when he does, they must then slay him and the filthy humans Petra has with her and who dared strike down my dear Draugur!" Valdis Ezelle spoke in a voice so pained it sounded more like a growl. "Now go and do your deed!"

"Outstanding!" said Arnleaf, taking hold of his Queen lovingly, his eyes following the white dot in the sky." The Gudmaour must be killed before he learns his strength!"

"As do the humans before they reach the southern plains, if that is what she planned for them. We cannot have all humans in GrænnFlugvélar rise against us while the Beasts prepare for war."

"As always, my love, you are perfectly right!"

$* * *$

What a beautiful morning! Thought Trevor as he made his way between the many shabby tents towards the central tent. There, his Syll had been waiting for him since the battle that had trapped her between life and death. Weeks had passed since then, yet Trevor only now dared to go to her to say his long-delayed goodbyes.

Lost in thought, he slowly moved closer to his lost friend and lover; his mind conjuring memories of her, keeping his heart in a perpetual ache. Sorrow, regret, and guilt were at work in Trevor's darkest depths as he remembered Syllvia's constant pursuit of him, her beauty, her kindness, her touch.

Her fall.

The blow that was destined to take his life, decided to punish him much worse by killing her. He should have been the one wasting away in a cot never to wake again. He should have been the one about to die, not Syll. But the Gods were but mean children, playing with the lives of men, squashing them, stretching them, breaking them for their sole amusement.

The noise of shifting rocks under rushed footsteps made Trevor cast away the daydreams his mind forged. He was almost at the entrance of the large tent when he caught sight of a young man walking through the camp towards him; his gait rushed. Trevor wondered what had happened that made the boy walk so purposefully towards him. A moment later, it became apparent that the young man was too, heading for the central tent; his hands loaded with a heavy bundle.

"Hey, you!" bellowed Trevor after the boy who must have been still a few years too young to bear a weapon. The young boy stopped in shock at the sight of Trevor whom all the Turmenn knew was of ill-temper and worse, ill will.

"What is that you carry?"

"F…f…food," the boy stammered. "For Petra and the others!"

"Who sent you?" Trevor asked, looking closer to the boy. His face was covered in so much dust and soot, it made it almost impossible to recognise.

"My father!" the boy answered wholeheartedly, shifting the weight of the bundle he still lugged.

Trevor looked at the boy then nodded, offering to take his load.

The boy shook his head.

"You are from Bells, aren't you, boy? I know you! What's your name?" Trevor asked, smiling at the frightened soul before him. Trevor could barely remember how good it felt to smile, to help.

"Elijah" muttered the boy sheepishly, letting go of the bundle he so protectively carried.

"Don't worry, Elijah! I'll take care of these!" The boy nodded quickly then, just as fast, turned on his heels and disappeared through the maze of tents. Somewhere in that direction, someone was waiting for their son to come back home. Trevor found himself smiling at the thought.

"Trevor!" shrieked Grov, hugging his old friend to the point of breaking his bones. "I knew it was you!" Taro nodded and shook Trevor's hand eagerly. The two young men had not seen Trevor roam about the camp in weeks.

"I need a favour, boys!" he said, his face serious once more. "I need to see her before Petra finds me here."

Trevor did not know what reaction to expect from his two friends. Happiness to help, anger for the way he treated them the past few weeks, pity? But the two simply remained dead quiet, their eyes staring at the bundle Trevor carried in his hands.

Grov's belly was the first to rumble. The smell that drifted from the parcel he had taken from the boy named Elijah simply bewitched the two young men before him.

It was now, Trevor realised, that in his hands, wrapped in a knitted blanket, a few warm loaves of bread steamed in the morning air. His mind had been so busy he did not acknowledge the rare gift nesting in his hands.

"You can have them if you let me in," said Trevor flatly. No food, no matter how tempting would cause him delay.

"We can't," said Grov halfheartedly as he battled between hunger and duty. "Petra is to bless all food!"

Taro closed his eyes in resolution to his friend's difficult, yet truthful, words.

"Here! Have one, you idiots! You'll soon collapse if you don't eat! Let Petra bless the rest of them!" and with one hand he handed over a warm brick-sized loaf of bread. Before the boys could turn him down, Trevor had already vanished through the entrance of the tent. Taro turned to follow him when Grov grabbed him.

"Let him be. He has the right to see her all alone."

If the central tent looked vast compared to the other many tents that spread throughout the Turmenn's circular encampment, its inside was, if possible, even larger. Carts turned on their sides and boxes had been used to form the tent's wide skeleton. Blankets, furs, and cloths wrapped over the wooden frame so that it formed an empty space inside away from wind, dust, and cold. In there, secluded from the many prying eyes, Petra tended to the wounded as well as blessed the camp's entire food stocks. Somewhere among the many cots and blankets, Syll was waiting, Trevor knew.

Oil lamps adorned the inner structure of the tent, but only one now burned at the small entrance behind Trevor, its yellow-dirty light casting deep shadows but feet ahead of him. A gloomy air hung in the tent as if a great disease had fallen upon it. Hidden within the safety of the darkness, the ill Turmenn shifted their weight on their cots, their breaths wheezing, their lungs coughing.

Slowly, Trevor walked towards the furthest side of the tent, determined to find Syll. Inside, buried under thick layers of cloth and furs, away from the sun and moon, time seemed to have stopped. But Trevor knew that his time there alone would quickly pass and he would have to leave. He had to find her. He had to see her.

Trevor's eyes soon adjusted to the lack of light just enough to see the cots and navigate between them without crashing. With every step, his heart grew heavier, afraid he had waited too long to come, and Syll had passed away. Trevor knew his friends or brothers would have told him, yet the thought made him feel ill, as if his flesh began to shrink around his bones and choke him.

"Where are you Syllvia?" he asked under his breath. There were, but a few cots left between him and the pitch-black cloth that made the tent's far wall.

But as if some higher force had heard him, a cough broke nearby, and as he looked to see who made the wretched sounds, he saw her. Beautiful as he had always seen her, Syll slept peacefully, or so she seemed. With two strides he was upon her cot, his hands holding hers, his eyes raining tears over her white face.

Unable to suppress his need to know, his curiosity, Trevor lifted gingerly the cloth that covered the wound caused by the High Counsellor's blow. Horrified of what he might find, Trevor looked unsure at Syll's bare shoulder. Nothing but a pink scar of new skin to greet him. Trevor felt both relieved and deeply troubled; the contradicting feelings clashing with each other as he tried to understand his friend's plight.

"Why wouldn't you wake up my love? Why now, before we even had a chance to start a family of our own, you chose to leave me?" Trevor found himself talking to Syll as if she was but resting. "Why did you take my place before that blow? I would have died for you, I would have died for any of you."

Trevor was now crying, so heartbroken, he found he could not form more words. So he grabbed her face between his palms and kissed her on the lips, and wondered why he had waited so long to do it. He was in love with her, he had always been, yet only now, when Syll was lost in death, he had the courage to accept his feelings for her. He felt like a fool.

Again he kissed Syll's lips, pressed his forehead against hers, and stood there in heavenly silence.

The loud creaking of a cot drifted through the dark air of the tent. Trevor thought he must have woken up one of the other Turmenn, but when the sound came clearer, louder but moments later, he turned his head to see. The darkness shifted as he stared at it. Something within it stirred.

Trevor released Syll's face and straightened up to better see what made the growing noises. His right hand quickly rested on his long sword's hilt.

"That will be unnecessary…" came an unmistakable voice.

Trevor flinched as he realised who had spoken from within the veil of blackness.

"…your visit here is most welcome, Trevor."

But then he saw her, slowly advancing towards him, a shadow, a shimmering contour, a much older Petra.

"How long have you been hiding in the darkness?" he demanded, his hand still holding his sword.

"Hiding?" Petra chuckled, "This is my home, but I did not wish to startle you! Everything creaks and groans much like myself."

Trevor fell silent for a moment, feeling his anger rise within his broken frame, bubbling to the surface from some rotten corners of his self.

"You planned this," he said flatly thinking of how stupid he had been to fall in such a simple trap. The thought that his friend had betrayed him for her, made him want to cut her right in half, right there before Syll's glued-shut eyes.

"She needs you, Trevor! I know you blame me for what happened to your father, but she is still alive!"

"You old barf!" Trevor boomed, losing the little command he still had over his senses. "I don't blame you for what happened to father! I blame you for every damned bad thing that happened since we went to Brim! Hundreds have died because of you! HUNDREDS!"

Petra did not speak, regardless of how much Trevor wanted her to. She simply stared at him with those cold emerald-green eyes.

"How can you sleep at night? How can you close your eyes and not see their dead faces?"

Petra did reply this time, but Trevor could not hear her. As soon as her lips parted, a choking sound came from behind the two, followed by a fleshy thud and then a mindless shriek.

Instinctively, both Trevor and Petra turned to see what made those dreadful noises. Then they saw the entrance of the tent torn open. Half in, half out, Taro's thin torso lay inside the dim-lit tent. Before either of them could as much as react, a green foamy substance bubbled uncontrollably from Taro's gaping mouth and over his own hands which lay rigid, clenched around his throat. He looked as if he had tried to rip his own throat open, but choked before he could.

Then, moments later, through the tent's torn entrance, came Grov thrashing left and right, his eyes bloodshot with shock, but also fury.

"What happened," demanded Petra, rushing over to Taro's lifeless body. But Grov had his eyes set upon his friend standing before him.

"You killed him!" he shrieked from the edge of madness as he threw half of the loaf of bread Trevor had given them to eat at him.

"Oh no!" Petra cried, dropping next to Taro.

Angels are Coming

"Mother, you know that you're not safe here."

"This is my home, son. What am I supposed to do? Leave you and your father because of an old legend?" What you have read in all those books the Queen has in her Tower, are nothing but some fool's imagination."

"You are wrong, mother. What we deem as our past is nothing but a forgery, a careful construction to hide the truth from us all. Even father knows more than he lets us believe."

"Vondur knows better than to anger the Gods."

"Since you last saw him, father has changed, mother. The shadows speak in Seribu Menara of a new High Counsellor."

"He would never!"

"I will know soon enough. We are to go to Undirheim to burry the last remnants of the truth."

"You ought to be careful, Eldur!"

"You ought to forget Ophidia, and leave. I do not know what we will find up in the desert, but no good will come of it!"

"Be careful, son."

Mother and son

Anonymous

"It's done." Concluded Bathilda, serious and cold.

"She should have died years ago. Our beloved husbands should have had Bells' leadership, not her!" Elfredda added, hacking thunderously as if she had felt something good within her wretched self and tried urgently to expel it. A dark coloured glob soon sizzled in the burning coals before her.

The Greed sisters sat around a large fire as they often did in the early hours of the day, going through the things their gang had stolen from the Turmenn. With them were Burt and Martens. They had all heard, but moments before, the shrieking cry that had announced Petra's demise. As Bathilda and Elfredda Greed spoke of Petra's death and knitted plans of how to take the Turmenn's reins, Martens looked up at Burt unsure of herself. Maybe she had sided with the wrong people, she thought, after all, her poison was what took a life that morning. Burt met her gaze unwavering; his eyes cold with resolve, but said nothing. His mind was busy working out where his son was. And soon, as if nothing had happened, Elijah appeared from behind a row of tents, his hands tucked into his shirt, his stride untroubled.

"Son!" exhaled Burt with relief. He had been holding that breath in since his Elijah left to take the bread for Petra's blessing. "What took you so long?!" But before Burt to reach his son and see he was alright, Bathilda stepped between them, one clawed hand on the boy's shoulder, the other on his jaw.

"Has anybody seen you, boy?" Elijah flinched, turning his head away from Bathilda's touch. He remembered he had been instructed not to let himself be seen by anyone.

"Speak!" she bellowed, pushing her rotten talons into his young flesh, turning his head so that he faced her. Their faces were but inches apart.

"Let him be!" growled Burt, but knew the old woman would not stop until her questions were answered.

"Yes," muttered the boy barely able to form the words; Bathilda's claws dug deep into his jaw.

"Who saw you? Petra? Her damned guards?" Elijah tried to shake his head, but the old woman's grip was far too strong.

"Trevor," the boy said, forcing the words through Bathilda's clenched skeletal hand around his mouth.

"Stupid!" she growled, lifting her other hand to smack the young boy down. Her hand levitated in midair before finally, she let him go.

"Maybe this isn't all so bad, sister!" came Elfredda's high-pitched voice from behind. The Greed sisters 'gaze met.

"That stupid man hates her as much as we do! We should use that!"

"He also hates us, sister! But you're right. We'll make him help us return home!"

"Get out of here!" came Burt's rough voice as he pushed his son towards their tent once he had escaped Bathilda's iron grip. The boy's face returned a looked of disgruntlement as he, without doubt, thought he should have been congratulated for his deed that morning. However, the elders 'reaction could not have been more different. Both Burt and the Greed sisters had instructed young Elijah to go in secrecy and return unseen, but the boy failed to do so, and for that, the Greeds were furious. Burt bore the weight of that morning's events solely on his shoulders. Elijah did not know, nor needed to, that he had killed a soul that day; the bread he carried, carried death in them.

* * *

Trevor stared perplexed at Grov, his eyes drifting up and down from his friend's livid face to Taro's sprawled, dead body. Curiously, Petra touched the foamy fluids coming out of Taro's mouth, smelling her fingers, staring intently in the young man's face.

"He has been poisoned," she said quietly, her green eyes glistening with tears.

"I don't know what happened!" said Trevor in shock; his head shaking, his hands involuntarily wiping on his shirt.

"You killed my friend!" cried Grov, blind with fury.

"Where did you get these loaves of bread?" asked Petra flatly examining the knitted blanket that contained a dozen other poisoned bread. "Who gave them to you?" she growled.

"I will kill you!" shrieked Grov pulling his sword free.

"I don't know—"

"Who?" boomed Petra. Grov, however, had heard enough and attacked.

"Grov stop!" yelled Trevor releasing his own sword. "It was an accident!"

Grov paused in his charge, just short of Trevor. "I don't care! For weeks we work without your help! And now that you're back, he's gone! Look at him!"

"You two stop it!" bellowed Petra from the tent's torn entrance.

"I am sorry!"

"LOOK AT HIM!" and the tent rang with the clash of metal. Sparks flew around them, lamps got knocked over, fists came in contact with chins. The two men, one a few good years older, the other twice as large, collided thunderously and fought for dear life.

"Stop that right now!" boomed Petra so loud, her words reverberated through their flesh.

The two men stopped, their swords still pointed at each other. "You will not fight in my tent! If you wish so much to kill each other, please do it outside. There are wounded people in here, children, Syllvia! And there's the dead body of a friend! This was no accident!"

"Who would want to kill Taro?" asked Grov lowering his sword, Trevor contemplating the same thing.

"The poison was no accident, that Taro consumed it was," Petra concluded, pulling out of the bundle Trevor had brought in, one of the loaves. "These were meant for me."

"What you're saying is murder!"

"Yes, Trevor, someone most definitely wants me dead."

"Those cursed Greeds!" hissed Trevor through clenched teeth.

"How do you know it was them?" asked Grov who although calmer, had something that tasted like revenge in his tongue.

"When I was walking here, I met a boy from Bells that had that bundle with him," he pointed at Petra's hands. "He said his name was Elijah, but I did not recognise him until now. He is…"

"Burt's son!" finished both Trevor and Petra together.

"And we all know where Burt's allegiance lies," he added, moving past Grov and towards his now dead friend.

Trevor felt the blood boil in his veins as he stared into his friend's gaunt face. He was going to find the Greeds, not for Petra, for whom he was no longer loyal, but for Taro. He would make them pay for what they did.

"I'll kill them!" said Grov plainly, heading towards the entrance of the tent.

"Grov, you can't; not like that." Trevor grabbed his friend by the arm and pulled him to a halt.

There in the gloomy insides of the central tent, over their friend's rigid body, Petra, Trevor and Grov stared into each other's faces while their minds forged plans to make the Greeds pay for their deed.

"Let me go," said Grov in a low, trembling voice.

"You can't storm into their camp!" Trevor exclaimed in an attempt to make his friend see sense. "They have men and weapons! We need to be smarter."

"Turmenn cannot know that food was poisoned. You are barely holding them together as it is. If they cannot trust the little food they get, they will march back to Bells and all this…" Petra pointed at the many cots around her, "…would have been in vain."

"And why would that be bad?" Trevor challenged Petra, feeling his anger rise. "No one is hunting us down now! We can go home!" Grov moved his gaze from Taro's lifeless body to Trevor, whose words for the first time in weeks, made sense. They could go home; back to their beautiful Bells, to soft beds and warm food, to their old lives.

"I think we should!" Grov nodded slowly.

"We — must — not," said Petra softly, stressing each word.

"Haven't enough died for this quest of yours?" bellowed Trevor, losing his temper. "Haven't we paid enough? Byard, father, Syll, and now Taro, and so many others we swore to protect! When will this end? Our men are barely standing! We are hungry, we are tired. You would sooner see us all like father…" he boomed, pointing at the desert beyond, "…than take us back home!"

"You are a fool, boy! You think we're safe? You think this is over? You have been daydreaming for weeks, and clearly, you still are. Wake up! This is war and look at us! We cannot fight the Sorcerers, we would be dead if just one of their Draugur found us now!"

"Then what? We wait for them to find us?"

"We cannot go back home, nor can we stay here. We need to reach the southern plains. The Sorcerers will not be able to wage war with both the Beasts and Humans."

"You are mad! If you are not willing to take us home, I will!" And with that, Trevor stormed out of the tent into the pale morning.

* * *

"Surprised to see you here, friend!" came Erlend's voice as the two men almost collided with each other.

"Not now!" growled Trevor. But Erlend's eyes drifted behind him, where through the tent's torn entrance, Petra and Grov kneeled by something the resembled a set of legs. Erlend's mind froze.

"What….what happened?" he whispered in shock, and he too dropped to the ground at the young man's feet. "Who did this to him?" Now, Erlend could see Taro's whole body sprawled onto the floor, half outside, half into the ill-lit tent, but clearly dead.

"We need to pull him inside, we need to talk."

"Who did this?" Erlend demanded, but Petra's gaze settled not on his face but on his hands.

"Where did you get THAT?" Erlend followed Petra's stare to the knitted blanket he had brought with him, where inside warm bread awaited to be eaten.

"The Greeds—" And then realisation struck him like a lightning bolt. "You think they did this!"

"We know they did this." Petra corrected. "Now help us pull his body inside, I need to examine him. Trevor, you too!" There had always been something in Petra's voice that could command even the most rebellious, so

Trevor helped put Taro's body in an empty cot by the entrance, where two lamps now burned and exposed their friend's poisoned body to them all.

He looked pale and rigid, petrified in an expression of pure agony. His hands frozen in time as he tried to rip his own throat open; his face a contorted gargoyle's.

"He needs a burial!" said Grov solemnly, his voice tearing at the heavy silence that had befallen all of them.

"Once I find what did this to him, so he shall!" Petra was already undoing his shirt, her hands brandishing a few small empty phials.

"This has gone too far!" Erlend's rough voice came as he hung white sheets around the cot and Petra, secluding them from the rest of the tent.

Coughs came, raspy and faint, from the wounded who, although they had witnessed Taro's death, were too weak and too addled to make sense of it.

"What about the others?" asked Grov, "They ought to have heard."

"Don't worry about them, half of them are dying, and half of them are mad. If we keep others from coming in, no one will know what happened."

"But Petra! We must tell others!" came Grov's voice.

"Until we know what did this, until we know no other food has been poisoned, no one must know!"

"What about the Greeds, then?" asked Trevor from across the cot.

"As far as they are concerned maybe it's best we let them think Petra is dead!" said Erlend calmly. "Maybe that way they will not poison more food."

"So what, we act as if nothing has happened? We lost a friend!"

"I know Trevor…" said Petra as she collected some of the green substance that had come out Taro's mouth in one of those small bottles. "…but for now we must! Once I find out what cursed substance they used, we can lay him to rest."

"We need, at least, to tell Daniel and Sam! Taro was their friend too!"

"Leave my brothers out of this!" said Trevor angrily.

"That I am afraid I cannot do. We need their help. We need more eyes out there while I play dead in here."

"You will kill us all," said Trevor unwavering.

"Trevor!"

"No, Erlend! You can follow her blindly, but I cannot! And nor will my little brothers! Once this is done, we're going home!" And he stormed out of the tent. But as he rushed towards the bright outside, he cast one last glance to Syll's shrouded-in-darkness cot. Somewhere in there, his love lay in a death-like slumber, and Trevor wondered if she dreamt of him as he dreamt of her every night.

* * *

Sara woke up alone, in the tent she shared with Erlend. He had awakened early again to check the camp, she knew, but selfishly wished he had stayed with her. Since the Turmenn had erected the camp, the two barely saw each other. She was always busy helping Petra tending to the wounded, while Erlend ran errands throughout the encampment. Still, she wished he had been there next to her, holding her, kissing her, today more than ever.

Sara was shaking both from cold and fright. She had been having dreams again, dreams of death, but had not yet gathered the courage to tell either Erlend or Petra. She feared them thinking she was slowly going mad. After all, she was not sure of her own sanity anymore.

Cold seemed to creep into her soul through the sodden clothes she had on, the mattress beneath her wet;

the dreams that came to her becoming worse with every passing night.

Clouds, leaden and black, gathered around the Turmenn's camp from all around, closing on them like a snare. Thunder reverberated through her bones and shook the very fabric of the realm. Sara had dreamt such things for weeks now.

Sands that shifted, blackened dunes that rolled towards their tents, birds circled above them in their hundreds. Nature itself seemed to have turned against them, intent on their destruction.

Cracking sounds of grinding, breaking bones filled the heavy air, while black birds swooped lower excitedly awaiting their heavenly feast. Ragged shadows walked through the billowing desert towards them.

And through the blackened skies, amid the many birds, they came, winged and merciless. The messengers and executioners of a God Sara wished not to meet. Through crying eyes, she watched them all amass around them, from the side, from beneath, from above.

Death was in the air, death was in the ground, death was everywhere. Angels were coming.

First Day of Training

"But mother!" cried Aerö childishly. "I don't want to go down there!"

"We have discussed this already. We cannot wait any longer for you to grow up. I have treated you favourably since you came here, but that cannot go on. I see now, as Finndôra crudely pointed out, that that was my mistake. You need to take your place within the Lair, Aerö."

"But mother!"

"And from now, you will address me as your Queen," she said coldly. But a quiver in her voice betrayed her true emotions. She felt terrible pushing her son away like this, but she no longer had a choice — much like Aerö. She was the Beast Lords' rightful Queen, their leader, but she too, had to obey the Lair's collective mind. And they had spoken, loud and clear, that the boy Skeggor foresaw millennia ago, would have to live and work and train like one of them.

Estrelle, of course, knew they were right. After all, had it not been her own son causing all the quarrels among the Beast Lords, she would have been the first to order them to follow the Beasts Lords' code. But it was Aerö, her lost son, and pushing him away like this felt more painful than the wound she cradled in her arm day and night. She had sent him away before, an act that took fourteen long years to negate.

Estrelle commanded her thoughts to return to order. She had to stay strong, for both of them to succeed.

"Now go! Your training starts today. Hïldúúr will be waiting for you down in the training grounds within the hour."

Aerö felt suddenly sick. Like some wounded animal, he looked into his mother's eyes, hoping to break the barrier she had erected against him. Her cold stare met his, and he knew he had no chance but to obey her. He would try again tomorrow if he survived today.

The only things Aerö could think of as he descended the long staircase to the lower level where his mother's and his own rooms were, was Hïldúúr and his terrifying Hound. The tall, broad Beast Lord and his Beast, second in command after Estrelle, had powers no other had in Undirheim, they could turn young Aer'ös bones into mush. Just thinking of them made him feel lightheaded, ill; his own legs fought his orders to go on and tried to trip him, stop him.

"He would not harm me! He would not harm me…" Aerö repeated louder and louder, trying to convince himself that there was nothing to be afraid of in the training grounds. But then, Finndôra's actions came to him, her angry shouts, her stare, and worst, her Feond's grip around his legs. She had not feared harming him in front of his own mother, her Queen; what would they do to him so deep beneath her throne room, so far from her eyes. Aerö shivered at the very thought. A few more steps and he would reach the hallway to his room and from there a labyrinth unknown. Aerö wondered if anyone would come for him if he hid in his room.

The bright orange light of Estrelle's chambers radiated up ahead. Aerö stopped to listen for other sounds of footsteps, but he could only hear the echoes of his own. He was alone.

Unwilling to risk awakening his powers, which only seemed to know how to kill, Aerö decided it was better to run quickly to his room, or better, to the other one in which he left the book Nóór chose for him, and hide. The thought quickly rooted in his mind, and without delay, he broke into a run down the last flight of steps and down the hallway. But as he reached the bottom of the stairs and turned sharply to his left, an obstacle waited for him there, an impediment he had no time to avoid.

With a loud crash, he collided with the object that had been so foolishly left on the floor. Aerö cried, a growl responded and a yap. Aerö shook his head wearily to cast away the lightheadedness the impact shrouded his mind in. He opened his eyes and saw the smooth ceiling of the corridor.

"Get off me!" came Nóór's muffled voice from somewhere beneath Aerö. And a shrill bark echoed through the long tunnel from a ball of fur near him.

"Are you mad? What are you running from?" Nóór asked, pulling himself free from the entanglement of limbs and torsos.

"Oh, nothing.But what were YOU doing there? I thought you had training every morning!"

"WE have training every morning," corrected Nóór through a grin that split his face in two. "Father asked me to come and take you to the grounds today, so you don't get lost."

Aerö sighed at his friend, who did not even try to conceal his excitement. He had tried to persuade Aerö to train with him and Ári for days, but Aerö was too terrified of his own powers.

Now he had no choice but to follow Nóór into the training grounds and train with Hïldúúr and his Beast.

The only hallway Aerö knew in the whole of Undirheim vanished behind them as Nóór and Ári took him ever deeper into the lone mountain. No lamps or torches burned, so far away from his small chamber, as the only ones who used these passageways needed no light to see. Somewhere to his left, Aerö remembered, was the smaller tunnel Nóór had shown him days before and the dried-up well they climbed into to reach the Beasts' forbidden Nursery. There, from under the protection of the deepest shadows, the two boys had witnessed Ári's birth.

Nóór pressed on, moving swiftly through the Lair's dark bowels, pulling Aerö after him. Ári's yaps echoed ahead as he led the way. Every so often, Aerö tripped or brushed against the tunnel's walls, he simply could not see. Nóór turned sharply to the right and Aerö, who was still attached to his right hand, joined his shoulder with the wall in a sore embrace. This was the third time.

"Watch where you're running!" said Nóór as Aerö moaned in pain.

"It's pitch-black in here," Aerö said, rubbing his bruised shoulder with his free hand. "How can YOU see where we're going?"

"Ári…" said Nóór matter-of-factly, yet his voice implied he was expecting Aerö to know that. "I see through his eyes, of course." Ári's shrill bark came from somewhere up ahead, and Nóór broke into a run once more.

Aerö could feel the tunnel slope beneath his feet as the two of them, and Ári, moved ever deeper. It was also getting warmer, stuffier and Aerö knew why. The deeper they went, the closer they got to the giant orange veins that heated up the immeasurable depths of Undirheim.

Then, as expected, images of the Verndari showed themselves to him, floating in midair, stretching their long tentacles towards him.

Aer'ös thoughts returned to the black tunnels Nóór was navigating through, as his eyes began to see his friend's contour before him. Light was pouring up into their tunnel up ahead, orange and bright.

"Up ahead," said Nóór excited, moving at a more manageable pace.

"Why are the training grounds so far away from the throne room?" Aerö asked, now that he could see where he was going. "It takes forever to get down here and back up!"

"You'll see," answered his friend excitedly. "I cannot wait to see what Father teaches us today!" Ári yelped ahead.

When Aerö saw the opening before him, he understood why the Beasts Lords had chosen a place so far away from where they lived to use as training grounds. If the cave Aerö had seen the spider-monkeys and the Verndari in, was large, this was of altogether different proportions. Orange light pulsated from thick veins that webbed the walls and ceiling of the empty space; their aura uniformly colouring the place an eerie amber. Aerö found the cave unusually bright for where it was — under a mountain.

Bangs and crashes echoed through the leaden-with-heat air as a few dozen Beast Lords, and their growling Beasts, fought against each other.

It was only when Nóór stopped at the edge of the vast room, that Aerö realised that the Beast Lords fought against their Beasts most seriously; their swords slashing through the air, their brows glistening with sweat.

Hounds, stags, bears, and Feonds unforgivingly attacked the ones they called their Masters, biting, tearing, slashing at the air between them. And in the middle of it all, Hïldúúr and his nightmare Hound watched the pairs battle.

Unlike the other giant cavern Nóór had taken him to, here no water filtered through the vaulted ceilings and noisily exploded into steam, but rather a suffocating fever reigned in the place. He could feel his skin turn sticky within moments of their arrival.

"You'll get used to it," said Nóór as he saw Aerö undo his shirt. Through the opening, a golden chain glistened in the orange light of the cave.

Aerö nodded, unfocused, his eyes tracing the web of throbbing fire-veins above and around them. He instantly thought of the bowl-shaped cages Trevor used to catch rabbits at the edge of Wündalær. His eyes slowly descended from the glowing dome, towards the flat span of rock on which the Beast Lords and their Beasts exchanged crippling blows. But as he looked for Nóór, who sat in front of him but moments earlier, his eyes rested on a large, dark blur. Aerö wiped sweat off his eyes with the back of his hand. When he looked again, two cold-yellow eyes gleamed at him from the amassed shadow of its body. Aerö instinctively stepped backwards and stumbled; his lungs gasping for air.

"So you've come," said Hïldúúr somewhat amused at the sight before him - their foretold saviour crumpled at his feet.

Aerö heard Nóór's father speak, yet he could not command his eyes to look away from the huge wolf-like creature before him. Hïldúúr's Hound - which reached the man's chest and was as tall as he was while standing, growled, bare-toothed, from an arm's distance.

"Good! There's much you need to learn. Let's go!" But Aerö did not move. The Hound watched him patiently, waiting for him to flinch.

"Ashäël…" hissed Hïldúúr at his Beast. "…as do I, but we need his help, and for that, he needs ours first." Ashäël seemed to weigh his options; to eat the frightened neither sorcerer, nor human boy before him or to obey his Master's words. Finally, the Beast snorted, annoyed, and moved slowly behind Hïldúúr.

"Thank you, old friend," Hïldúúr whispered petting the great Hound's head; then turned his attention back to Aerö.

"Well?" he asked, "Are you coming?"

Reluctantly, Aerö followed. Somewhere to his right, Nóór chased Ári along with a few other young Beast Lords. Their odd game of chase sending echoes of rolling laughter through the empty cavern. Aerö wished he could go play with them. Their loud chortle unearthed memories of friends and games he used to play in Bells.

Aerö did not know where Hïldúúr planned on taking him, least what the broad Beast Lord wished to teach him, yet he followed obediently; his thoughts lighter than they were when he had reached the grounds.

At the fringes of the cavern, at the meeting point of the flat ground and the great luminous cage, dimples patterned the floor. The depressions seemed to have been meticulously dug into the hard rock, or better, formed under the weight of a great Beast. To Aerö they looked like giant nests scattered for as far as he could see. Hïldúúr led the way, moving further away from the battling pairs and the raucous young ones.

"This will do," he said, stopping next to a large pothole. Ashäël sniffed at the air inside it and sneezed as if some fetid smell Aerö could not perceive, drifted upwards from within. Unsatisfied, Hïldúúr's Hound moved on, tasting the air within each dimple. Hïldúúr, however, did not follow, but slid gently to the bottom of his chosen nest.

"Come."

Aerö skidded to a halt next to the Beast Lords' second in command. A wide grin stretched across his face. Despite his fears of the Beast Lords and their Beasts, and of his own powers, Aerö was happy to be out of the dark rooms in which he constantly lurked.

His elation, however, was short-lived, as from behind came the screech of claws on smooth rock. Ashäël descended next to him. Aerö froze as the large Hound levelled with him, just as tall as he was, just as menacing-looking as always. Ashäël's large, yellow eyes blinked at Aerö coldly, his huge snout so close to him, Aerö could feel his whiskers tickle his face, but not the laughing kind. A chill crept up young Aer'ös skin as the Hound released a low, guttural growl that reverberated painfully throughout his body.

"That's enough, Ashäël," said Hïldúúr grabbing Ashäël by one alert ear and pulling him away from Aerö. "Don't mind him, boy, he doesn't like anyone, really. He's old and ill-tempered—and wise," he added after Ashäël released a louder growl this time aimed at his Master.

"The Queen asked me to teach you the ways of our kind, but mind you boy…" Hïldúúr said plainly, "…not everybody under Undirheim believes that you're the one, our saviour. I, for one, do not believe in prophecies. But I have seen you fight, we all have; and while we do not know exactly what you are, an Elemental, a human, or a Beast Lord, we need your help. However, if there's any sign to make me think that you're a spy for the Betrayers, despite my love for our Queen, I will kill you." Ashäel growled again making himself noticed that he too would slay him if given any motive.

Aerö swallowed hard and nodded, unsure what he should say.

"Good!" said Hïldúúr with finality on the matter and seeing Aerö look around the bowl-shaped depression they were in, he added. "We use these for one-to-ones. We train here to fight our own kind, our companions, without interference or help. We fight in here until one can no longer stand."

Aerö felt his knees buckle under his own weight. He now understood why Hïldúúr had brought him there, far away from any prying eyes or curious ears. He was there to fight the Beast Lord or his hellish Beast, or both.

"Sit!" came Hïldúúr's somewhat bored voice as he dropped to his knees, settling as comfortably as possible on the hard surface. Ashäel paced around the two until satisfied with a spot at his Master's right he also settled; his large head resting on his clawed front paws.

Aerö watched the two relax, Ashäel even seemed to have fallen asleep, before he sat down slowly to face them.

"How much do you know or understand your powers?" asked Hïldúúr, genuinely interested. Aerö instinctively touched his chest, where under his plain shirt, rested the egg-sized scarlet gem his father had bequeathed him.

"Not those powers boy, with them I cannot help you. What do you know of talking to the Beasts?" Aerö considered the question and shook his head. He knew he did command the Beasts to leave the throne room just before he had unleashed his purging flames and saved their lives, but all seemed to come to him through the translucent veil of a long had dream; remembered, yet devoid of detail.

"Then we have a lot of work to do," said Hïldúúr patiently, his right hand, as always, petting his old companion's large head. Ashäel did not even seem to notice.

"To understand your gifts, you have to understand yourself, said Skeggor Skalidur in front of the gathered masses at his coronation," began Hïldúúr in a calm voice and Aerö understood why the Beast Lord had chosen the sunken nest to train him. Here, away from the clashing of swords and claws, of battle cries and the shrieking of children, they could speak in peace.

"Our skills are not to rule the Beasts, but help each other, understand each other. We hear their thoughts as they hear ours, and for that, no secrets can be held from one another. We pair for life as children, a match made by two minds, a bond that can be broken only by death. So you must understand that only minds alike can bond, good with good, evil with evil, bad-tempered with bad-tempered," Hïldúúr said, shifting his gaze upon his sleeping Beast. "Skeggor's words still make, millennia after their utterance, the foundations of our Lair. There can be no secrets between a Beast Lord and his Beast."

Aerö listened, absorbed, to Hïldúúr's soft-spoken words, his cadence slow, yet passionate.

"But do you see now why all the souls that live under this mountain are afraid of you? Well most," he corrected himself, allowing a small smile to paint his lips, "We do not,…" he added roughly pulling on Ashäël's furry ears, "…and neither does Nóór and Ári." Aerö shook his head again.

"It's because of what you did inside the throne room."

Aerö shrugged, clasping his father's pendulum through his shirt as he remembered the inferno it contained.

Hïldúúr shook his head. "What you did with your mind boy!" he said louder, his calm demeanour slowly cracking, peeling away. Ashäël opened one yellow eye then shut it again sighing.

Seeing that Aerö did not understand, Hïldúúr
continued.

"The Beast Lords and their Beasts have always lived a
life with one linked mind. Their thoughts, their feelings,
even their fears shared with their companion's. We could
never have secrets from our furry friends, but we enjoyed
each other's thoughts without other Beast Lords or their
Beasts listening in. Until you came. What you did, albeit
unwillingly, is shatter our very privacy and way of life.
For the few short seconds you reached our minds to
deliver your message, our thoughts and fears were all
yours to know. Beast and Beast Lord ran to safety, not
only from your flames, but from your thoughts as well."
Hïldúúr's words drifted away, lazily through the cave's
leaden air. Ashäël's bright eyes watched closely Aer'Ös
every move.

This is why they were so hostile towards him, this was
the reason of their fright. And for the first time since he
had to give away his life above the sands, Aerö
understood the Beasts and their Masters.

Golden Living Things

Tired and with his mind saturated with questions, Aerö returned to his cool, dark room. The training grounds had been abandoned by the time Hïldúúr allowed him to turn in for the night. It must have been late for his supper lay cold by his cot, placed there, no doubt, hours earlier.

Questions burned brightly in his mind, keeping tiredness at bay. Slowly, Aerö changed his damp clothes and readied himself for bed. The heat that he'd withstood all day had drunk, thirstily, the water from his body. He sat on the edge of his mattress and thought of all the things Hïldúúr's had shared with him. Although he had spent all day in the training grounds, he felt alert and curious. An emotion he had not allowed himself to feel in months filled his being; the excitement for what was to come.

There he lay, alone in his cot, a lone candle flickering next to him, its licking flame projecting light and shadows across the cramped room. Aerö could not sleep. His thoughts wandered free across all of Urukk, from Bells to Undirheim, to Seribu Menara, and back again, never to settle. Faces of people he once knew flashed before his mind's eye and vanished just as quickly; people he loved, people he loathed, people he trusted. Aer'ös mind spiralled faster and faster through memories, and things imagined, from his dreams of death and silver lakes to Petra. She was still alive, he knew that, Estrelle had told him so, yet she would not allow him to go see her.

This will not work, thought Aerö as he realised that sleep was something he would not achieve. He was too worked up by Hïldúúr's words. Then it occurred to him. Maybe if he tried his mind by reading a few pages, or at least until his candle died out, then maybe his thoughts would settle, and he could get some rest. There was no doubt that Hïldúúr would expect him to be ready at dawn.

Slowly, he made his way across the hallway, to the other room where Estrelle's library was, his bare feet slapping the cold stone beneath them. Candle in hand, he entered the shelved room where he had spent most of his time since his arrival in Undirheim. Somewhere at the far end of the room, Aerö remembered to have abandoned the book Nóór suggested he should read. With the book under his arm and his candle tightly clasped in one hand, Aerö returned to his small room. Triumphant, and with a few breaths left in his black-wax candle, Aerö climbed in his cot to read and hopefully manage to get some sleep.

Heavy and old, the large tome rested in Aer'ös lap, every so often his fingers tracing protruding petrified rings on its covers where snail-like creatures had, until recently, been resting. Aerö turned the book in his hands, observing its cover, its binding; then resting it on his knees, he carefully peeled away its front cover. With a sharp, tearing sound, the book opened itself to Aerö and allowed things it had been deprived of for long centuries — light and warmth — to permeate its age-old insides. Crinkled and brittle, dark yellow pages whispered at him from his lap.

Magical Creatures and the Kingdom of Peace were written in Greindur Gamall's fluid hand, which Aerö recognised easily; he had been reading the old sorcerer's writings for weeks now. Beautiful and cursive, Greindur's words stared back at Aerö from the delicate pages in his lap. Aerö threw a quick glance at the candle at his right to evaluate how much life it still had left; then, satisfied, he returned his attention to the book.

Magical Creatures and the Kingdom of Peace

In a land much different from our own, where magic had not yet been conquered by men, creatures ruled the world in its entirety. Beasts, the likes we fail to imagine, roamed those realms. Ancient in their age, kind in their nature and of such intelligence no anthropoid would ever come to know.

Untold millennia had shaped their Realm, yet the ancient creatures never changed their way. They had ruled their Kingdom throughout their extraordinary lengthy lives with kindness and not wars. They had no kings, nor queens, nor any overlord, but rather, they all ruled in harmony their blessed Kingdom of Peace.

Long forgotten, and with great difficulty unearthed, tales spoke of their strange world, legends of such beauty, my imagination still fails to paint them fairly.

It was in my long wanders that curiosity kept taught my sails to follow the odd stories, to chase them, and if in luck, discover their true meaning. My thirst for the forgotten knowledge the realm might have still possessed, had taken me as far as the White Shores up north, or beyond the ever-growing desert to the East. Far I went and read whatever writings I could find. Had there been records of fallen cities or tales of demonic creatures, I devoured all of them. The further my attraction for the peculiar took me, the wilder the stories grew, and stranger the ones who remembered them.

And I think, as I write these accounts of the bizarre, of mad Syngja-Vatn, the captain of a sun-bleached shipwreck in the middle of Endalausir Desert, and his many tales. There he stood, and I can still see him through my mind's eye, on the high mast of his ship half-swallowed by sands; always looking at the sea of dust around him.

At night he would come down to rest, weary and parched, or maybe only brought by my food's rising scents; tiny, invisible wisps that conquered him through his burnt nose and grabbed his guts for them to order. Like a bone-white lizard, he would descend, spiralling towards me slow and frightened; his feet-long, age-whitened hair coiling like a serpent at the proud mast's base. Naked and dark, with skin resembling crumpled, dry paper, and eyes as white as snow, the old captain of a boat that had not moved through water in millennia shared his stories in exchange for food.

Syngja-Vatn was, by any reckoning, utterly strange, yet stranger still were his accounts of the things he had witnessed.

Night and night again, he crept next to my fire with stories old and new; and for a fortnight we enjoyed each other's company, I for his yarns, Syngja-Vatn for my food and friendship. In a place like that, not many got to gaze upon the carcass of a ship and its unusual commander.

Yet one story left his lips more often than any other as an answer to my constant questions for his reasons to kept watch atop the erect mast. His response was always "The Singing Waves".

"They came at night from deep beneath the blackened surface of the sea, their presence hidden by the mirrored stars and pale-white moon. They drifted slowly to the surface from unknown depths and gently took hold of our minds, so none of us could fend ourselves against them.

I was high up inside the crow's nest, as I am sitting every day since then, watching the waveless sea, when sung whispers started to echo through the night. We all welcomed their sweet words and listened to them merrily; but as we did so, our thoughts grew heavy and dragged us to them. I was young then, with a whole life left for me. When I awoke, I was like this, alone and ancient on this yellow sea. But late at night, I can just hear them, singing from afar, the waves that took my crew and my life with them."

That was the story Syngja-Vatn shared with me, among so many others, yet this one remained with me for many years to come. Centuries have passed since then, and now, when I recall those *memories, I feel as if I never left the man who sailed the sea of sand and watched for Singing Waves. He was Syngja-Vatn the observant, or maybe he was simply Syngja-Vatn the mad.*

But not all my quests that took me far and wide began as such, as a wander, but rather as a question. The first curious creatures to wonder upon their origins were not mountains apart from my own home, but rather inside it.

They had been brought by Skeggor Skalidur himself into the city, three creatures of such unusualness, no one had ever seen before, or for that matter after, despite my many journeys to reveal their past and birthplace...

With a loud, slapping sound, the large book slid from Aer'ös hands and hit the floor. Startled, he looked around, but could not see a thing. His eyes blinked from behind a thick black veil. It was darker than the black of night. Aer'ös candle must have burnt itself whole as he read from the thick book Nóór gave him; and in the blackness that followed, he most certainly had fallen asleep. Aerö had no other source of light he could conjure, so he left the book where it had fallen and turned in for the night. It was late, closer to dawn than dusk, and Aerö knew he had to get some rest, for when the Feonds 'cry would herald the new morning, his training with Hïldúúr would begin again.

Morning came as quickly as Aer'ös eyes closed. The Feonds' high-pitched, painful cry reverberated through Undirheim's bones for all to hear. Dawn had arrived.

Aerö grunted as he turned inside his cot, tired, as if he had not slept, eyes glued, his body begging for more rest.

Moments seemed to pass while Aer'ös mind produced excuses to not wake and go, like every other Beast Lord, to the training grounds. But as he lay in pitch-black darkness in his cot, thinking of the many reasons he could give Hïldúúr for his now decided, inevitable absence, the stone door that separated him from the rest of the Lair opened. Aerö got up hastily on his elbows to see who had come. Light poured into his tiny room from burning lamps outside, a silhouetted figure watched him from the wide-open doorway.

"You'll be late, and father does not like it," came Nóór's voice, and a second later, a tiny yelp from Ári. Before Aerö could even muster a reply, the pup sprinted, moving like a shadow through the slice of light that cut his room in two, and jumped in his cot, excited. Aerö traced the outline of the Beast before him; watching him pant, his yellow eyes ablaze upon him while Nóór placed next to his bed, the dreaded breakfast they had every day.

"Eat that quickly and let's go!"

Aerö wanted to say no, to tell his friend to leave him be, to lie that he was ill or that he simply did not want to go, but for some reason, he did not. Aerö picked up his food and ate it without speaking. Mushrooms and fruit, the same food every day, but despite his acute dislike for it, he was glad to not feel hunger the way he had so often up in Bells.

Aerö did not know why he did it, why while he ate his food, he stretched his hand and petted Ári on his head as if it were a dog and not a soon-to-be merciless Beast. The pup's warm body, his short fur, his lolling tongue shifted something inside Aerö, and he found himself smiling at the thought that he might actually like the little Beast. Dressed and fed, Aerö, Nóór, and Ári left the tiny room for the Beast Lords' training grounds.

"I wish father would let you play with us soon," said Nóór, as the three navigated through the maze of tunnels beneath Undirheim. Unlike the previous day when Ári led the way in pitch-black darkness, dim lamps rested on the tunnels' walls, for which Aerö was grateful. They moved swiftly down the narrow passageways and reached the training grounds in half the time they'd needed the previous day. No fresh bruises marked Aer'ös shoulders as the three emerged into the bright-lit cavern the Beast Lords and their Beasts used for their training.

"Me too," muttered Aerö, feeling his hope fade as Hïldúúr made his way towards them. Ashäël walked slowly at his side, his gait heavy, painful.

"What happened to him?" asked Nóór, failing to catch Ári from dashing between his feet to Hïldúúr's Beast.

"We all train, son," said Hïldúúr, at which Ashäël growled low and swung his giant head to touch his Master. Hïldúúr instinctively rested his hand on the Hound's head. Ári moved between the large Beast's legs at such a speed, that tracking him proved difficult to Aerö. "Now go and train with the others. Aerö, come with me."

The glowing, entwined veins that lined the walls and lit the place, wrapped around Aerö as Hïldúúr led the way towards the nest-like pits they'd trained in previously. Beyond the fighting pairs of Beast Lords and their Beasts scattered over the stone plane, passed the few children and their ever raucous games. Aerö found himself sliding again towards the bottom of a smooth depression Hïldúúr and his Beast had already reached.

"Good," said Hïldúúr taking yet again the kneeling position he'd taught Aerö. Just like the previous day, Ashäël moved slowly, but this time clearly in pain, around the two until he too dropped to the ground next to his Master. Aerö took the same position as Hïldúúr before him, feet under him, hands on his knees.

"Today we'll try to see if you can use your mind to reach that of the others. Well—today just mine and Ashäël's." Hïldúúr added, and a tiny smile betrayed his face, but then added, serious as always, "But for that, I'll need you to do something first! I want you to take off your gem."

Aerö stared into Hïldúúr's eyes, unsure, but as he tried to fathom why the Beast Lord wanted such a thing, the memories returned to him, as they always seemed to do from the deepest recesses of his mind. Woods burning right before his eyes, Rokksvaart's inn roofless and charred, the whole desert blackened by his flames. Aerö nodded obediently, as memories of Undirheim, spewing tongues of flames through every crack and tunnel, washed over him. Slowly he undid his shirt and pulled the cold stone away from his warm body.

Aerö felt somehow naked, exposed, as the scarlet gem came to rest on the floor beside him with a silver ring. He could not even remember the last time the golden chain did not touch his skin. A feeling he did not like, despite his inability of commanding its raging flames. After all, the pendulum was the only physical thing Aerö had left from his murdered father. Eldur's diary flashed before his mind's eye, the other thing his father had bequeathed to him, but which now most probably lay on his old room's floor among many other forsaken things of his old life. Bells had been left abandoned by the very villagers it struggled to protect, this much Aerö knew from Estrelle, images of empty streets and decrepit houses forming in his mind. The house he shared with Petra looked worse than most, slowly crumbling under its own weight. In their tiny room, the stalagmites of books and parchments that rose in piles from its floor turned steadily to dust. There, among the many leathery corpses of old tomes, his father's journal decomposed just like the rest of them.

"Boy, are you ready?" Hïldúúr's voice drifted sluggishly and Aerö realised his mind had taken him again on one of its wild wanders. Hïldúúr stared at Aerö, waiting for him to reply.

"Ummm…" Aerö hesitated.

"I know you're scared. I understand, but you have to try. You have to focus," Hïldúúr said, patiently petting Ashäël's giant head. The Beast seemed to enjoy a rather restful sleep. Only the rhythmic rise and fall of his large ribcage to betray his stillness.

"Empty your mind of any thought and try to see in mine. Listen to my thoughts."

Aerö tried to keep his thoughts at bay, to push them out of his wandering mind, but that proved far more difficult than he had expected. Thoughts of things he knew or dreamt about came crushing into his mind, a vertigo of images he had no command over. The harder he tried, the louder his mind grew.

"Come on! Try harder!" Aerö could hear Hïldúúr's words over the pandemonium unleashing in his head. "Harder!" And how he tried. Aerö struggled to rein in his screaming thoughts, only to hear them bellow louder.

"You can do it, Aerö! Try harder, you can do it! I know you can!"

But fruitlessly did Aerö tense his every muscle, his every nerve, for he had less control over his thoughts than a parent with a rotten-spoiled child. He was hopeless.

"You can do it!" Hïldúúr boomed.

"NO, I CAN'T!" cried Aerö, tears leaping from his eyes as he slapped the floor with his hands. His fingers quickly found the scarlet gem that always managed to comfort him. Both Hïldúúr and Ashäël stared at him with their cold eyes. The Beast Lord scrutinised his every breath, his every falling tear; his Beast bared his dagger-teeth and snarled at him.

Upset, but mostly frustrated, he stood up and ran up the slope outside the giant dimple in the stone.

Swifter than Ári, he ran passed the yelling youths who quickly fell dead silent, leaving behind the radiating-orange training grounds. Aerö only looked behind once he had reached the tunnel that would take him, after navigating through the maze of passageways by the burning lamps that now adorned their walls, to his small room and solitude. He was expecting to see Hïldúúr and Ashäël speeding after him, but there was no one chasing him.

His room welcomed him, cool and dim-lit, a lone lamp flickered on the small table by the door as he rushed in.

How could they all know better than he did about his supposed powers? Why couldn't they just leave him be? Hadn't he saved them once already? Aero's selfish thoughts screamed at him as he lay down onto his cot.

Aerö felt his frustration eat at him as he remembered the many times Velas had tried, just as Hïldúúr now did, to teach him to control his gifts. The powers they all thought he had, but never managed to summon them at will. But that was untruthful, and Aerö knew it. He was too angry to accept that he failed to awaken his foretold powers, not because he lacked them, but because he had been too afraid to summon them.

From beneath the carelessly folded woollen blanket, Aerö retrieved the old book Nóór had given him and hoped that its strange tales would help to silence his lour thoughts.

Aerö peeled the book's dry covers to reveal its yellow flesh inside, and started to read again the page he fell asleep pouring over the previous night.

But not all my quests that took me far and wide began as such, as a wander, but rather as a question. The first curious creatures to wonder upon their origins were not mountains apart from my own home, but rather inside it.

They had been brought by Skeggor Skalidur himself into the city, three creatures of such unusualness, no one had ever seen before, or for that matter after, despite my many journeys to reveal their

*past and birthplace. It was they who made me question our
knowledge of the old. Three creatures of such calmness and patience
one could only wonder at the intelligence hidden beneath their golden
skins.*

*They were the Golden Oaks Skeggor Skalidur brought with
him on his return to Seribu Menara, three ancient beings who had
forsaken their true home to guard their first King's tower. They were
the ones that showed me just how little our understanding of the
world was. We saw ourselves as the natural leaders of the realm, so
we adorned our heads with crowns, our hands with whips. Our long
lives and powers made us believe we were in charge. But how wrong
we had been to revel in such mistaken beliefs.*

*I can still remember the day the ancient Oaks came into the city
with Skeggor Skalidur, their heavy crawl before the Order's eyes,
their precious bodies swaying, carried by thick walking roots. Years
rose and fell beyond the Wall since their arrival, as I stood before
them every day and questioned them, but on no occasion did they
answer back. They only obeyed their King and King alone. Stoically
they guarded his tall tower with their bodies rooted in place; their
millions of golden leaves sparkling and clinking in the wind. They
were magnificent.*

The high pitch call of the Feonds startled Aerö as he
read, totally trapped by Greindur Gamall's words, the
reverberating shriek that announced noon made him
question how long had he been back inside his room.
Slowly he lowered his eyes back upon the open book
before him, his mind slowly letting go of the vague
memory of his run from Hïldúúr that seemed to have

happened in another life, not merely bells before. The old sorcerer's grip onto his mind was absolute.

But when the other two decided they would slay their friend and King so they could have his throne, the Golden Oaks finally answered my decades of questions; their voices loud and pained, and ringing still in my old mind.

Ancient though we are as we are gilded,

Such treachery we have yet to observe.

Betrayal is a mortal sin, they knew, and still,

They chose to cowardly snare him and kill.

Down came the blade they so skilfully wielded,

No punishment sufficient for what they honestly deserve.

We thought, as did so many others,

That your Order needed our skill and aid.

To live in peace and not by harsh command,

But your kind is too foolish and too young to understand.

We gave you our knowledge, our homes and brothers,

So that the two can have you all and us enslaved.

In our hidden world we lived since long ago,

With sparkling, mirrored, full of wonders seas,

Tall mountains and caverns of unfathomable depths,

With creatures that would never give their final breaths.

Such is our secret, beautiful Kingdom of Peace,

A place your kind will never come to know.

Aerö read a few times, the rhymes in Greindur Gamall's book, looking to see if he could find any concealed meaning. The words, he could imagine being sung by the three Golden Oaks he met in Seribu Menara. Then too, they sang to him and whispered, deep voices carried by the winds; their message urging him to run as far away as his legs took him from the two who promised help but meant no word of it. Run he did, and by some miracle, he did survive the King and Queen's deceit, the three enormous creatures' voices still ringing in his head as they did in Greindur Gamal"'s long after they had been sung.

The heavy door that isolated Aerö from the rest of Undirheim began to slowly swing inwards, the force behind it breaking the seal he had hoped to maintain until at least the next day. Aerö barely had time to close the old book shut and shove it under his blanket before the door stopped moving. Across the room, it now gaped open at him. Aerö was expecting Hïldúúr to come for him, angry for his running off and most probably determined to punish him twice as hard. But when Estrelle walked slowly, in her White Wolf form, he knew he was in far more trouble than he thought.

"Follow me," she growled. The words formed with great difficulty on her protruding jaws. Aerö knew better than to disobey her direct order.

She led the way, and the two walked in silence through the quiet hallways, Estrelle's large furry body moving like a silver cloud against the dark tunnel. The absolute silence of the place struck Aerö as odd as he followed his mother towards her throne room above, as if the Beasts' Lair had fallen asleep despite being but hours after noon.

Estrelle climbed the winding stairs slowly ahead of Aerö, and he knew that she still felt the pain from Velastrum's poisoned blade.

"Sit!" she said roughly climbing onto her throne of skulls. Aerö dropped to his knees where he waited, unsure and somewhat afraid of what was to come.

"I thought I asked you to train every day with Hïldúúr like the rest of us," the White Wolf spoke slow and laborious, but finished in Estrelle's feminine tongue as she changed back into her human form. Naked, she sat on her terrifying seat, with nothing but a white fur mantle covering her shoulders. Pale-skinned and slim, beautiful and cold, she watched her son before her.

"Mother—"

"I know you ran from your training earlier today, and I know why, but I don't think you do."

Aer'ös hands and feet began to tremble, hearing Estrelle talk. He tried to tell her how he felt, about how Hïldúúr reminded him of Velas and his training deep in Wündalær, how he too tried to force him to awake his slumbering powers. But despite it all, Aerö choked on his own words which stubbornly refused to part from him.

"Mother—" Aerö tried again to speak, but barely managed to vomit the one word before he heard them. The unmistakable sounds of claws on polished stone echoed through the air, drifting from the spiralling staircase they had climbed but moments earlier. Aer'ös hairs stood on end as the scratching noises grew closer and louder.

He turned around to face the dark stairs although he knew too well who made those sounds. Ashäël emerged through the gaping archway, large and soot coloured. Behind him followed Hïldúúr at his usual leisurely pace. Aerö expected to see anger on his face or at least disappointment, but saw none, the Beast Lord appeared lost in thought.

"My Queen," he muttered distracted, his gaze measuring the throne room, his cold stare washing over Aerö without focusing on him. Ashäël moved close to Estrelle and bowed his giant head, close enough for her to stretch a pale hand and stroke him gingerly. At her touch, the Hound released a low, intimidating growl and Aerö tensed.

"You're purring!" Hïldúúr's voice came down like a blade, but also sounding amused. Ashäël snorted and moved away, embarrassed to have let himself enjoy her touch.

"Do you know why we're here, Aerö?" asked Estrelle, shifting in her seat. Aerö nodded slowly, not trusting himself to speak.

"He does not." Hïldúúr's words crept like ice beneath his skin.

Aerö raised his gaze to meet the Beast Lord's, but he too was facing naked Estrelle, who slowly wrapped her white fur mantle around her. The only eyes on him were Ashäël's.

"I do!" said Aerö, annoyed that Hïldúúr did not even bother to turn around and speak to him directly. "It's because I ran away because I didn't listen."

"That is not why, son. You are here because of what happened in the training grounds."

"But nothing happened!" Aerö heard himself say. "I am sorry. I shouldn't have run." His strained, high-pitched words echoed, multiplied throughout the empty room.

"Fool! Listen to her!" Aerö heard Hïldúúr speak again facing Estrelle, only Ashäël's eyes on him. The Beast watched him intently, every now and then flashing his fangs at him threateningly. Aerö could feel Ashäël's anger fill him, but not just that, he thought he also saw fear in him.

"We don't have time for this!" bellowed Hïldúúr angrily.

Estrelle merely watched her second in command, but did not say a word.

To Aer'ös shock, she seemed to smile at the Beast Lord before her, her head nodded, satisfied. Aerö felt stung by her reaction. He knew he had been wrong to leave the training grounds despite his promise to her, but wished she had defended him in front of Hïldúúr.

"He's wasting our time!"

"I AM SORRY!" yelled Aerö tearfully, but this time no echoes travelled thorough the vaulted room. He could suddenly feel all eyes on him, searching, staring, piercing him.

"Incredible," came Estrelle's muffled words. Her face was suddenly lit up; sitting on the edge of her throne, she stared at her son in disbelief.

Aerö felt his skin warm up, his eyes swell with tears as he felt their heavy stares. He stood up, ready to run and hide inside his room.

"Aerö, son, I had to know that Hïldúúr's claims were true. You have made such wonderful progress!"

Aerö stared at Estrelle; for the life in him, he could not understand.

"You still don't see it do you?" said Hïldúúr, for the first time facing him.

Aerö shook his head.

"Those were Hïldúúr's only words since you came in here." Aerö watched his mother smile at him, her complexion healthier than he had seen her in weeks.

"Son, the exchange of words you two had down in the training grounds and now in here, were…" she stopped to find her words. "… You talked through thoughts Aerö, something no Beast Lord has managed to do since Skeggor Skalidur! You are his grandson, you are in truth his foretold heir!"

Each With Their Demons

Consume me now, oh Gods of Old,

For all that I have done

Has brought but pain and death and mould

To those I swore to guard.

Oh, Gods of Old, what have I done?

A Mother's Prayer

Harrubea, The Matriarch

Sara found herself changing into dry clothes as she had been increasingly doing since the battle of the Kórr Mountains. A new day was being born outside her tent, when Sara peeled away her sodden blouse and trousers. Hunched, with barely enough room to extricate herself from her constricting garments, she pulled free from their wet grip, pushing against the small tent's walls like a soon-to-be newborn positioning itself to leave behind the safety of the womb. Still feeling damp, but mostly frightened, Sara emerged through the tent's slit entrance to find Petra and start tending to the many wounded.

A few days had passed since Taro found his end, as Petra and Erlend suspected, poisoned by the Greeds. A few days during which she had to witness constant arguments between Petra and Trevor, Trevor and Grov, Trevor and his brothers; no peaceful end in sight. Petra, as she had ordered, remained confined to the insides of her tent, no soul apart from the few trusted ones to lay their eyes on her. She believed that everybody would be safer with the Greed sisters believing they had managed to succeed in killing her. So, every day, Sara awoke from nightmares of her mind, to ones observed by her own eyes. Mothers trying to smother their babies, husbands their wives, friends turned foes, siblings trying to stab each other. And now her own friends and family threw threats much heavier than stones across the central tent, gloating in the hope that their last blow inflicted the most damage. Life in the encampment had been hard, and Sara blamed most things on it. The lack of food, of shelter; the absence of intimacy was slowly turning all of them into more primal selves.

Standing there in front of her small tent, Sara welcomed the crispness of the failing night, its freshness somehow tightening the strings of her being, smothering out the creases that the restless nights and days had made. *Waking up before the others had its benefits*, thought Sara as she gazed across the span of tents and smoking fires. Only in the early hours of the day, the camp did not appear as if built from scraps, but rather like a peaceful sanctuary. The encampment revealed itself through the morning's veil of pinks and blues like the magical home of fairies Sara enjoyed reading of as a child.

Today, more than ever, Sara wished Erlend had stayed with her all morning. The world-ending nightmares that had troubled her for weeks turned into a nightly occurrence, especially after she dreamed of blackened seas and angels. Yet she failed to tell a soul of them, afraid of what her loved ones might think of her, scared they would tie her to a cot in Petra's tent, like they did with those who had descended into madness. With Erlend leaving their hard bed of old hemp sacks filled with straw, early before dawn, Sara was left to fight off the bad dreams on her own. While she yearned for her husband's loving touch and kisses, shivers and wet cloth caressed her skin. But they all had their burdens to carry, their errands to run; and Erlend more than most now that Petra played dead inside her tent. Few knew of the Greeds' unforgivable actions, but most wondered where their leader was.

"She's busy," Erlend would then say over and over again as faces peered out of shabby tents; their voices rough and hollow. And while most did trust his word, Erlend could see increasingly, doubt on the people's faces.

Sara stretched and yawned, welcoming in the new day's freshness, her memories of nightmares-past slowly receding deep enough for her to finally forget, but not sufficient for them to never crawl back up again.

Muffled shuffling sounds from somewhere nearby startled Sara, who had been enjoying the absolute silence the early hour provided. Instinctively she turned around to see where the rustling sounds might be coming from. Slowly, she revolved a second time, searching for movement through the pastel coloured haze, when from two tents away, Adriana's bronze face peered through the ash-covered flaps of her shelter.

Sara almost rushed back into her tent, but Adriana's hazel eyes focused on her the minute she emerged. She did like Woods' late leader's daughter and appreciated her hard work and help, but the many rumours that encircled the beautiful young woman made Sara uneasy. But she had been too slow, and now Adriana, who wiggled herself out of her tent, approached her smiling, pleased to see a friendly face at such an early hour. Sara could only smile back at the olive-skinned, fiery woman.

"You can't sleep either?" asked Adriana, although there was no question in her words. Not many managed to still get a full night's rest.

Sara nodded as Adriana covered, barefooted, the distance between them.

"There are many who need help inside," said Sara gesturing towards the central tent, forcing a smile. "the earlier, the better."

But Adriana did not smile back. Her shiny face, with her high cheekbones, dark red lips, and eyes the colour of amber, stared at Sara silently.

"You look terrible!" she said with such finality, Sara felt taken aback and speechless. "You ought to get some rest," Adriana added, scrutinising Sara with her bright eyes.

The urge to run away and hide inside her tent washed over Sara as the dark-skinned woman examined her intently. Adriana was so close to her now that she could smell the woman's skin, fragrant and sweet, and could not but wonder how she managed it. None of them had had a real bath in more than two months.

"I've had some trouble sleeping lately," mumbled Sara shyly, combing her hair with her bare fingers in an attempt to brush away the tiredness that stuck to her like burrs. The loose shirt Sara wore tightened around her frame unknowingly to her. Only when Adriana's alert eyes traced her contour, did she realise and lowered her arms and crossed them in front of her, hugging herself. Sara felt self-conscious about her looks for the first time since she left Bells.

"I should go," she said, trying to escape the young woman's piercing gaze.

"Don't be silly! You cannot go like that. Your hair is damp, and you look like you need to talk to someone. Too many things have happened lately—the war, the Beasts, the poison,…" she said in a low voice. "…We need to stick together more than ever."

"I shouldn't. She's waiting for me." Sara lied, implying that Petra, who now lived entirely within the confines of her tent, awaited her. But Adriana had something that Sara mostly lacked; the power of convincing. Before she knew it, Sara found herself stooping behind Adriana as the two entered her tent.

Sara had never seen the insides of Adriana's tent, nor had she ever wondered what it must be like. They had all built their shelters out of the few things they owned, wood and rocks. In the few that Sara went into, the same sense of suffocating came to her, accentuated by the piles and piles of useless things the Turmenn brought with them, blinded by mammon. Sara could even remember the clock someone had hauled all the way from Bells, their backs bent under the tremendous weight of time. And there was the smell.

Most lived in filth, same rags worn day and night for weeks. Sara could see it in the people around her, in the villagers from Woods and Brim, but also in the faces she had known in Bells. The subtle change in their mien the longer they were in that camp; the return to savageness, the slow undoing of everything that made them, them. None of the living conditions the Turmenn had had in their villages were part of their life within the round encampment; even the beggars and the maimed had it better back in Bells. Sara could only hope that Adriana's tent was not like those others she had seen.

But how little she should have worried. Adriana's tent was realms apart from the grimy tents she knew within the camp, even from her own which she was rather proud of, bright and tidy, always aired. But the shelter she found herself in, was something she could only awe at.

The fragrance of burning, scented wood forced itself into Sara as she entered the small tent. Like the palaces she always fantasised of, coloured spans of cloth adorned the walls, red and maroon, green and yellow. The beautiful fabrics covered the walls and floor, even the flat mattress Adriana used as her cot. Lightheaded, Sara looked around the unusual tent, searching for the source of the scented smoke. Strong and sickeningly sweet, transparent tendrils embraced Sara and enslaved her mind, a sense of blissfulness pouring into her parched body.

Sara sat down on her knees, unsteadily, as her mind and soul revelled in the smoke-infused euphoria. Nothing but the shadow of a thought to cross her mind of where she was or what she was doing.

Adriana dropped next to her, in her hands two dented mugs. More smoke seemed to billow from them.

"It's just tea," said Adriana reading Sara's mind. "With all the wounded, dead, and now the ones that try to poison us, you need to take it easy." Sara nodded obediently.

Tired, Sara cupped her face into her hands and understood why Adriana always smelled so sweet and strong of spices unknown to her. The hanging wisps of smoke permeated not only the air within the tent, but also everything within it; the fabrics, their clothes, their skin. Feeling more peaceful than she had in weeks, Sara looked around at the oddness of the place. Adriana not only looked different than the rest of the Turmenn, but also seemed to live unlike the rest of them. And then she saw it. Resting on a small box at the opposite side of the tent, behind Adriana, a brass-coloured bowl belched pale-blue smoke into the already scent-saturated air.

Minutes passed without either of them speaking a word. Adriana unpinned a large red blanket from above her cot, while Sara happily sat and let her mind go blank.

"Here," said Adriana handing Sara the woven red cloth she'd so gracefully unfastened moments prior. Sara took hold of it, unsure of what to make of it. It was so beautiful and delicate, so soft to touch the clothes she wore suddenly clawed at her skin.

"Change into that, you'll feel much better." Adriana nudged Sara with her words. "I promise."

Sara petted the soft cloth reluctantly. She felt shy, uneasy about changing before anyone else but Erlend, and especially before the dark-skinned woman staring at her. People said a lot of things in anger or frustration, in fear or out of spite, but this one even Sara thought of being true; as did Petra. The Turmenn spoke of Adriana being what they called a kynlï. But the attractive young woman had helped them in their fight against the Sorcerers and now was helping Petra with her plan to reach the Southern Plains. For that, Sara trusted her. Not for what the Turmenn said she was, but for who she was.

Slowly, the rough clothes Sara wore peeled away from her pale skin, nothing but the folded cloth of crimson-red that rested on her lap to cover her. Under Adriana's gaze, Sara wrapped the soft cloth around her, light and sweetly scented; a gift for which she instantly felt grateful. She had never owned nor worn such cloth, least now when such sumptuous things had no place in the Turmenn's world of ash and famine. Yet, in that very moment, Sara felt happy and peaceful, but most of all, attractive.

"Thank you," she said softly, smiling at herself. It is very pretty."

"I don't get to wear them. From where I come from, you see, they are worn by the leader's family. That, I no longer have."

"I am sorry." Sara heard herself say. "It's been hard on all of us, but that pales compared to what your people went through." Sara thought about the distant place Adriana's family must have come from for such clothing was not something that the northerners of Urukk wore. She wondered how the woman before her, who was always clad in garments made of leather and wore daggers at her belt, would look in such beautiful clothes. She must look like a princess, Sara concluded.

"We are survivors. Woods never had Bells' impenetrable fences, nor Brim's iron-hand rulership, but we survived for all these generations. We will survive this too." Adriana said as she removed the glowing amber from within the brass bowl to make it stop spewing more blue smoke. The tent was already permeated with it. "But I feel there's something else troubling you, Sara."

Sara gazed away from the steaming mug between her hands, her eyes tracing the wisps of fumes as they vanished into thin air, much like the Turmenn's hopes.

"I am afraid," she whispered. "I am scared for our survival, I fear for our future, I dread my dreams."

"Aren't we all?"

"Maybe." Sara said in an even lower voice. "But my worst dreams tend to come true. I am cursed to dream the deaths of those I cherish most," she added before she could stop herself. Until now, she had never dared to share that with anyone. Erlend and Petra knew about her nightmares, but Sara learned to conceal the dreadful things her mind was showing her.

Adriana watched her quietly, her face not spilling any clue as to what her mind was churning. Sara lowered her eyes back onto the dented mug, embarrassed. She could hear in her head how mad her own words sounded, but for reasons unknown to her, she knew Adriana would not deem her so. Maybe the dark girl, better than most, understood how it felt to be different.

"That sounds like a gift to me. A painful, horrible one, but a gift no less. It must be terrible to dream your loved ones' deaths, but while the rest of us walk blindly all our lives not knowing when we might wake up alone, you, my dear, know when that might happen. Despite the pain they cause, maybe these dreams are with you for a reason, maybe they come to you to help you change the Gods' unfathomable plans."

Sara felt her eyes swell with tears, for never before had she opened herself to someone other than Erlend and Petra, yet this strange woman before her made her speak her heart.

More moments of silence passed before the two as they both seemed to chase thoughts of their own, but Sara could not but appreciate the genuine nature of the woman before her. She had lead whatever was left of her people across sands and battlefields driven by sheer courage, and now was lending all her help to see the Turmenn reach their yearned safety. She had renounced the leadership over her people to Petra on nothing else but trust. She was a warrior, a leader, and by the looks of her tent, a princess too.

"I envy you, you know," said Sara shyly, looking into Adriana's bright-gold eyes.

"Envy me?" she roared, throwing her head back, exuding overpowering femininity. "You have what most of us can only dream of. You have your family, your husband, you have friends. If someone is to be envied here, that is you, my dear!" And Adriana released another merry laugh.

"That is not what I meant.—I wish I was more like you." Sara added, looking away from a wide-eyed Adriana. "I trust Petra with my life, and I want to help. I believe she can take us to safety, but I'm weak."

Adriana giggled again.

"It is incredible how those who shine the most are blind to their own brilliance. Stars can never look upon themselves."

"Like my dear Erlend and Trevor, and of course, Petra, you are a born leader. I, on the other hand, am good at sowing, tending to the wounded," said Sara with a sigh. "Sometimes, I wish I was more like you, free to do what I think is important and courageous enough to actually pursue it."

"Oh, Sara! This journey has not yet stripped you of your innocence. And that's why you can't see it. But I will help you realise how wrong you are."

Sara felt her face change colour as Adriana smiled at her so honestly, her own face smiled back at her. And despite it all, despite the malicious rumours circling Adriana or her past, Sara could not help but see a bridge erecting between them. She could feel that fluttering of wings deep in her being as a friendship was born.

When Sara walked out of Adriana's tent, the world seemed to have changed, the sun was brighter, the sky deeper, the faces staring at her happier. Like a barrier, the tent's entrance separated two very different realms, one ruled by black ash and ill feelings, hunger and dislike; and the brighter, colourful refuge of Adriana's tent. Within the smaller world, Sara had found a friend, someone she knew she could talk to and who would understand.

* * *

"How long do they plan to keep her body hidden?" spat Elfredda, throwing yet another wooden toy onto the roaring fire before her. Petra's undoing had been celebrated with yet more looting from the poor. Bags of clothes and toys awaited to be burned between Bathilda and Elfredda Greed.

"They'll keep it hidden for as long as they can. Their lives are the only things that keep this camp together. We must be patient sister. Let them undo the trust the people have in them, themselves. We shall be there to lead the Turmenn back to Bells." Elfredda grinned, throwing a bundle of someone else's clothes into the licking flames.

"Sooner or later these stupid people will realise she is long gone. She got what she deserved."

Somewhere behind them, inside her tent, Martens listened to the Greed sisters, trembling hands wrapped around her mouth to stifle her sobs. Faced with the choice of being alone and cold, with no family of hers to have survived Woods' massacre, or inclusion into the Greeds' group of misfits, Martens had chosen the latter. But now she knew that had been a mistake. Woods old apothecary wished she had never made the poison that the Greeds requested her to make. A woman she never liked nor disliked, died by her own hands, the leader of so many. As always, regrets come far too late to make a difference. The leader's death could never be undone, just as her guilt could never be absolved. Not only that, but because of her concoction, an innocent soul had performed the greatest sin. Burt's son, Elijah, too young to even understand the gravity of his blameless actions, had delivered the killing blow; his hands forever stained with the black mark of murder.

So Martens cried her swollen eyes out day and night, thinking of ways to desert the Greed's treacherous group, but knew too well she would not be allowed to. She joined them because she feared being all alone, now she feared being with them.

"Twenty more have joined our group this morning. They know we have both food and water. Soon we will be able to go back to our lives," came Burt's rough voice from behind the two old women as they fed the fire before them with more toys.

"Good, Burt, good!" said Elfredda, satisfied. A tiny sculptured horse cracked open in the fire, and through the gaping gash, incandescent sparks rose to the skies like fragments of its soul. Elfredda beamed.

"Then our plan to starve them is finally working out," said Bathilda plainly. "They'll do anything to keep their bellies tamed, their sprog from crying. You have done well, Burt!"

"Thank you."

"Remember, be patient, and those fools will come themselves to us. Nothing makes them more obedient than misplaced trust in do-gooders," she croaked, and both sisters' hunched backs shook with laughter.

* * *

Inside the central tent, Petra discussed with Erlend their next plan of action. They knew they were running out of time, yet no other option seemed to show itself to them, but wait.

"More and more people ask of you throughout the camp, Petra. We ought to do something!"

"We cannot let them know I'm still alive, not until I know I can detect the poison in our food. We cannot have more die because of them."

"We could go and confront them, banish them," said Sam and Daniel from the entrance of the tent.

"They have too many under their command for us to hope they would just leave without a fight. And we cannot start waging wars among ourselves, not unless we cannot avoid it any longer," said Erlend calmly. But Erlend understood the young warrior's passion; he felt it himself, but this was a war of whispers and poisons, not blades and battle cries.

"We could kill them," said Grov flatly.

"Grov!" said Sara sharply, as she entered the large tent followed by Adriana; all eyes glued on them.

"That's alright," came Petra's raspy voice. "We have all thought about it. That would cause more bloodshed, more chaos." Petra pondered aloud. All stared at Sara, who walked in wearing the red dress Adriana had gifted her.

"My love!" Erlend gasped at the sight of his wife. Sara looked radiant as she advanced towards him between the empty beds at the front of the large structure. Adriana stopped beside Sam and Daniel, and although she did not look at them, she could feel Sam's gaze upon her.

"Has anyone seen Trevor?"

"No," responded Erlend, distracted; his hand searching for Sara's who stopped beside him. Despite the early morning, Erlend had already done his round of the village. "He's nowhere to be seen."

A flash of anger crossed Petra's face, but her demeanour changed as soon as her eyes sank to the fresh patch of soil where once stood her cot. There lay Taro's body, buried secretly by his close friends. A rectangle of darker soil stared at them, reminding them of what was decomposing right beneath their feet.

"May Narrū take care of your soul, Taro," muttered Petra under her breath. And even though no one had heard her, she knew they all said prayers of their own.

"Petra…" said Adriana slowly, her voice cutting through the deathly silence. "…if all we hear is true about the Greeds and their growing band of traitors, we need to leave this camp of death and edge closer to the southern plains. We need to start marching again, or we will never reach them."

"That, of course, is true. I will need a few more days to work out this damn poison, then once I have the cure, I'll show those Greeds who is the leader of this camp," Petra hissed with renewed conviction. Adriana had always had a gift of looking past the noise and staying focused.

"But Petra, Are we really ready to fight them? Are we to kill our own people?"

"My dear Erlend, maybe it's time I showed those two my real nature. You are all right to fear the fight against our own, but if we let the Greeds persuade enough to follow them to Bells, they'll all be dead regardless. I ask of you to be patient." Grov watched Sam and Daniel across the room; the two brothers had told their friend the truth about their leader, about her past and all she had kept secret from them. Grov still could not believe that there had been a sorcerer amongst them all these years.

"I'll do all I can to keep things quiet with my people. But even they are curious of your late vanishing," said Adriana nodding.

"As will we," said Erlend looking at Sam and Daniel across the room. The two boys nodded soberly.

Within minutes Erlend, Sam, Daniel, Adriana, and Grov all left the tent to patrol the camp and make sure no one caused more trouble. There had been more whispers of robbing and stealing from the poor with every passing night. And all knew who was guilty of them all.

"We need to find Trevor, brother," said Daniel, checking their older brother's spot where he had wasted away for weeks before his bread killed Taro.

"I hope he's smart enough and has not sided with them—"

"I hope that too, brother, for I don't think any of us can fight against him."

Slowly, the two made their way around the camp, threading carefully between the clutter of tents, watching the Turmenn's faces scowl at their sight. People they had known since they were children, parents of their friends of old, now stared at them in fright, but worst of all, disgust.

"Ali!" cried Daniel at the sight of their old friend from Bells. "Ali! It's us!" he boomed, waving a hand at a tall figure, some tents away. Ali looked like a standing sack of bones. Seeing the two wave, the boy's eyebrows and upper lip bunched in the middle of his face, a reaction Sam and Daniel saw much too often lately. A moment later, before the two could knit their way between the tents towards their friend, Ali's father emerged behind his son from their ash-covered shelter.

"Mind your business elsewhere!" he bellowed, placing two skeletal hands on Ali's thin shoulders. Sam and Daniel steered away from their course. The camp was turning against them faster than they expected.

"What's wrong with them?" asked Daniel, a sting of anger in his voice. "We work ourselves to the bone for them, and still, they are the ones unhappy."

"Adriana was right. We do not have much time before we have a full-blown war amongst ourselves. We'll be lucky if we can keep things quiet a few more days."

More faces frowned at them as the two brothers moved along the southern edge of the camp, advancing carefully towards the Greed's dominion. But the boys had no intention of confronting them. They were there to look across the infinite span of blackened sands that stretched from the camp's southern border all the way south. Just as they did most days, Sam and Daniel stopped to watch the battlefield reveal itself through billowing clouds of sand and ash.

"We need you, father," said Daniel hoarsely; squinting at the never-ending sea of dunes before them. Somewhere in there, lost within the waves of gore and ash and dried-up limbs, Alistair's severed body lay, taken from them, swallowed. His remains were still hidden from them despite the many searches. Black shadows in the distance, protruding from the ash, marked Alistair's and many others 'resting place.

* * *

Petra moved between the many occupied cots inside her tent, checking the wounded. There were still so many who had tried to harm themselves or others, people she once knew from Bells, others from the other villages up north. Most of them were dying from their own self-inflicted wounds, cuts on their wrists or inner thighs, ingested poisons, or covered in skin-crawling burns from throwing themselves into the fire. All lay motionless on their mattresses, but for the seldom grunts and laboured breathing to give away their presence; Petra had them all under her spell, a concoction of Rana and sleep herbs. Those who tasted the bitter drop fell into a Syll-like, stir-less sleep with no control over their minds and bodies.

"What will we do with them?" asked Sara, placing a hand onto a young man's forehead. "We can't abandon them."

"Those who have healed enough to walk, I shall awaken before we leave—the others—we might have no other choice." Petra responded without straightening. She was bent low above the girl whose mother tried to burn her alive.

"We can't do that!" Sara exclaimed, horrified.

"Who would carry them across the realm, child? Most Turmenn can barely carry their own bones least others." Sara stared across the cots at Petra who oiled the burned girl's skin. Suddenly Sara felt faint, or ill, or both, she could not tell. Her lungs refused to breathe in air as the walls of Petra's tent shrunk around her. Dropping the pile of rags she had been gathering from the many wounded, she stormed out of the tent in a flurry of billowing crimson.

Petra looked around as Sara pushed away the entrance of the tent.

"I need some air," she managed to hiss as her red form vanished. Petra considered following her, but she knew Sara needed time to accept the consequences of their actions as leaders of the Turmenn. She was too good, her heart too pure, to leave their own people behind; maybe she was too weak, but Petra saw it, just as Adriana had, much more hiding just beneath her skin.

Left alone in the central tent, Petra checked all other cots before stopping beside the only one she wished to wake, not drown deeper in slumber. Tighter than Rana, Syll's mind trapped her body in a prison of her own making. Gently, Petra peeled away Syll's blanket to reveal the place where Vondur Blöö's long sword, Petra's own husband and father of their son, cut deep into her neck and shoulder. A long, pink scar marked the place like a pale memory of the gruesome wound that weeks before adorned Syll's skin.

"You have to wake up, child," said Petra softly, petting, gingerly, Syll's forehead. "You can no longer drift between the worlds of the living and that of the dead. Trevor needs you now more than ever. Wake up!" But Syll remained as still as she had been since Vondur dropped his sword upon her.

* * *

"Our plans are working better than we hoped!" exclaimed Elfredda happily, watching the long row of people waiting to be given food and water.

"Indeed, sister," croaked Bathilda. "But we must make sure they are not discovered by her stupid men."

"Our own will tell us if they plan to visit us. All these weeks of taking all their food only to have them come and beg for it has worked out nicely!" And they both grinned, satisfied with the number of people waiting obediently to receive their ration. They would soon have enslaved their own army.

Sounds of shuffling naked feet and rubbing sores drifted through the fragrant air that announced the new morning. The smell of baking bread pulling the hungry like invisible threads. No one spoke or tried to get in front, but waited patiently like lambs for their turn to receive their food. But there were other sounds now being carried by the morning air, noises of slow feet. Both Bathilda and Elfredda turned around at once, expecting to have been discovered. However, instead of the long-sworded, strong-handed, broad-shouldered men that still acted as if their leader was alive, an old woman threaded slowly a few tents behind, poking through the small tent's flaps with her walking stick.

"You! What are you doing?" shrieked Bathilda at the woman who walked almost completely bent by old age.

"Oh!" exclaimed the old woman struggling to lift her head enough to see who yelled at her, but failed miserably to straighten but one inch.

"You have no business there, old prune!" Elfredda spat.

"I'm sorry..." said a raspy voice. And the woman edged towards the two slower than a sand-snail. "I'm sorry...".

Moments later, under the disgusted look of the Greed sisters, the old woman reached them; out of breath despite the slowness of her gait.

"What are you looking for?" asked Bathilda bluntly, losing her patience. Her bulbous eyes staring at the woman's back before her. She must have been so old she had not gazed at the vast skies in decades.

"Food, my dears, some crumbs for an old soul like me."

"If food is what you want, then get in line!" Bathilda hissed, stepping away to reveal the stream of people in their tens behind her.

"Oh, but I'm so old, have mercy—"

"We have no need for you, old rag! Get in line if you want food, if not go to your leader. After all, it's her duty to keep us all alive! She must have food in that large tent of hers!" Bathilda and Elfredda croaked turning their backs to the poor woman who's eyes saw but their dirty feet.

"Thank you, my dears!" said the old woman, pleased, and slogged away from them.

Silver Sparkling Ponds

Aerö spent the rest of the day buried deep inside his room. Estrelle, his mother and Queen, had granted him a day away from the training grounds, Hïldúúr, and his Hound, Ashäël. She said he well deserved it after all the progress he had made, and beamed at him proudly, Aerö felt his eyes swell up with tears.

But Aerö did not feel proud of himself. The more he learned about his gifts, the more he learned to use his powers, the more the Beast Lords and their Beasts seemed to hate him, fear him. His unusual skill of listening to others' thoughts and feelings made him feel more isolated, rather than included. No one wanted him to pry into their most intimate of places, and Aerö could not blame them. No one could hide a thing from him. Nor could the Beasts.

Alone, he lay in his cot staring at the ceiling, the lone candle burned beside his mattress and projected dancing shadows on his small room's walls. Aerö found them oddly enticing, and if he stared at them enough, oddly soporific. Every now and then, sounds of footsteps echoed through the hallway outside his door, and every time he tensed, much like the rabbits Bells' old butcher bred when Aerö went to see them play. He had never taken one to have it killed and skinned and turned in Petra's tasty stew, yet the little furry creatures regarded him with utter fright. He never understood it until now, as he lay under his blanket and twitched each time someone walked passed his room.

SCRATCH …SCRATCH …SCRATCH the sounds of claws on stone seeped through Aer'ös walls. Footsteps soon followed, rushed and loud. Aerö held his breath and waited quietly for whoever prowled the tunnel to walk past his room. SCRATCH…SCRATCH… the noises stopped outside his room mere moments before the large door that stood between Aerö and the rest of Undirheim slid open.

Aerö instinctively pulled his blanket to his face and closed his eyes in a failed attempt to seem asleep, yet he had been too late.

"It's far too early for that," came Nóór's hushed voice as he closed the door behind him. Ári jumped onto Aer'ös cot and yapped excited, his little paws clawing at him. Aerö had no choice but to emerge from under the thick covers.

"Oh it's you…" said Aerö quietly, as he sat up. "Shouldn't you two be training?"

"They let us all leave early today. Too much distraction," Nóór added grinning, the candlelight amplifying his broad smile. "Everybody is talking about you!"

Nóór sounded excited. Even Ári barked and clawed at the blanket again for Aerö's attention. Aerö felt his heart sink lower and lower. The thought of every Beast and Beast Lord talking about him made him feel nauseous. If by some miracle there had been someone who was not afraid of him, now they most definitely would be. He could hear their thoughts, he alone had the potential to see them for who they truly were.

Yet Nóór and Ári did not seem to be affected by it. Had they been able to read his thoughts, wouldn't he feel scared? Wouldn't he want to stay away from them? Aerö knew he would.

"So? Is it true?" asked Nóór genuinely seeing Aerö drown in the cobwebs of his mind. Aerö focused on the Beast before him, slowly comprehending what his friend had asked.

"So?" Nóór repeated, and Ári released yet another high-pitched bark. "Did you read my fathers mind and Ashäël's?"

"Umm…I don't know…" Aerö said coyly. "…I think so."

"I knew it! I knew it!"

"Aren't you scared?"

"Scared?" asked Nóór confused, looking at Ári, and Aerö knew his friend asked his young Hound if he was.

"Yes…I felt it in both your father and Ashäël. They are scared of me, of what I might see in their hearts." Nóór seemed to consider Aer'ös words and even Ári stared at him intently.

"We have nothing to hide, none of us have, especially my father."

Aerö looked at his friend, but said nothing. He should not plant the seed of doubt in his friend's heart.

"If anyone had doubts about you being Skeggor's heir…" continued Nóór, "…they no longer do."

Nóór's Beast tested the blanket gingerly, before he lay down, muzzle on his paws, atop of Aerö's legs. Aerö had a sudden urge to touch the little Hound, to pet him as he sighed and closed his eyes.

"We came because we want you to try it on us," came Nóór's words, as if from far away, as Aerö looked at the slowly breathing creature in his lap. Aerö met his only friend's eyes.

"No."

"You need to train now more than ever, Aerö!"

"Your father's taking care of that," Aerö said in a low voice not wanting to disturb Ári. Nóór chuckled, and Aerö could not fight the grin that stretched across his face.

"Both Ári and I want to see what it's like," added Nóór still smiling, beaming excited at him.

Aerö could only think of what a bad idea that was. Nóór was his friend, his only one, and Aerö did not want to change that. Who knows what he would see in the young Beast Lord's mind. But Nóór was not to be dissuaded, even Ári was now panting excitedly, whip-like tail wagging, tongue lolling, his snout stretched in a silly grin.

"I really think this is a bad idea," he said finally, his right hand stretched involuntarily to touch the pup before him. Only when Ári's soft, wet tongue licked at his fingers, did Aerö realised what he had done.

"Come on! It will be fun!" pleaded Nóór climbing onto Aer'ös cot. Three very different beings crammed together in the smallest of beds; a Sorcerer, a Beast Lord, and a Hound.

"Fine…" Aerö caved in. Nóór and Ári gleamed at him.

"What do we need to do?" Nóór asked excited, pulling on Ári's ears.

Nothing, thought Aerö, trying to remember what he had done with Hïldúúr.

"Just think of something," he said vaguely, and then grinned. No matter what, he could always count on Nóór to put a big smile on his face.

Slowly, the tiny room drowned in silence as Aerö closed his eyes and focused on his gift. He did not yet know how to make it work, but listening intently seemed like the right thing to do. Nóór and Ári's breathing stopped as did his own, he realised, along with all other sounds. A sense of floating swallowed Aerö as the whole room vanished, and he thought he had fallen asleep. But in the absolute emptiness that held him, Aerö began to see the sparkling of tiny lights, the twinkling of stars, and then feel the unmistakable presence of others.

Aerö opened his eyes only to see Nóór stare back at him unsure, and Ári's yellow eyes fixed on him. They were both as silent as the black mountain above them, yet Aerö could hear them all too well.

"So?" asked Nóór out loud, breaking the grave-like silence. Aerö did not reply, but kept on watching his friend and his Beast, and more importantly, listening to them.

Aerö could feel their curiosity, hear their pondered questions, enjoy their puzzlement. He looked closer at the two, focusing his mind's eye on their shining lights within the utter darkness, but no matter how deep he looked, how intently he listened, Aerö could not find a trace of fright in them. The two filled him with their unwavering love and loyalty for each other. Tears swelled in Aer'ös eyes.

"Is everything alright?" Nóór asked alarmed. Aerö had already seen the question in the young Beast Lord's mind form like a concoction of words and feelings, images too, moments before he uttered it. But when Aerö answered with his mind, both Nóór and Ári gaped at him bewildered.

"This is how it feels to talk through thoughts. Please don't be scared." Aerö pushed his thoughts into Nóór and Ári's minds and felt their initial valour crack. Ári barked, Aerö could hear him far away, the Beast's mind much louder than his voice. Ári was scared, not terrified of him, just nervous of another's mind apart from Nóór's inside him. Aerö stretched his open hand to touch the small Hound's head. The Beast flinched, but just as quickly licked his outstretched fingers.

"It's alright, little one," Aerö heard himself saying as Ári worked hard at his fingers.

"This is amazing!" Nóór yelled in his head, a little too excited, and Aerö pulled away. It felt so intimate talking to other minds; their fears, their thoughts, their most hidden emotions all his to pry into.

All noises of the outside world returned to Aerö as he peeled away from his friends' minds, gifting them back the privacy of their own thoughts.

"How did you do that?" Nóór asked, his face split in half by a wide grin. "How long have you been able to? Is it difficult? How far do you think it works?" He spewed every single question that came to him, and Aerö was pleased to be out of his mind, or he would hear them twice, at least.

"I don't know," he muttered, his own voice resonating weirdly in his ears. Ári barked as Aerö pulled away his hand from the Beast's head.

"Tomorrow you must come down to the training grounds. Everybody will be there, even the Queen!" Nóór announced, excited.

Aerö could think of few things he would enjoy less.

"Maybe father will let us train together."

"Maybe…" Aerö responded doubtfully. Híldúúr would keep him busy for years if he could before he would allow Aerö to play catch with the other youngsters in the Lair.

"We should go," Nóór said aloud, although he was talking to Ári, who was already prepared to take off. The little Beast licked Aer'ös hand one more time, before dashing to the door. Standing up, Nóór noticed the large book lying under Aerö's cot that he had told his friend to read.

"Have you finished it? Have you read about them?" he asked with the most curious of expressions and pointed at his feet.

Aerö shook his head. "What…not yet. Your father's been keeping me busy!"

"Oh—right. Well, see you tomorrow, Andlegûr!" Nóór said, smiling, clearly enjoying Aer'ös puzzled cast.

" Andl…what?"

"That's what everybody now calls you, Mind-Talker, Aeröl!" Nóór answered, grinning even wider, and then was out the door, Ári barked from somewhere down the hallway. Aerö had not even seen the agile Beast dart out between his Master's feet.

Aerö found himself staring back at his room's ceiling, tracing the joyful shadows dancing for him, his candle but a stub. He only had a few more hours before it would die and with it yet another day. The time Nóór and Ári spent with him while he showed them his gift, had flown by far too quickly. And as he lay there on his back, he could not but smile at the thought that he had truly found a friend. Both Ári and Nóór had welcomed him inside their minds, and he had seen them in their purest form. He had pried into their souls and found nothing but friendship, loyalty and trust.

From beneath his cot, Greindur Gamall's black tome whispered Aer'ös name. Its old pages cracked as he peeled them one by one. Passages of the book he already read, jumped at him from its yellow pages, tales of old of creatures he failed to even picture how magnificent and strange they were. Aer'ös eyes lingered on Syngja-Vatn's account of his vanished crew, and he wondered if Greindur's portrayal of the man as old and mad was accurate. Aerö himself found the story hard to believe, but so were most of Greindur Gamall's tales. If he were to believe any of them, surely he should all. More stories flashed before Aer'ös eyes as he made his way through the old book, the Golden Oaks, he himself had met, brought memories of their encounter, of their chants and their strange gift to him.

Finally, Aer'ös fingers settled on the page he intended to read. Bold, beautifully drawn letters jumped at him from the top of the page, the title alone sending Aer'ös mind spinning back to Bells, to his awakening in that forsaken cavern, to Velas and his promises that later turned to be just lies, to Wündalær.

The Creature in the Silver Pond. Aerö read the six words inked on the top of the page, over and over again yet his mind failed to absorb them. From the moment he saw them, his mind chased scattered thoughts, unable to hold one more than a few moments. Like a child who tries to catch bright-coloured butterflies with his small hands, every now and then stopping to look inside their clasped-tight hands for the soft creatures, only to realise that they were just too fast, so did Aerö fail to catch his fleeting thoughts. Unable to make them still, he followed them deeper, hoping they would stop to rest so he could then entrap them. Wündalær, the edgeless forest, wrapped around Aerö. A blink of his mind's eyes and he was in its midst once again. A great glade blossomed around him with crisp grass and white flowers tickling at his feet. Aerö looked at his two hands in disbelief. It seemed so real, it felt so real he struggled for a few moments to remind himself that this was just a daydream. Almost instantly, he spun around looking for Velas who had found him there after his failed escape. But there was no one chasing him this time. Again he looked around and marvelled at the beauty that surrounded him, the clear blue sky, the wall of trees, the blanket of grass so soft and fresh he felt sorry to squash it beneath his feet. Staring at it through his mind's eye, Aerö decided that the place was the most beautiful of places he had ever seen. Maybe it was the lack of all of those miracles he once took for granted that made him think so, trees and grass and colours he had been deprived of since he buried himself under the black mountain. Aerö could even feel the sun's warm rays kiss his bruised skin, and the gentle gusts of air that made their way beneath his shirt and tickled.

A purple, sparkling bird dived in front of Aerö from the great blue opening above, and he knew he no longer was alone to enjoy the glade's breathtaking beauty.

Just as he remembered it, the silver pond that had appeared to him on two previous occasions gleamed from where, but moments before, was nothing other than grass. Tentatively, he approached it, as he had done before, his eyes darting at the joyful coloured birds that swarmed above it. There, it lay still as a great mirror on the face of the glade. It truly was a wonder to behold, even the cotton clouds stopped from their march across the sky to gaze upon themselves in its silvery surface.

Slowly, Aerö knelt before the depth-less lake to gaze into its sheen, expecting to see again the visions he failed to grasp before. But unlike the times the lake had shown itself to him, now it remained as still and flat as the King and Queen's high-polished floor at the top of their tower. Aerö stretched one trembling hand and touched the pond's shimmering substance.

At last, Aer'ös mind managed to catch his scurrying thoughts and was able to return to his room. Eyes squinting at the ill-lit chamber, his skin cold from the suddenly vanished sun that blessed him with its touch in his strange daydream, Aerö stared at the bold words written in blank ink.

The Creature in the Silver Pond.

Ever since the Golden Oaks spoke to me about their much-loved Kingdom of Peace, I have travelled long and wide to find it. I even climbed through Skeggor Skalidur's mountain of books only to find no reference of it. But try I did, and although I came across a wealth of strange tales and even stranger creatures, it was not until the end of my long journey that they showed themselves to me.

I was already older than whoever made me, planned for me to be, yet aeons I still had ahead of me. During the same travels far beyond the borders of the realm, I discovered and perfected my most precious skill. The means to cheat the Goddess of Death's summon.

Out of the Initial Three, only Skeggor Skalidur the Beast appreciated my strange gift, the other two dismissing it as a deceitful way of gaining power. Power I had plentiful as the King's High Counsellor. But the other two, I came to understand much later and very much too late, were jealous of what I had discovered. They clung with all their might to their fading perfection and craved my ever-lasting youth; a gift they will do anything for, I am now sure. As I am writing my long travels for whoever might be interested in reading them, I know my end will come too soon by their innocent hands. They will take along with my long life the soul severing powers I possess.

Centuries after my first interaction with the Golden Oaks, before Arnleaf and Valdis's attempted to slay their King, the most incredible of creatures showed themselves to me. Deep inside the woodlands that surround the city of the Healers, on a day like any other, I found myself lost in a glade I had never before come across the many times I crossed them. There, I sat and wondered at its

*beauty, as I am sure you reader will try to form inside your mind
and fail. No man's imagination can fathom its absolute perfection.*

Aerö read Greindur Gamall's words and knew the old
sorcerer was right. He had seen the glade with his own
eyes, and still, he caught himself wondering if he had
truly seen or merely dreamt it. Every time he tried to
picture it inside his mind, its colours appeared duller, its
beauty less, as if his mind could simply not produce such
utter flawlessness.

*Neither could it grasp the peculiarity of the creature that lived
there. A stain of melted silver formed on the glade's green carpet, it's
surface still and shiny as a mirror's. Intrigued, I approached it,
doubting my own senses, watching it grow before my eyes. Birds with
plumage of deepest colours swooped around the newly formed,
expanding pond, inching ever closer to its shine but never daring to
touch it.*

*Time stopped as I peered over the lake's brim, the clouds
stopped rolling, the wind stopped blowing, even the birds that so
noisily fluttered all around froze in mid-flight. The only things still
moving were myself and my clear reflection in the pond. And that is
when I saw her…*

*There, beneath the mirror-like surface lived Naga, the woman
of the silver lake, Queen among all creatures.*

Aerö stared at Greindur's words for what felt like
hours. His mind once again raced thought after thought,
memories of his encounter with the molten-silver pond.

Something was troubling him. Although Aerö had peered into the pond's reflective surface and watched the world turn up-side-down, he had not seen the woman that lived beneath its sheen. But he had seen far stranger things lurk beneath the lake's waveless polish.

Sounds of footsteps echoed slowly from outside his room, and Aerö had a moment to pull the blanket over Greindur Gamall's tome before the door swung opened. Through the shifting darkness, a tall figure moved. Aerö straightened in his cot. Confusion washed over him as he tried to measure the time of the day, or night, he was not sure. Time seemed to seep through the many cracks in his room's walls when he read the old sorcerer's tales.

Estrelle's thin figure formed out of the blackest black, her pale complexion radiating, almost casting her own glow. Aerö released the breath he had been unknowingly holding.

"Come with me Aerö," she said, barely making any sound, then turned around and vanished into the blinding darkness she had just taken form out of. "Quickly!"

Aerö followed, leaving, under the protection of his cot and blanket, Greindur's book of marvellous mythical creatures.

Eldur's Son

Wait we shall, and wait we must, but mark my words, the
Færa-há will rule once more over the Realms.

Anonymous

Aerö followed Estrelle through the gaping door, out
into the dark hallway. The lamps that still hung from the
sculptured walls lay fast asleep, their orange brilliance
extinguished. It must have been the dead of night for the
whole mountain to be in such slumber. Aerö tried to
remember hearing the Feonds' calls, but failed. He had
been so engrossed in Greindur's book, he had completely
lost all sense of time.

Estrelle's pale contour floated through Undirheim's
tunnels, her warm grip wrapped around her young son's
wrist. Although Aerö could barely make her vague shape
before him, the Beast Lords' Queen navigated through
the Lair's bowels as if the lamps were still ablaze. Aerö
thought of Ári, whose eyes, too, could cut the darkest
shadows. Estrelle moved swiftly towards the winding

stairs that lead to her throne room. "Where are we going?" asked Aerö, out of breath as he fought the urge to stop. Running through the night-swallowed tunnels at such speed required a great amount of trust in the hand that pulled and guided him.

"Ssshhh," whispered Estrelle. But instead of turning right, to where Aerö though the access to the throne room was, his mother turned sharply left and entered her own chambers. Here, light flooded the interconnected rooms Estrelle used as her own. Lamps and coloured veils covered the black walls Aerö knew but vaguely. He had been inside a few times, but never long enough to marvel at their beauty. Estrelle's chambers were like no other in the whole of Undirheim.

Aerö squinted as they plunged into a bright-lit room. Estrelle's grip pulled him deeper, but her pace had slowed, and he remembered that those very chambers had been Skeggor Skalidur's. The first Beast Lord and King over Urukk, God among his people and legend for the rest. Aerö had spent many a night since his arrival in the Beasts' Lair thinking of his grandfather, imaging the time he ruled over the realm. Yet despite his legacy, not many wished to talk about him as a man. Maybe no one remembered, after all, it had been many centuries ago.

"Mother—"

"I know it's late, my son, and I am sorry, but there are things that you must do. Things that require utmost secrecy." Estrelle spoke, kneeling before her son. Aerö looked into her beautiful face. Her eyes were his, her skin and hair were his, but he had someone else's traits as well. The only thing amiss upon her otherwise flawless face was the cross-shaped scar that Velas put upon her brow but days after his birth.

"But before we start, I have something that I wish to show you." She stood up and walked into an adjacent room, just as beautiful. Aerö followed her, curious.

More painted fabric embellished the glossy-black walls while low tables and fat pillows made of the same beautiful cloth lay empty around the room, and Aerö wondered just how many used to live down here. The room could comfortably sit at least a couple of dozen. Objects he could place, and others he had never seen their kind before, gathered dust on the many surfaces, from books and lamps and phials — just like Velas', to objects forged of metal, but of questionable use. Things that looked like golden claws, fist-size gems, and a crown, lay abandoned on the closest table to Aerö, while the deeper he looked into the odd room, more peculiar objects jumped at him. Somewhere ahead, to where Estrelle now was, a giant skull gaped at him from afar, human in shape but fuller, wider. The more Aerö looked at it, the more it seemed impossible that such a thing had ever lived. By the size of its head, the creature who once bore it on its shoulders must have stood at least twenty feet tall. Aerö looked somewhat closer pondering if it belonged to a Feond, but it looked too human, with its normally shaped jaw and mouth and not the side-to-side, wide grin of the Beast's.

"They are your grandfather's. Things he brought from his long travels and managed to keep safe from Valdis and Arnleaf's grasp."

Aerö spun around, trying to see them all, inhaling the subtly fragrant air of scent-wood, attempting to imagine Skeggor Skalidur collect them.

"I kept this room as he made it. A reminder of the man he was." Then seeing Aer'ös keen desire to know more, she added, "He was of no desire to gather the realm's riches, but he was loved…so loved, all these precious things are gifts offered to him by men and creatures…most of them." Her eyes drifted to the giant skull.

Aerö tentatively touched, on one of the tables, a glass ball so pure and polished it gleamed at him like a gigantic bubble of soap.

"That one is the eye of a Hafgufa."

Aerö pulled his hand, as if the ball had burned him. He had no idea what a Hafgufa was or looked like, but he knew too well that such an eye could not have come from any creature he had seen nor wished he would. Estrelle chuckled.

"Follow me." She disappeared into yet a deeper room.

A small hallway opened before Aerö, to his right his mother's room for he could see her bed, to his left yet another chamber in which Estrelle went. Smaller and darker than the others, the room smelled strongly of the same burnt scent-wood.

"I know you must be wondering why I brought you here, son, but I trust you will understand. What lies ahead will be the hardest thing we've ever done, and for you harder than most. I want you to know who you are, son. I want you to know that this war is worth fighting, and for the most of us, die for."

Aerö looked at his mother, ready to shout that they will all be fine, but he knew better. Wars meant death.

"Before we go into the throne room, there is something I want you to see." She peeled away the only veil that adorned the small room's walls.

A life-size painting of a man looked down at Aerö from his painted throne. His hair was long and black as was his beard which obscured most of his face. To Aerö, the man looked savage, wild. His large hands and torso made him look like a giant.

"This is your grandfather, Aerö. This is Skeggor Skalidur the first Lord over all Beasts."

Aerö stared into the painted face of his forefather, his eyes tracing his figure, searching for any signs that he could truly be the man the Beast Lords spoke so proudly of. No jewels or crown embellished the man's body, nor any other kingly details one might expect. The man before him was as different from Arnleaf Uriel as night from day.

"He was a great leader, an even greater father and a loved friend, but he was also ruthless. For centuries, he sought all Beasts to bring them under his banner, and while most were persuaded to follow him, others were not, so Skeggor forced them. He was strong and understood before all others that the world the Beasts had ruled was coming to an end. The time of the sorcerers had arrived, and if the Beasts wanted a part of it, they had to be united. Battles broke out, and Beast Lords died as did too many creatures, but Skeggor had been right. To survive the coming of the sorcerers, they had to be as one or all of them would die."

Aerö listened to Estrelle recall the times her father was still King over the whole of Urukk, and for the first time wondered just how old she was.

"But when the other two, his friends, tried to take his crown and slaughter all who bowed their heads before him, Skeggor Skalidur's true rage came forth, something, I am sure, those betrayers still tremble at the thought of. My father was a Beast in every way and would have much rather seen the realm burn than his own people, the very creatures who swore their allegiance to him, die without a fight."

Aer'ös eyes moved lazily across the painted wall. The man before him, his grandfather, looked nothing like Estrelle; or she, like him. Where she was white, he was of blackest black. While she looked gentle, slender and royal, he looked like the monsters Petra scared him with. But the more he looked, the more he saw also resemblance. Like Estrelle, Skeggor wore a mantle of thick fur clasped around his shoulders; and then there were his eyes. Green like the youngest leaves and cold, calculating just like his mother's.

"He fought and died so that the rest of us could live, Aerö, and we must now do the same so that our children have a future too. You are so young, my son, and I am wrong to ask of you to fight alongside us, I know, but without you, we stand no chance."

"Thank you," said Aerö calmly. "Thank you for showing me this."

Estrelle approached him and kneeling before him, hugged him un-queen-like but very motherly.

"Let's go in the throne room, but quietly," she said, trying to keep her tears at bay.

The warm, comforting light of the many lamps that blazed inside Estrelle's chambers died, smothered by the cold night that ruled Undirheim's tunnels. Past the coiling stairs, the throne room welcomed them, large and hollow. A greenish light descended from the vaulted ceiling like raining lustre, turning everything it touched a deep shade of green.

Aerö looked between the rows of pillars, as he always did, trying to see the end of the large room, but only found, like every time, more shadow-eaten pillars. Lagging behind Estrelle, he made his way toward the throne of skulls, but that was not where she had walked to. Instead, his mother kept on walking deeper into the room. They both walked in silence. Every so often, Aerö spun around to look behind, his skin prickled from the vastness of the chamber behind him. The encroaching shadows followed growing thicker in his wake. To Aerö, it felt as if they had been walking for hours. Identical pillars, born out of the blackest floor and vanishing into the dark ceiling, came and went at equal intervals; the silent maze they formed, infinite and damp, broken only by the echoes of their footsteps.

At last, once she had put enough distance between them and the entrance to the throne room, Estrelle stopped. Her green-tinted body knelt in the middle of a large flat square that spanned between four of Undirheim's moss-covered shoulders. Aerö stopped before her. The place seemed even darker than the rest of the throne room. The pillars that surrounded them looked charred, even the floor had signs that flames had licked at them.

"Sit down, Aerö," she said no longer in a whisper but in her full, clear voice. The thickly-pillared room returned her words tenfold.

"Why are we here, mother?" Aerö asked, looking over his shoulder for the fiftieth time.

Estrelle followed his gaze, her luminous eyes piercing the room's darkness. Then she focused those same eyes on him.

"I need your help, son. My people think I'm growing weak,..." she said, her right hand touching gingerly below her ribs where Velas's poisoned blade cut deeply into her, "...and they might choose to put someone still whole to lead them into battle. Of course, Hildúúr would be that."

"They can't do that! You are Skeggor's daughter. You are their Queen!" Aerö tried to sound strong, but his voice failed him. Something in him hurt each time his mother winced at her own fingers touching the unsealable wound. Estrelle paid little attention to Aer'ös words.

"If they think I am no longer able to assure their survival, then they should. One law rules all other, and that is preservation, son. But before that happens, if that happens, I need to make sure we can fulfil my father's prophecy and win this war once and for all. Hiding can no longer save us. They will find us, Arnleaf and Valdis, and we must be prepared."

"They are all training so hard,"

"Yet they will stand no chance," Estrelle said flatly. "If they ask me to renounce my crown, they will not welcome you among their ranks, and that would be their downfall. You are the power that will help us win this war, I know it, but they are far too afraid of you to trust you with their lives."

"I want to help," said Aerö, and was surprised at how easy the words came out. "But they don't like me, never did, least now when I can read their minds."

Estrelle smiled at him. "Aerö, they may dislike your gift of seeing into their hearts, but that is not why they are afraid of you. They are afraid you truly are my father's heir, and even more so, because of the gift Eldur bestowed upon you." Aer'ös thoughts drifted to Bells and his father's abandoned journal, but his right hand petted the answer through his shirt. Aerö pulled out his father's scarlet gem, the dormant pendulum that so easily burned villages and armies when awakened.

"Your father trained in this same place," Estrelle said slowly, as she looked around, and Aerö knew she relived some cherished memory of Eldur. "And I have watched him many times perform his blazing skill. That's why I brought you here, son. I want to give you all the knowledge I possess of Eldur's flames and train with you."

Aerö felt his heart fall into the deepest hollow of his being, like the rocks he threw with Nóór down ancient wells and never heard them reach their bottom. If the Beast Lords were scared of his father's flames, he was terrified.

"We can't let anybody know. They would banish both of us if they knew we dared rouse those powers you possess."

Aerö nodded.

"Shall we begin?" she asked, beaming at him.

Aerö nodded again, but thinking of the times, the pendulum answered his call, said in a muffled voice. "I don't know if I can control them. You shouldn't be so close."

Estrelle stretched both hands and cupped his face. "You are your father's son, they will obey you."

With trembling hands, Aerö held the egg-size crimson crystal as if it were a wounded animal.

Estrelle watched him calmly from one mere foot in front of him. If the pendulum did as much as cough one flame, she would be burned.

"I saw your father do this a million times," she said, smiling. "Hold it there and wake it up. Don't be afraid if the gem starts to burn. It will not harm you."

Aerö stared at the precious pendulum cupped in his palms and thought of Eldur.

For what felt like hours, although he knew only moments passed, Aerö waited for the gem to burst into flames. Nothing happened. Then just as Woods came back to him, the battlefield, then Rokksvaart, his thoughts exploding with the happenings inside that very throne room, the crystal warmed inside his hands. A quiet yawn drifted from it as the pendulum answered his call and touch, and with the flimsiest of sparks, it burst ablaze. Aerö almost dropped his father's mighty weapon. The gem felt warm and quivering against his skin and memories of the many times he felt it on his chest, beating franticly like a tiny heart overwhelmed him. Aerö felt the urge to smother the small flames leaping from it.

"Don't," Estrelle called, beaming with pride. "You two are one, just as we are with our Beasts. Let it feel you, let it see you are its worthy wielder."

Aerö slackened his grip around the ruby gem, allowing it to burn.

"I'm scared…" Aerö muttered instinctively, but as the words parted his lips, he felt the gem's warmth seep into his flesh, igniting his every nerve and muscle. Aerö expected to be afraid as anybody with their hands enveloped in red flames would be, yet he felt none. As if something had changed inside his body, as if some part of him refused to give up, he stared down at his burning hands and marvelled. Tongues of scarlet flames flickered between his fingers and around his wrists, licking at his skin, hissing as they came in contact with the damp cold air. Aerö was no longer afraid of his own gift, not for his life at least. The gem filled him with warmth, not heat, but warmth, the kind you feel inside your soul, and Aerö felt his eyes swell up with tears.

"That is Eldur's son," Estrelle announced, smiling widely at him; her somewhat-sharper-than-they-should-be teeth gleamed orange from his flames.

"Now try to make it stop. You have to have complete control over your flames before we can go further." Aerö nodded and instead of clasping his hands around the burning crystal to smother it, he opened them and asked of it to stop.

A second must have passed before the gem quenched its flames and finally returned to its inactive state. The times he called upon them, they only stopped when he no longer had the strength to bear his weight. But now, they finally obeyed him.

"Light it again." Aerö did as asked.

"Put it out."

"Again."

"Again."

"Again."

With every try, with each new cycle, on and off, ablaze then quietly still, Aerö found his father's crystal quicker and more willing to obey his thoughts. The gem lit up blood-red then darkened at Aer'ös lightest mental touch.

"I am so proud of you, son," said Estrelle grabbing his face between her palms and pulling him towards her. With his hands holding his finally awakened gem and with no way of bracing himself, Aerö fell head first towards his mother. Estrelle held her son between her palms then when he was near enough, she planted a loud kiss onto his brow. Aerö felt utterly embarrassed yet inexplicably content.

Without realising, Estrelle's heart opened to him, allowing Aerö to feel as if his own, her most hidden of parts. He had never felt a mother's kiss before, and despite the years spent apart, Aerö now knew her love for him was unbreakable.

"Go and get some sleep, son. You've made more progress than I dared to hope. Tomorrow after your training in the lower grounds with Hïldúúr, I want to see you again. Come here after the night call."

"Yes, mother," said Aerö between yawns. He had no clue of how long they had been in the throne room nor how much sleep he would get. But if his levels of excitement were a measure for it, he would guess that none.

* * *

Up in the Ivory Tower, Valdis Ezelle paced the polished floor anxiously. From his velvet seat, Arnleaf watched his Queen move aimlessly around the room, her hands brandishing her jewelled dagger.

"Why haven't they reported yet!" she howled in frustration. "They should have done by now!"

"Patience, my love, give them time. Your white creature must have just reached them."

"I want her dead! I want them all dead!" she cried like a spoiled child, stamping her bare feet. The golden floor rippled like a mass of water from the place she stood. The King stepped off his throne and wrapped his arms around her.

"And once she's in our grasp so will be that wretch of a child." Valdis' thin lips stretched into a feeble smile, then returned to their pursed-with-disgust shape.

"What about your beloved angels? Any news from them?"

"None. But that is how they work. They only contact me once their deed is done." The Queen grumbled, then fell still in her King's arms.

"You are my all," she said, burying her face into his chest.

"As you are mine, my love," he whispered, kissing her luminous-white head. Then as they stood there, merged as one, entangled in their robes and jewelled arms, the Queen spoke in her usual cold voice.

"If we fail again, I'll bring *him* back to raise an army in my name and let them lay ruin to this world."

Arnleaf tightened his hold around Valdis, but said nothing. He knew that, after waiting for millennia for Skeggor's heir to come and end the war they started between sorcerers and Beasts, she would not flinch at the destruction of their realm. And neither would he.

A Brewing Storm over the Horizon

A new dawn began to stretch over the eastern edges of Urukk, its pale light eating slowly at the veil of darkness that enveloped the world. Night had its reign, but the glorious sun would soon ascend onto its conquered welkin and feed the spans of land and water with its blissful light. But its strength was weakened by the months of summer, and in but a few more weeks, it would give up supreme reign over Urukk to night, and winter.

Despite the insufferable kiln the desert turned into during the day, the Turmenn feared the coming of winter. Days so cold, fires would need to be kept ablaze throughout the camp, while once the night would fall, not even burning coals would help. If winter caught them out there in the open, many feared they would not survive it. They had good reasons to feel cold shivers, even on a summer day like this. Even when they had homes with walls and stoves and wood to burn, winters claimed too many; young and old, women and men, it claimed their lives indiscriminately. Whispers traveled through the failing night as the Turmenn stirred from their unrestful sleep, hungry and angry.

They would not succeed in keeping them obedient and quiet for much longer, thought Sam and Daniel as they made their round through the poverty-stricken camp. Almost none who saw them walk between their tents smiled at them or wished them good morning. They had lost all their allies and would soon lose the camp.

"What is happening there?" Daniel pointed over the sea of rags and wood that made up their makeshift village.

"I really hope they're not turning against us already. Petra needs more time." Daniel rolled his eyes at Petra's name.

"You still doubt her, brother?" asked Sam, somewhat amused.

"Always!" replied his brother.

Sam could not but laugh. It was no longer about taking sides or listening to orders; the world they now lived in was ruled by just one law: survival. The Beasts they'd feared all their lives were keeping them alive by bringing food from deep within Wündalær. Petra, their own leader, was a Healer. While all around their ugly camp, a war they would but surely lose was ominously nearing. Nothing was now about mindless trust, but rather choosing the best partner for the ultimate game of chance.

Ahead, a few dozen tents away, Adriana and her group of warriors from Woods, all trusted and brave, talked to a gathering crowd. The two brothers quickened their pace to lend their aid in calming the fermenting tempers of the Turmenn.

"Where is she?" cried a woman clutching at her baby as if Adriana tried to snatch it from her.

"Please calm down." Tarn's daughter tried in vain to placate the growing numbers of angry Turmenn around her. She had but five of her people with her. The crowd would soon be ten times as large, and far more dangerous.

"I bet she lives inside her tent, like royalty!" bellowed another woman. Adriana knew how wrong they were. Petra had been starving herself, so that they had food to eat, while working day and night to heal the wounded and now to find the poison that threatened to kill them all.

"Yeah! She's fattening herself while our children starve!"

"Please!" pleaded Adriana. Her right hand strategically placed on the pommel of her sword in case the Turmenn turned to real violence, not just hostile words.

"You are not convincing anyone! We will not be scared into obedience!" A large man pushed himself towards the front of the crowd. Women with children clinging by their skirts peeled away from his path. For a second, Adriana thought the man would keep on walking straight through her and her small group of men. But the man did stop, albeit but feet away from them.

"We want to see her!"

"You cannot go storming into her tent. She mustn't be disturbed."

"YOU, will not tell us what we can or can't do!" He moved one step closer to Adriana. Men and women joined with their own voices the already rowdy wakeup call.

"We will have to stop you," Adriana exclaimed while trying to keep calm, but even she knew they could not fulfil such a task if the enraged masses decided to assail Petra's tent. The large man laughed, a healthy, full chuckle.

"If I were you, I would be more concerned with my own safety. We know who you are, Woods' cowards. We might be farmers and fools, but we know what you are, girl! And we do not like your kind, kynli!" Shouts died to whispers, confusion turned to focused anger towards Tarn's daughter. Adriana could even feel her warrior's cold eyes set on her from behind. Her face hardened at the crude word the man used.

"Step away, sinner!" Adriana tightened her grip around her sword, her thoughts fighting an inner battle of their own. To slay the man before her and silence him for good, or let him badmouth her and try to reason.

"You look like you need some help here!" shouted a young woman over the growing racket. Behind her, another girl, just as young, and two men released their swords. Red flowers of rust sparkled on their blades.

"You can't cut anything with those! Put them away, child, before you harm yourself!" bellowed the man who had been advancing towards Adriana. But he stopped and turned to face his new opponents.

"It may not cut you, but I am pretty sure you'll feel it when I drop it on your head," the woman said without the faintest of fear in her eyes. Her mouth curved in a satisfied, and very attractive, grin. Her three companions brandished their swords in turn.

The broad man darkened with anger.

"Who are you?" asked Adriana feeling grateful for their interruption, yet curious for not knowing who they were. She had never laid eyes on the woman before her, she was sure of it.

"We are from Brim," the young woman said, her smile melting off her face. " I am Ishim, and this is my sister, Ezkiel." She pointed at the other equally attractive woman beside her.

The large man took one small step towards them.

"Come closer, old man, and you shall feel its weight onto your forehead," Ezkiel said coldly.

"How dare you!" he bellowed inching closer. Adriana watched, amazed, at the two young women before her. They seemed so frail, so small in comparison with the mountain of a man slowly closing on them, but there was also something overpowering about their presence. Was it their confidence, was it their yet-to-be-seen talent at wielding their blunt blades, or was it just their gobsmacking attractiveness? Adriana could not yet decide.

Sam and Daniel arrived at last and stopped beside Adriana. Before them, the mass of Turmenn swelled with anger at those who had sworn to protect them.

"What is going on?" asked Sam, but his voice could not match that of the yelling mothers, crying babies and their booming men. Adriana did not even notice them; her eyes scrutinised the newly arrived courageous, or incredibly foolish, young women.

Through the gathering masses, ripples formed as a group of Turmenn ploughed through them. At their front, the Greed sisters, offering as they passed, bread and fruit to the starving people.

"There is plenty for everyone!" Bathilda cried over the tumultuous voices.

"Don't fight! There is enough!" Elfredda said, offloading her arms, burdened with goods.

But living like this, at the edge of savageness, people turned into mindless brutes, kicking, elbowing, stamping over each other to snatch whatever food they could.

Adriana, Sam, Daniel, and the two fiery women from Brim watched the Turmenn encircle the Greeds and their band of thieves. They took their food and kissed their hands in misplaced appreciation. Little did they know that those same men and women stole that very food from Petra and by extent, from them. They were the ones who starved them and their children only to offer them the food they should have had already.

And the Greeds' plan worked. People swarmed around them, first in tens then hundreds. Bathilda and Elfredda's grip around the Turmenn — absolute.

"Where do they have all this food?" asked Daniel.

Adriana, for the first time, noticed them behind her. She looked at them wide-eyed.

"We are losing them," she murmured. The words died as soon as they formed inside her throat, but Sam read her crimson-coloured lips and nodded.

"They must have stolen it," said Daniel with finality, looking past Adriana to the Greeds who still had food to give.

"Those vipers!" hissed Adriana.

"I wish Trevor had slain them months ago in Bells when he still had his wits about him. Then none of this would happen. All they've done is poison people's minds." Daniel spat, appalled by what he saw.

Sam looked at his younger brother and thought of Taro. Their friend had truly been poisoned by those two, yet none of them could do one thing about it. But maybe soon they will. At the speed at which the Turmenn turned towards their new good-doers, they would soon have a conflict on their hands. If not to stop the Greeds then for their very safety.

"There is enough for all of you!" Bathilda shrieked, showing her rotten teeth as she smiled broadly. Her face crumpled hideously as she forced the one expression she had never genuinely felt.

"Thank you! Thank you!" whimpered the Turmenn with gratitude, as they clung to the goods they'd managed to secure.

"Gods bless you!" The Greed sisters reveled in the appreciation showering upon them.

Slowly, Bathilda and Elfredda's group moved towards the Turmenn's guardians, smug-faced. The tens and tens of people moving with them like a torrent ready to envelop the few who stood in their way. Adriana, Sam, and Daniel watched the masses swell around them, as did Adriana's men and the two young women from Brim.

"Where is your leader now?" bellowed Bathilda with venom. "Where is your beloved Petra?"

The masses cheered.

"You know what I think? I think she's dead and you have lied to all of us to keep us quiet, tamed like cattle before slaughter!" The Greed sister crowed, delighted as the Turmenn roared louder.

For the guardians, their chance to appease the Turmenn was swiftly shrinking right before their eyes. Within minutes, a full-blown uproar would tear through the encampment if they could not make the Turmenn calm down. From behind another voice boomed over the building clamour.

"I am afraid I have to disappoint you, Bathilda!" the voice rose over the advancing sea of angered Turmenn.

The masses stopped as did the Greeds. From her guardians' thick shadow, Petra walked into the light; her sole presence causing gasps to ripple through the gathered villagers of burnt Woods, lost Brim, and abandoned Bells.

"You!" gasped Bathilda and Elfredda. "You should be dead!"

"I guess I should," said Petra airily. "But next time do not rely on a young boy to do your bidding, and deliver the poison yourselves."

Somewhere, swallowed by the Turmenn's noise, Martens sighed, relieved. She had regretted making the damned poison from the moment Bathilda laced the bread she planned to give their leader.

The Greed sisters glared at Petra.

"Your venom, however, did claim one innocent life, and for that, you will pay in due time."

Sam, Daniel, and Adriana loosened their swords, expecting the two to command the Turmenn to attack.

"This is not over!" Bathilda barked and spat at Petra. "You don't know it, but you have already lost!"

Petra watched Bathilda and Elfredda Greed return to their dangerous band of traitors. The battle she'd tried to avoid would not take place that day — but soon.

"Turmenn!" she cried when the mass of people before her looked around after the Greeds.

"Turmenn! Go back to your tents and families and hold them dearly. Before the seventh sun climbs high into the heavens, we are leaving this cursed place behind and push towards Caraa."

"Caraa?!" a few of the Turmenn gasped slapping their hands over their gaping mouths.

"That place is worse than here! If anything the merchants said about the place is true, I do not want to be near it!" cried a woman holding tightly to two children just old enough to stand.

"Gods help our wives and daughters!"

"We mustn't go there—"

"We have no choice," Petra concluded, dismissing the Turmenn's founded fright. Caraa was dangerous, she knew too well, but they had run out of options.

The Turmenn looked as if they were about to start a fight, but slowly, from the edges of the mass of bodies, limbs, and heads, people began to peel away and head for their loved ones. As much as they now disliked Petra and her warriors, the fear of being left behind made them obey her command.

"This is not over!" Petra could still hear Bathilda's high-pitched words inside her head and thought, *it has not even started.*

Away from the dispersing crowd, Trevor walked towards Petra's large tent, his eyes set onto its unguarded entrance. Briefly, his thoughts turned to his two brothers and to Grov who always sat outside defending Petra's secrets, but as he reached the flaps that would grant him entry, his thoughts settled on the young boy with the poisoned bread and then on Taro. Trevor remembered every detail of that accursed morning when, because of him or at least with his help, Taro died right there where he now stood.

The insides of Petra's tent lay hidden in semi-darkness. No lamps diffused warm light from their suspended bodies, no sounds reached his ears, but the seldom rise and fall of weakened lungs. Trevor made his way towards the back of the tent, where, in the deepest shadow, lay his love. Syll had been asleep for weeks, and even though he knew Petra had done all that she could to save her, Syllvia refused to wake.

Blindly, he found her cot, drawn to her by unseen forces. Trevor could still taste her smell in the air, her shape, protruding from beneath the woollen blankets, known to him. He sat next to her on her small mattress, gingerly caressing her warm brow, his other hand curiously peeling away her coverings. There it was, pink and fragile-looking, the scar that caused him so much pain. He should have been the one wearing it around his shoulder and not Syll. She was just another one of the bodies around him, his father after distracting him in battle, and recently, Taro poisoned by the bread he insisted on him having. When Syll had come up with the plan to have the last black rider killed, Trevor decided that he should be the one struck down by his long blade. As brother, lover, and leader in his group, he should have sacrificed himself for them, but Syll was always faster. She had pushed him aside and welcomed Vondur's blow upon her skin so that the others lived.

Trevor had wasted days and nights drowning in the regrets. So much hurt caused because of him, some even dead, and all because he trusted Petra and her orders. Had he never wanted to ride to Brim. They might never have found out about the Beasts or the black riders. What if Petra had been wrong and Bells' walls would have saved them; maybe the Greeds and the others who opposed Petra's decision had been right.

"I will take you home, my sweet," he whispered in her ear, "So we can live in our old, beautiful Bells." Tears prickled in his eyes as he lay there with his head pressed in the crook of her neck. What if she will never come back to him?

"That would be such a shame…" a voice drifted dry and weightless from behind and Trevor jumped to face whomever was there. Fighting back his tears, he looked around the dark innards of the tent for the one who spoke, but there was no one he could see.

"...after all we've sacrificed to leave that place behind..." the raspy voice spoke again but this time from the opposite direction. Trevor turned around only to face more darkness.

He turned a third time before he realised that the voice came not from within the shadows, but from Syll. Surprised, he stumbled standing up fumbling for a lamp to kindle and flood the room with light. No sooner that the wick caught fire that he saw Syll's eyes staring back at him from her small bed.

"Syllvia!" he cried, dropping the lamp and running to embrace her. She grunted in pain. After all the weeks she had been lying in her cot, her skin was painted in raw bruises. She ached from doing nothing, yet she smiled at him.

"Thank the Gods! Thank Narrū for keeping you alive!" he said, kissing her on her pale lips, something he had never dared do while she was whole. Tears, heavy and real, fell freely from his eyes.

"I'm so glad you're back, Syll!"

"As am I, Trevor..." she said in her new, harsh voice. "...I did not think I would survive his blow." Then she coughed so badly it made Trevor wince with pain.

"Don't talk," he said, caressing her face and naked shoulders; feeling her thin frame.

"Where am I? How long have I been gone? Is everybody safe? Did we succeed?" she coughed the words with strain. Although her body was painfully broken from the weeks of inactivity and lack of proper food, Syll's eyes were bright with questions and with life. Trevor kissed her lips again, making her stop. He came to realise how much he loved her, only after her courageous fall in battle. But those were questions he did not know how to answer, so he kissed her, and he held her in his arms in silence. Right then and there it was just the two of them and nothing else.

"If Vondur's blade did not manage to kill her, you will by crushing her to death, boy!" Petra's unmistakable voice came from behind, and Trevor turned to face her. His plan had been to come and see Syll sleep then go away before she found him lurking in her tent.

"Petra…" he muttered, but she was already past him and next to Syll who smiled at her wearily.

As if inspecting some rare creature, Petra touched Syll's brow and hands, looked at her eyes and inside her ears, even smelled her skin. Then she, too, smiled, relieved.

"What happened? Did we succeed?" Syll murmured, lifting herself onto one elbow. But Petra grabbed her shoulder and pinned her back to the cot.

"Everything is fine, but now you have to rest, child. You have finally come back, but you're in no position to stand yet. As for you…" Petra pointed at Trevor, "…you, follow me!"

"What have you done to her? How did you wake her?" Petra barked as soon as the two plunged into the bright new day outside. "What did you do?" she asked, pulling Trevor's arm so that he faced her. He was at least two heads taller than her and quite a bit broader, but that did not make Petra less formidable.

"Speak!"

"Nothing!" Trevor replied, pulling his arm free from her iron grip. "She came round just like that."

"Just like that…" Petra repeated, unconvinced.

"Will she be alright?" he asked, taking a step away from Petra who still regarded him with doubt.

"I do not know. Whatever trapped her in that wake-less slumber is still there in her—but she seems out of it now," Petra added, knowing Trevor's feelings for Syll.

"I want to take care of her, make sure nothing happens to her," Trevor announced, turning around towards the entrance of Petra's large tent.

But Petra wrapped her claw around his arm again and this time held it tight.

"You will do no such thing, Trevor. Her body needs tending by someone…well, someone more appropriate."

"More appropriate?! I'll do anything for her." Trevor snorted angry, holding her cold stare.

"She'll be naked and uncovered so her sores can heal. So yes, someone more suitable is required," Petra answered matter-of-factly. "Sara will take good care of her that I promise." She turned around, releasing Trevor's arm and stepped into the shadows of her tent.

Trevor was left staring at Petra as she vanished through the heavy flaps, his mind still not quite capable of grasping the miracle he had just witnessed.

* * *

Inside the central tent, Petra and Sara rubbed Syll's back and limbs with oils. Through muffled moans, Syll fired questions at the two about what happened to the

Turmenn since the battle that had crippled her, but neither answered. Sara and Petra's hands worked fast, spreading the tinctures all over Syll's blistered body. Sara winced as she wiped her hands clean on a rag at her side. But despite the rawness of her back, Syll would be back on her unused legs in days.

* * *

The sun climbed into the vast skies and watched the spread of Urukk unfold before its might. From there, the realm seemed reigned by peace and beauty, a world apart from how the Turmenn felt. War was brewing throughout Urukk; Beasts and sorcerers and men revealed their last secrets before their armies would collide and drown the world in blood.

One by one, the Turmenn's no longer wanted guardians returned to Petra's tent. They needed her wise steering for the restless days to follow. The first to enter the large construction was Adriana, closely flowed by Sam and Daniel, and then by Erlend and Grov. The last two, despite not having been present at the Turmenn's uproar, knew all about it. The whole camp now talked about Petra's last order.

It was with great happiness that they found Syll had finally stirred from her dead-like sleep, and for a few short moments, they all forgot the difficult times approaching. But mirth had no hold on their souls as dread and questions filled them.

"What is the plan?" asked Adriana matter-of-factly; turning away from Syll to face Petra. The others mirrored her and surrounded their old leader, waiting for her orders.

"We cannot stay here much longer, that you know. And now that Syll has returned to her body, there is nothing keeping us in this cursed place. Begin to gather the supplies and to convince the people that the Greeds are wrong just as they were in Bells. Narrū seems to have blessed us with Syll's miraculous return, but also opportunity…" she spoke, lowering herself into her cot. "…Arnleaf and Valdis could have had us dead by now, yet we are not. Maybe they need more time to prepare for war, maybe they simply sat and watched us struggle for survival, but this is our chance. We will march past the Healer's City, to Caraa. If we manage that we might still have a chance."

"Caraa…is it true what they say about it?" murmured Adriana watching Petra's reaction.

"Yes," she sighed. "Caraa is a terrible place. But its danger and lawlessness might just be our salvation. Not

even the King and Queen have a footing in that place."
Adriana nodded. The others merely blinked.

"Erlend and Grov, I want you to be in charge of the
supplies. We need to be ready. Adriana, you and the
boys…" she looked at Sam and Daniel, "…will continue
to look after the Turmenn and keep an eye on the
Greeds." Again Adriana nodded, her mind working fast
at what lay ahead.

"Sara and I will tend to Syll and talk to the Turmenn."

"What about the others?" Sara asked, looking around
the room at the other wounded. Petra considered for a
moment, thinking of the last time Sara asked her the
same thing and then burst out of the tent nauseous and
angry.

"If they cannot carry their own weight, then I will take
care of it." The room fell even quieter if that were
possible as her words sank in. Eyes stared at her,
bewildered.

"You cannot, Petra…" said Sara roughly. Tears were
clawing at her throat as she tried to swallow them.

"We cannot carry the gravely ill or the demented. I will
take care of them and will make sure they go in peace.
That will be my sin to carry."

* * *

Outside the sullen tent, the warriors from Bells, Brim, and Woods awaited their commanders, as did the two young women Adriana had welcomed into her group. They needed all those able to wield swords to help them rein in the increasingly more violent Turmenn and the Greeds. Adriana thought that at least one good thing came out of the morning's uproar. New allies.

* * *

"How dare she!" stormed Bathilda through the compactly built tents at the southern edges of the camp. "How comes she's not dead?"

"She must have known the food was poisoned when that other died," Elfredda spat. "All the work, all the planning…".

"She will die even if I have to slit her throat with my own hands!" Bathilda hissed, kicking at one of the tents, not caring if her feet trampled to death someone's innocent baby.

A few tents away, a hunched shape scavenged through a pile of discarded, stolen items the Greeds' brutes brought back the night before and now smoked peacefully among charred toys and bones.

"Oi! What are you doing there?" Bathilda crowed at the bent over, black shape.

"I thought we told you there is nothing here for you!" Yelled Elfredda at the old woman they had mauled at the previous morning.

"Put down whatever you've stolen and leave."

The old woman pocketed whatever she had found and moved slowly away from the two.

But the Greeds were not to be insulted a second time that day. Within moments, Bathilda and Elfredda clawed at the crooked woman roughly.

"We told you to not come back here!"

"Please forgive an old soul like me," the woman begged, her head covered in a ragged hood, her face pointing at her bare feet.

"You dare to steal from us?" Elfredda barked, jerking the old woman by the only thing she seemed to own, the dirty clothes on her humped back.

"Never." the woman moaned leaning in her wooden stick. "Never!"

"Lies! We saw you! Give it back!" Elfredda shook the woman more vigorously.

"Please have mercy," the woman pleaded. But before the Greeds had time to answer and harass her further, the woman slashed the air with her walking stick, bringing it squarely onto Elfredda's outstretched arm.

Elfredda howled in pain as she retracted her bruised limb.

"You will pay for that!" Bathilda hissed, but the old woman seized her chance and moved away from them. Both Greed sisters stared at Elfredda's arm as a purple-black bruise grew slowly like a serpent rising from beneath her skin.

"You're dead!" Elfredda cried.

The old woman vanished through the maze of tents. Her fingers caressed, deep in her pockets, the things she managed to take from them.

Skrímsli

Aerö woke at the Feonds' call with the feeling that he had not slept at all. His mind still worked at the happenings of the previous night, as it had done since Estrelle ended his secret training. He felt elated, despite the lack of rest. For the first time since he'd found out what the scarlet pendulum could do, many weeks before in Woods, Aerö felt blessed to have it hanging by his neck.

Confident, he pulled the gem free from beneath his shirt and held it in his hands the way his mother taught him. The crystal felt warm to the touch, alive; a subtle quiver growing from within as his hands stroked it. Aerö stared at the marvellous, yet deadly thing before him, mesmerised by the joyful flicker of his candle on its chiselled faces. The gem sparkled more beautifully than he had ever seen it before.

With his thoughts turned to the incredible previous night and his heart swollen with a feeling of accomplishment, Aerö moved away from his cot, putting as much distance between him and any flammable objects as he could. His room was small, but if he failed to contain the gem's blood-coloured flames, it would not matter anyway, thought Aerö, gazing at the pendulum nested in his hands. Confident, he asked it to rouse.

Bright red tongues of fire licked at his skin with nothing but the faintest heat to touch his hands. Aerö gazed at the miracle he held and could not help but feel stronger. With it obeying his will, Aerö knew he could now contribute to the soon-to-be-unleashed war between his mother's people and the King and Queen's. Amused, Aerö tried to put himself in one of the two camps but failed. He was neither a Beast Lord, nor was he a sorcerer, but something of the both. A Beast-Sorcerer.he laughed at his own joke. Was he the first of a new breed of people? Or the last of some freak accident of nature? Aerö shrugged and asked the gem to sleep until after the night call when they would once again train with Estelle. With the pendulum safely tucked beneath his shirt, Aerö emerged into the lit hallway ready for another day of training deep in Undirheim's bowels.

"I'm a Beast-Sorcerer!" he said out loud, and smiled.

In the distance, the training grounds glowed bright orange. For the first time, Aerö found his own way to the lower chambers of the Lair the Beast Lords and their Beasts used to learn and sharpen their skills. No sooner had he emerged into the large, circular room, that a shadowed figure moved towards him. Aerö expected Hildúúr to still be angry with him after his last time in. Seeing him, Aerö quickened his pace, unlike on their previous interactions, he no longer doubted his own skills. Within days since his training started, Aerö had awakened both his gifts. One that allowed him to hear other creature's thoughts and another to control his father's gem.

Feet away from the tall silhouette, Aer'ös heart skipped a beat as he realised that whoever awaited him inside the bursting with light chamber was not broad-shouldered Hïldúúr."I see you're gracing us with your presence today, your majesty," said Finndôra mockingly, bowing her head at Aerö. "I thought we would never see you again down here." A gigantic shadow moved behind Aerö and stood between him and the only way out. Finndôra's Feond kept his beady eyes on him, unblinking. Aerö felt his innards tremble.

"I still have much to learn," coughed Aerö, finding his voice after it had scurried somewhere deep into his being.

Finndôra moved closer to him, and Aerö trembled as her long shadow embraced him."We don't want you here," she said plainly, gesturing to the entire Lair, not just the training grounds around them. "Estrelle might think you're our only hope in battle, but I disagree."

Aerö noticed how Finndôra referred to his mother by the name, not title. Were the Beast Lords already working to remove her from her rightful place upon their throne just as she had predicted? Aerö felt a pang of anger bubble in his guts. The pendulum quivered against his chest.

"You are not one of us," she added, but Aerö focused on her thoughts, not words. He let his mind reach out and touch Finndôra and her Beast.

Anger and fear seemed to mix into a dangerous concoction inside the two, but Aerö did not pull away. Instead, he pushed his senses deeper into their beings with not the faintest of remorse. He invaded the most guarded corners of their minds.

Finndôra seemed to notice his attempt and pointlessly tried to hide her true emotions. But she did not know how his powers worked. Like little lights inside pure darkness, her thoughts ignited as she tried to drown them deeper in her mind, but all her efforts only aided Aerö. He did not even have to search for what he wanted as she led his mind straight to them.

"Get out!" she bellowed, snatching his thin shoulders. But she was too late. Her true feelings flowed into Aerö, and he understood.

Angered, Finndôra ordered her Feond to grab him in its giant fist and crush him to death. But as the Beast stretched out its arms, Aerö commanded it to stop, then pulled his thoughts away.

Har-úgur, Finndôra's Beast, stopped with its hands but inches away from him. The look on the female Beast Lord, one of absolute shock.

"You…you…" she mumbled incomprehensibly, still clutching at his shoulders. "How dare you?"

"You gave him no choice," came a man's voice from behind Finndôra. Aerö instantly recognised it as Hïldúúr's. Ashäël growled threateningly from somewhere nearby.

"No one commands my dear Har-úgur, but me!" she hissed, releasing Aerö and turning to face her husband. "No one!".

"You're lucky the boy did not order him to do to you what you had planned for him," he said amused, willingly pulling at Finndôra's already taut cords.

Aerö ordered his own mind to remember Hïldúúr's words.

"You, out of all people, should know better than to side with her!"

"She is your Queen, Finndôra! Show your respect."

"Not for much longer," she hissed at him.

Aerö watched the two duel with words and wondered how did they manage to have Nóór. They seemed to hate each other, but Aerö had seen into both their hearts and knew their feelings for each other and towards the rest of their kind.

"Enough!" Hïldúúr boomed. And behind him, all the fighting stopped. All Beast Lords now observed the two Beast Lords and their Beasts growl at each other.

"Aerö, come," the second in command Beast Lord ordered as he turned his back to his much loved, but volatile-tempered, wife.

Aerö followed mindlessly.

Aerö expected Hïldúúr to take him back to the bowl-shaped dimple in the ground the two had used before, but instead, the Beast Lord walked towards the centre of the cavernous chamber. Hïldúúr petted his Beast's head, and Ashäël released a roar that filled the underground room.

Then, before them, the Beast Lords gathered, old and young. Even Finndôra and Har-úgur joined their commander's summoning, a look of pure indignation on Nóór's mother's face.

Aerö looked from face to face as the adults formed a neat row with their Beasts at their side; and for the first time, he could see just how few of them there were. Not even two dozen adult Beast Lords with just as many Beasts awaited Hïldúúr's words. Then the young came. A handful at most and some too young for battle among which his friend joined carrying his Hound.

Ári growled madly as Nóór kept him tight against his chest, the pup squirming to get free. But then wasn't he too young for battle? thought Aerö as he counted the few who lived under Undirheim.

The young joined their parents in the line that curved around Hïldúúr and Aerö. Beast Lord and Beast alternated before Aerö, tall and proud, yet savage looking. Aer'ös eyes drifted from Beast to Beast. Hounds, Feonds, stags, and bears, even the gigantic serpent he had seen inside the throne room now awaited as if on display. Aerö felt a chill creep up his spine as he felt their yellow eyes focus on him. Even without using his gift, he knew they were apprehensive of him. Their fear-fuelled ferocity piling just beneath their calm appearance. Aerö shook away the darkening thoughts and looked at Nóór, who smiled broadly at him.

Ashäel roared again and every eye, human and Beast settled on Hïldúúr.

"This is Aerö." Hïldúúr commenced placing a heavy hand on Aer'ös shoulder, which only accentuated the growing nausea he felt stirring in his body.

"He is our Queen's son and Skeggor Skalidur's true heir. This, you already know. What you don't know, or stubbornly refuse to believe…" he shifted his gaze upon his wife, "…is that the boy is our only hope to win this war. The Queen knows it as I know it in my soul."

The Beast Lords and their Beasts shifted their weight as they took in their commander's words. Aerö could see a few nods break the stillness of the group, but most looked angry.

"I also know you have been training hard for this one final battle that awaits us, but now it's time you learn to fight as one. From now on, all of you shall train with Aerö under my command."

"Are you confident that this is the right thing to do?" asked the Beast Lord with the giant snake coiled around his body. "He is not one of us. He has no Beast."

Finndôra smiled.

"He might not have a Beast, but he is one of us, that I am certain," Hïldúúr said calmly.

"Is it true that he can steal our thoughts?" asked another whom Aerö recognised as the woman with the stag that almost ran him over in the tunnel outside his room.

"That he cannot. Not exactly. But he can hear your thoughts the same way you can hear Cęrreb's."

Aerö watched, intently, the white stag-like creature named Cęrreb. Of all the Beasts that lived under the mountain, that one was his favourite. Tall and white, it bore its crown of antlers, aware of its beauty. But there was something in the Beast's eyes that he had yet to see in any other. They glistened with intelligence rather than ferociousness.

A wave of muted sounds followed Hïldúúr's words as each Beast Lord, apart from Nóór, shook their heads in disagreement. Their Beasts lent their growls and hisses to their Masters' whispers of annoyance.

"I will do no such thing," announced the man with the wet-looking serpent.

"Neither will I!"

"Nor I!"

Hïldúúr watched his Beast Lords refuse his direct order with a calmness that challenged the large snake's.

Aerö, in comparison, trembled with concern from the angered Beasts and Beast Lords before him and from the quivering pendulum hidden under his shirt. He prayed the gem would not wake.

"I did not ask you to agree, my brothers. You will willingly train with him as equals, or he shall use his gifts on you as foes." From Hïldúúr's other side, Ashäël growled, threateningly, emphasising his Master's command. With that, all whispers died.

"Who shall go first?" asked Hïldúúr as if all the others had agreed. But before he had the time to choose from the row of sullen Beast Lords before him, Nóór stepped forward still clutching Ári at his breast.

With the corner of her eye, Finndôra saw her son step forward. A low hiss passed her white lips in strong disapproval. Nóór did not even seem to notice, or chose not to show it.

"Very well."

Nóór did not wait for Hïldúúr to explain the rules they would obey while training with Andlegûr, the Mind-Talker.

Aerö let his mind open with ease, he was quickly getting the hang of it. Instantly, a wave of noises, thoughts, and feeling poured into his mind. The door to his thoughts, for that, is how Aerö imagined his mind-reading gift, was far easier to open than to shut. He closed his eyes and focused on the only minds he wished to hear, Nóór's and Ári's.

Like two tiny sparks their minds ignited in the vast emptiness of the world of thoughts Aerö had access to. Their minds and hearts became his to know, their absolute love for each other, his to feel. Aerö let them fill him with their warmth.

"We've tried to see you, but mother has kept a close eye on us. She does not like our friendship." Nóór said apologetically, and Aerö could feel his honesty, raw as if his own.

"It's alright," Aerö sent forth his thoughts. "Father likes you! The others say you did something to his head."

Aerö could not but smile. He barely knew how to erect the bridge between his mind and that of others', yet the Beast Lords reckoned he could plant thoughts in their minds.

"They've spent too much time trapped beneath this mountain." And now it was Nóór who laughed out loud. The other Beast Lords looked at them some curious, some angered.

One by one, the Beast Lords trained with Aerö, trying, just like Finndôra, to hide away their thoughts — only to lead his mind straight to them. They fought and swore and threatened him with their scurrying minds, their most intimate of thoughts escaping the flawed prison they erected to protect them. Their Beasts, however, allowed Aerö to touch their minds more willingly, to them his skill was the infallible proof that he was truly Skeggor's heir, the only one who had been known to have such a gift.

When Finndôra's turn came, she simply turned around and walked towards the exit. She had already failed to guard her thoughts and feelings from him. No one said a word, instead they expected Hïldúúr to order her to stay. But he knew best which wars were worth fighting. That one was not one of them.

Aerö felt tired and was happy the training was over. The Beast Lords and their Beasts trained with him then left. Only Hïldúúr remained at his side, where he had been since the summoning. Aerö turned, expecting the broad Beast Lord to open his mind. But he did not.

"Thank you," he said, using his vocal cords.

Aerö looked at him, confused. He was glad the Beast Lord in command chose not to use his thoughts.

"They might refuse to show it, but they will accept you, boy. They are stubborn, but they are no fools. Thank you for being patient. And do not mind Finndôra, she is just…spirited," and for the first time, Aerö saw him grin. The resemblance with Nóór striking.

"I should thank you…" Aerö said thoughtfully, "…for siding with my mother."

Hïldúúr ruffled Aerö hair and laughed.

It was late by the time Aerö returned to his small room. A new candle, clean clothes, and food had been left piled neatly on his cot. He was starving.

The plate of fruit, mushrooms, and nuts lost its contents within seconds of Aer'ös arrival in his room. Tonight, stronger than ever, he wished he could have had some meat or bread at dinner, and memories of Petra's dishes wafted around him. Aerö then thought of the Beast Lords and how different they were from how they seemed. Mean, wild and scary-looking, yet they refused to taste the flesh of any Beast. They lived off fruit and nuts brought in by Beasts, but mainly hand-size mushrooms that grew right in their Lair in many of those hot and humid chambers down below. And Aerö, too, started to lose the taste for meat the longer he lived in Undirheim. Maybe it was the lack of it, or perhaps it was the awakening of his gifts that brought the change. The more he entered the Beasts 'minds, the less he craved their flesh. They were intelligent creatures, they were friends to those whom they partnered with, and that made it wrong in Aer'ös mind to eat them. Even the memories of lesser ones, the rabbits and the birds he had enjoyed before, now tasted bitter as he imagined touching their small minds, seeing their lives unravel, feeling their fright become his.

It was still hours before the Feonds' call to sleep, and Aerö already felt exhausted. The many minds he'd touched down in the training grounds had stripped him of some unknown energy. He still had to train with Estrelle in the vast throne room above. Aerö sighed at the thought and crashed atop his bed. He was excited by what Estrelle would teach him that night, yet wished he could just sleep.

Something hard poked at his legs from beneath his blanket and Aerö peeled the woollen coverings away. Wrapped in its black binder, Greindur's tome gleamed at him.

Aerö looked at the old thing, slowly caressing its leathery faces, his fingers tracing some of those petrified circles the rock snails left behind. Tonight, he did not want to swim in Greindur's seas of riddles. Yet somehow, absentminded, he opened it; his hands doing all the work without him even asking them. Pages cracked and turned until one word jumped back at him, a word he did not know, yet somehow his wandering mind was fully aware of. Skrímsli.

Minutes passed as Aerö tried to remember where and when he'd heard the word, but after a few long moments, he had to accept defeat. The memory tempted his thoughts to follow it, to try and find it, but whenever he got close enough to feel the answer, just one thought away, it managed to evade him.

"Skrímsli," he said aloud, but no light flickered in his tired mind. But curiosity nibbled at his senses, and despite his tiredness, he pulled the book onto his lap and began to read Greindur Gamall's millennia-old words.

Skrímsli

Many Gods blessed this world with their innocent presence and lived among us, helping their children prosper. Beast or human they regarded all as equal, good or bad, peaceful or brutes, they gave all purpose. From the shadows, they nudged us on the right path, helped us when we stumbled and encouraged us when life turned harsh. They have watched over their various creations with patience and with trust that we would live. And rarely, when the world fell out of order, they kindly restored it. Such Gods have roamed the world since its inception, beings of absolute strength and skill, of love for their young hatchlings.

As ages turned the world from lush to ash to lush again, we somehow forgot about their presence and their strength, and soon believed we were ourselves Gods over the lesser creatures. But much like parents who's love for their young is unwavering, they never left us out of sight, and even now they guide us to become what they had always planned for us. They are as many as they are old, like the Lady of the Silver Lake or the Golden Oaks or the so many others that I have yet to chance on.

However, reader, do not naively believe that all the ancient beings that live in the most hidden of places in this world are good. Some, as with everything, are the ones that balance all kindness and love bestowed upon us by our creators. They do not believe the world should have been gifted, but instead forever held onto for their own enjoyment. Such beings, unlike their gentle siblings who gave their world to us to see us thrive, never do interfere in the lives of beasts or men and would joyfully sit on their old thrones and watch us squirm. They are creatures of the cruellest kind.

But from all the evil Gods that ever came to be, none are like the Skrímsli.

Just like every other time he read from Greindur's tome, Aerö felt he was unable to take his eyes away from the old sorcerer's writings. They trapped his mind into the world they so skilfully conjured and made him question everything he knew about the world. And just as it happened when he read about the silver pond or about Syngja-Vatn's tales, Aerö wondered if there was a pit of truth in all of it, or were they but delirious conceptions of a tired mind.

Rule the world they did for many ages until the other Gods renounced their home and forced them into hiding, to build a kingdom of their own beneath the surface of the world. There they live still, brutes that dwell in darkness. Millennia they dug a world just for themselves away from all the other Gods, away from the new masters of the realms, away from men and beasts. Their cities span beneath Urukk and beyond, large mazes cut in stone that never surface, unending galleries that allow them to roam free from Wündalær to the Wall and to the Taðr Sea. Vast is their underground realm as are themselves, the Skrimsli - the Hollowers built for themselves, a world like no other and where they cannot be disturbed.

Not many know about their presence far beneath our feet, and even writings have been hard to find, but HE managed to find them and make them do his bidding. Skeggor Skalidur, the true master of all beasts and men, sought out their help to build a better world.

Help they gave, but they are the most treacherous of beings and tried to have him slain. Skeggor, however, knew their nature, and prepared, he made them build an everlasting home, a city carved under a mountain. The Gods obeyed and build they did a place called Undirheim, a capital for their underground realm. But Skeggor had a different plan, that was to be his home, a labyrinth of caverns safely isolated from the world in which he and his growing kind could live in peace.

But the Hollowers did not take kindly to his deceit, for they were sole inhabitants and Gods beneath the surface. They tried to fight him off, but failed, and when their King was speared by Skeggor in their final battle, he made him swear he will allow the

Beast Lords to live in Undirheim in exchange for his life. The King agreed and sealed off the Beast Lords' mountain from their world. Millennia have passed since then, yet anger boils still beneath the world's surface. The King of the Skrímsli, God among Gods, will have his revenge.

Now you know of the most dangerous of creatures to have ruled the world, and rule they still in their sunken kingdom. But reader, may my words carve in your mind the way the Skrímsli carved their cities in black rock. Never have them sought. Never have them found, for they will kill you.

Aerö closed the book and put it on the floor. He had read enough. Without hearing the Feonds' call, he stepped outside his room and ventured to the throne room where he knew he would find Estrelle. There was no time to lose.

Old Friends, New Enemies

The Turmenn's camp fermented with the happenings of the past days. Groups soon formed out of the masses, some defended Petra and her guardians while others cursed their names and blamed them for their wretched lives. The Greed sisters watched with glee as those who still stood by their leader faltered under the sheer numbers of the opposition. Women wept as their men bellowed at each other, covering their children's eyes as fists were thrown and noses broken. The young wailed as the angered noises swallowed the whole camp.

"This is better than stealing from them," sniggered Elfredda as she watched the southern part of the encampment drown in rage and fights. "We should have done this earlier!"

"That stupid Petra will have to march on her own all the way to Caraa. Not one soul will follow her."

"Just her and her stupid guards!" spat Elfredda.

"They would be so proud of us—"

"And they will be avenged, sister. Petra will pay for our husbands' deaths!"

Behind them, Burt walked towards them purposefully, followed by a miserable-looking Martens. The two had become, despite Marten's desire to not be involved, Bathilda's and Elfredda's right hands.

"You've come to enjoy the view! Good!" said Bathilda smiling, flashing her corroded teeth at them.

"We're here to see if you need anything done."

"Maybe there is…" Bathilda thought aloud. Elfredda turned to watch her sister, her expression puzzled, her left hand tightly held against her chest, on it a raw-looking, purple bruise brought colour to her ash-white skin.

"We saw an old woman scavenging through our things; stealing from us. I want you to find her." Burt nodded while Martens looked away. She did not want to know what the Greed sisters had planned for the poor woman.

"She can barely walk. I don't know how she survived the journey here, but she has something that is ours. Find her!"

"Maybe one of those stupid boys carried her all the way here," Elfredda said, caressing, gingerly, her swollen limb.

"We'll find her," growled Burt in his rough voice and grabbed Martens by the elbow. "Come," he hissed and pulled her after him.

* * *

In Petra's tent, Sara helped Syll with her clothes. A few days had passed since she woke up from her long sleep.

"I still think this is too soon!" she pleaded.

"Sara, I cannot bear to sit another day in bed. I need to move, to walk."

"But your back…"

"She will be fine, child," came Petra's voice as she moved like a shadow from cot to cot examining the wounded.

"She needs to move or will not manage the march to Caraa. But no running or fighting, Syll! Promise me!"

"I'll be careful, Petra."

"Be back by nightfall. You must sleep here until your back is healed."

"I will, I will," Syll replied, already walking towards the exit.

"Are you sure this is a good idea? We don't know where she'll go. What if she gets in trouble with the Greeds? She cannot fight like that."

"Sara, my child…" said Petra grabbing her hands in hers. "…I know exactly where she'll be". Sara looked at her curiously.

"If you had been asleep for weeks on end, where would you go?"

"Erlend of course…"

"Exactly!" Petra said, smiling. "She will be with Trevor, out of harm's way."

"You think he'll tell her?"

"I hope he does. That would make them both feel better. The weeks she's missed, the Beasts, and now Taro; she needs to know. We cannot hide them from her any longer."

"Will she be ready?"

"If it was anyone but her, I would not know, but she will."

"I hope you're right, Petra, I really do."

So do I…thought Petra as Sara walked out of the tent.

The central tent was once again conquered by silence. Nothing but the seldom wheezy breaths to remind Petra that she was not alone inside the large structure. Slowly she moved from lamp to lamp, smothering them to conserve the little oil they still had. The journey the Turmenn started back in Bells was nowhere near its end. The tent descended into darkness, patch by patch, until only the corner where Petra's cot stood was still blessed with light.

Heavily, she dropped into her bed, her centuries-old bones cracking from the effort.

"Humph!" she grumbled as her joints complained louder than ever.

"Not long my dears, not long. Once we get everyone to Stórvatn, you won't have to move again." Petra spoke softly, caressing her knees. "But until then, no more complaints!" She grinned.

With both Sara and Syll gone for some time, Petra enjoyed the quietness and solitude her tent provided. She knew there would not be much of it in the weeks to follow. They would soon pack, once again, everything they owned and leave these lands behind in the hope that they would reach the city of Caraa in safety. Her eyes drifted to the patch of dirt that marked Taro's crude grave. She should have been more careful, more vigilant.

Taking her eyes away from the dark mark upon the ground, Petra bent over and pulled from beneath her cot a wooden trunk just large enough to hold under key the few possessions she dared bring with her. Slowly, she unlocked it and pried its lid open.

Phials filled with liquids only she knew, occupied the top of the chest. Carefully she relocated them onto her bed so she could free a smaller wooden box. Petra remembered the last time she used the box weeks back in Bells, when Sara had her first of many terrifying dreams. With the box resting next to the sparkling phials, Petra could now unearth what she was after. A handful of books gleamed at her from the bottom of the trunk, all leather-bound and old. Ancient tomes she'd managed to salvage from Bells. Among them was the one she wished to hold.

The Unreadable Book nested in her lap as it had done all the way from Bells. Black and neatly bound, the book lacked any seams or clasp from where one could force it open. Greindur Gamall's last creation, and maybe his most potent, would only share its knowledge on its own accord. No matter how much force or spells would try to crack it open, the book would not be tamed into revealing its protected secrets.

Petra stroked the black book as if it were a child, gentle and loving. The tome, despite its unobtrusiveness, was truly a living thing. Greindur Gamall's genius had been to bind a living soul to the bundle of paper and leather that composed his masterpiece. He had been the first to create such a thing, a living object. Those who witnessed its creation, quickly separated into two groups, the ones who saw it as an infallible solution to protect the most dangerous of knowledge, even if it meant sacrificing something as pure as a soul. And the others, lead by Arnleaf and Valdis, who called it an abomination, not because it had a soul, but for the knowledge it contained, the truth about their poisonous existence, about their treason and attempt to kill their very friend. The two groups argued over the true value of Greindur's creation, but when it became clear that the King and Queen would not allow such profanity to defy the very things they worked so hard to grasp, Greindur created five Unreadable Books and hid them from his Lords. For millennia they searched for them only to find four; the fifth adamantly out of their reach. But such treachery was to be punished, and the King and Queen tortured old Greindur until not a trace of him was left.

The fifth and last of the Unreadable Books eluded Valdis's and Arnleaf's tormented hunt by hiding in plain sight, moving from hand to hand through Urukk until finally, it found the one to keep it safe.

"How long has it been since you found me?" asked Petra, petting the black book. Her mind fishing from the deepest parts of her being the memories of their first encounter.

"It was before my awakening, that I remember, but far too many years passed since then. Soon you'll have to take on another guardian." The book almost quivered, Petra thought, but otherwise remained as lifeless as the tomes it so skilfully impersonated. It had already shown its secrets to her twice, and Petra knew that she would never stare again at its living, breathing pages.

* * *

Sara wandered through the camp, unable to decide what she should do. She did not want to be alone, but could not bear to tend to the many broken Turmenn in Petra's tent, when none of them would be allowed to live less than a week from now. For a few times, she walked past her own tent, checking to see if Erlend had returned; guiltily hoping he had given up his duties for the day so they could be together. Sara felt pangs of conscience the moment her mind formed the selfish thought. There were so many others in far greater need than her, Turmenn that had nothing and no one to hold them at night, people whom she knew from Bells that had lost everything, just as the many unfortunate others from Brim and Woods.

Sara turned around abruptly as her head finally cleared. She only wasted precious time wandering about the camp instead of helping others, or herself for that matter. Solitude was the worst of cures for the kind of wound her heart was bleeding from. Briskly she walked again past her small tent, her direction set for Petra's. But as she moved swiftly between the rows of shelters, her red dress billowing around her, a familiar voice called Sara's name.

Adriana walked towards her tent, olive-skinned and shining bronze-like, closely followed by two other women and two men.

"Sara! Wait up! There's someone I want you to meet!" Adriana called, and Sara waited for her to catch up.

"Is everything alright?"

"Oh...yes..." Sara stuttered, shaking away the last of the bad thoughts and smiled. "Just needed a walk."

Adriana nodded but did not return her smile. She offered Sara a look that said clearly - *I don't believe you, and I'll find out.* But then added, turning her around by the arm.

"I want you to meet Ishim and Ezkiel. And these are their friends from Brim."

Sara shook the young women's hands and smiled. Adriana had already spoken of them to the gathered guardians in Petra's tent that morning.

"Thank you for helping us," Sara said, smiling broadly, mesmerised by the girls' radiant beauty. They were as beautiful as they were courageous, and she understood why Adriana spoke so highly of them. Sara also noticed that the two men were carrying big bundles that they now had at their feet as they shook hands and rested.

"Ishim and Ezkiel are moving closer to the central tent so they can answer Petra's call when needed. They were camped at the eastern edge, and from there it's a long way here, not to mention slow."

"You can pitch your tent between mine and Adriana's…" said Sara, pointing at a spot already cluttered with too many shelters. "…It'll be tight, but it's the best spot in the camp."

The two sisters flashed their teeth and thanked Sara for her selflessness. Adriana also smiled, pleased.

Sara watched Tarn's daughter cast side looks to the two sisters, especially to Ishim who acted as the older of the two although they looked so much alike they could have shared a womb. Sara followed their expressions, their quirky mien with each other; an idea forming slowly in her mind. It rose from the depths of her being, conjured out of nothing, but once it had formed, it felt watertight. Sara smiled instinctively as she heard her name called. She blinked away the web of thoughts she'd pieced together only to find the group moving away from her and towards the small patch of trampled dirt she'd offered the two sisters.

The men spread out the few possessions they had carried and began to build the young women's tent. It also occurred to Sara, as she rejoined the group, that the men had only brought Ishim and Ezkiel's belongings. The two of them were not about to move closer to Petra and her guardians.

"The sun has done you good," said Adriana looking at Sara, examining her from head to toe. "You spend too much time inside that tent, away from light."

"You are right," replied Sara, smoothing her hair self-consciously. It felt good to sit outside under the full weight of the sun.

"How are the Turmenn?"

"Oh…they are still railed up by the Greeds, but they are not yet eager to fight us."

"The sooner we leave, the better," called Ishim from the midst of her slow-rising shelter.

Both Adriana and Sara turned towards her.

"They need something to do, something to keep them busy and their minds at rest," she added as if reading Sara's mind, then smiled again so honestly, Sara could not help but return it. And so did Adriana.

The two of them observed the erecting of the sisters' shelter, enjoying the gentle wind that crept under their shirts, loving the brilliant sun on their skin. It was a beautiful day.

But little did they know that not even the sun with all its strength and warmth could keep at bay the chilling plans unfolding in their camp. By nightfall two of those they swore to take care of and protect would lie in their own blood.

* * *

At the northern edge of the camp, closest to the jarring mountains and Wündalær, and in clear sight of prowling Beasts, Trevor poked at his long-dead fire. His hands worked hard at the white coals while his mind raced over Syll and Bells. They had been so happy back there when Alistair was still alive, when they still had their homes. But now all that was gone, some permanently ripped from him while others still waited quietly for their return. Despite all that he had seen, Trevor was now determined to go back to Bells and forge a life for himself and Syll, away from wars and Petra.

"Hey!" came the voice he never thought he would hear again. Trevor dropped the stick he was absentmindedly wielding and turned to see his Syll standing behind him.

"They say you've spent a lot of time here alone," Syll said in a rough voice, but a voice that now resembled her old one.

Trevor looked at her, taken aback. He still had not quite worked out if her awakening was a miracle or something his broken mind had conjured in a delusional attempt to keep it whole.

"Hey," was all he managed to cough out.

"Hey!" she repeated, smiling at him and, shifting all her weight onto his shoulder, she lowered herself down next to him. Syll winced as the blistered skin on her back and legs stretched painfully.

"She let you out?"

"Don't sound so surprised, I'm not a prisoner." Then, without hesitation, she leaned over and kissed Trevor's brow. She had been waiting for a long time to do it.

And so had he. Trevor felt his strength seep through his skin as he leaned against her lips and sobbed. His iron-cast will, the impenetrable wall he had erected around his shattered heart crumbled at her touch. There he lay, emotionally naked in Syll's arms, and cried all the tears he had held back, for his father, for Taro, and for her.

After a while, Trevor dislodged himself from Syll's embrace and faced her.

She looked at him through puffy eyes and smiled.

This was the moment they had both awaited, to seal the love they bore for one another. Trevor's arms wrapped gingerly around Syll's body. Eyes closed, lips parted, he leaned over and kissed her on her ruby lips. The taste of her was like nothing his mind would have ever managed to imagine. Sweet, warm, and soft. He wished their lips would never have to part. Minutes passed, but time was known to spare true lovers. The two released each other from their prison of kisses and each stared into the other's eyes, tearful and happy.

"I thought I had lost you."

"I thought I would lose you when I took that blow."

"You shouldn't have pushed me…it should have been me."

"It was my plan, Trevor. I did it so that you, the boys, and the rest of the Turmenn would have a chance to live."

"And what a life we've had since that damned battle…" Trevor snapped a twig between his fingers. His old anger returning to him.

Syll shifted her gaze to the sky-tearing cliffs above them. She still remembered vividly, the first time her eyes fell upon them, how defiant they appeared to be, how rooted in this world. They still inspired her with awe as she lost herself under their heavy shadow.

"I need to know," she said finally. "I need to know how long it's been since the fight and what has happened since. Neither Petra nor Sara wish to tell me, and I came to believe they want me to hear it from you."

Trevor swallowed what felt like a fistful of sand.

"Father has been dead for close to six weeks," he said levelly, his own eyes now measuring the height and depth of the Korr Mountains.

"Six weeks…" Syll repeated voicelessly. "…Such a long time to sleep, and yet I feel as if the battle ended yesterday. What happened to me?"

"Petra believes the blade was poisoned or that it damaged something more than flesh within you. Maybe both."

Syll crept a hand beneath her shirt and touched the long scar that cut down her neck, shoulder and chest.

"After the battle was over, we tried to find their bodies, father's, Byard's, and the others we knew from Bells, but never managed to. They are still out there, trapped within that blackened sand. We had no strength to keep on marching, no food or water, no will, so we built this camp out of what we could salvage."

303

Syll looked at him in silence, her eyes wet with tears. When Trevor stopped, she urged him to continue.

"Since then the Beasts have brought us food and water, helped us gather our wits so that Petra can go on on her demented journey, and drag all of us with her."

At this, Syll looked up at him unflinching, her stare an obvious disapproval of his tone.

"We healed, but soon, others began to work at the dispirited Turmenn. The Greeds have gathered a whole army of those who no longer trust Petra and her plan."

"Surely you and the boys tried to stop them!" Syll cried, aghast at the grim news.

"We thought a battle from within would do us far more harm, but the Greeds had bigger plans than that." Trevor stopped, running a hand through his dirty hair, thinking of how to best deliver the last bit of bad news.

"They thought that having Petra killed would grant them rulership over the rest of the Turmenn, so they poisoned some of our food."

Syll no longer could contain her tears. Heavy, crystalline boulders rolled off her face in streams.

"No one knew that was their plan, so we did not question when fresh bread was taken to Petra to be split in rations. Taro and Grov had been keeping guard at

Petra's tent that morning—" Trevor stopped, swallowing hard.

Syll drew sharp breaths of air.

"…they were starving, so they had some. Taro ate his and then died mere moments later. Grov almost killed me by your cot." Trevor was the one to now shed tears, not of sadness but unforgivable guilt.

"Oh no…" Syll whimpered. "…it wasn't your fault, Trevor!"

"But it was. I was the one to give him that poisoned bread and forced him to eat it. I killed him, Syll! I killed him!" he howled and crumbled into her arms.

They lay like that for hours, not a word passing their lips. Syll kissed his head and held him, knowing just how guilty he must feel. She would have blamed herself had she served Taro the same deadly meal. So she kept him close to her and sobbed alongside him, sharing the pain and sorrow of losing one of their dearest friends.

The sun was already drowning in the Taðr Sea by the time either of them dared to speak. Their eyes had long since shed all their tears, yet their hearts still ached. A missing part of their souls seemed to have been taken from them with the death of Taro, a hole that seemed impossible to fill back in.

"I cannot keep on going Syll…" whispered Trevor, looking Syll in her big eyes. "…I am no longer able to obey her orders and march on to our deaths."

Syll tried to stop him there, but Trevor pressed on. "…I plan to go back to our Bells and live the life we always dreamt of. Come with me, Syll, come back home and away from all this death and pain. Come to Bells with me." He pleaded, squeezing her closer to him so he could land a kiss onto her brow.

Syll barely felt the kiss caress her skin as ice seemed to have formed beneath her skin and rooted her in place. If somewhere deep inside her, she still believed that she could not have been asleep for weeks on end, now she was certain. The Trevor she knew would have never abandoned his leader, his brothers, and his men. He would not have even flinched if his life was required for any of them to live. But this Trevor was a different Trevor than the one she knew.

"Will you come with me, my love? I beg of you!" But Syll stood up without saying one word. The pain she felt from her raw back and legs was gone, replaced by something far more consuming and profound.

"I was afraid I was the one who'd changed after my dreamless wanders, but it is you who's lost his way. I will not follow you, Trevor, in the midst of a battle to protect the ones we swore to keep safe. My path is with Petra and the Turmenn wherever that will take us. If yours is to Bells, then this is farewell."

* * *

Dark enveloped the realm of Urukk through and through. With the death of the sun, roaring fires sprung to life around the Turmenn's encampment, their lashing tongues of flame fighting away the settling chill. Beyond, uncountable gems twinkled on the blackened sky, their beauty utterly unseen by the angered masses far below. The Turmenn were gathering again, but this time, determined to take their survival into their own hands.

The Greed sisters laughed gleefully at the billowing sight.

"Soon, my dear, we shall have what should have been our beloved husbands' rulership over these stupid men," Bathilda said, smiling.

* * *

A dark figure moved between the many tents and fires, towards the central tent.

Inside, Petra and Sara tended to Syll's wounds, unaware that all their oils and tinctures could not alleviate the throbbing pain in her heart.

"Your wounds look so much better, Syll!" said Sara as she finished dousing her back and legs and allowed her to put her clothes back on. Syll smiled wearily.

"Thank you," she whispered, then turned her back to the two and cried in silence. Her heart felt like it was tearing itself to pieces.

With Syll fast asleep, or so they thought, Petra and Sara checked on the other wounded before calling it a night.

Outside the tent, in the dark, a hunched figure drew closer to the entrance, her walking stick slack in her arm, the other wielding something in her pocket. She pushed the flaps aside and entered.

* * *

Bathilda and Elfredda watched the Turmenn fight amongst themselves and wished the night would never stop. But despite their pleasure in seeing men and women fight over what would happen to them, they needed all of them to follow them to Bells and claim back their homes and lives. At least most of them, they grinned. Nothing could spoil such a beautiful night.

As expected, Grov, Sam and Daniel, Ariana too, followed by their armed guardians, soon arrived to calm the Turmenn. But the Greeds knew that the masses were beyond appeasing. So they sat and enjoyed the sight unravelling before them.

From beyond the shouting crowds, Burt and Martens ran to the two sisters, out of breath. At this, Bathilda and Elfredda reacted. They had given the two an order and knew they were now coming with news.

"We saw her!" Burt spurted, catching his breath. Martens coughed looking purple even in the lack of light.

"She entered Petra's tent!"

"Did she!" Bathilda exclaimed. "Then this might just be our lucky evening!". The two looked at her with an expression of total confusion. Elfredda grinned even wider, her slack face making her look like a deflated toad.

"Turmenn!" Bathilda bellowed over the rising turmoil.

"If we are to live the lives we fought so hard to deserve, we need to take them!"

The Turmenn yelled together, no longer fighting amongst themselves.

"She took them from us! She must give them back!"
The assembled masses yelled again in unison.

"Follow me, Turmenn! To Petra!"

* * *

In the dim-lit tent, Petra and Sara tended to the wounded. Syll sobbed, pretending to be fast asleep, while the humped old woman advanced noiselessly into their midst.

As if some foulness had spoiled the air inside the tent, both Sara and Petra gazed up and at each other, then towards the shifting darkness beyond the globe of orange light radiating from a lone lit lamp.

"Is anybody there?" called Sara timidly, her tone half afraid, half-conscious of the sleeping sick Turmenn around them.

"Can we help you?" called Petra coldly. "It's rather late…"

"Oh…help, you can…" came a woman's voice from within the deepest shadows. The hunched shape of the old woman stepped carefully within the island of light where, in its centre, Sara and Petra awaited.

"Oh, my dear, how long I've been waiting for this day," the woman spoke again in her old and raspy tongue. But there was something else jarring the edges of her words; poorly concealed excitement.

"What do you need?" asked Sara stepping forward to help the old woman who sought their aid. Her eyes tried to see some damage, some disease, but only saw her severely humped back and her trembling hand upon a walking stick.

No more than a few paces was Sara allowed to take before Petra's hand raised in her path, signalling her to stop. Sara looked at Petra sideways, but she had her eyes glued to the bundled shape before them.

"Who are you?" Petra demanded, losing her patience with the woman who seemed to revel in the confusion her presence created.

"Have you truly forgotten me, dear?" the voice came again. The bent-over woman slowly began to straighten and rise to her unconstrained-by-age full height. White, timeless locks flowed from beneath the deep hood that obscured the woman's face. The tent echoed with the cracking sound of rearranging bones as she shifted into a completely different form than the one in which she had entered.

Petra felt her strength leave her body as the woman before her dropped her walking stick and grabbed the hem of her hood. The taller, prouder the shape became, the older and more tired Petra felt. Curiosity no longer nibbled at her mind, but fear. This woman before them was no ordinary Turmenn, was not one of them at all, but something very different and far more dangerous.

Sara, beside her, shook with fear as she watched the woman unwrap herself and shed her feigned demeanour.

Syll turned around to see what the bizarre exchange of words was all about, just in time to witness the dark shape's complete reveal.

Gasps emerged from Sara's white-with-fear lips as Petra stepped in front of her.

"No. It can't be you!" Petra whispered hoarsely.

A black face emerged from within the many folds of her hood, not naturally coloured like Adriana's, but dark with ink. Layers upon layers of lines and symbols painted grotesquely on the woman's face; glinting wet-like in the lamp's flickering light.

Sara felt a wave of nausea wash over her as the sorceress unmasked herself to them.

"It's been too long, Petra," the old Healer hissed, pleased.

"…Nephthys…" Petra said aghast. "…Priestess…"

Syll covered her mouth with one hand as her body shook with horror, the other searching frantically for her blade. All thoughts of Trevor now forgotten, she rose from her cot and stepped in front of Sara, next to Petra. Syll waited for Petra to tell her off and urge her to her bed, but the command never arrived. Petra's colour drained from her flesh.

"Why are you here?" she asked.

"You must know why I'm here, old friend." Nephthys croaked, smiling at her. Sara moved to the other side of Petra. The presence of another sorceress, a Healer, inside their encampment meant but one thing. They had been found. The war the Turmenn started by defending themselves against the King and Queen's dark riders was about to claim even more lives. More men and mothers, more children and old would most definitely find their end in the same sands their loved ones perished weeks before.

This time, Petra did break the eye contact with the unwelcomed Healer to gaze at Syll and Sara.

"You two must run," she whispered. "You must make sure the Turmenn are kept safe and far away from here. Go!" she urged.

"That will not save anyone, dear…" Nephthys slurred through her wide grin.

"Leave the others! Do your deed and take me to your Queen!"

"Embarrassing… I once thought you were my most gifted student, Petra. What happened to you?" Nephthys asked, but before Petra answered, she went on no longer grinning at her.

"You've melded with these revolting apes, old friend. They've closed your mind and dumbed you down. How could you put yourself at their filthy feet when they should be the ones kneeled before you?" the old Healer's voice now boomed with outrage.

"You are a God compared to them! You have dishonoured your Order and yourself!" she howled.

"Just let them live." Petra insisted. "Take me to her, but let them live!"

"The Queen has not sent me to fetch you, Petra! She has no wish to lay her eyes upon your wretched self. She wants you dead!" she laughed madly.

"All of you, dead!"

* * *

"Follow me, Turmenn!" Bathilda bellowed as she led the gathering masses towards Petra's large tent. Little did they know that out of all the nights they could have chosen to banish their leader, the Turmenn picked the one in which they should, instead, run far and hide. By some perverse plan of the Gods, they marched to their own demise.

"Do not wait for her to come to you with other lies, go into her tent and seize her!" The Turmenn roared.

Every soul soon joined; like a flood, they gathered speed and force, from but few, now hundreds answered the Greeds' call.

Adriana and her warriors, Grov, Daniel, and Sam, tried to make the people stop, but they were vastly outnumbered. All they could do was run alongside them and wish that when they did reach Petra, she would manage to bring sense to them.

"Shouldn't we try to fight them off?" growled Daniel from the midst of the stampede.

"We can't, brother! Remember Petra's words! We have promised to protect them, not kill them with our blades!"

"He's right!" called Ezkiel, who ran with Adriana. "We cannot fight them even if we wished to! They are now too many."

"Make sure they do not enter Petra's tent!" Adriana shouted.

* * *

"Why are you so afraid of us?" demanded Syll lifting her sword. The sharpened metal felt much heavier in her hands than she remembered it to be. The many weeks she wasted in her bed had made her weak.

"Afraid?" howled Nephthys, genuinely amused.

"We are not scared of you, filth! You have no place to claim our lands as if they're yours. Your very existence is an insult to the Gods!"

"You're mad!"

"Syll!" muttered Petra. "Take Sara and run! Leave me and run!" But it was too late to escape the inevitable. Syll knew, just as Petra did, that their option to run had vanished the moment Nephthys walked inside the tent.

If the old sorceress had enjoyed playing with her prey, now she stared at them full of malice. She was ready to fulfil the task bestowed upon her by the Queen herself.

"You must be craving death," she said as she focused her cold eyes on Petra. Her left hand vanished into a pocket and emerged holding a curved dagger, black and oily, much like the Draugurs' swords. The blade glistened thirstily at them.

"Why now?" asked Petra trying to win some time for the two young women to escape. "Why kill us now?"

"Oh…only your heathen pets will die tonight. For you, old friend, I planned something far greater. We will use you to make that godless heir of yours come out so that the King and Queen can slay him."

Petra shook as Nephthys's words cut her insides like blades. They knew where Aerö was, and they wanted him dead. Arnleaf and Valdis themselves sought to crush him before he could grow strong enough to fight them. Sara released a low cry as she understood the venom in the sorceress's words.

"It's time," Nephthys announced as she looked behind her and towards the rising clamour of voices outside.

Syll knew she had but one shot at slaying her. If she failed to dig her sword deep into her body, the sorceress's black blade would no doubt find her flesh and this time kill her for good.

* * *

Children wept in their mothers' arms, men bellowed, women wailed as the angered mass of bodies reached Petra's tent. It was dark, yet the shelter glowed in the Turmenn's many blazing torches. Between the raging torrent of limbs and clubs, and the entrance to the central tent, a row of courageous warriors stood rooted in place and awaited the forceful impact with the very ones they wanted to protect.

"Stop!" cried the guardians, who had been joined by Erlend. He, too, failed to stop the gathering Turmenn at the northern edges of the camp. From all sides, a sea of torches encircled Petra's tent. Trevor crept behind the central tent and watched the masses bellow. He would not stand aside and let his little brothers die, nor Syll, but unless a fight broke out and they were put in danger, he was on the Turmenn's side. Just like them, he had grown tired of Petra's orders and sick of the life he now had. He shared the same misguided beliefs with the Greed sisters, the very ones who he once almost killed for their poisonous tongues.

"Don't listen to them! Don't believe their lies!" Elfredda shrieked over the thunder that echoed through the camp.

"Turmenn, stop!" tried Sam and Daniel in vain to pacify the masses, but this time they would not be so easily stopped. They advanced slower now, yet more compact towards their believed enemy with nothing but the thought to have their leader banished, raging through their minds. The Greeds however had a different plan for her. Far colder and more final than that.

* * *

Petra, Syll, and Sara watched the sorceress brandish her black dagger between her hands, probably debating with herself on how to kill them most pleasurably. The tent that was but moments earlier governed by darkness, now glowed orange at them, like some monstrous womb keeping them imprisoned.

"How fitting!" exclaimed Nephthys to herself. "You humans truly are the stupidest of creatures. Only the Gods know how you managed to survive this long."

The moment Nephthys looked behind again, listening to the deafening uproar that reverberated through the fabric of the tent, Syll took her chance. She leapt before Petra could stop her, blade aimed at the old woman's heart, all her strength and weight behind it.

Time seemed to elongate as she charged towards her, but the old Priestess was not to be slain so easily. With her eyes away from Syll, she stepped sideways. Syll stumbled forward, slowly through the distorted time, as her sword did not managed to meet its target. Then before she could regain her footing, Nephthys's movements regained their normal speed, and it was over.

With incredible speed, Nephthys's dagger slashed through the air, its hilt meeting Syll's left temple with a muffled thud. Sara blinked, and Syllvia's body was already on the ground. Sara yelled. The glowing tent seemed to shimmer as the Priestess moved towards Petra and Sara, a cloud of smoke, a billowing shadow moving so fast they stood no chance. The dagger materialised again at Petra's throat while the other hand hit Sara so hard in the jaw she crashed through Syll's now empty cot.

"You come with me old friend, or I shall kill them all! You know I can!" Nephthys hissed pressing the tip of her dagger in Petra's jugular.

"You won't mind if I take them too, would you? I die of curiosity about how such abominations work." Petra winced at her old Master's words.

"Please Nephthys! Take me but let them live."

The Priestess laughed at her.

* * *

Outside, the guardians turned to Sara's cry, but Erlend was already almost through the flaps of the large shelter. Trevor pulled his blade and cut straight through the side of the tent. If Sara was in danger, so was Syll.

"Stop him!" bellowed Bathilda, but Erlend was already in. She and Elfredda stumbled forward after him.

Both men gasped at the sight of Petra's tent. From the knocked down cots, to Syll and Sara, to the woman dragging Petra by her hair.

"Syll!" Trevor cried, feeling his insides squirm at the sight of her.

"What is this? …Who are you!" Erlend boomed blocking Nephthys's path with his broad frame. "Release her!"

"Step aside ape," she said, almost bored.

"Who are you?"

"You really should cherish the last breaths you have," the Priestess added moving towards him, her gait just as determined to walk out the tent.

"There's no way you can leave this place still whole! There are a thousand people outside—"

"They are all here to skin her. I'm doing them a favour," she laughed. "But if you're all so eager to see beyond the veil of death, I can certainly help." And she dug her free hand in her pocket. She smiled as she saw the patch of fresh dirt at her right. *What fools bury their dead inside their tents? The soul still lingers…they cannot even grasp what they have bought upon themselves. This makes the ritual so, so much easier…*

A fistful of broken bones and ash scattered before her as she chanted madly; her hoarse voice rising and falling in an enchanting rhythm.

"Rise my beautiful! Rise and kill them all!"

Nothing seemed to happen. The crowds still roared outside, louder than ever, their fires still painted the whole tent orange while the black-faced woman dragged Petra towards Erlend and the exit behind him.

* * *

Bathilda and Elfredda would not let the many weeks of planning go to waste. They charged towards Petra's tent aware of the row of warriors awaiting them.

"Grab her!" Bathilda shrieked, and the masses swarmed upon their protectors. Chaos broke, as everybody threw their fists, clubs, and torches at the few who stood defiantly in their path. But as the masses reached the guardians, cries of terror rippled through the enraged Turmenn and confusion took hold of the camp.

* * *

Erlend froze in place as the most unnatural of noises filled the tent, just as the Turmenn began their assault beyond its thin fabric walls.

Trevor checked on Sara who was crying, hidden under the remnants of Syll's cot.

Syll, however, was still lying on the floor not moving, between Erlend and the woman Trevor did not recognise. He did not care why Petra was being dragged by her hair, her hands limp by her body, or why crunching sounds echoed louder in the room; all he could focus on was his Syll.

Then, as shrieks began to rise above all other sounds outside the tent, both Trevor and Erlend saw him. First, a hand, then his head, until he was fully emerged from the hole they'd put him in.

Trevor lost his balance, as before him, Taro stood, or what was left of him after the worms and earth had feasted on him. Trevor was trapped.

Erlend felt like pinching the insides of his arms to make himself wake up. But no matter how much pain he caused himself, he could not make the repulsive image go away. Taro stood before him, facing Trevor with a long blade trapped in his skeletal hand. More shrieks came from outside.

"Sara, stay where you are!" he bellowed as he saw her move with the corner of his eye. By the sounds coming from outside and the impossibly cruel things happening before them, she was safest where she was.

"You're all going to die!" laughed Nephthys, hysterically.

Trevor pulled out his sword hastily as Taro wielded his.

"Taro, it's me!" cried Trevor trying to make his friend see sense. But Taro had been rotting in the ground for days. Before him was no friend of his, but something the black-faced witch had summoned to do her bidding; an abomination.

"Taro!" he bellowed, but the terror of bones and rotten flesh was not willing, or able to listen. Taro raised his blade determined and precise.

"Taro! It's me!" Trevor repeated, dodging his dead friend's blows. Taro however threw blow after blow without mercy.

* * *

Bodies fell as swords cut through their flesh with ease. Yells of horror rippled through the running Turmenn. From within the darkness that surrounded the bright dome of light their torches spewed, ten dead bodies of their friends and loved ones slashed at them indiscriminately. Some of them were husbands, some of them were wives, some were even children; each of them wielding a weapon that did not stop from hacking. The Turmenn stampeded in all directions, trampling on the slow or old, the disoriented or wounded. None still cared about their renounced leader or her guardians, but the Greed sisters. As Turmenn died all around, unable to defend themselves, and with Petra's warriors busy fighting off the unnatural assailants, Bathilda and Elfredda moved towards the entrance of the central tent willing to risk it all to have her killed and their loved husbands finally avenged.

* * *

"How do we kill them?" bellowed Adriana in Sam's direction, dodging yet another murderous blow cast by one of the formerly dead Turmenn.

"How should I know? I don't even understand what they are!"

"They're the dead, dear brother!" said Daniel mocking from a few feet away, where he and Grov duelled another one of the horrendous, walking things.

"I think I saw old mister Hempps back there…you know, the old preacher," continued Daniel, driving his sword straight through his opponent which caused no damage to the putrescent creature.

"Are you sure, brother?"

"Sam, I am sure! He still had his cloak and beads on him, but this time he wasn't running sermons that much, he was busy cutting someone up!"

"Boys! How do we kill them?" roared Adriana, who fought alongside Ishim and her sister.

"I don't think that's your best plan yet, Adriana!" bellowed Daniel. "Hempps died seven weeks ago!"

"Oh, will you be serious!" hissed Sam, trying to show Adriana that he was not as senseless as his younger brother, but beneath his serious mien, he too laughed at Daniel's terrible jokes. Maybe there was something truly wrong with both of them to love a good fight, but that was what they knew best.

Ishim and Ezkiel both fought valiantly, but even they could not manage to slay one of the risen dead.

"We can't keep going like this!" How do we stop them?" repeated Adriana for the millionth time.

"We've tried cutting them, chopping them, stabbing them…"

"I even set one on fire!" yelled Grov, in his high voice.

"…But nothing worked!" finished Sam.

"I've got an idea!" roared Daniel, turning away from the enemy he was fighting off alongside his brother.

"Hey! Come back here!" But Sam had to fight the flesh-dangling brute all by himself. The Turmenn were slowly dispersing through the cluttered camp as their guardians battled the monsters. They may have not been able to stop any of them from fighting, but they succeed in keeping them away from the defenceless.

Sam almost gagged at the sight of his opponent as they spun around, still fighting, into the brighter light of a nearby fire. The woman's face, Sam was certain the creature had once been a woman, was fleshless and brown from rot. A hysterical grin stretched upon her face as she fought, not flawlessly, but without fear of pain or damage. Every time her blade hit Sam's, her loose jaw would clatter away happily, in a mad laughter. Sam felt revulsion just from looking at her, but there was also the smell.

Against his will, his eyes slid down from the jaw-dropping head and to the woman's eaten away throat and shoulders. When he reached her breasts, he could no longer hold his meagre dinner in. Sam stooped evading yet another crippling blow.

From behind, just in time, Daniel appeared wielding a long beam from one of the carts nearby. With a wide swing that caused a few of his friends to curse, he rammed the thing in Sam's assailant's head, sending it rolling across the camp. Sam crouched down and spilled his guts from what his eyes had seen. The putrid body of the woman crumbled to the ground, as if the inner strings that kept the thing together snapped.

"Are you alright?" asked Daniel offering his hand. Sam took it and stood up. He was feeling queasy, yet he still broke into a laugh.

"You are mad!" he declared.

"Or a genius!"

"A mad genius!" and they both roared in laughter.

"Use something longer than their blades to cut their heads off!" boomed the two, as they moved towards the others who were slowly losing. Unlike their attackers, they did get tired and wounded.

Grov shrieked as he slammed into one of those creatures with his massive body, folding the dead arms long enough so he could tear its head off barehanded. Mysterious fluids ran on his hands and forearms and everyone who saw it happen, retched. Two were dead-dead, plenty more to go.

"Boys!" roared Adriana as she sent another head tumbling between the tents. "You really are mad! But I am so happy to fight alongside you!"

Daniel grinned at Sam whose blushed face reached new depths of red.

"What?" Sam hissed. Daniel grinned wider.

"Let her go!" bellowed Erlend at the dark figure before him, as she dragged Petra behind her.

"We are Gods compared to you, ape! Step aside," the Priestess said, dismissing Erlend. Yet the man refused to budge. Nephthys regarded his foolish courage with curiosity.

More yells came from outside, horrifying, blood-gurgling sounds. She stopped as isolated cheers drifted to her through the tent's lit walls. If she was to do the Queen's bidding, but also bring some entertainment to her sisters, Nephthys needed to leave. Those damned apes, she thought, must have found the way to stop her beloved puppets. She still had time before all ten of them were sent back to their graves.

Trevor dodged another well-aimed blow at his side. Taro was relentlessly thrusting his sword at Trevor's heart.

"Erlend! Give me a hand! I can't reach Syll!" Erlend watched him briefly, but his eyes returned to the woman before him. She was very old, yet she was capable of holding Petra by her hair with ease, she was also responsible for the abomination fighting Trevor. What else was she capable of, he thought.

"Erlend! Help me!"

"I am sorry, Trevor, but I cannot let her leave."

"You bastard!"

"I was going to take the women, you know…" said Nephthys looking at the unconscious Syll and then at Sara.

"…But I think I would much prefer to have one of the other sex as well," she grinned at him, white teeth gleaming, contoured by her inked-black face, and stepped towards Erlend and the entrance behind.

Erlend raised his sword and threatened the advancing woman with it. She laughed, then moved so fast, he blinked and she was already standing right beside him.

At her feet, Syll groaned as she came back to her senses.

"Useless…" she muttered as Erlend spun round to cut her with his blade. But the Priestess was expecting that and with barely any effort, she hit Erlend in the back of his head. The world spiralled out of view, and Erlend hit the ground.

In that very moment, when Trevor blocked another one of Taro's relentless blows, and Sara gasped as her beloved husband crumbled next to Syll, two outlines tore open the tent's entrance.

* * *

"How many?" crowed Adriana at her warriors.

"I think there are only a few left!" answered Grov, covered in rotten fluids. His method of separating the dead Turmenn's heads from their bodies was barbaric and disgusting, but also highly effective.

"Brother!" called Daniel swinging the long beam he carried. "We need to hurry."

"I am rather busy!" shouted Sam, as he tried to hit his rather short opponent in the head.

"Brother, don't you find it odd—"

"Not now! Help me here or go fight another one of these foul things!"

"Sam!" Daniel bellowed, and this time Sam's beam smashed with full force into his opponent's head.

"Don't you find it odd that we haven't seen either Petra, Erlend, or Trevor?"

"Damn it!" Sam growled and ran towards the central tent.

* * *

"Who are you?" shrieked Bathilda as she and her sister almost ran into the old Healer. It took them a few good moments to realise what was unfolding around them. The tattooed woman, the fallen bodies at their feet, the clashing sounds of swords and shouts as Trevor fought one of those things.

They gasped in horror.

"Oh, my dears…" Nephthys croaked and hunched her back.

"You…you…" Elfredda stuttered incomprehensibly, while her hands clawed themselves to blood.

"You are that thief!" spat Bathilda.

"A thief! The monkey dares to call me a thief!" Nephthys shrieked at the two. "But I have right here what I took…" she added regaining her amused demeanour. "…You can have them back."

Nephthys rummaged through her pockets while still holding Petra. Another fistful of bones and ashes scattered in the tent.

"Come forth, my beautiful!" she called.

The tent drowned in silence as the Greeds stared at the inked woman before them, their eyes darting from her blackened face to the scattered bones on the floor.

Nothing happened. Only Trevor's shouts pierced the palpable tension from where he was fighting Taro, begging him to stop.

"Run, fools..." growled Petra. The sound of something cutting through the tent's taut walls startled the two sisters. The infinitesimal chance they had to turn around and run, and hopefully escape Nephthys' dark arts was gone. They never listened to Petra's advice, just as they did not now, a defiance that would cost them greatly.

The tearing sounds rippled through the tent, then stopped as whatever made them managed to break in. From the dark corners of the tent, something moved towards them, slow and lumbering as their legs carried their bodies awkwardly.

If defiance painted Bathilda and Elfredda's faces moments prior, now terror reigned. From behind Trevor and Taro, who were still sparring , two figures moved into the light, ash-covered and dark, their clothes torn and stained by time and blood.

"It can't be," wailed the two sisters, taking hold of each other's hands.

"My love!" shrieked Elfredda as their two husbands stopped alongside Nephthys. The two made a few feeble steps towards them.

"Is that really you?" cried Bathilda, hysterically. The two figures looked at them through hollow eyes. Unlike Taro, whose flesh had been eaten away by worms, the two Greed brothers looked still whole; their skin still stretched over their bones like a tarp. From afar they looked alive.

"The sands have been merciful with them," said the Priestess, caressing one's sunken cheek with her free hand. Bathilda and Elfredda cried in blind happiness for their reunion with their loved ones.

"My love…" Bathilda hiccupped shaking from all joints. "You've come back to me!" and moved one step closer.

"Go…" Nephthys whispered, taking her hand away, her voice calm and motherly.

The Greed brothers moved one step at a time towards their wives, their gait heavy, their hands wrapped around long swords. Bathilda and Elfredda opened their arms to welcome back their husbands.

"Run!" hissed Petra, but her call was wasted on the sisters. They stood arms wide apart, awaiting their loved ones' embrace.

Their swords rose swiftly and slashed everything before them in tandem, cutting air, cloth, and flesh with ease.

Petra gave a faint cry as her ears heard what her eyes failed to see.

Bathilda and Elfredda stood as they were, arms apart and smiling at their husbands, but their flesh and bones could no longer bear their weight and keep them upright. A red sliver blossomed on their throats and faces as their brown clothes fell severed in half. Without delay, their bodies followed, splitting down the middle, peeling from each other gruesomely.

Nephthys smiled as the four halves splattered wetly onto the ground, atop Erlend and Syll.

"Bring them, we need to go!" the Priestess ordered her devoted puppets, and walked deeper into the tent. Petra stumbled in her wake as he tried to regain her footing.

Once out of the globe of orange light, their bodies merged into the thick darkness beyond it, vanishing from sight.

"Come on!" yelled Sam at Daniel, as he sped towards the central tent.

"We are so stupid! This was another of the Greeds' distractions!"

"But Sam, the dead—"

"I know, but I can feel that they are behind all this."

"They couldn't, brother—" but his words died in his throat as they burst through the tent's entrance.

The image of the halved Greed sisters hit them in the guts, their innards, brains, and bowels spread across the floor. The boys felt their own entrails squirm as they recognised the four half-faces staring back at them. Horrified, they looked around for Petra, Syll, and Sara, but instead saw their older brother fighting one of those dead things. Both Sam and Daniel spilled their guts as Taro walked into the light.

"Get away from here!" bellowed Trevor at them, barely managing to form the words.

Taro slashed his sword at him with no sign of exhaustion.

Daniel wiped his mouth onto his sleeve and grabbed his sword.

"Run, brother!" roared Trevor.

"I am sorry, Taro!" Daniel growled between thick tears and cut straight through his friend's skeletal neck. Just as it had happened with the others, the strings that held together Taro's bones suddenly snapped, sending his putrefied limbs and torso to the ground.

"Brother, where are they?" Sam couldn't take his eyes away from the mess around them. Trevor had already run out into the night.

"Trevor!"

Deeper Still

"Do you really trust her, my King?"

"As much as one can trust a God, I guess. But do not feel discouraged, my dear Örn. What I now ask of you is of most importance."

"Still—to walk straight into their trap with only her word for it—"

"We have been blessed with endless life, we ought to be patient, and you, my dear, must be more patient than most. Await for him, sharpen your skills, my heir shall come."

"Centuries on that damned island with the wolves…"

"Four thousand years, if you must."

The Falcon and the Bear

Örn, The Teacher

His room vanished in his wake as Aerö ran along the narrow hallway to the stairs that would take him to

Estrelle's throne room. To his left, his mother's chambers spilled warm light ahead of him, casting an amber glow onto the stairs he turned to climb, two at a time. He was early for his training with Estrelle, but he needed to find answers for the questions that burned brightly in his mind.

A noisy draught moved the mildew-scented air inside the Beasts' vast lair, as if the whole of Undirheim was one enormous creature breathing, snoring. Its many galleries and tunnels turned to windpipes in the quietness of the night.

Aerö sped toward the throne room in great haste. He was eager to find Estrelle, but also wished to reach her without being seen. The slapping of his feet was the one thing that could betray his presence.

The twisting staircase finally opened before him with a yawn, spitting him inside the endless chamber. Estrelle sat on her throne of bones, no other soul in sight. She stared as her young son stumbled into the room.

"You're early," she said softly, crossing her arms in front of her.

"I fell asleep…" Aerö lied, "…and didn't know if the night call rang."

Estrelle nodded, unimpressed.

"How was your day down in the training grounds? I hear you had quite a few opponents," she smiled, wrapping her white mantle tighter around her body. A chill had settled in the throne room.

"Did you ask him—?"

"Oh no, I was quite against it, but he thought otherwise, and I know better than to interfere with his teaching." She chuckled.

"So? How did it go?"

"The others do not like me to look inside their minds, especially Nóór's mother."

"Finndôra has always been the wildest of us all. But she will come 'round, for our people. She does not trust any of us." She laughed again.

"I've thought about the times I saw your father train, and I have a few things I want you to try." Aerö nodded obediently. He would learn as much as he could from his mother before asking her about the book she did not wish him to read— not yet at least. He knew this would be the last time he would train with her.

Aerö followed the Queen of the Beast Lords through the equally spaced forest of pillars to the blackened spot they'd used before to awaken his skills, and where Eldur had practiced years prior.

Estrelle walked slowly under the cascading pale-green light that turned the throne room into a seemingly underwater chamber. Aerö tried to gauge the height and width of the throne room each time he found himself in it, but always failed to attain its true dimensions. Shades and sourceless shards of light played tricks in Aer'ös eyes as he looked up to the high vaulted ceiling.

How many times had Eldur walk between these pillars just as he did now? Aerö thought, looking at the enormous place. *How many nights did he spend sharpening his skills or learning new ones away from the unfriendly eyes of the Beast Lords?* Aerö walked in Estrelle's wake thinking of the father he never met, a man some called a traitor, a deserter, while others, just as his mother did, remembered him as nothing less than a true hero. Aerö might have never met him, yet he knew his father had been a great sorcerer. Good or bad was just a point of view.

Ahead of Estrelle, in the petrified, surreal forest the two walked through, Aerö saw the blackened patch. The Queen of the Beast Lords slowed down and then stopped in the very spot she did the night before, dropping to her knees in preparation for her young son's training.

Aerö followed suit and took his place in front of her.

"Let's start with the things you already know."

Aerö placed a hand beneath his shirt and took out his father's scarlet gem. The rock trembled in his hand, excited.

Before Estrelle could ask of him to rouse the pendulum between his palms, he asked its flames to come forth. Without a moment's delay, his hands burst into flames, blood-red tongues of fire hissing as they came alive.

"Very good, Aerö," she said, pleased, smiling at him proudly.

Aerö then made the pendulum stifle its flames, repeating the cycle a few times before Estrelle spoke again.

"You've been practising," she said, piercing him with her cold stare.

Aerö nodded, but did not apologize. He needed to be strong for what he had planned next. As he did for the war.

"I will not ask of you to stop, but you must promise me you will not burn one thing or hurt a soul within this Lair with your flames, son. The secret of your awakened elemental powers will be your greatest weapon against the King and Queen."

"I promise," said Aerö without hesitation. In but a few hours, he would no longer be inside the Beast Lord's ' Lair to be able to hurt them.

"Now…" Estrelle said grinning, "…I want you to learn one of your father's favourite spells." Aerö smiled at her. Complete trust in his father's pendulum filled him as he listened to Estrelle. Where once was but terror, now understanding and acceptance reigned in his heart.

We can do it! He projected his unwavering thoughts to the gleaming gem between his palms. The pendulum quivered.

"This was one of your father's most feared gifts, a power you already summoned in the battle with Velas." Estrelle spoke slow and calm.

"The ability to conjure flames from thin air and from afar." Aerö thought about the battle with his friend, turned foe, inside that very chamber weeks before. Blurry images of Velas spitting out the truth he had hidden from him, tore open wounds Aerö naively thought had healed. Tears stung his eyes, as they did that night, when Velas stabbed his mother right before him. And then came the flames.

Like a roar from deep inside him, they rose and bubbled beneath his skin. Aerö could still feel the unbearable scorch that pulsated from somewhere within him. Through teary eyes, he saw pockets of flames appear in the room moments before Velas was sealed inside the blazing coffin Aerö had put him in.

"Aerö!" Estrelle yelled, moving away from her son.

When Aerö came back to his senses, Estrelle was feet away from where she had been sitting. It took him a few more moments to realise what had alarmed her.

Bright red, liquid flames covered his whole body, dripping molten to the now burning floor beneath him. In his grip, Eldur's pendulum trembled with suppressed power.

Nothing survived the flames' raw touch; his clothes turned into smoke, not even ash was left behind.

"Aerö, make them stop!" Estrelle cried.

But Aerö was again in full control of the merciless flames and wondered if he could now summon Eldur's feared skill.

"Aerö!" she yelled again, moving even further away from him.

A ring of flames was spreading, radiating from where Aerö stood. Yet Aerö knew he had to try. The pendulum's wildest explosions happened when he thought he was about to die. For more powerful manifestations of his father's flames, he needed much stronger emotions than the ones he conjured while training.

Aerö closed his eyes and thought about the King and Queen, Arnleaf Uriel and Valdis Ezelle, the betrayers, the unfaithful, the undying. Stronger the torrent of flames that channeled through him grew, burning hotter and brighter. Aerö knew he'd reached his limit when his body cried in pain.

"Aerö!" Estrelle yelled again, more alarmed than ever, but her son refused to stop the scarlet gem from spewing flames.

Velas and the Draugur showed themselves to Aerö before his mind's eye, then the High Counsellor, followed yet again by Arnleaf and Valdis who smiled broadly at him.

Then, when the flames became too fierce to bear, Aerö released them, focusing on a green spot a few good feet away from him and his, now frightened, mother. Nothing seemed to happen for a few long moments. Estrelle still yelled at him, the pendulum still trembled in his hands, the floor beneath him bathed in scarlet flames. But then the shadows began to move and shimmer all around them, hooded faces, paws and fangs advancing onto them in haste. When they were just about to step outside the obscuring darkness into light, a globe of fire burst to life three feet up from the floor in the same spot, Aerö focused his gaze on.

The contoured shadows of the Beast Lords and their Beasts stopped outside of the pulsating sphere of bright red light floating before them. They stared at it in absolute terror. The newborn sun inside the throne room cast red light onto the many pillars that spanned from floor to ceiling, morphing it from eerie-green, moss-covered into a surreal, bloody red. Aerö could now see the yellow eyes of every Beast upon him as he kneeled onto the burning floor. His nakedness covered not by modesty, but lack of strength left in his limbs to carry him. He gazed into the angered faces all around and understood their sentiments. Aerö knew he would be just as scared and maddened as they were if anyone threatened to harm his mother. Then as he saw more faces come into the crimson light his conjured sun released, the scarlet gem went back to sleep and took all light and warmth it had created.

Aerö came 'round in the roaring voices of many men and women. He opened his eyes to find himself lying on the cold surface of the Beast Lords' throne of bones, with no recollection of him getting there. He was still naked, but a dark cloak had been placed atop of him. Aerö felt a wave of gratitude towards whomever lent their clothing to him. The racket of voices grew as Aerö lifted himself up to face the angered gathering of Beasts and Beast Lords. In front of him, standing before the thundering men and women, Estrelle faced her people trying to calm them down. But the Beast Lords would not be easily appeased.

"You shouldn't have encouraged him to summon those cursed flames in our home, Estrelle!" bellowed Finndôra, whose voice Aerö recognised with ease.

"Choose your allegiance, daughter of Skeggor Skalidur the First!" roared the Beast Lord whose Beast was a giant yellow snake wrapped around his body. "Us or him!" he bellowed, pointing at Aerö, who was coming to his senses. Estrelle turned to see her son sit up onto the throne, she may not own much longer.

"He should have never been allowed into our home," said Finndôra coldly. "We've hidden from them for centuries, and we have prospered! How can you give all that away?"

"Prospered?" asked Estrelle incredulously.
"Prospered? Have you not seen how few of us still roam these halls? How few of us bear children? My father's line will not survive another generation without new blood. If you fail to see that, Finndôra, than you're blinder than I thought!"

"How dare you?" Finndôra growled and Har-úgur, her Feond, stomped the floor in anger. "How dare you judge my loyalty towards my own?"

"Let me ask you one question. Had Nóór been taken from you by Arnleaf and Valdis, would you just sit and watch? Would you just hide away under this prison we've been living in for long millennia?"

"My son is one of us, a Beast Lord, not a filthy sorcerer like him!" Finndôra hissed, pointing at Aerö, who watched the Beast Lords' seethe around him and Estrelle, who sat before him like a hen before its chicks.

"Watch your tongue, Finndôra," said Hïldúúr calmly. With one hand he petted Ashäël, the other held Nóór close to him.

"He needs to leave!" she spat.

"You cannot—" Estrelle began, but the voices of the other Beast Lords drowned her own.

"We agree!" they chanted.

Aerö could feel the Beast Lords' rage inside his body, as their feelings merged with his. He could sense their fear, their disgust, their utter horror of him, as if he too felt all those things about himself. But above all else, he felt Estrelle's sadness tear her apart as she weighed her choices. Either she sided with her people and banished Aerö away from Undirheim where he most certainly would fall into the betrayers' trap, or she sided with her son and ran away with him. However difficult the decision may be, none of the choices given to her by her people would have them survive the war. Estrelle knew that without Aerö, none of them stood any chance against their armies, least their skills. No matter who she sided with, the Beast Lords would be dead. The only soul she could actually protect and maybe save was Aer'ös.

"If you cast him out from our home, I shall go with him. I will not let my only son walk to his death and do nothing!" Estrelle growled at the united Beast Lords before her. Aerö could feel how deeply their betrayal had wounded her. But she was resolute. She would give up all for him, her only son and Skeggor's foretold heir.

"Then so be it!" hissed Finndôra before Hïldúúr could stop her. Estrelle was right, they were too few to banish any of them. To Hïldúúr, Aerö too was one of them.

"Agreed!" chanted the Beast Lords in unison. Estrelle bowed her head to them and turned towards the throne. Aerö, however, was no longer on it, but standing beside her, gem in hand spewing scarlet flames.

"No, son," she said calmly.

Aerö could now see all the Beast Lords and their Beasts arranged into a crescent around the two of them. Nóór was there too, close to him, between Finndôra and his father, images of Aerö's room drifting on his friend's wandering thoughts.

"How dare you treat your Queen like that? Have you forgotten who she is? Are we to banish Skeggor's daughter and thin our numbers still?" Hïldúúr bellowed, and Ashäël growled threateningly at the few who feared Aerö so completely, they were willing to sacrifice their own Queen to have him leave the rock they had been hiding under for centuries.

"Aerö, stop," Estrelle repeated, placing a hand onto his shoulders, but Aerö made the flames grow fiercer. She pulled her hand away.

"He must leave before dawn," said Finndôra, ignoring both Estrelle and Hïldúúr, but focusing her stare onto the boy with burning hands before her.

Nóór glared at his mother.

"Choose well, Skeggor's daughter," said the woman Beast Lord with the stag like creature called Cẹrreb.

"Leave us!" Estrelle ordered.

"My Queen…" said Hïldúúr, clearly upset by how the others treated her, but not even he could stand between her and the will of the Lair. That was the way of the Beast Lords. One would reign over them as long as the others allowed them to do so.

"Leave!" she growled through elongating jaws as her body changed into that of the White Wolf.

The Beast Lords cleared the room, but their voices carried long after they left Estrelle and Aerö all alone.

"Choose well, Estrelle… choose well."

Aerö returned his father's scarlet gem beneath the black cloak where it dozed happily.

* * *

"Are you really going to send them away?" Nóór asked his mother as she dragged him towards their chambers. Hïldúúr walked a few steps behind them, angry at his hot-blooded Finndôra.

"We need to protect our own. That is our most important duty," she said coldly.

"But mother—"

"The boy is not one of us, he's a cursed sorcerer and has no place in our home."

"You are wrong, Finndôra." Hïldúúr spoke for the first time since they'd left the throne room. "The boy is one of us, regardless of your fears. We cannot banish him."

"The Lair has spoken!"

"Soon there'll be no Lair to speak of if we start fighting amongst ourselves. Isn't it enough that we are at war with the betrayers, now you wish to fight for the throne too?"

"The Lair has decided, Hïldúúr. The boy goes, and she does too if she so chooses."

"You've all gone mad."

"You've gone soft, fiercest Beast Lord in Urukk," she said mockingly.

Neither Hïldúúr, nor Nóór said another word. The young Beast Lord allowed his mother to drag him through darkened hallways to his room, while his mind joined Ári's and worked on their escape.

* * *

"We need to leave, son," she said, finally taking hold of her emotions and returning to her human form.

"Mother—"

"We will not be safe until we reach Wündalær."

"Mother—"

"Then cross the Korr Mountains and head for Caraa."

"Mother—"

"Then cross the sea towards the southern plains where Arnleaf and Valdis have no eyes nor rule."

"Mother!" Aerö yelled, cutting through Estrelle's string of thoughts.

"They are right, I must leave, but not because of them."

Estrelle looked at Aerö curiously. Her anger to her own people was quickly replaced by puzzlement.

"You know I want to help you win the war. But you are too few to stand a chance against their endless armies. I have seen them gather in Seribu Menara, mother, there are thousands and thousands of Healers and Elementals, uncountable Draugur. They will slaughter every one of you." Estrelle stared at her own son speaking with such an iciness in his voice, she almost did not recognise him.

"Finndôra was right that day inside the throne room."

Estrelle shook her head, failing to understand him.

"We need help, mother!" Aerö said abruptly.

"Help? There's no one who will join us in this war, Aerö—"

"There are. Just as Skeggor found them and then bound them to offer their much-needed aid, so shall I."

"Aerö," Estrelle gasped. "You cannot possibly be talking of the…where did you learn of them?"

"I read Greindur Gamall's book of Magical Creatures…"

"How did you get to that book?" she spoke so short of breath, Aerö almost did not hear her utter the words.

"They are just legends, Aerö, they are not true. No one has ever seen nor heard of them apart from my father, or so Greindur Gamall claimed."

"They are real, mother," Aerö said calmly. "Many of the creatures in that book I've seen, the Skrímsli must be real too."

"I cannot allow you—"

"I've learned so much since I came here, mother, but now it's time to leave. The Beast Lords are getting increasingly restless, the longer I am here." Aerö pulled the pendulum from beneath the black cloak he had wrapped around him, the gem ignited in his hand.

"I cannot let you leave, son, if they are true and really roam the deepest depths of Urukk, then they will not take kindly to you. If I can't stop you, then I'll join you."

"You cannot," he said with such finality, Estrelle stared at him, taken aback.

"You must make sure the Beast Lords are preparing for the battle that will surely come. They need you to lead them, mother."

Estrelle's fair face glistened with falling tears as she felt her son slip, yet again, away from her.

"I've just found you, son!"

"I will come back, I promise," he added, extinguishing his flaming hand and hugging his mother lovingly.

"I know now who I am and what I am to do. I will find them, mother, and I shall make them help set free the realm."

"Please, son...stay a little longer..." Estrelle shook with sadness but knew Aerö would be gone before the Feonds' call at dawn.

* * *

Through the dimly lit hallways, Aerö walked towards his room. At his right, his mother's chambers spilled bright light onto the spiralling stairs he had just descended. Estrelle remained up in the throne room, alone, but with her thoughts. Her people's betrayal, her only son's decision to go search for the most feared beings in the realm would surely keep her up all night.

Aerö felt his own heart start to ache as all the courage he had mustered in front of Estrelle slowly drained from him. He felt pained to leave her, but also excited to finally leave the Lair behind, regardless that the tunnels would most definitely take him but deeper underground. Aerö also had another hope, one that he'd nourished since he'd read about the mysterious creatures. Maybe the Skrímsli will allow him passage so that he could go and see his friends, his Petra. Perhaps they too were trapped beneath the King and Queen's dominion of Urukk, maybe they were dying out just like the Beast Lords, lonely too. Aerö suddenly found a new resolve to find them, even help them if he could.

Ahead, the lamps that threw their orange light dotted the tunnel's walls. His room's door opened at his right, the blackness within inviting him to safety. Aerö had grown to like his tiny room in the weeks he hid in there from Beasts and Beast Lords. The black walls, his cot, even his lone candle, all welcomed him into their midst. They had been his sole companions for many days and kept him safe and warm at night.

The large door ground shut behind Aerö, the little amber light that entered his room was now gone.

As if Aerö could see through the darkness, he walked to his cot and grabbed his candle, which he lit. He almost dropped it as he stumbled backwards at the sight of something moving in the darkness.

"Shhhhhh!" hissed Nóór pressing a hand on Aerö's lips. Ári jumped onto his cot, wiggling his slender tail energetically.

"Why are you here?!" Aerö sent his thoughts towards his friend and his Beast. His tone clearly annoyed for the scare they gave him.

"We can't just let them send you away! Father says you and the Queen must stay." Aerö felt his friend's words and emotions fill him. He shook his head.

"Maybe if we hide you somewhere for a few days while mother and the others see how wrong they were—"

"Nóór…" the young Beast Lord looked up at Aerö. "… I am leaving tonight."

"Father believes that once you emerge at the surface, they'll kill you."

"I will be fine," Aerö lied and wondered if the two he had projected his thoughts to, could tell.

"You are not going up, are you?" Nóór asked incredulously, yet a smile betrayed the corners of his mouth.

Aerö would have to remember that as he could tell when the others he listened to, lied, so could they if he did.

"Nóór…no," Aerö said as he saw the idea form inside his friend's mind even before he knew it.

"You think they're real? You think they built this place for Skeggor? You want to find them?" Nóór opened his mind to let all questions flow straight into Aerö.

"They are real, and I will find them," Aerö said lightheaded from the many questions swirling around from his friend.

Ári nibbled at Aer'ös hand.

"Then we'll come too," they announced

"You can't, Nóór. You and Ári still have years of training ahead of you. If your parents knew what you are planning, they'd kill me just to know you're safe!"

"Do you really think they'll let me go to war when that day comes? You've met my mother." He chuckled, yet his thoughts remained ice-cold.

"You cannot go alone. We are coming! Plus you'll need our help."

Aerö looked at Nóór doubtfully.

"We can see in the darkness, we can sense if other Beasts are close. We can fight," he added, but could tell that Aerö was still not convinced.

"But if you still refuse to take us with you, I will tell father what your plan is and where he can find you!"

"How would you know where to find me?" asked Aerö, puzzled, although a thought was edging towards him, shouldered in darkness, but about to pop like an amber in the night.

"Oh…I might know a way to go even deeper under Undirheim then the Nursery caves…"

Aerö stared at his friend, amazed. Nóór truly was unlike the other Beast Lords.

"So…?" Nóór grinned.

"If I can't stop you from coming, then promise me you'll do everything I ask of you. If the Hollowers are real, we might be in greater danger than in Seribu Menara."

"I promise," Nóór said, and Aerö knew he told the truth. He could feel fear eat away at the edges of his friend's heart. Ári yelped excitedly, muzzling at Aerö. Aerö could not but grab the young Hound's head between his hands and ruffle him. The young Beast growled joyfully.

"Then, we leave now. We won't need warmer clothes as down there will be hotter than the desert above us."

"We need water and food," said Nóór, a little too excited for the dangerous journey they were about to embark on.

"I've saved some fruit and nuts from my last meals. Water we need to grab on our way down there."

"We'll pass right by the lower storerooms. We'll find plenty to eat and drink there."

"Then let's go," announced Aerö, using words this time, once he had changed into some clothes that fitted him much better than the shrouded cloak he had on.

Ári jumped on him just as excited as his Master was.

* * *

"Where are they?" boomed Finndôra from the top of her lungs as she and Hïldúúr entered the throne room.

Estrelle looked up at them from her seat of bones, unsure why they were back.

"Where?" Finndôra shrieked.

"My Queen…" said Hïldúúr lowering his head. "Both Nóór and Ári are missing."

"Where is that son of yours? I'm sure they are with him!" barked Finndôra. If she had had the tiniest amount of respect for her Queen, now even that was gone. Instead, raw anger punctuated her loud voice.

"Oh no…" Estrelle managed to say, and Finndôra almost released her blade.

"Finndôra!" bellowed Hïldúúr. "Control yourself!"

"We need to move quickly!" Estrelle said, finally.

"My Queen?" asked Hïldúúr puzzled.

"Aerö has read about the Skrímsli and decided to go ask for their help. If Nóór went with him, we must find them immediately!"

"This is your fault!" cried Finndôra, unrestrained.

"I can control what he does with his life just as much as what you do with yours. He is stronger than us all, he was stronger than one of Arnleaf's most talented sorcerers, and he was the one to save us all from certain death. Do not forget that so easily, Finndôra! None of us can stand between him and his foretold fate. But we can still stop Nóór from getting in harm's way."

* * *

Nóór and Aerö followed Ári through the pitch-black tunnels that would take them to the narrow well they'd once before climbed down to reach the Beast's forbidden nursery. They moved swiftly through the dark, united by Aer'ös gift and Ári's night-piercing vision. They used untravelled tunnels so that no wandering soul would stumble upon them as they ventured deeper under Undirheim.

"Just a little further ahead," said Nóór inside his head. The three of them shared Ári's eyes so they moved as quickly as they could. Their thoughts formed cobwebs inside Aer'ös mind as the three passed emotions, thoughts and feelings from one to another.

"Tell me more about this place you know," said Aerö refraining from diving on his own through Nóór's own thoughts.

"It's always been there. A crack of sorts into the wall. We scare each other with stories of monsters lurking in there. The adults investigated it many times, but it's too small for them to go in."

"So it's just a crack into the rock," Aerö repeated.

"Yes, but sometimes you can feel a draught whistling through it. There must be some other place beyond, for the wind to come from."

"Ah!" Aerö exclaimed.

"Ári's much smaller than the other Beasts so he can scout and tell us what he sees," Nóór went on; his thoughts, initially but disjointed half-formed ideas, now linked together at great speed to form a plan. Aerö was pleased to have his friend with him.

The two young men turned a few times, sharply, following Ári, who turned and bent confusingly until the old well came in sight.

Nóór did not even stop to look around. He scooped up his Beast and jumped onto the ring of rocks that hugged the terrifying hole into the floor, holding onto the knotted rope with one hand and Ári with the other. Nóór descended swiftly, his pace measurable by the quickly fading echoes of his effort.

"Come!" Aerö heard inside his mind as his friend called out for him. Aerö, however, was not nearly as good as his friend at climbing down the rope. But moments later, he too reached the bottom of the well where Nóór and Ári waited in absolute darkness.

No lamps or torches ever burned this deep into the Lair. Seeing through somebody else's eyes made walking rather interesting. Both Aerö and Nóór could only see what Ári looked at, and remember every obstacle that stood in their way. If the Beast decided to sniff at the ground before it, the boys too, saw only that. Sometimes it felt nauseous having no control over what one could see. Still, it was amazing to be able to share such skill. Without Nóór and Ári, Aerö thought, it would have taken him at least twice as long to travel the same distance. Even if he was willing to ignite his father's gem inside the Lair, Aerö had little control over the strength of its burgeoning flames. They had to stay hidden, they had to move in secret, and most importantly, he did not want to accidentally scorch his friends.

The air began to thicken as the party moved towards the lower storerooms to acquire their much-needed food and water for the journey ahead. Hotter and more humid, the air grew inside the dark galleries they navigated. They were edging closer to those giant orange veins that turned rivers of water into steam. Aerö remembered the vast chambers where Nóór had taken him to witness Ári'a birth. The spider-monkeys and the cave-cows flashed before his mind's eyes, fragile creatures on thin legs and bulbous caterpillars the size of houses moving up and down the walls. And then came the visions of the Verndari, guardians of the Beasts' most inner chambers and nursery of their young, creatures so odd looking, Aerö had trouble picturing in great detail. Transparent bodies suspended in midair, they swayed their long translucent tentacles, trying to catch and feed on other creature's thoughts. They were the most bizarre things Aerö had witnessed since he had arrived in the Beast's Lair.

* * *

"Where would they have gone?" asked Finndôra angrily, as she and Hïldúúr ran towards the lower chambers after Nóór and Aerö. Estrelle ran ahead of them, in her White Wolf form, tasting the air for their sweet scent to follow.

"That way!" Hïldúúr pointed at a tunnel that bent to their left.

"We know they went towards the nursery. But they will need food and water for their journey, our best chance of finding them will be at the lower storerooms," said Estrelle in the low guttural voice of the Beast. The words rolled with great difficulty on her sharp-toothed jaws.

"Quickly, then!"

* * *

Nóór and Aerö reached the lower storerooms, tired and beaded with sweat. The condensed humidity rained on them from the tunnel's ceiling, soaking them to the skin. Ahead lay the large doors to the chambers where the Beasts gathered and stored the food needed for winter and for those too young to go hunt on their own. Nóór peeled open the double doors, making just enough room for Ári to squeeze through and see if there was anyone in there. The young Beast's mind blossomed with relief and Nóór, and Aerö quickly followed him inside.

The storerooms were like other storerooms Aerö had seen in Bells and Woods, large chambers piled with goods. The room was also colder than the outside, which meant that rivulets of condensed water ran from the curved walls to large puddles perfectly circular in shape.

"Be careful, they're deep…" said Nóór following Aer'ös gaze. "We call them auga, eyes."

Aerö nodded, touching the still water with his hand. It felt cold and fresh.

"We should hurry," said Aerö. But Nóór had already returned holding in his hand a large waterskin. While he filled it from the brim of one of the auga, Aerö packed his pockets with fruit and nuts, enough to keep them going for a few days, he reckoned. The three of them ate as much as they felt was appropriate for the long march through boiling caves that will surely follow, quenched their thirst with fresh water, then stood ready to find the crack in the wall and their exit from the Beast's Lair.

"How far is it?" asked Aerö, patting his pockets with his palms to make sure they were safely sealed.

"Just down the hallway and to the left."

"Isn't that the way to the nursery?" asked Aerö, fear nibbling at his thoughts.

"Oh," said Nóór shyly. "I might have forgotten to say that we'll need to move unseen past the Verndari."

"You forgot?" Aerö cried, mingling thoughts of fear and anger spreading from him to the other two minds open to him.

"Will be fine as long as we don't think of harming anyone,"

Aerö said nothing. The last time they had to move beyond the place they guarded, one of the Verndari almost wrapped its ghostly tentacles around him. Aerö shuddered at the memory and could feel the other two share his emotion. The Verndari were not like all other Beasts under the Beast Lords' rulership but served the Beasts themselves. They were mindless sentinels who would extend their scary limbs onto whoever dared to have threatening thoughts in their presence.

* * *

"The storerooms are just ahead," growled Estrelle, panting. "Their scent is strong," she added, licking her snout clean of the beads of water condensing on it and her fur. She looked malnourished with her fur glued to her skin.

"I am going to kill that son of yours!" hissed Finndôra. "If anything happens to my Nóór, I will crush him!"

"Enough, Finndôra!" hissed Hïldúúr. "Let's focus on finding them first."

Within moments, the two Beast Lords, led by the White Wolf, reached the large doors of the storerooms. Hïldúúr pushed them apart the second his hands met their chiselled surface. A second later, the vast chamber opened itself to them, filled with food and pools of water, but no boys. Estrelle howled in frustration.

"Their scent is still strong, but vanishing quickly in this humid air. Follow me!"

* * *

To their right, the long tunnel Nóór and Aerö had followed Ári through, opened into the cavern cobwebbed with orange veins and the Verndari. Ári stopped at the entrance, wiggling his whip-like tail. Aerö felt cold chills travel beneath his sweaty skin.

"We're lucky! They are asleep" said Nóór pointing at the far left side of the cavern.

"That is where we need to go. But we'll have to be quiet." Aerö followed his friend's finger to a spot but feet beneath one of the transparent, tentacled creatures. The Verndari swayed gently, suspended in midair, kept aloft by scalding, heated air. If it was asleep, Aerö could not tell, for it looked just as it had the last time he laid his eyes on them.

"Maybe you should turn around and go back, Nóór!" said Aerö. "It's mad what I'm about to do. Go back." But that very moment, a loud roar echoed through the tunnel behind them. The thick air rushed into the cavern as if frightened by whoever made that noise, waking up the creatures that were fast asleep. Spider-monkeys scurried up the wall away from Nóór and Aerö as did the nearby giant caterpillars, wriggling as fast as they could. Then the Verndari moved, and the boys shared the same feeling of their breaths stolen from them.

"Run!" yelled Nóór, this time out loud, pushing Aerö into the orange-laced chamber and towards the Verndari. "We can reach the gap before they're roused if we hurry!"

Behind them, Estelle, in her Wolf form, pounded at the ground beneath her paws to catch up with them. Hïldúúr and Finndôra ran a few paces behind.

The boys sped after Ári, who was dashing in and out of view between boulders and rocks. Their lungs breathed in fire, and their skins turned red-hot under the heat of the dome's blazing veins.

"Stop!" yelled Finndôra, but her voice barely travelled through the solid air.

The Verndari stretched its limbs and began to glide towards the running Hound and the two young boys behind.

"Faster!" cried Nóór, who ran alongside Aerö. From behind, Estrelle was closing in, her body but a silver cloud inside the orange chamber. None of the boys dared to look behind.

The Verndari began its descent onto its victims. It could taste their frightened thoughts with its transparent tentacles. Ári was the first to reach the crack in the wall after he nearly crashed into one of the creatures' swaying limbs. The young Hound dived deep into the lightless space within.

Nóór and Aerö were next. The boys ducked one of the descending tentacles, lunged forward, stumbled, crashed, then got back on their feet.

Estrelle was but feet behind, charging after them.

Another tentacle came down upon them, and the boys turned left nearer the wall; Aer'ös shoulder grazed the chiselled rock, scuffing his skin straight through his shirt. Estrelle ducked the Verndari's limb without slowing down.

When a third tentacle swung towards them, Aerö kneeled below the swinging, see-through limb while Nóór jumped over it. The young Beast Lord's legs got caught by the Verndari's limb and he fell.

Aerö turned to see his friend, imagining him suspended by his legs by the Verndari, but Nóór was already back onto his feet and jamming himself through the narrow crack into the wall.

"Aerö!" he yelled, panting.

Estrelle growled at the Verndari who was now attacking her, forcing her to stop her pursuit. Aerö also stopped and looked behind, at his mother, snapping her huge jaws at the blind creature.

"Leave!" she barked at the transparent guardian, but the creature continued to thrash with its many elongated limbs.

"Aerö!" she called.

"I am sorry, mother," he projected his thoughts to her as he vanished through the gap in the rock.

* * *

Hïldúúr and Finndôra reached Estrelle and the retreating Verndari, just in time to see Aer'**ö**s body wiggle into the tight space. They had no hope of following them in.

"Nóór!" Finndôra called, heartbroken, after her young son. Hïldúúr wrapped his hands around her as she sobbed.

"Why would you leave your people for him?"

"I'm doing this for our people, mother…" Nóór's thoughts echoed to the three Beast Lords gathered outside the gap in the wall, carried by Aer'**ö**s gift.

"Please come back, son, come back…" Finndôra pleaded, but no other thought or sound came from the two boys and their Hound.

The three managed what no other had; they found a way out of the Lair and into the vast unknown beyond.

The Chase

A full moon reigned over the world from its diamond-encrusted welkin. Its bright silvery glow illuminated uncountable miles below, the sea of sand that stretched from the Korr Mountains to the Wall. From its high place, the moon observed the world unfold impervious to the pain and suffering of the many souls that showered in its light. A tiny orange dot was all that marked the Turmenn's encampment from such height, an incomprehensible gathering of worthless souls and things.

Among those worthless souls, Trevor, followed by his younger brothers, Sam and Daniel, burst out of the central tent and ran after the dark figure that took with her, Petra, Erlend, and Syll. Sara stumbled out of the tent, lightheaded from the blow she took, just as the three brothers almost collided with Adriana, Grov, and the other guardians, including the newly welcomed amongst them, Ishim and Ezkiel.

"Hey!" yelled Adriana as Trevor pushed her roughly aside.

"Someone took Petra while we were fighting those damned things outside!" called Sam, apologetically, as he and his younger brother tried to catch up with Trevor. In this dark, if they lost sight of him for just one moment, they would not know where he ran.

"What about the others?"

"Dunno!" barked Daniel.

"Syll and Erlend, she took them too!" said Sara between heavy breaths as she reached the remaining warriors. They all looked around confused. "She had the Greed brothers help them! The dead Greed brothers!... And then Taro..." she sobbed.

"Oh! We fought a dozen or so of those things out here too. But if she's not alone, then the boys need our help!" said Adriana ready to follow Sam and Daniel into the night.

"Yeah!" cried Grov putting his sword away.

"No." came Sara's broken voice. "You can't go." The warriors all turned their eyes on Sara as she uttered the words.

"We can't stay here and do nothing! We have to help them!" Adriana spun around towards the running Sam and Daniel whom she could already barely see. Sara grabbed her by the elbow, forcing her to stop.

"No, Adriana! If they know where we are, they'll come in greater numbers after the rest of us. We can't stay here any longer, we have to leave."

"But they've got Petra!"

"They've got my Erlend too!" cried Sara. "But we are now in charge of all these souls and not just our own. We cannot wait. We cannot stay. We have to reach Caraa," Sara said softly, still holding onto Adriana's arm, not to restrain her, but to hold herself upright.

"And the others?"

"I pray that the boys will bring them back unharmed. But we need to leave as soon as possible. Wake up the few who are sleeping, gather the ones that have run away. We leave at dawn." Sara retreated into the large tent that had been used to heal the wounded, which now only sheltered death.

Inside the tent, the full image of the past events revealed itself to Sara. Gore, guts, and brains covered the floor inside the tent, blood still oozing from the cut-in-half Greed sisters. The blades that had severed them perfectly in half, sprayed the taut tarp above, dark red. More blood trickled from the few cots that had held wounded Turmenn in their wraps; deep gashes yawned at Sara from shrivelled chests and lifeless limbs. Taro's body, reanimated and manipulated like a worthless puppet by the sorceress that brought death upon them all, had cut through everything that stood between him and his unwilling opponent, Trevor.

The sweet scent of death hung heavily inside Petra's tent, and for the first time, Sara wished the horrid scenes would have come to her in the form of those terrible nightmares. Regardless of how mad that made her, dreaming of such sickening things, maybe then she would have managed to avoid this slaughter. Consumed, she dropped onto one of the empty cots, unable to hold back the tears any longer. There she lay, sobbing for Erlend, for Petra, and Syll, for all those dead whose deserved rest had been taken from them, for the many new souls who found their grave that night; she even cried for Elfredda and Bathilda. Death brought a fresh perspective to the lost lives of others.

What will she do without her Erlend, without Petra's wisdom? What will come of the collection of villagers of Bells, Brim, and Woods? How could they survive the desert and reach safety without their most trusted guardians?

Sara sobbed alone in Petra's tent, unable to find answers to any of her questions. For the first time since the world began to crumble around her, Sara felt utterly lost, separated from those who kept her rooted. The realm became suddenly a great deal scarier without Petra and Erlend at her side.

Two hands rested on Sara's shoulders from behind, which made her skin crawl towards the back of her head. Surprised, she turned around to see Adriana staring at the chaos around her. Her unusual beauty was drowned entirely in tears, her dark, olive skin soaked in them. She simply could not take her eyes away from the display of unthinkable savageness before her.

"Oh no…" she whimpered, squeezing Sara's shoulders. "Why? Why would anyone do this?"

"She came for Petra," mumbled Sara voicelessly. "She came for her and took Erlend and Syll for her own pleasure. My Erlend!" she sobbed heartbroken.

Adriana felt her own heart sink ever deeper as despair poured into her. If one could do such unimaginable things, what could an army of them do? Adriana shuddered at the thought.

"Where are the others?" Sara asked, trying to put her mind to work on other things than the certain death that awaited them.

"They're rounding up the Turmenn and whatever belongings they can carry. Most of these things…" Adriana pointed at the tent and cots around them, "…we cannot take with us. It's been weeks since we ate the last of our horses." Sara nodded solemnly.

"We'll be ready to leave at dawn." Sara nodded again.

* * *

Through the silvery illuminated dunes of the Great
Desert, Nephthys moved purposefully, pulling a tied
Petra after her. At her sides, the Greed brothers pulled
after them, Erlend and Syll, all three prisoners tied to
each other with the same silver thread. Behind them,
Trevor, Sam, and Daniel sped across the infinite span of
sand, determined to fight the sorceress and her animated
puppets in order to save Syll, Erlend, and Petra.

"Hurry, brothers! We mustn't lose them!" bellowed
Trevor to Sam and Daniel, who were already exhausted
from the fight they had just ended.

"Brother, how far do you think she'll be able to walk in
this?"

"Don't be fools! She did not walk from their damned
city all the way to our camp! We must hurry and get her
back!" Sam and Daniel both thought of Petra, but knew
that their brother only intended to rescue Syll. The other
two were their responsibility.

The three brothers could see some distance ahead, the
vague shapes of the High Priestess's group. But no
matter how fast they ran, the distance between them
remained the same, if not expanding. Running through

the fine sand proved impossible to sustain. Shin-deep they sank in it with every step they took, stumbling, falling; cursing the very nature that stubbornly tried to stop them from their quest. Still, they ran and fell and cursed some more. Giving up meant abandoning their friends, their leader and their loved ones.

* * *

"Please let them go, Nephthys." Petra pleaded to her old Master. "You want me, not them."

"Silence!" the High Priestess hissed, tugging the thread that wrapped around her three prisoners. "Walk faster, or I'll make you see your beating hearts." The three captives quickened their pace.

"Please!" Petra tried again to persuade the very sorceress who taught her everything she knew about her own powers.

"You've really lost your touch, Petra! Vondur was right after all. I need you to fulfil my Queen's desire, that is true, but I also want your friends." She laughed sickly. "After that elusive grandson of yours comes out of that tomb the Beasts call home to save you, and I kill him, then I shall take my time with them two."

"What could you possibly gain from them?" Petra asked, trying her best to not let Valdis' sly plan to slaughter Aerö drive her mad.

"Oh..there's so much my beloved High Priestesses and I can learn from them." Nephthys laughed again. "Now let's get moving faster! We are expected."

* * *

"Brother!" called Daniel with effort. "What if she has more of those things? What if she can bring back more of those we knew and fought alongside?" he asked, holding a hand around his throat as if to keep it whole. The words clawed at his insides as they formed. Sam looked sideways to his younger brother and knew the moment their eyes met that Daniel, just like him, had the same terrible thought. What if the sorceress would bring back Alistair, their father. Could they fight him, could they look into his once bright-blue, now hollow, eyes and run their blades straight through his neck? Could Trevor face their father after he had been the one to shout his name in battle, a mistake that cost their father his life? The young brothers nodded at each other as the weight of the thought pushed their feet deeper in the sand, slowing them down. Trevor however said nothing. He quickened his pace.

"I do not care who she can bring back from the dead, brothers. All I want is to bring her back. Run faster or go back, I do not need your help."

* * *

Sara grabbed the few things of value from Petra's tent and put them in a bundle. To her left, the rectangle of dark soil, where days before they had put in Taro's lifeless body, stared at her heaped to one side. The grave was now empty, her friend's remains lay scattered a few feet away. What other powers had the sorcerers, that she could not even begin to comprehend? Sara looked around the death-saturated shelter one more time before she stepped out into the night.

Fires roared throughout the Turmenn's encampment as the frightened masses gathered the few belongings they still owned. Shouts and wails echoed as Adriana, Grov, and the rest of the guardians urged them to hurry. If the Turmenn had been ready to fight Petra's warriors in order to banish her, but moments before, now they followed their command unquestioningly. Their thirst for blood forever quenched.

* * *

The three prisoners walked in silence behind Nephthys, and her two raised corpses. Petra stared into the dark horizon thinking of Aerö, of how her own son before him went to live with the Beast Lords, a treachery Valdis and Arnleaf would wait decades to punish him for. Now fourteen years later, his son sought to live with his kind under the lone mountain. But unlike what they had done with Eldur, they were not about to wait for him to grow to his full strength and come for him themselves, they'd hatched a different plan to have him killed. They would use her, his grandmother, to drag him out of safety years before he could even hope of defeating them. She should have known they would not wait, she should have never come on her own accord closer to her old home. Decades had gone by since she abandoned the Order, decades since she ran away from Nephthys and her kind. She had watched children grow old in the many years she'd hid among the humans up in Bells, decades to make one forget too many things. But for the sorcerers that was not nearly long enough to disregard her sins. Sorcerers had all the time in the world to feed their ancient hearts with hatred and plans of sweet revenge. Had she done things differently, Erlend and Syll would now be with their loved ones, not trudging to their death.

Behind Petra, Syll and Erlend, flanked by the dead Greed brothers, turned their thoughts to the two souls their hearts cared most for. But unlike Erlend who hoped that Sara and the rest of the Turmenn would be safe, Syll thought of ways to slay the ones that took them prisoners.

Erlend's eyes met Syll's and saw the bold determination to escape. He shook his head, afraid that she would die much sooner than the sorceress had planned for them. Maybe a real opportunity to run would come, but only if the warrior beside him could muster some patience.

Syll surreptitiously rummaged through her garments for the dagger she held hidden at her belt.

Syll would rather die trying to escape than wait for Erlend's miracle that would allow them to outlive the night.

"Move!" barked Nephthys pulling on the silver thread that held her prisoners in place. Petra, Syl and Erlend's minds snapped like rubber back to where they were, or worse, to where they were going.

* * *

From behind Nephthys's cortège, the rustling of metal and leather drifted through the night. Trevor was not willing to go back without his Syll. Behind him, Sam and

Daniel ran as fast as they could to aid their brother in the battle that would inevitably break out.

* * *

"How dare they!" the High Priestess growled looking back over her prisoners, tied securely, and towards the filthy camp of the half-apes.

Syll and Erlend tried to look behind, but the Greed brothers pulled them forward by their silver threads.

"They really wish to die." Nephthys hissed, pulling out her dagger and a single bone. She only had one other corpse to summon. She cut her palm with her own blade, closing her bleeding fist around the remaining bone she had left to use.

Nephthys's raspy voice rose and fell as she invoked her devastating spell.

"Please don't!" said Petra, horrified of losing even more of her friends that night.

Nephthys ignored her and continued to chant madly at her oozing fist.

Trevor advanced towards the High Priestess' group, his own sword in hand. He had no plan, but one had always come to him when most needed, and so it would be now, he trusted mindlessly. Behind him, Sam and Daniel unsheathed their own swords.

Nephthys threw the fistful of black blood and bone to the ground in an ecstasy of yells and grunts. She turned her split-open face to Petra.

"Oh, don't worry. Once Eldur's son comes forth and dies, you shall meet them in the afterlife," she said, regaining her demeanour. "If there is such a thing."

* * *

Sam and Daniel almost caught up with their older brother when, from behind, the unmistakable sounds of feet ploughing through sand reached them. They turned around and stared into the darkness while still running, but there was nothing they could see between them and the orange-glowing dot that was their camp. They ran on.

* * *

Syll and Erlend could now clearly hear the rattle of heavy breathing behind them. Checking to see if the

Priestess' animated puppets looked at her, Syll turned her head towards the sound. Her mouth fell open as she recognised the shape charging towards her.

"Oh no…" she whispered, searching frantically for her hidden dagger. Both Petra and Erlend turned to face the darkness and their far-away camp. They all recognised Trevor and his two younger brothers speeding towards them.

Nephthys had stopped moments before to cast her spell and now sat waiting for the foolish humans to attack her. She could easily defeat them on her own, but she needed to be more careful now. The Queen had been too clear with her orders. Either the boy would die or she would, along with her Priestesses. So, Nephthys waited patiently for the few who followed her to reach them.

"Now you shall see what happens to those who defy me!" she groaned at her prisoners.

"Make sure they watch!" she ordered her two standing corpses. The Greed brothers showed no sign to have understood Nephthys's command, but pulled the silver thread and the three prisoners it held, closer to them.

* * *

Closer and louder, the galloping sound that unnerved Sam and Daniel, echoed through the stillness of the night. Even over their heavy breathing and clinking of their swords, the boys could hear the thing approaching them so fast it almost whistled.

"What is that?" croaked Sam casting looks over his shoulder. Still, he could not see anything but the orange camp and the many silver stars pierce the wall of blackness.

"No matter what it is, it has more feet than two," answered Daniel. "If she could summon more of those dead things, it does not mean they have to be all human. Maybe she needs a piece of them or something…"

"There's plenty of bones drowned in sand since the battle…" said Sam more to himself than to his younger brother. And then, is when they saw it.

Like a bullet of bones held together by rotten flesh and worms-infested muscles, a large Hound materialised but feet behind them. The boys drew their swords and turned around to face the nightmarish creature. Trevor, too, had stopped a short distance away, not for the putrid Hound, but for the sorceress and her just as dead two servants.

"Release them!" he bellowed brandishing his blade. Nephthys smiled at him unfazed.

"Kill him," she said, almost bored.

The two Greed brothers released the silver thread and stepped between their master and the livid-looking man.

"Run back!" cried Syll. But the words had barely left her lips when the skeletal fist of one of the dead brothers hit her in the gut. She bent over coughing painfully. Erlend pulled at the rope that tied them by their hands, trying to free himself to help blood-spewing Syll.

"You'll die for this!" Trevor roared at the smiling sorceress who held her gaze aloft. Her right hand wrapped around her dagger.

* * *

Sam and Daniel had no time to make a plan. Without thinking, they dodged the speeding mass of decayed Hound only to find themselves separated from their older brother by the thing.

Puss, dark and retched, flowed out of the Beast's jaws; its fangs much longer now that no flesh coated them. The creature snarled at them threateningly, its eyes but in their memory still bright and yellow, now they were but hollows in its skull.

"We need to help Trevor," hissed Sam seeing his older brother encircled by the two Greed brothers up ahead.

"We are busy, haven't you noticed?"

"We can do this, brother!" Daniel had no time to reply as the Hound charged again, this time at half the speed but twice as precise. The Beast's fangs caught Daniel in the leg, and they both collapsed to the ground, one growling, hissing ball of murderous intent.

Sam slashed his blade at the maddened creature to give Daniel enough time to get back on his feet.

"Brother! Are you alright?"

"Yes, I think so…" he swayed back and forth. "It caught me by my trousers." The boys smiled, but the Hound was on its feet as well, angrier than ever.

"What are these things?" Sam asked, planting his feet deeper into the sand in expectation of the attack to follow.

"Can't you ask yourself these things after we've killed it?" Daniel snapped. "Let's cut its head off and then we can debate whether it was already dead or just pretending!" Sam chuckled.

"What do you propose?"

"I haven't got it yet…but unlike the other ones, this is too fast to simply sneak behind and finish…" Daniel's words gathered in his throat, refusing to slip past his lips as the dead creature charged again.

Out of the many different Beast's the boys had hunted in Wündalær for their hides and flesh, none had been so easily slaughtered as the rotted men. Unlike all other creatures, men were by far the squishiest and most prone to die among them. The millennia of living in lasting societies had killed their instinct for survival. But the Hound before them was of a very different nature than its dead cousins had been. It wished to kill despite the orders that the sorceress had surely given it.

The Hound sped towards the two brothers, widening its jaws so that this time they would tear flesh as well. Daniel jumped sideways just in time while Sam stabbed the sand with his sword. The Hound was far too fast for them.

* * *

The two unearthed Greed brothers watched Trevor patiently through their rotten eyes. Behind him, his younger brothers fought on their own a monster of a Beast.

"Release them!" Trevor bellowed again. Still, no one moved.

"Go." Was all that Nephthys said to her two mindless puppets and the Greed brothers moved stiffly towards him.

Swords sprayed red sparks into the night before Erlend had even time to realise what had just happened. The apparent slow-moving corpses were capable of speeds beyond those of their human origin. Within a blink of an eye, they covered the distance between them and Trevor and clashed their swords against his.

Petra closed her eyes, expecting to see Trevor crumble to the ground, but he would not lie dead just yet. He pushed the two decomposing old villagers from Bells aside, attacking them furiously.

"Finish him!" commanded Nephthys from Petra's side.

"I hope you're watching," she added grinning, taking hold of Petra's jaw with the blooded hand. "This is all because of you."

* * *

Sam and Daniel evaded attack after attack from the maddened Hound. Their clothing was torn, and a few gashes bled nastily on their legs, yet no wound they managed to inflict.

"Is this your plan, brother?" asked Sam throwing blows at the impossibly fast creature. "You plan to tire it to death? I'm not sure who will give up first!"

"Maybe you should come up with a plan, Sam!" Daniel snapped, although his lips grinned involuntarily at his brother's joke. The Beast attacked again.

* * *

Syll was still bent, kneeling on the sand, coughing and choking on her own blood. Erlend wrestled the rope that tied his hands, but now that the Greed brothers were busy fighting, he had managed to creep next to her.

"Syll, are you alright?"

She nodded, placing a hand to her mouth, the other rummaged at her belt. Finally, her dagger came free of the entanglement of her clothes; their only weapon safely in her hand. Without looking up, she pressed the blade against the silver thread and started cutting at it. Erlend kept watch while she worked. But the thin rope was not of human make and cutting it was far more difficult, despite its fragile look. Like everything that came from sorcerers, things were never what they seemed.

After a few more failed attempts, Syll looked up at Erlend, then Petra who shook her head at her and Syll knew that her plan would not work.

Neither Trevor nor his brothers could defeat their resurrected opponents. Swords chimed as they struck against each other. Sparks flew, blood splattered the fine sand beneath the three boys' feet. The High Priestess watched the battle unfold, her mouth set into a euphoric grin. There was something primal and enjoying in watching creatures fight to their death. Nephthys licked her thin, blackened lips with pleasure.

"Keep watching!" she told Petra holding her by the jaw.

"It won't last long, enjoy it." Petra felt warm tears break the prison of her will and wash over her face. Nephthys' hand retracted as if burned.

"You've grown weak!" she spat, disgusted. Her moment of euphoria observing the men fight was gone.

* * *

"Daniel!" yelled Sam, swinging his sword at the Beast, but managed to slay but the crisp air. The boys revolved around the creature trapped between them.

"Be careful of the tail!" he added as the Hound used its bone and skin, thin tail as a whip. The thing cracked and whistled as it sought to split their skin. The Beast spun madly, unsure whom it would finish first. The boys spun with it.

"Oi!" yelled Daniel. "Oi, you stupid Beast!"

"What are you doing?" hissed Sam. "Isn't it angry enough?"

"I have an idea…sort of…"

"Oh, great!" exclaimed Sam. "And does this plan of yours involve using one of us as prey?"

"I did say sort of a plan…"

"Let me guess…that someone will be me."

"Actually it will be both," Daniel said matter-of-factly.

"You only come up with suicidal plans, you know that?"

"It's the only plan that I have," Daniel said, explaining briefly what they needed to do to position themselves close enough to the Hound to slay it.

"If this kills me, brother, I will haunt you, I swear to Narrū!"

"If this doesn't work, we're both dead, so we can haunt each other for eternity." Daniel chuckled, jumping to the side as the Beast attacked again. Sam stabbed at the sand in order to distract the Beast from tearing Daniel to shreds.

"Funny," hissed Sam seriously. "Are you ready?"

"Here goes nothing…"

* * *

Syll and Erlend clustered together on the ground, their hopes defeated by the silver thread that refused to free them. Erlend placed his hands onto Syll's shoulder to comfort her.

"We'll be alright," he lied.

A muffled sound came from nearby, and the two lifted their eyes from the fine sand.

"What are you two doing?" snapped Nephthys, looming over them, her hand still clawed around Petra's month. Slowly she released her so that she could pull the magic-strengthened rope and the two weak humans to her. Syll fumbled to hide the dagger she had in her hand.

"What is that?" the High Priestess asked, looking amused at Syll.

"A weapon?" she laughed. "That will not help you, ape! We are Gods!" And she pulled the precious-looking rope so forcefully, both Syll and Erlend stumbled forward and then fell.

Slowly, Nephthys approached the two. Syll expected to be hit again, and when that moment came, she would then drive her blade inside Nephthys. No matter where, regardless of how much or little pain, she managed to cause. She would push her dagger through her flesh.

But the High Priestess did not stop next to her to apply her punishment. Instead, she stepped onto Syll's neck with all her weight and force. Syll's face dug painfully into the sand beneath her, her hands struggling to keep her above the smothering dust. Syll breathed in mouthfuls of sand and felt like she was drowning, choking, her coughing muffled by the particles that stuck to the inside of her mouth like glue.

* * *

Erlend half-stood to fight off the Healer, but the High Priestess hit him again on the head with her dagger-holding hand. He stumbled sideways dizzily.

Petra begged to let them go back to their families and friends.

"Leave her alone!" bellowed Trevor, but his two opponents stopped him from running to Syll's aid.

Nephthys crouched from where she stood perched onto Syll's neck, and grabbed the blade from her right hand. The High Priestess laughed, inspecting the poorly made weapon.

"Filth!" she said, throwing the thing away, then moved back to observe the unfolding battle. Erlend rushed, lightheaded, back to Syll to help her extricate herself from the shifting grave of sand.

Feet away, Trevor fought the two Greed brothers for his life. The two already dead men threw blows at him unfazed by the seldom times Trevor's blade managed to touch their rotten flesh.

Another blow hit Trevor on his side, knocking the wind out of him. He bent slightly, but regained his defence against the rain of swords that fell on him unmercifully. He could not last much longer.

"Run, Trevor!" yelled Syll, vomiting mouthfuls of sand. "Leave!" But Trevor fought still. Had there not been two of them against him, he would have managed to separate their heads from the magically held together torsos.

"I cannot wait to see what ticks inside those apes," said Nephthys slowly.

Petra held her breath and hoped the boys would manage to escape. The Turmenn needed them to lead them to safety more than ever now that war had undoubtedly begun.

* * *

"Run, Sam!" shrieked Daniel from ahead. "RUN!" His brother pushed against the sand with all his might, but running through the desert was impossible when rested, worse when they had spent their strength fighting the Hound.

"It's now or never!" bellowed Sam, catching up with Daniel and with the creature at his heels.

The ear-throbbing silence of the night made all other sounds so much more powerful. The boys' breaths and the slapping of their scabbards against their legs, the crunching, shifting noises of the desert trying to entrap them in its sands. Worst of all, the night amplified the noises made by the attacking Hound. It gurgled in its innards as it felt its prey so near it could almost lick Sam's blood-splattering legs. Its long tail whooshed and cracked, excited for the feast that would soon come. Unlike the unearthed men and women that attacked their own friends and families mindlessly inside their camp, the Beast still held to its murderous instincts from before its death. It felt hunger ravage through its broken body.

"Now!" yelled Sam, forcing his body to crouch on the ground. The Beast was far too close behind him to manage to stop in time and sink its fangs into his flesh. The Hound jumped over Sam like a ball of tensed muscle, determined to land on its slower prey. But this was Daniel's plan all along. He turned around and threw himself with his back towards the ground, just as the Hound descended upon him from its crushing jump. In mid-air, the creature could no longer evade Daniel's, at the ready, sword. With the Beast plummeting towards him, Daniel slashed his blade at the right time, cutting straight through the Hound's head and neck.

The thing split in half, then crashed full upon Daniel.

"No!" bellowed Nephthys angrily. "Finish them!" she growled like an animal at the Greed brothers. The two soulless men attacked Trevor faster if possible, their blows heavier.

"We are leaving!" she said, dissatisfied, pulling the silver thread after her and the three prisoners with it.

"Daniel!" cried Sam, running to his brother.

"Daniel!" But he was in no shape to stand, least fight.

"Go help Trevor," he mumbled, pulling himself free from the collapsed, lifeless Beast. Its bones and flesh, no longer held together by the High Priestess' spell, tore free at his touch. Sam covered his mouth as he felt acid bubble inside him. He vomited.

"Go!" yelled Daniel again, feeling his own body convulse from the decomposing mess that landed onto him.

"Trevor!" yelled Sam charging to his brother's aid.

"They're leaving! Help me stop them, Sam!"

The two brothers fought alongside each other, both exhausted and wounded, both thinking of the same thing. They had spent too much of their limited strength during this battle. What would they do once they managed to put to rest the Greeds? The sorceress was still their most formidable opponent, and they could not even get close enough to throw their swords at her.

But they still had to separate two heads before they could chase the High Priestess and her captives.

* * *

Some distance away, Nephthys lead a tied up Petra, Syll, and Erlend away from the commotion of the fight. Within the deepest blacks, tall shadows lurked.

* * *

"We need to make them fight back to back!" yelled Sam over the ear-ringing cries of their clashing swords. Trevor threw a puzzled look at his young brother, but in the absence of a better plan, he began to steer his opponent towards the other one Sam struggled to keep in place.

"What now?" asked Trevor as they managed to steer the two brothers in place.

"Now?" Sam yelled, "Now we send these two back to the graves they climbed out of!" And Trevor understood.

They both slashed with their blades at the dead brothers' throats from opposite directions, forcing the Greeds to bend their heads the other way to avoid the crippling blows. But as Trevor's opponent ducked away from his blade, Sam's blade cut straight through from behind, as did his to Sam's adversary. The Greeds' heads flew through the air some ten feet away, their bodies collapsing onto themselves where they stood.

At that very moment, a cry they wished they had not heard, rippled through the night.

"No!" cried Trevor. "Syllvia!" And with that, he ran after the High Priestess.

But he was too late. Nephthys, Petra, Syll, and Erlend sat on Nightlings of their own, all but the High Priestess chained securely on their backs. Before Trevor and Sam could take two steps, the cursed beasts neighed and they were gone, galloping so fast, no other Beast could catch them.

Trevor failed to save his friends, his leader, his soul-brother, and his love. He collapsed, just like the Greeds, onto the barren ground, however, unlike them, he did not lose his head, only his heart.

Sam placed a hand onto his shoulder just as Daniel words came from behind.

"I'm sorry, brother."

Ophidia

"What better way to die than by your Goddess' sweet kiss?"

"Death tastes just as bitter, be it a kiss, a blade, or old age."

"Has She not shown you the raw power we shall inherit in the afterlife?"

"I'll rather keep my beating heart than trade it for that power."

"You've changed, old friend."

"You have not, High Priestess."

They Are Fools

Greindur Gamall

Never before had Syll and Erlend travelled at such speed. They rode their Nightlings low, holding to them with all the strength they had left. Repeatedly, the two tried to look at the blurry world around them, but their eyes and faces stung, slapped by the night's cold winds.

Syll worked at the fastenings that held her on the speeding beast, but after a dozen failed attempts, she gave up on that too. The two prisoners rode, terrified, hugging their Nightlings, nothing but their thoughts still theirs to rule.

Ahead of Syll and Erlend, Petra rode hunched down, but watching, carefully, the world speed up around her as her Nightling ploughed through night and desert at an impossible pace. Many seasons had turned since the last time she'd made this very journey, yet she remembered every detail of it. Last time, however, when she rode across the desert in such haste, she was riding towards Bells.

The world through which the Nightlings galloped was entirely composed of blacks and greys. But even with such lack of depth and colour, one could clearly see the unnatural haste with which they travelled. Petra observed the northern parts of Urukk, and her home for the last half a century, vanish out of sight, even the gargantuan Korr Mountains shrunk away from them, their blackened contour but a shallow ridge against the diamond-dotted sky.

As the other two she sentenced to this death thought of their loved ones, Petra thought of Aerö and her son, thought of the Beast Lords deep under their mountain, thought of all the other creatures, men and Beasts that would be slaughtered by Arnleaf and Valdis' monstrous plan. Had everything she put the Turmenn through, and before them, the villagers of Bells, been worth it? Had she done what the Beast Lords did and hide from those who meant them harm, would then the Turmenn and her grandson still be safe and whole together with their loved ones? Possibly, but at what cost and for how long? Petra knew too well that the King and Queen could wait another thousand years to eradicate them all and wipe their whole existence from the realm they believed was theirs. To choose to lead them to death so that future generations can be born, or to hide far away from danger knowing that there will be none of them left throughout Urukk, was a difficult choice to make, yet Petra chose tomorrow for the painful price of today.

All around the speeding Nightlings, the Great Desert spread its dunes of sand, the uncrossable millions of humps and valleys taking all hope of return from the hearts of the three prisoners.

Ahead, rode Nephthys on her beast, a billowing black shape, her thoughts turned to the reward the Queen had promised her for laying Aerö's trap.

Exhaustion, numbness, and the constant rocking of the beasts beneath them, made the three captives fall victims to a restless sleep. Petra's last sight of the vast span before them was the glowing dot on the shores of Taðr Sea, their hopeless destination.

* * *

Dawn roared over the realm of Urukk, purple and bright. Beneath the encroaching cracks of colour, the Turmenn's camp fermented with movement. The many frightened souls carried bundles to the western edges of the encampment, where Sara commanded the masses to gather. She had been Petra's right hand along with Erlend and with both of them now gone, she had assumed the responsibility to take them to safety. No one opposed her claim to leadership, at least not yet; the Turmenn were simply too frightened from the happening of the previous night. Yet alone, she could not rule, Sara knew that, but with Adriana's friendship and the guardian's respect, she felt confident that they would follow her to Caraa and beyond.

Women dragged their children after them towards the meeting point, while the men carried bundles with their few belongings, clothes, and food. The few riches the Turmenn took with them from their villages had long since burned or had been traded, only to be left behind inside the forlorn camp. No one wished to bear the weight of things they would not need for their survival now that war had found them once again. They were all heart-shatteringly terrified by what lay ahead.

"What do we do with all the rest?" asked Grov in his high voice, pointing at the sea of tents and things people abandoned.

"Let the sands have them," said Adriana dismissively, searching the breadth of the camp for any latecomers.

"If we find safety, then one day we might come back," said Sara putting a hand around Grov's shoulders. Adriana placed hers onto Sara's. From the gruesome remains of the night's events, a strong bond formed between them, a common desire to outrun their deaths and live for those they lost.

"The last of them are here," came Ishim's voice from behind. She and her sister, Ezkiel, had been rounding up the few who wished to stay behind and die next to their loved ones.

"And the ones that ran away last night?" asked Sara.

"Few made it far enough. Without food, and especially water, they sat down, exhausted on the sand and waited for their end. Ezkiel and a few of the other warriors quickly brought them back."

"Good!" said Adriana smiling at her. Ishim flashed her teeth in return.

"What about the Greeds' followers?"

"They joined the rest," answered Ishim. "I think they are more terrified of walking on their own back to their villages with those things coming after them then joining you to Caraa."

"We should have banished them after what they did to Taro!" hissed Grov angrily.

"I know. But our numbers are shrinking by the day. If we will not be able to form a thriving village after all we've been through, then why are we doing this?"

"They're murderers!" growled Grov.

"Aren't we all?" asked Adriana. "Sara's right, we need to stay united."

Grov nodded in defeat.

"I'll go check on our food stores and the water we have gathered, and we are set to go." Adriana squeezed Grov and Sara's shoulders.

"Perfect."

Grov turned his back to Sara, his eyes searching in the distance. Golden light now fell upon the ground through purple clouds. Beyond the Turmenn's camp, the Korr Mountains loomed barren over them, and further to the East, Wündalær gleamed, a sea of dark-green that obscured their home. Bells hid somewhere far beyond into the distance. No matter how far they had travelled, he still found his eyes drawn to it. But there was something else missing from the vista before him.

"Is there something wrong?" asked Sara measuring the span of land between the camp and Wündalær.

"Ummm…I'm not sure."

"I noticed it too," said Adriana startling the other two.

Sara's eyes widened as realisation dawned to her.

"The Beasts!" she murmured. "They're gone!"

"I haven't seen one in days."

"Then it's a good thing we are leaving. Without them, we would not last another week." Sara turned around to watch the gathered massed readying themselves for the long march to Caraa.

"What do you think happened to Trevor and the boys?" asked Grov peeling his eyes away from the forest.

"I hope they did not reach the High Priestess," Sara said flatly.

Grov and Adriana stared at her.

"Then maybe they are still alive." She walked away to address the frightened men and women. The red dress she wore, the one she'd received from Adriana, billowed mesmerisingly in her wake. Compared to the rest of the

Turmenn who wore clothes dyed brown or grey, she stood out like a princess. Her red form, unusual and beautiful against the bleak world around her.

Sara had dreaded this moment since she'd taken charge of the Turmenn's destiny the night before, but the masses needed someone to give them confidence and hope. They needed someone they could trust and later blame for their misfortunes. It had happened to Petra, and it would happen to her, but Sara did not plan to be their leader for longer than needed. Upon reaching the safety of the southern plains, others, more fitting, would take the duty of being the leaders of the group.

"Turmenn!" Sara spoke loud and slow so that the few hundreds of souls remaining of their villages could hear her. She was amazed at how easily the words came out, a feeling of some other mind talking through her, washing over her.

"We have lost yet more of our brothers and sisters, and our loved ones, but we will find safety. We have a long journey ahead of us to Caraa, a tough, perilous march, but together we will reach its walls. Follow me and those who have sworn to protect you, and no more of us shall die. We will look out for each other, share our food and water, and survive together. We are all that is left of our villages, we must make sure our legacy lives on!"

No one cheered, no one said one word, but nodded obediently. Their will had been broken by last night's events, and all they wished was not to see another sorcerer again. They were incredibly naive in thinking that, Sara knew.

The Turmenn funnelled orderly, out of their home for the past weeks, obeying their guardians' orders to stay together. Nothing could be seen around their crawling procession but the golden desert and the looming mountains to their right. But the guardians knew too well that danger lurked all around them. They would not be safe until they reach their destination. Ahead of them all, a crimson coloured Sara led the way into the unknown. None of those she shepherded towards safety had seen so much of the world they lived in.

Like a beacon of hope, Sara walked, joined by Adriana who swore not to leave her side. She needed to be protected just as much as the other Turmenn did, if not more. Unlike the warriors and some of the other men, Sara bore no weapon with her, nor had she the skill to fend herself. Sara appreciated Adriana's offer to walk with her despite her deeper desire to be closer to the other guardians, especially Ishim.

"I don't need you to walk with me, Adriana," Sara said softly, piercing her with her stare.

"Of course you do. All the others are spread out along the Turmenn, and whoever could be spared have been sent to watch our back." Adriana smiled at her knowingly, and Sara felt a pang of shame churn in her stomach.

"You are a good friend, Sara, and a leader to be reckoned with. Never forget that."

"I am no leader, but I'll do my best to see us reach the southern plains, I promise you that. As for your friend, I should be the one to thank you. Without you, I would have been lost. All my life I've had Petra, and then Erlend, by my side."

"I still bear hope for them. Petra has resources we cannot even begin to comprehend. She'll find a way to bring back Erlend and Syll."

"I am afraid to hold such hope, but thank you. If the Gods bless us with peace among ourselves, we have a chance."

Adriana looked in the distance absentminded. She could swear that she had seen black shimmers far away.

"I wish the world was a better place where we could all live peacefully with our people. No good will come of this damned war." Adriana spoke again, but her eyes never left the shining golden surface of the desert.

"Someday it will," said Sara thoughtfully. "But despite the many we have lost and our lives abandoned, we have found each other. Never before have all the villages united under the same banner. We will find a better place and make another life for ourselves. Just as Petra did, I now see it too."

Adriana laughed.

"Not many can keep a light heart in such times, Sara," she chuckled again, her olive complexion amplified by the golden reflection of the sand.

Sara blushed.

"If anyone had told me months ago, while we were still in Bells, that I will get to lead the greatest gathering of humans, I would have deemed them mad. There is danger all around us, Death herself is watching every single one of us, waiting to fail, but there is also hope." Sara smiled at her, a full, genuine smile that pierced Adriana.

Was Sara staggeringly optimistic in their collective will or was she incredibly naive to hold such hopes. Regardless, Adriana loved her for everything she was, compassionate and strong, even if Sara herself failed to see that she was made of something different from the rest of them.

Again, Adriana stared into the distance as her eyes played tricks on her. Repeatedly, the shimmering dark stains appeared and then disappeared, only showing themselves to her when she was not looking for them.

Maybe it was the lack of shade; still Adriana searched the vast span of sand.

"What is it?" came Sara's voice and Adriana realised she had been walking while staring vaguely, lost in her own thoughts. She said nothing. Again the blotches showed themselves to her, and this time closer. Adriana felt a hand wrap tightly around her throat, suffocating her.

"Look!" she gasped. "LOOK!!!" she yelled, pointing at the three dark shapes walking towards them from their left.

Sara almost stumbled as her knees wobbled at what Adriana was pointing at.

"It's them!" Adriana hissed still too shocked to breathe. Sara felt a sickening mix of happiness and dread fill her, the boys were still alive, but her Erlend, Petra, and Syll were nowhere to be seen. They had failed to bring them back. Still, they were alive.

"There are still Gods that watch over us."

"Hey! Hey!" Adriana cried waving a hand and Sara joined her, momentarily suppressing her tears. There will be time to cry tonight, not now. The three shapes waved back at them.

"Trevor! Sam! Daniel!" Sara hugged the boys dearly, tears trickling down her face.

"Thank the Gods you're back!" Adriana slapped the boys on the back. "What happened?"

The boys looked exhausted, wounded, and heartbroken.

"We should stop," said Sara, seeing them so worn out. She knew they had fought with everything they had to save their friends.

"No." croaked Daniel and Sam, leaning against each other as they walked. "We mustn't stop."

"What happened?" Sara asked Trevor, trapping him with her gaze.

The boys told them the dreadful things they had witnessed the previous night.

"They are gone, Sara, I am sorry," said Trevor in a low voice. Sara's eyes swelled with tears.

"You were the one to keep believing in Syll even when I had lost all faith. I wish I could have saved them. But we cannot linger here any longer. They are too strong for us to fight them, we need to reach Caraa as soon as our bones will take us," Trevor added, wiping his own tears from his sunburnt face.

Sara nodded and hugged him, lovingly.

"I am so glad you came back, boys!"

Neither of the brothers said another thing. They had wounds to heal and hearts to piece together.

They all resumed their walking towards Caraa, towards what they all hoped would be their long-sought safety.

* * *

"Wake up!" came Nephthys' displeased voice from behind the world of restless dreams.

Syll and Erlend stirred on their Nightlings, unwilling to rouse to what they knew would be the home of the Healers.

"Welcome back home, Petra!" she hissed, hitting her cursed beast over the muzzle. The creature neighed and shook in pain.

Petra came 'round to a world bleached in its entirety. She dragged her hands over her face, unsure is she had gone blind or if the world ceased to exist while she dozed off. Slowly the outline of the Nightling beneath her formed out of the sea of white, then Nephthys and her friends. Petra turned around and gasped at the sight of her old home, revealing itself to her wall by wall, majestic building by majestic building. The three of them, Petra,

Syll, and Erlend stared at the city before them in amazement and in shock.

Ophidia loomed over them like a snowcapped cliff. Its bright white walls rose high between the shores of the Taðr Sea and Naga's Forest, a flabbergasting mix of sky-high towers and colossal constructions like the ones Agür-y-Hadën once contained.

The three prisoners shielded their eyes to look upon Ophidia's walls. To Petra, the sight of the grand city brought memories she had long buried deep inside her. She never thought she would again lay eyes on the majestic structures, home of the Healers and the second-largest city in Urukk. She felt tears swell inside her eyes as she relived the two centuries she'd wandered through its streets.

Erlend and Syll just stared at it, their minds unable to find the words to best describe the miracle before them. Ophidia was of a beauty grander than their minds could ever conjure.

Fragrant winds caressed their tired bodies, zephyrs carrying the scents of the sea beyond the blinding walls, and that of flowers from the forest at their right. Syll felt lightheaded as she devoured the sense-trapping perfume. What lay before them was worlds apart from what they knew as beauty.

"Get down!" came Nephthys's voice again, and the three captives were reminded why they were absorbing such perfection. They lowered their eyes to the black-clad woman who had singlehandedly undone the Turmenn's whole defence.

"Now!" she growled.

The three dismounted their tall beasts, their hands still tied by the thin silver thread which Syll and Erlend now observed was made of a braided, transparent fibre, similar to that of spider's web. Nephthys pulled on the thread, and the three stumbled forward.

"My sisters are dying to meet you!" she said, enthused.

Petra frowned at her welcome back to the place she had called home for centuries. Then again, she'd run from them, disobeying her Queen's orders. Fifty years had passed since then, yet she remembered the vast city brick by brick.

Two large gates opened before them, welcoming them inside. The city buzzed with movement as they passed its gates, sorcerers from young to old, minding their own business in the early hours of the day. They all stopped from their feverish runs to watch Nephthys bring into their midst, three prisoners the likes they had not seen among them. No humans stepped within the city's walls in millennia.

For the briefest of moments, Syll and Erlend sighed with relief as they saw the enormous city spread before them, only to be reminded that if they had failed to escape when but three others guarded them, they stood no chance now that they reached Ophidia. The two of them, Erlend and Syll, stood out like a sore thumb with their black hair among the silver-maned sorcerers.

The masses stopped and watched them walk toward the inner parts of the city, and even though Petra refused to lift her gaze from the white stone beneath her feet, she knew her brothers and sisters recognised her. In a place where all lived in abundance and long-lasting peace, with nothing to perturb their placid existence, no span of time could erase their memories of blasphemous long-past events. They all remembered her betraying them, her Queen and God, just as she did, in its detailed totality.

Nephthys lead the way between the staring masses, smiling broadly as she pulled her prisoners behind her. Faces snarled at them, some even spat as they passed. With every sorcerer that stopped and showed their disgust at the three captives, Nephthys's blackened face cracked even wider with delight. The news that she'd managed to trap the one who had betrayed them would reach the furthest edges of Ophidia before they even reached its midst. The High Priestess gleamed with pride.

Above the solemnly marching Petra, Syll, and Erlend, the city rose to meet the very heavens. Towers made of the same brilliant rock stretched upwards into the skies, while larger, domed buildings filled the spaces in between. Even the most basic of constructions were of unimaginable beauty in Ophidia.

Nephthys turned and bent around the colossal buildings, not once checking on her prisoners, for she knew, just as they did, that they had no chance of escape.

The sounds of spat curses mixed with those of the churning sea beyond the city's walls, into a rhythmic, mind-ensnaring chant. For Syll and Erlend who had never heard nor seen the sea before, the noises took hold of their thoughts and washed away with them. They walked mindlessly in Petra's wake.

Petra, on the other hand, focused on the direction they were walking. She still remembered the city's layout from the many decades she had walked its streets, but many things had changed in fifty years, among which, the new building before them.

It rose slowly from the ground, a blemish of a building unlike anything around it or within the Healers' city for that matter. A large, polished sphere, half of which hid from the sun beneath Ophidia's fomenting streets. It gradually revealed itself to Petra as she walked, holding her gaze as low as she could, the unusualness of the construction challenged only by the fact that she had never laid her eyes on it before. This was the first building Petra heard of to be newly constructed by the

Order in millennia. It looked nothing like the forest of pinnacle-like towers that formed the rest of the city.

Nephthys walked towards the swollen construction. For the first time since they were dragged into the city, the High Priestess turned and looked at her captives happily. Immediately, she saw Petra stare beyond the many hooded shapes around them and straight at the dome-like structure in their path.

"We built it after you abandoned your faith, Petra." said the High Priestess, thrilled.

"While most of our kind strive to live high into the towers, myself and my sisters prefer to be below the ground," she added, stepping into the shadow of the building.

Before them, a tall, narrow slit in its otherwise seamless surface absorbed all light. Nephthys walked into it dragging Petra, Syll and Erlend after her.

If Ophidia was the most beautiful of thing they had laid their eyes on, grand a bright, the inside of the dome was nothing less than an enormous tomb. Hollow and dark, the structure acted as an oversized lid to the sunken home of the High Priestess.

"Welcome to your new home," she beamed at them. The place was cold and ill-lit, with not a single thing adorning its stark walls.

A deep staircase yawned at them in the middle of the cavernous place, a tunnel that descended into the depths of the city. Syll and Erlend measured, wearily, the insides of the structure, trying to shield their hearts the best they could from the ominous weight it pressed upon their shoulders. Nothing felt right about the place.

They were now being led down the endless stairs that took them ever deeper into the bowels of Ophidia. With every step they took, the cold that thrived beneath the spheric structure crept ever deeper into the three prisoners' tired frames. They were lead away from any prying eyes, away from light and warmth. Nothing good could come from it.

Faint chants drifted through the emptiness before them, soft and subtle echoes bouncing off invisible walls. Petra tried to calm her mind from racing, but she knew too well the kind of place Nephthys was taking them to.

After the long descent that seemed to take them miles through the dark and mouldy insides of the world, Nephthys finally stepped into the illuminated chamber at the bottom of the stairs.

The second Petra, Syll, and Erlend walked into it, all three of them wished they had been thrown into the darkest prison in the Realm than be there.

A cavern dug into the rocky shores of the Taðr Sea opened before them, a monstrosity of a chamber fit for the deranged, the mad, or for the ones who sought pleasure from the torturing of both the soul and the flesh. Chains hung from the ceiling and the looming walls in their hundreds, most waiting to take hold of flesh while some still held, in their locked shackles, disembodied wrists. Syll and Erlend almost spilled their guts at the sight; that was before they looked beyond the draping chains.

Spikes and cages, packed with long dead creatures, had been stacked against the walls, their putrid remains gaping at the three who stared in horror at the room they had been brought into. Syll shook with the convulsions of her insides.

In the centre of the room, ten tables made out of stone rose seamlessly from the floor, ten slabs of blackest rock waiting to suck the warmth out of living bodies. They spread in a large circle, radiating from the middle of the room towards the walls, all fitted with manacles and chains to hold tightly to their victims. In the middle of them all, inside a dimple in the floor large enough for a few people to bathe in, five or so black shapes clustered together singing madly, unaware of the horrified looks upon them. Nephthys waited patiently for them to finish. When they did, they turned and faced their leader, unknown faces hidden deep into black folds.

"What is this?" asked Petra aghast over the echoing remnants of the chants.

"This is your new home while we wait for your grandson to answer our call. Once he is dead, you'll join him. Until then, we have exciting work to do!" Nephthys said grinning and spreading her arms so that the five obscured shapes could kiss them adoringly.

"You have returned, High Priestess!" spoke the five masked shapes with nothing less than worship in their voices.

"I have," she revelled in her sister's adulation for her.

"And I brought with me what I have promised you!" Nephthys added while the five shapes still kissed her blackened hands.

From the far end of the room, where it was feasting on a rotting carcass, a white bird flew and perched itself on Nephthys' shoulder. The High Priestess pulled her hands away from her sisters' hungry lips and took the bird with care.

"You need to fly to your Master and tell her we have caught the traitor," Nephthys said gently to the bird who kept her beady red eyes on her. The white raven screeched and flapped its bleached wings for the High Priestess to let go. Like a white arrow, the bird shot through the room and up the dark staircase; flying hurriedly to Valdis, who expected news. The five hooded shapes clasped their hands in awe.

While every eye was on the High Priestess before her, Petra used the chance to search the room for anything she could use to escape. The braids of chains hanging from the walls and ceiling glistened at her as her eyes darted from side to side with speed. She tried to avoid staring at the death-filled human-size cages piled against the walls all around her, but she needn't worry. She found something worse than them to fear. The whole far wall, beyond the circle of stone tables, featured more chains and cages. Hundreds of skulls, bleached and clean adorned it like some sick collection of trophies. Without doubt, many of the unlucky, putrid bodies in the cages had their heads on that vast wall. These sorcerers, for Petra, could no longer call them Healers, worshipped something far more sinister than Valdis.

"Prepare them," commanded Nephthys absentmindedly, casting a look to Petra and her two terrified companions. Her words burned through Petra's focus on her surroundings like acid. The High Priestess' gaze lingered on Petra, then she turned around and vanished through another door at the far side of the chamber.

Greedy hands stretched from beneath the black robes to grab them. Shrivelled hands with black tattoos advanced toward them. Petra, Syll, and Erlend backed away in panic, tripping, stumbling on each other as they tried to put some distance between them and the advancing hooded shapes.

"The stairs!" hissed Petra at the two behind her.

As Petra, Syll, and Erlend turned to run that way, the leading shape, the one closest to Petra, stopped from chasing them. For the briefest of moments, Petra and her friends thought they had a chance of at least returning to the surface, but then the hooded figure bent and grabbed the silver thread that held the three captives securely.

With a jolt, all three collapsed into the entanglement of hands and claws that desperately wished to hold them, prod them.

"No!" hissed Petra kicking and fighting the black shapes.

"NO!"

But their resistance was futile. Within seconds the three were dragged roughly back towards the stone tables at the centre of the room. Black robes billowed around them. Then from above, chains flashed before their eyes, shackles clamped around their wrists.

Panting, the three prisoners shook with all their might, the thick chains that held them, cursing and spitting at the inked faces, that with much curiosity, peered over them.

"Release us!" groaned Erlend, who tried to punch the shape that stood above him. The chain that held him captive was too short, and his arm bounced back painfully. Blood showered over him as the manacle around his wrist cut deep into his flesh.

"Let us go!"

But the hooded Priestesses had no intention of releasing them.

Petra turned her head away from the hood that peered over her, searching for Syll and Erlend. The three of them lay tied to black stone tables, one next to the other, their heads towards the centre of the room so that they could not escape seeing each other's pain. Petra felt her tears choke her. She had brought this upon them; because of her, the Priestesses had them entrapped.

A hand materialised above Syll's face, stroking her pale skin.

"Crying won't save you," she sang happily. Syll shook her head away from it with renewed power, but another hand took hold of her. For the first time, Syll could see the woman's face within the many folds of her hood. A thin tongue flashed and licked black lips with pleasure. Syll stared at her horrified.

"Let them go!" Petra boomed, shaking the heavy chains. "You have me! Let them go!"

All five black shapes stopped from caressing their stretched prisoners and laughed.

"Let them go?" the one that loomed over Petra asked.

"Let them go?" she shrieked hysterically. "You were once one of us! Have you forgotten who we are? What is our purpose?"

"No! Please do what you must with me, but let them go!"

"Yell as much as you like, dear…" the shape spoke patiently, "…but you and your friends are ours to keep."

Through the door she had vanished moments earlier, Nephthys returned dressed in the same immaculate, black robes her sisters wore. The High Priestess, however, was unmasked. Silver-white hair flowed down to her shoulders, a mane so pure it haloed her and almost radiated its own light. She had shed the mien she had worn inside the Turmenn's camp, much like a snake moults its old scales.

"Now, now…" she said motherly, placing a hand on Petra's brow. "You knew this day would come the moment you ran off and renounced your Gods! No soul in Ophidia will save you."

Petra spat the High Priestess in the face.

"Make sure she watches her dear friends, sisters. She abandoned so much for them, make her remember them blooded and dead!" More tongues licked hidden lips beneath black hoods.

On each side of Petra's sprawled body, Syll and Erlend waited, in the same unnatural position, for the sorcerers to take their lives.

All five hooded shapes gathered, summoned by their High Priestess, around Syll.

Petra hesitated, then turned her head away from her and towards Erlend. Nephthys hissed, and a hand grabbed her by the jaw and made her watch.

At her right, Erlend pulled at his restraints, ignoring his own pain, but the bonds that held them tight to the ice-cold table would not give.

An enraged cry escaped Syll's lips the moment ten skeletal hands began to strip her clothes away. Within moments her naked body lay on the cold table hopelessly.

"No…no…" she whimpered, but the Priestesses were not to be put off by her pained wails. Contrarily, they gleamed with rapture at the squirming human before them. They watched and waited eagerly for Nephthys' next command.

The High Priestess' tattooed hands touched Syll's tears, moving slowly down her neck and to the gruesome scar she bore from her shoulder to her breasts.

From where she lay, forced to watch her friend be tortured, Petra saw a sick curiosity sparkle in the High

Priestess' cold eyes. She shuddered at the thought of what was to come next.

The lights dimmed and flickered as the Priestesses started to chant again. Slow at the beginning, then faster and faster, powered by their palpable desire to release their skills. Nephthys rolled up her sleeves so they would not get stained with blood.

"Where should we begin?" asked the High Priestess, elated, her face set into a grimace of pure pleasure.

"The arms!"

"I want to see the colour of her blood!" hissed another hooded Priestess, almost drooling.

"Yes! Yes! Let's see the blood!" agreed the obscured shapes.

"Seems fitting," said Nephthys, nodding at her devoted Priestesses. "The hands seem like a great place to start, for someone who had barely crawled from under some god-forsaken rock, yet think they are entitled to our world."

Louder, the hooded figures sang. The few torches that lit into the room, flickered close to extinction.

Syll's naked body shook with cold and terror as the six sorceresses summoned their spells.

"No! Noooo!" she pleaded futilely, for Nephthys' mercy.

"Don't worry, ape! I will not let you die this easily!" And with one hand, she held Syll by the jaw, forcing her claws into her face to make her mouth stay open, while with the other poured the green contents of a phial down her throat.

Syll coughed, spat, and moaned, but the substance was already inside her.

Nephthys released her and resumed her chants.

Words, sung in unknown tongues, bounced off the skull-clad walls, black robes billowed, a black dagger flashed before Syll's eyes. She shrieked and squirmed away from it, but Nephthys' hand brandished the blade with the precision of centuries-old practice.

Petra winced as she recognised the acrid stench of the substance Syll, was forced to drink. The venom from the Dreki serpent could keep their prey alive and conscious for weeks while its young ones hatched and ate their way inside their warm insides. The tormented creature that would hatch the Dreki's eggs, would only be allowed to die by the serpent's crushing jaws as it replenished its own strength with its. Then Petra saw the dagger approach Syll's shackled arms.

The blade danced in Nephthys' hand, up and down onto Syll's skin, cutting through layer after layer of her flesh.

Both Petra and Erlend felt their innards squirm as they watched the Priestess peel away the skin, then muscle from their friend's trembling arm.

Syll roared in pain, and Petra knew the yells would only get worse. The Dreki's venom made it impossible for their victims to give up and faint.

The gathered shapes hissed and moaned with pleasure as they watched their leader work her dagger. Blood began to flow freely from Syll's arm. Tiny rivulets of crimson fluid racing down the table, guided by precisely chiselled grooves in its smooth surface. Before long, Syll's life trickled away from her, down the stone table, and pooled into the disc-like dimple in the middle of the ring of torture beds.

Syll continued to scream madly.

One table away, Erlend pulled onto the tight restraints with newfound strength.

At the speed the Priestesses carved flesh away from bones, they would all be dead before nightfall.

Slowly, Nephthys made her way down Syll's mutilated arm, passed her elbow and towards her ribcage. More blood fled her body in a cowardly attempt to leave the failing pitcher that contained it.

On, Syll cried and begged for them to stop.

Nephthys sighed, satisfied, as her dagger reached Syll's shoulder.

The five hooded shapes gasped in awe every time the High Priestess' blade opened up another section of Syll's arm. Some of them pressed clawed fingers in the wounds, prodding, touching.

"Oh, High, Priestess!" they whispered breathlessly.

"Their insides are as fascinating as you've promised!"

"I want to see the muscles in her legs!" hissed one of the hooded sorceresses.

"Or maybe her bowels!"

"No! Her heart! I want to see her beating heart!" snapped another, placing a shrivelled finger between Syll's naked breasts.

The Priestesses all turned and waited for Nephthys to choose for them. The High Priestess turned the blade between her fingers, thick drops of blood splattering onto the table and rejoining their fleeing kind towards the puddle that had formed at its end. Nephthys's eyes shone with a sickening lust for knowledge.

"I, for one wish to unravel how they work. What makes these apes believe they own our Urukk. Their brains will hold my answers, but I shall take my time and learn all there is to them, from their frail bodies first. We must allow the Beasts the time to send that wretched boy to us to try to save them, but their skulls will soon be on that wall, fear not my sisters!"

The hooded Priestesses nodded in agreement excitedly.

"I'll now study their legs, but some of you should start the work on the male. We will amass far deeper knowledge if we can compare the sexes."

The sorceresses nodded again. Their hands immediately vanished deep beneath their robes to fetch their daggers.

"Freyja, I trust you to conduct it."

To four of the Priestesses disappointment, the fifth had been chosen to apply her skill and dagger to Erlend's already bleeding arm.

Petra turned to face him. Through streams of tears, she saw her most trusted friend lose the last of colour he still had. His whitened frame in contrast to the deep black table beneath him. Petra howled as six hands began to tear the clothing off his body just as they had done, moments before, to Syll.

"Noooo…" she cried, but no one listened. The Priestesses were too engrossed in their abominable study of the human body.

Petra and Erlend stared into each other's eyes, Petra begging for forgiveness while pale Erlend smiled at her with hope. Syll and Erlend would keep the hooded figures focused for as long as their minds stayed with them before they would retreat into sweet insanity. They would accept the pain, they would sacrifice their bodies so that Petra could find a way to escape. Petra shook her head at him, but Erlend smiled at her and nodded.

"You have to…" his lips moved without making a noise.

"…you have to take them to safety." Then he turned his eyes upon the hanging chains above him and awaited the excruciating pain to come. What did, however, hit him first was the acidic taste of the same gloopy, greenish substance Nephthys had forced Syll to drink. He swallowed bitterly.

Petra stared at him a while longer and felt proud of his sheer courage. But despite his offering, she saw no way out of the tomb Nephthys had put them in. Syll and Erlend's groans echoed through the room and forced her thoughts to focus on them.

At her left, Syll's legs were slowly being opened, gashing cuts cut deeply in her limbs. At her right, Erlend was experiencing what Syll had when the High Priestess, exposed her arms' white bones to the elements. Petra could only imagine what they went through.

Blood now flowed from both Erlend and Syll; dark, thick gore, trickling slowly down their black tables and into the filling pool between them. Again, the Priestesses exclaimed in awe at the nauseous workings of Syll's peeled back legs. Petra rattled her taut chains futilely to make them stop. They did not so much as look at her.

Torches continued to flicker for what seemed like hours, as the Priestesses used their skills on Syll and Erlend, their hushed voices growing in intensity while their blades made their way from arms to legs, and now towards their torsos. The two Turmenn, and before that villagers of Bells, roared unceasingly from the pain the black-robed figures brought to them.

"Good…good!" Nephthys beamed at her devoted minions, especially to Freyja who had followed her precise instructions and managed to perfectly split open Erlend's arms and legs. His hairy, naked body lay slumped and blooded onto the black table under him.

"What now, High Priestess?" asked Freyja shaking with the excitement from her work on Erlend.

Petra felt her innards tremble loosely in her frame, then scurry, frightened, somewhere where no blade could find them. Nephthys glanced at the two bodies before her. With the back of her hand, she touched their brows, then looked closely at their eyes. Petra judged she gauged how little life they still had in them. Slowly she retracted her hand from their cold bodies looking past them and her five mad Healers, to the pool of blood their bodies had created.

"We'll stop here for today," she said absentmindedly.

"Another cut and we might lose them despite all the Dreki venom I have given them." She glanced again at the mirror-like surface of the accumulated gore.

"Is it time, then?" asked Freyja, taking hold of her own hood.

"It is."

And without another word all sorceresses, led by Nephthys, unfastened their robes and let them fall off their own naked bodies. Petra watched in horror as the six, blackened by ink, bodies stepped, elated, into the round pool of blood.

"What is this?" Petra said, horrified by the barbaric ritual unravelling beside her. But her words were drowned by the six's joyful chants.

Thick blood splattered all around them. With cupped hands, they washed themselves in Syll and Erlend's blood, covering their whole old bodies with it. Then the

High Priestess stood up, crimson coloured and laughing, caressing lovingly, the heads of her five followers.

"Take our offering, ruler of all. You, who singlehandedly decides who lives and dies throughout your glorious kingdom. Izanami, our souls are yours as are the ones of those we wish to offer you!" Nephthys roared, lifting her hands above her head.

"May Death allow our servitude in the afterlife!"

"May Death allow our servitude in the afterlife!" the five Priestesses repeated in a mad frenzy.

Petra felt her body go ice-cold as she now understood the depth of their madness, but also the breadth of their horrendous powers. Nephthys had sold her soul to Izanami, the Death Goddess.

The Priestess' ritual ended as quickly as it had started. Their chants faded, then died away. The torches burning on the walls now spilled their orange light with renewed power.

Petra kept her head turned towards Nephthys and her five followers despite the acute pain in her neck. She feared that if she as much as blinked, some valuable aspect of their act would be lost on her. If by some miracle she managed to escape, others would need to know the atrocities the sorceresses of Ophidia did.

While Petra stared at her six sisters of the Order, from her left and right, her two butchered friends coughed painfully on their own blood. They should have been dead from their extensive wounds, but the potion Nephthys gave them, kept them conscious and alive even when death seemed much more appealing. Petra did not take her eyes away from the six figures covered in Erlend and Syll's fresh blood.

Suddenly, Nephthys started chanting yet again. Her voice rose and fell in the rhythm of her Priestesses' hums. The lights began again to flicker, terrified by the High Priestess's skills.

"Our souls are yours! Our lives are yours! Our past and future, has and always will be yours, Izanami!" Nephthys cried, rubbing her hands onto her soaked-in-gore naked body. Her hands then fell and settled at her side, her palms faced outwards while her head pushed back to stare at the chain-cluttered, high ceiling. With an image of total worship, Nephthys brought her hands together.

A monstrous clap, a thunder of a sound rippled through the Priestesses' torture chamber, bouncing ten more times before fading away. The few lights that dared to burn inside the room went out, then sprung back to life on their own volition.

It took Petra a few moments to realise what spell Nephthys had summoned. Then, slowly at first, but gathering speed, the blood that covered her and the

Priestesses whole bodies slid away from their inked skins. Within seconds, it had once again puddled, smooth and still, in the dimple in the ground. Nephthys clapped again and, pulled by some unknown witchery, the blood slid upwards on the black stone tables and forced itself back into Syll and Erlend's gaping wounds. The two winced in pain as the blood gurgled back into their bodies.

The High Priestess clapped a final time, and Petra watched in shock as her friends' flesh bound itself together in a spectacle of healing sorcery.

"Rest!" Nephthys commanded, moving closer to her three captives. Slowly, almost motherly, she placed a skeletal hand onto Syll's shaking shoulder.

"You will need your strength. Tomorrow we start again!" Then she walked away from them, closely followed by her five devoted Priestesses.

Petra, Syll and Erlend were left alone to their healed, yet still excruciating, wounds. Spells like those the Priestesses had summoned damaged them much deeper than their flesh.

The Summoning

About the same time as Petra, Syll, and Erlend woke up and found themselves in the shadow of the Healers' city, a group of hooded Draugur sped across the barren lands between Seribu Menara and Rokksvaart, carried, faster than any other beast could match, by Nightlings. Three tiny black marks raced between the incomprehensible span of desert to the right, and the mind-boggling Wall to the left. What would have taken a week to cross on horses, the cursed beasts reached Rokksvaart in mere hours.

The gates of the Order's source of gems opened gracefully before the three Draugur. Their Nightlings stomped the dusty road beneath their hooves eager to take their riders in.

Rokksvaart expelled black smoke and sparks through a forest of tall chimneys. Here were the Order's mines that brought to light the precious stone the sorcerers chiselled and baked into swords and daggers, but also into pendulums and rings. The Elementals' gems they used to channel their powerful skills, all came from Rokksvaart.

The three Draugur moved slowly through the opened gates towards the centre of the ash-covered city. All sorcerers halted from their feverish duties to watch the three hooded riders. Heads turned and bowed, some sorcerers even knelt before them as they passed, all measuring the Queen's mysterious fighters with fright but also curiosity. Never before had she sent them to their city.

Increasingly more sorcerers gathered around the carefully treading three Nightlings. Their hooves announced their arrival and called upon all those who heard them to turn and watch. Snow-white eyebrows peered through black-stained windows at the mounted Draugur, one by one answering their summoning.

Soon the whole of Rokksvaart funnelled out into the open space between the many smelters and the city's only inn.

The *Hounds and the Bear* stood against the blackness of the Wall, a patch of colour against the soot-covered city all around it. Its tinted windows of stained glass sparkled in the morning sun most brilliantly. Here, many weeks before, Velas, accompanied by Aerö, sought warm food and beds, a night of rest from their long journey across the Great Desert. It was in *The Hounds and the Bear* that Aerö's powers flared once more to defend him from the sorcerers who recognised him as Eldur's son; whom they all hated for his treason against his King and kind. Although Aerö had burned the inn in its entirety, *The Hounds and the Bear* still stood as it had for countless centuries before and just as many yet to come, rebuilt by

Rokksvaart's skilful sorcerers. No one in the whole of Urukk could work the black rock as they did.

The last to walk out of the inn was the broad sorcerer in charge of it. Looinn stopped in the doorway, measuring the three riders before him. Just like everybody else, Looinn had never heard of Draugur riding to their small city on their own. Whatever duty was with them, it was not good.

The three, fully-cloaked riders stopped their Nightlings in the middle of the rumbling, amassed white heads. Their cursed beasts neighed and stomped their hooves to call for silence. The murmuring sorcerers all stopped and listened to the Draugur speak.

"The Queen has sent us to deliver you a message," they hissed from under their black hoods. "The war against those who are spoiling our lands has started. Armies gather as we speak inside our great Seribu Menara to purge our realm once and for all of the Beasts and humans." Their breathless voices carried over the secular sorcerers before them.

"The King and Queen ask of you to join their holy ranks. You have a fortnight to answer their summoning and bring all gems and swords to them! The time has come to claim back our realm. The impure will feel the full wrath of the Order. Be in Seribu Menara in a fortnight!" they repeated.

"What about our families?" the sorcerers asked; their voices multiplying into a rumbling clamour.

"The King and Queen expect you all inside the Capital within a fortnight," the Draugur answered calmly.

"What about our young?"

"The King and Queen expects you all to answer their summoning," the Draugur repeated then turned their Nightlings around, leaving the gathered masses to mumble in their wake.

The sorcerers shouted more questions with newfound strength, but before they could get their sought answers, the Queen's soulless disciples kicked their Nightlings and broke into a run. They delivered the Queen's message just as she had asked.

Looinn turned his back to the rising voices and bubbling tempers, and stepped into the dimly-lit interior of his inn. The time had come for all of them to answer their duty's roaring call.

Unhurriedly, Looinn moved between tables covered in half-emptied mugs of mead and unfinished plates of food; all of them unoccupied. Their owners had answered the three Draugurs' call, leaving them all behind. Gently, he placed the rag he twisted in his hands onto the long, worn bar. Without stopping, he moved towards the far end of the room, his feet echoing loudly in the empty inn, his hands searching beneath his shirt for something only he knew he had there. His grubby hands clasped finally the thin chain suspended by his neck. He pulled on it until it came free of the entanglement of clothes. A tiny golden key hung at the end of it.

Without hearing the inn's doors open, Looinn placed the key into the lock. With a little push, the door creaked open.

"What are you doing?" came a man's voice from behind and Looinn knew precisely who it belonged to. Gourn stood tall and broad in the cone of light that now entered the inn through the large door that had been left ajar.

Looinn turned around calmly, to face the sorcerer. The light behind the man was bright and turned his body in a faceless, shapeless contour, but Looinn could see the orange gem that shone on what would be the man's broad chest.

"Well?" Gourn demanded in his spiteful voice. Looinn never liked the sorcerer, even less after but weeks before his inn had almost burned completely to the ground because of him. Still, he was Looinn's best customer. Gourn waited impatiently for Looinn to answer.

"The King needs all the gems in Rokksvaart," Looinn said thoughtfully, putting the golden key securely deep beneath his shirt. "But I have kept this inn for many decades now, I have nothing I could offer him. I have no skills in battle, and I doubt he'll want my mead." He chuckled, pointing at the barrels beneath the bar. "But I can make him one more gem, the kind no other has been made in centuries. I plan to have one done before we leave for Seribu Menara."

Looinn could feel Gourn's drunken eyes focus on him with great difficulty. They darted left and right, drawn by the abandoned treasures all around him. The innkeeper did not need to wait too long for Gourn to find the many mugs still filled with mead more worthy of his stare. The Elemental managed a few wobbly steps before he collapsed at the nearest table. Chairs creaked, mugs spilled their golden innards as he crashed atop of them. Like a creature whose evolution has yet to provide a spine, Gourn sat hunched, his hands limp at his side, his forehead against the wooden table, while his mouth and tongue worked hard to drink the spilled goodness beneath him.

Looinn shook his head at the sight. How could such beings of such power be so weak, he wondered. Then he reminded himself, grinning, that he was making a good living on their unquenchable thirst.

Loud, the door that opened at the far end of the inn, cried to be left shut. Cobwebs and grime had glued it to its frame harder than nails. Still Looinn pushed, forcing it to crack just wide enough for him to squeeze through.

The inn had been constructed, decades before, in front of his old workshop. Looinn patted his broad chest and the golden key beneath, then crossed the barrier he himself, had put in place between his new life and his old. He locked the door behind him.

Lamps burst to life inside the small room he had not stepped in for almost a century. Bright and golden, their flameless, magical insides flooded the workshop with light. Before him lay, dormant, his old life. A large furnace slumbered, covered by the dust and grime that had gathered in the many decades it had not been used, flanked by large stone tables; they, too, hidden entirely by the passing of time. Many tools and objects could be seen drowned in soot and dust atop the large black tables or hanging, looking ancient, on the walls. Looinn tread slowly towards his old stool. How many days had he spent in there, hunched over large blocks of stone, how many nights had he worked hard to keep the furnace burning? They all came back to him like dreams he knew he had, but could not quite remember.

Looinn moved around the room, touching the long-abandoned relics of his past, brushing dirt off, blowing away billowing clouds of dust. He had not been inside the room in decades, yet he remembered every tool it contained. He felt ashamed for his decision to renounce his gift in making gems, but after what had happened with his last one and its Master, he had not had much choice.

Without any resistance, the furnace door swung open. Through the large opening that formed, big enough for his whole body to crawl through — a thing he had done many time before to clean its insides — Looinn pushed an arm inside up to his shoulder. He felt the smelter's hearth with his bare hand, almost caressing it, but when it once again emerged into the lit room, his fist held something in it. Looinn stared at the small glass-like rock between his fingers, a glossy-black nugget the size of an egg. With his shirt, he wiped the stone clean and placed it on the worktable beside him. He stared at it for what felt like minutes, hours, days. On the table before him, dark and rough, stared back at him, the remaining half of the rock that gave birth to the strongest gem the Order ever come to have. The precious stone had been so powerful that no one dared to claim for decades. That was until *he* came and tamed it. Oh, the glorious things they had achieved together, gem and Elemental, a team so strong, the kind you only hear in legends. Looinn reminisced about the past events that changed the Order and his life forever.

From outside, the muffled voices of the sorcerers quarrelling about their future, drifted in. They all worshipped their all-knowing King and Queen, but being asked to take to war, their wives and children, was a hard command to mindlessly obey.

Looinn put his hands around the dark rock before him, thinking of what will come of it once it shed its impure skin and became, just as its other half had, the strongest stone in Urukk. There was much to do before that happened. A gem like that would take a long time to chisel, bake and polish, yet he had but days. Without looking, his hands grabbed his old tools from deep beneath the fuzzy layer of dust. Looinn found it incredible, if not somehow funny, how even after almost a century of abandonment, his hands still knew where his tools were without him even looking. With the war that was soon to start pressing heavily upon his thoughts, Looinn began the long and arduous work to turn the rock before him into something of great power.

* * *

From their Tower's arched windows, the King and Queen observed their armies gather outside their Inner City. Thousands of feet below them, Seribu Menara fermented with movement. Sorcerers, Healers, Elementals, and Draugur gathered and readied themselves for battle.

The sun's bright light fell from the heavens on the vast city before them. Its golden towers, walls, and roads made it shine brightly in the new day's light. Seribu Menara appeared like a giant gem encrusted in the black face of the Wall.

The King and Queen watched their devoted sorcerers prepare for what would be known, millennia to come, as the Second Great War. The conflict that would claim so many Sorcerers, Beast Lords, Beasts, and Humans, was brewing throughout Urukk. Greed, fright, and sheer stupidity had been at work in preparation for the devastating conflict that was soon to follow. They were all too ready to pick up their swords and fight. Was it for safety, for land, or simply pleasure, they all dreamt of the bright future they would have once everything got washed and cleansed with blood. But almost none thought of the sacrifices they will all be asked to make to see that future come, sacrifices beyond the most horrifying of nightmares.

Old and weary, Arnleaf Uriel and Valdis Ezelle stared at their kingdom from their heavenly throne room. Much time seemed to have passed since their youth and beauty had been stripped away from them by Skeggor's heir. Weeks and weeks of plotting the most cruel of deaths for the young boy who defied them. Anger flowed through their ancient veins instead of blood despite their cool composure.

"Your armies double with every coming dawn," sang Valdis to her King, her shrivelled fingers wrapped around his hand.

"All sorcerers throughout Urukk have answered our call, my love. Never before have such armies gathered since the War."

"And soon my sisters from Ophidia will join. Once they have killed that traitor and her filthy grandson, they shall lend their skills to you, my King!"

"Have the winds spoken of his return back to the surface?" asked Arnleaf petting her hand with his other, yet keeping his eyes on the tens of thousands of black dots assembling far below them.

"Not yet," she hissed and dug her claws into his flesh unknowingly.

The King kindly removed her hand.

"Your High Priestess should have managed to get hold of her by now."

Valdis nodded thoughtfully.

"What about your Seraphs?"

"You know their work. They will only return home once they have done their duty, or found their graves in foreign lands."

"There is, however, something we have yet to do and needs to be done. We need a leader for our gathered armies."

"You, of course, my love, are their true leader," whispered Valdis, leaning against him. The sun's warm rays blessed their old skin through the window they had perched on.

"That may be true, but I wish not to leave these walls unless utterly needed. Fear rules better than courage, my Queen," he said slowly. "And there is also the small matter with the Golden Oaks. They will not let us pass unnoticed."

"Damned traitors! When this is over, I will take their souls from them and lock them in the deepest depths of Urukk!" she growled. "Then they will have a whole eternity to ponder, bound to darkness, if betraying us was worth it!"

"Until then, however, we still need to find a leader of our army. Have you not thought of bringing Vondur back?"

Valdis stared at the golden vista before her seemingly absentminded.

"He has failed us too many times, my love," she said slowly. Her eyes were set coldly on the vast horizon, where in the Great Desert's golden sands, lay hidden, Undirheim.

"His punishment will be to drift without the substance of a body for eternity. Or at least until he learns, if there is such a thing, to bind his wretched soul to flesh."

Neither of them spoke again, but watched their city's streets and squares darken with hooded sorcerers. Their thoughts turned to their future kingdom, a realm cleansed of talking apes and Beasts. Yet not a single wandering idea of the seas of death they would soon cover the whole of Urukk, crossed their ancient minds.

The Dark Within the Darkness

"I am the Herald of Death, Illur! My skills are needed here!"

"Do not forget who you are talking to, Zarokk! The Queen has summoned you, you shall obey."

"I have not lain ruin to this Realm and waited four millennia to conquer Urda for nothing!"

"No, not for nothing, Zarokk. You have done what She has asked you, and you will continue to do so. The Queen has given you eternal life, and for an eternity, you shall obey her every word. Now go, and take with you Jurt, Jörðin and the twins."

"Gods, what's worse? To miss the end of this damned war, or to be stuck with those imbeciles?"

The Queen's Summoning

A maze of dark, damp tunnels burrowed through the black rock Aerö knew too well from Undirheim. Nóór, Ári, and Aerö had been walking for miles into the

unknown. Hours passed since the three left the Beasts
Lair's safety through the narrow crack into the wall,
chased by their parents attempting to stop them from
their mad endeavour. Water dripped from the galleries'
walls, soaking them to the skin as they advanced ever
deeper into the rock. Round and chiselled, the tunnels
took them further away from safety, away from family
and friends; their smooth surface making Aerö wonder
what had made them and what could be their purpose.

They had vanished through the narrow breach into the
lower chambers of the Lair, slamming blindly into the
hard walls, panting, cursing at the throbbing pain that
took hold of their arms and legs. It was then, when Nóór
asked Ári to lead them. But down there, away from any
source of light, not even the Hound could see before
him. Nóór's mind screamed in fear as his Beast failed to
see through the absolute darkness any better than he did.
He had never imagined that such blackness could exist.
Nóór leaned against the damp wall, unsure what they
should do. Chased by the White Wolf and his worried, if
not angered, parents, the three had dived at full speed
into the opening that promised their escape. They ran
and turned and hit more walls before they stopped to see
where they were going. Now the young Beast Lord feared
that without a way of seeing, they would be forever lost
and die like rats trapped in escape-less tunnels.

Aerö, however, never thought that Ári would be of
much help in navigating through the solid sea of
darkness. He had agreed to bring the two with him in this

terrifying search for help, only so they would show him where the gap inside the wall was. That and the fact that he knew, he had felt it in their hearts, that they would have not been deterred from following him.

With great satisfaction, Aerö pulled free his father's pendulum and commanded it to burst into flames. Instantly, a red glow leapt across the wet walls of the tunnel. Nóór's eyes lit with hope as he found his bearings in the globe of light.

"Wow!" he gasped, amazed at Aerö's skill. Ári's mind too, flourished with happiness at the light that licked the walls of the galleries around them.

Now, hours later, they still walked down unknown tunnels, slowly descending towards what felt like a great fire that burned deep underground. Slow as their progress seamed, with the boys' perception of time and distance altered by the twisting tunnels, they knew they had walked for miles. They were getting hungrier and more tired with every turn they followed of their endless road. The air also began to warm and thicken. Just as it did inside the Beasts Lair's lower chambers, the rainwater that seeped through rock from countless miles above them turned to steam in contact with the now too-hot-to-touch curved walls. Nóór and Ári followed Aerö, who commanded their sole light, ever further from their home.

Endless, the polished tunnels stretched in front of them; the two boys and their Hound turned and bent nauseatingly, yet never reaching a dead end. They had no way of knowing if they had been walking aimlessly in circles. Nothing but the change in temperature could they use to gauge their slow descent. Still, they marched on.

Then, hours after they had first immersed themselves into the darkness and the catacombs beyond, a gentle wind slapped at their faces. The three froze in place. The heated air whizzed passed them in the rhythm of a breathing, enormous lung. Again and again it came whistling through the ducts ahead of them. Aerö and Nóór - who had scooped up his young Hound and held it at his chest, glued themselves to the smooth walls and listened.

If there was wind rushing towards them from the unknown depths they were trudging towards, there could only be two explanations. Aerö shared his thoughts with his two friends, one hand holding Eldur's flaring pendulum, the other wrapped around Nóór's arm. They held their breaths and listened. Like clockwork, the air rushed and whistled.

The simplest reason for the wind was the existence of another opening ahead of them that connected this cavernous world with the surface. Aerö thought of it, even imagined stumbling out and see the vastness of the world before him, the wide spans of land and the vastness of the sky he took for granted as a child. Nóór and Ári shook with fear of such a place. They had been born and raised inside the confines of their Lair, never to feel the sun above them, not once to see the trees. Aerö's mind returned to the underworld the three explored, called back by yet another skin-prickling, passing breath.

The other explanation Aerö thought of, and found immensely more likely, was that somewhere before them were the things they had been looking for. Hope sprung into his heart, just as it vanished from the others. Aerö could see in his friends' souls, the hope they harboured that the ancient creatures he so desperately sought, would not be real.

Aerö pushed himself away from the wet wall and dragged Nóór, who did not wish to follow, after him . They were too deep into the tunnels for them to separate, least turn back.

The two boys and their accompanying Beast moved slowly at first, listening intently for whatever lay ahead. But when nothing seemed to happen, they resumed a healthy pace.

They seldomly talked, for their young voices travelled far and wide. Instead, they shared their thoughts with one other. They shared the food they'd stuffed their pockets with up in the Lair's storerooms and made good progress into the unknown, yet always inching closer to the source of those loud gusts of air, despite the turns they took.

They walked like that for hours before they had to stop and marvel at what hid so far beneath the humans', the sorcerers', and even the Beast Lords' feet.

The echoes of their feet onto the smooth floor slowly changed from closed and rapid, to seldom and hollow, as if bouncing off some greater walls. Still, ahead of them stood nothing but the immovable block of darkness. Slowly, Aerö's crimson flames licked at it, revealing partially, its immeasurable depth. Aerö stopped as did Nóór and Ári beside him.

The wind howled in the cavern before them, and even though they could not measure it, a sense of emptiness, of gargantuan nothingness, took hold of all their senses.

"What's wrong?" asked Nóór, ashamed of the slight tremble in his voice. His whisper carried far away.

"I don't know," muttered Aerö, wincing at the power of his own voice. "Move back," he commanded.

A second later, once Nóór and his Beast moved a few paces behind him, Aerö grabbed his father's stone with both his hands and summoned its roaring flames. The globe of light flickered as the pendulum answered his call. Before him, in the heart of the darkness, a tiny crimson spark ignited. Aerö focused on it, and another second later, it flared into a tiny sun suspended in midair. Aerö pumped his powers into the bright stone he cradled in his hands. Brighter and large the globe grew, eating away the darkness that enveloped everything in sight. Slowly, it began to push away the blackness. Above their heads, chiselled walls, wet and smooth, glinted in its light, yet nothing they could see below. They were standing on the brink of a large cavern, a gigantic hole inside the stone. The tunnel they had taken, ended abruptly, some ten feet ahead, vanishing into the nothingness of empty space.

"We can go a little further…" said Aerö, in the quietest of voices. His words tumbled like boulders through the cavernous emptiness before them. Slowly they treaded carefully towards the edge of the abyss. The further they went, the brighter Aerö's summoned sun shone. The heavy breaths they had been following for hours roared from some obscured lungs below. The two boys peered over the edge of their tunnel for them, but could only see the burning star Aerö had conjured.

"Turn it off," said Nóór quietly. Aerö looked at him puzzled but followed his advice, slowly choking the power he pushed forth into the stone.

"In places like this, light blinds worse than darkness," Nóór added, seeing Aer'ös confused look.

Aerö took a deep breath and commanded the pendulum to go to sleep. Absolute darkness enveloped the two boys and Ári. Aerö made a step backwards as the wall of nothingness surrounded him.

"Look!" Nóór hissed, pointing a finger Aerö simply could not see, least follow. "Look!" And Aerö saw it. Growing like a vine through the blackness, orange tentacles of light protruded through the empty space below, growing towards them. A globe of light, much fainter than the one his summoned star belched out, radiated from below, allowing the two boys to measure the cavern's true depth. The two felt faint by simply looking at it.

Miles and miles below, at the bottom of the pit, an amber coloured city spread. *It must be the size of the City of Sands*, Aerö pondered looking at it.

"Look!" Nóór hissed again, but Aer'ös mind was too entwined in the conflicting thoughts and feelings blowing through him for his eyes to follow.

"Look!" Nóór repeated, and Ári released a shrieking yap to make Aerö break contact with the unknown world below. This time Aer'ös eyes broke free of the hallucinating sight and followed his friend's finger.

"There's a path that goes around the wall and down into that city!" Aerö heard his own grasp as he realised what they had stumbled upon.

"What should we do?" asked the young Beast Lord, but Aerö had already moved closer to the thin ledge of stone that spiralled around the dome-like cavern and towards the amber city far below.

"We've found them!" Aerö hissed, half excited, while his other half trembled in fright.

The three began the coiling journey towards what Greindur Gamall wrote of, as the city of the creatures no one should disturb.

Gradually, the three followed the narrow ribbon of protruded stone, their eyes focused on the immeasurable depth of the pit at their right, while their hands gripped the best they could to the smooth wall at their left. With no barrier between them and the hollow space, Aerö, Nóór and Ári threaded carefully, afraid they might stumble or slip and fall to their death a few miles below.

Aerö pondered for a while what would be like to fall from such a height. Would he be able to observe the ground speed rapidly towards him, or would he be too afraid to watch?

Nóór hissed at him from behind. "Will you stop that!"

Aerö realised that they were still connected through their thoughts. He grinned at the thought of the things his friend feared, from the vast outside to the vast below, Nóór seemed to be scared of anything that seemed to have no limits. Aerö, on the other hand, was far more terrified by what was waiting for them at the end of the path.

Slowly, they descended, moving round and round the almost vertical wall, quietly approaching the amber-glowing city below. The closer they got, the harder the gusts of air rose from the bottom of the pit. They were almost halfway down before Nóór spoke again.

"What do you think is down there? Do you think they're real?" he asked timidly, trying his hardest to conceal the fear in his heart. Aerö however felt his true emotions.

He thought about Greindur Gamall's words before he answered. "They're probably creatures that have not seen the light of day in centuries, nor any other being but their own. They will be scared and most probably dangerous—" Aerö let the words hang heavily between them. "I must ask you to do everything I say, Nóór," he continued. "If they are as wicked as Greindur believed, they will not blink before they have you killed, that is if they have eyelids," he joked, but Nóór did not found any of it funny.

"They will listen to me," Aerö concluded confidently. But deep inside his chest, his heart quivered in fear. For all he knew, they would be slain the moment they would reach the bottom of the pit.

Further they went, hugging the outer wall, descending the steep spiral path before them. After a few hours, the bright city was in reach. From their vantage point, Aerö could see the bright city span for miles to his right. Amber-gold, tall, crude buildings rose above the otherwise shallow span of constructions. They all seemed to him, from still a sizeable height, to have been constructed out of some sort of rock that sparkled in the light of the entwining orange veins he had first seen in the Beasts' Lair. Tall, chimney-like constructions puffed smoke and steam through blackened lips. The now violent bursts of air, were coming from them, Aerö was certain of it.

"It's hideous, don't you think?" Nóór glanced at the closing breadth of buildings up ahead.

Aerö thought they were of a rather beautiful nature.

"It's so bright down there," Nóór continued, and Aerö understood his friend. He had lived all his life shielded from light and brightness, and now that they were steadily engulfed by the city's radiating glow, he felt unease. Aerö wondered what would be his genuine reaction, if he saw the brightness of the sun above the miles of rock and sand that separated them.

The Skrímsli's city widened beyond the boys' field of sight. Amber and sparkling like a giant gem, the span of buildings welcomed them inside their radiating glow. Aerö, Nóór, and even Ári, stared at them speechless. Before them, a sea of golden buildings gleamed at them. They had arrived into the Skrímsli's hidden city.

As they stood and watched, mouth-open, at the giant labyrinth of hovels, furnaces, and towers made of the brightest rock Aerö had seen, it dawned on him that everything before them had been erected out of purest gold. It was beyond his comprehension, the pricelessness of the place.

Nóór shielded his eyes with his left hand, his right clasped tightly around Aer'ös arm.

Aerö could feel him tremble beside him. Then his blood froze in his veins as a grunt echoed through the glowing light exuding from the city.

"Grrruhh! Grrruhh!" the voice echoed around them. It took Aerö a few moments to see the large, monstrous creature before him.

The Skrímsli stood a few feet away, clearly taken aback by the small, thin creatures that had materialised inside its city. Its beady eyes, small and wet, stared at them unblinkingly.

"I am Aerö, heir of Skeggor Skalidur," Aerö announced, moving in front of his frightened friend.

The being, several times larger than a grown man, stared at him startled. The Skrímsli reminded Aerö of the Feonds in the Beast Lords' Lair, large and naked, their only garment a roughly torn leather cloth around their groin. Aerö awaited it to answer him.

Nóór and Ári hid behind him, too afraid to look.

The Skrímsli grunted again, guttural and low, then bent forward as if to smell them. Instead, it roared so loud it hurt their ears.

The boys clasped their hands around their ears.

The Skrímsli bellowed louder, making Aerö and Nóór almost collapse with pain. Then Aerö realised the grave mistake he had made. He had naively assumed that the creature spoke the same tongue as he did. Instead, they did not seem to have yet conquered the most basic of words. Aerö opened his mind to the creature before him.

"I am Aerö, heir of Skeggor Skalidur," he repeated calmly.

At this, the beast stopped from roaring and glared at him. Its beady eyes set so coldly on him, Aerö felt suddenly scared the creature might just step towards them and crush their squishy bodies with one fist. The Skrímsli continued to stare at him.

"Can you understand me?" he asked, tentatively.

The Skrímsli opened its wide mouth and roared again.

Before the rumble could subdue, a hoard of Skrímsli joined the first and grabbed the boys roughly by their heads with hands as large as boulders.

The boys' cries echoed, muffled, from inside their leathery prisons.

Ári yapped once at the giant creatures taking hold of his young Master and his friend, then he too found himself trapped in a fist a hundred times larger than he was.

Things were not going the way Aerö had envisioned them.

More grunts drifted through the thick fists of the Skrímsli to the three captives, their incomprehensible tongue instilling fear around the trembling hearts of the small creatures in their grasp.

Aerö wiggled his body in an attempt to free himself, but stopped the moment Eldur's pendulum began to quiver and warm up against his chest. He needed the Skrímsli's help, not burn them into oblivion. Aerö decided to relax his body and wait to see where they were being taken. He opened his mind and searched for Nóór and Ári's bright specks of consciousness inside the immeasurable void of nothingness Aerö could tap in. A moment later, he found them, fighting to get free, shouting, kicking at the hunched creatures that held them in their fists.

"You need to relax," Aerö's thoughts drifted lazily to his two friends. Nothing but fear exuded from their minds.

"It's alright!" insisted Aerö. "They haven't killed us so they must be taking us to see their leader."

"Or to throw us in some deeper pit!" growled Nóór, but Aerö could feel that his friend stopped struggling.

"You should use your flames and get us out of here."

"We need their help, Nóór. We did not come all the way here, ran from our parents and your home, so that we can go back and live under the mountain as if nothing had happened. Plus, they've seen us in their city. Who knows what they will do now that they know their very existence is no longer lost to the minds of men? If everything in Greindur's tales is true, then they may very well be our enemies as well. That's why we're here! Like Skeggor did before, I must persuade them to help us!"

Nóór nodded, unconvinced.

The Skrímsli trudged through their bright city towards a hideously pointy building in its midst. Their small black eyes skipped lazily over the golden riches of their home, too used to its polished beauty to still marvel at it. They held aloft their giant fists in which they carried, roughly, their three prisoners.

Another rumbling grunt travelled through the tight fist that wrapped around Aerö's entire body. He could not see where they were being taken, nor how far into their city — if that is where they took them. Aerö hoped that the half-naked brutes would not simply throw them in some deeper hole as Nóór feared.

"Grruhhghh! Rrugghh!" Voices bellowed all around the squashed and blinded, three small creatures caught outside their city.

"Roghhhro gruhrrro ggrruh!"

"Grrohr! Grro!" And the fists that held Aerö and his friends tight in their hold, unwrapped and let them fall.

The two boys blinked and shook their heads to cast away the veil of blindness that had seized their senses. Slowly, the brightness of the golden-everything around them made its way into their eyes.

Aerö wiped his eyes again in disbelief of the odd mix of beautiful and staggeringly grotesque collection of buildings around them.

Nóór reeled around beside him, mumbling, frightened, at the things he saw.

Before the three, rose high towards the seemingly black sky, the oddest construction Aerö had ever seen. Made of gold just like everything else inside the Skrímsli's city, a collection of jarring spikes and polished edges hurt his eyes. The more he looked at it, the more it gathered itself together into something Aerö could vaguely comprehend. It looked as if some giant hand had swept together all the bits and pieces they had not found use for when they built their precious home. But the more he stared at it, the more it started to make sense, something greater took shape out of the monumental pile of golden metal.

Nóór, however, did not even notice the giant construction. Instead, his eyes refused to budge from the gathered Skrímsli behind them.

As Aerö sized up the haphazardly erected throne before them, more and more half-naked beasts answered some unheard call.

Nóór and Ári trembled in the shadow of the giant creatures.

A seat, a throne, stood erected before him, Aerö could clearly see, a gruesome pedestal amid the chaotic mass of golden spikes and blocks of chiselled metal. On it sat the largest, fattest being Aerö had ever seen or heard of. The thing made Finndôra's Har-úgur look small and ill-fed compared to it.

Both Aerö and Nóór now watched the creature, in awe of its sheer size. Aerö guessed that the sole purpose of the giant mess of a construction that rose behind the throne was to support the creature's staggering weight.

Behind Aerö and Nóór, who now held Ári at his chest, a good four dozen Skrímsli grunted angrily at them.

Their fat leader raised a hand.

"Grruhhlll!" it bellowed incomprehensibly.

Nóór, beside him, looked at Aerö, puzzled and scared.

Aerö took a deep breath as the rough voices of the Skrímsli died, and tapped into the empty void of thoughts and consciousness. Quicker than a blink of an eye, he found the leader's retched sentience. Dark, and filled with anger, it screamed inside Aerö's listening mind, putrid from the aeons of living in utter isolation from the above worlds they'd shunned themselves from. Aerö instantly felt pity for the creature who no longer had the capability to feel anything other than rage.

"Ghruh…grobhr," it spoke again in their crude tongue, but Aerö understood it. He still heard the beast grunt madly before him, but as his mind managed to understand the Beasts in Undirheim, so it did now with the large creature before him.

"Where did they come from?" it roared roughly.

"Above," grunted another just as harshly.

"Impossible! There are no tunnels to the surface. We closed them off thousands of years ago!"

"What are they?" asked another Skrímsli. In its giant hands, Aerö could see, it wielded a monstrous hammer.

"They look like they're meaty," another Skrímsli added licking its fat lips.

"Can we eat them?"

At this, Aerö could not stay quiet any longer.

Nóór also turned his eyes to Aerö, who had been conveying the creatures' thoughts to him and Ári.

"We are a Beast Lord and…" for a better word to describe himself he added, "…a sorcerer," said Aerö calmly.

The Skrímsli who had been arguing how to eat the three fell dead quiet.

"You're what?" grunted the brute that had carried Aerö through their city by his head. His thick fingers poking at his ribs with such force that Aerö stumbled forward.

The fat creature from the throne leaned forward as if to see him better.

"How…do you speak to us, vermin?" growled the large Skrímsli, his many folds of fat shaking on him violently. To Aerö, the brute looked like a giant gelatinous heap.

Nóór almost chuckled as he saw with his mind's eye the things that Aerö thought of.

"As my grandfather did before me. I am Aerö, Skeggor Skalidur's heir." Aerö said coolly and awaited the Skrímsli's reaction.

He did not have to wait long. The creature shook with even more force.

"How dare you bring his name inside my home?" it bellowed so loud, both the boys had to clasp their hands over their ears. The finger poked again at him.

"Speak!" it growled.

"I am Aerö, Skeggor's heir and I have come to ask you for your help."

If its face would have allowed it, the large creature would have looked at him incredulously.

"You dare to come inside my city with such lies?"

"Can we eat them now?" the Skrímsli behind Aerö asked its master impatiently.

"Soon…" it hissed. Then, to Aer'ös surprise and bewilderment, the creature rose from its piled-together throne and wobbled its way to them. It wrapped a large hand on Aerö's face, which vanished in its grip. It all happened fast, yet Aerö had plenty of time see the creature dash to him. Aerö blinked repeatedly, as if unsure of what his eyes had seen.

The Skrímsli's entire body was decorated with long belts of gold, not chains and bracelets, but whole bands, inlaid into its tremulous skin. The love for gold these creatures had, made Aerö fear them for the first time, but also gave him hope that there might be just enough room between those many folds of skin, for bargaining.

"If you are half of what you claim to be, then you know who I am." Aerö shook his head inside the Skrímsli's hand.

"I am Skel, King of the Skrímsli and the end of you! You are no heir of that betrayer, but no less you all shall die the most terrible of deaths!"

"Take them to the furnace!" it shrieked, so angered, its beady eyes turned in its gruesome head.

A small spark exploded in Aerö's mind. The gusts of air and smoke they felt on their descent were from the tall chimneys of the many furnaces that spread through the golden city around them. These creatures loved their gold above all else and smelted rivers of it.

Nóór's thoughts could only focus on the gathered giants around them. They should have listened to their Queen and turned back. There must be a reason why the Beast Lords kept the Skrímsli's whole existence secret. He began to see why.

"The boy speaks the truth," came a wheezy voice from somewhere behind Skel the King of the Skrímsli.

The fat creature turned around and glared towards its throne.

Next to the golden seat upon the golden mess of spikes and blocks, a golden stub of a tree trunk stood. It was crooked and only had one branch left from its glorious crown. Aerö felt pity for it. Like a landslide, the memories of the three Golden Oaks outside Seribu Menara's Inner City and its Ivory Tower washed over him and every creature linked to his thoughts.

Loud gasps echoed through the room.

"The outside…" one of the Skrímsli whispered in wonder.

"You have met my kind before, young one," the wheezy voice drifted again.

"What is this trickery?" Skel bellowed, moving a step closer to the ancient Golden Oak and away from Aerö.

"Speak, old one!"

"I did," said Aerö instead, managing to form the words inside his mind as he regained control over his thoughts.

"And I have proof." He produced, from inside his pocket, the golden leaf the Oaks had given him on his escape from Seribu Menara. He held it aloft, the precious gift sparkling before the muted mass of monsters.

"I asked you to take these liars to the smelter! If there's gold inside them, I want it all!" Skel roared with greed.

"Whoever they might be, they must DIE!"

But the Skrímsli hesitated. The image of the world above their own had a bigger impact on them than Aerö first realised.

"Skel, listen to the boy," chanted the old tree.

"NOW!" Skel bellowed. And this time, the same hand that had taken Aerö to the Skrímsli's King, wrapped around his body in a deadly crush.

"Please release me, and no one will get hurt," Aerö sent his thoughts through the cobweb of linked conscious minds.

In return, the brute tightened its grip around Aerö's whole body.

"Please, listen to us, King of the Hollowers."

But Skel was not to be deterred from squeezing every ounce of gold he could get his fat hands on.

"Hurt us?" the King choked with laughter.

Aerö hoped he would not have to prove himself to them, but more hands extended to take hold of Nóór and Ári. The Skrímsli had decided they had heard enough, and that was time to give them to the flames. Aerö wished they had not, but if flames they wanted, flames they shall all have. He called upon the quivering pendulum around his neck.

Before the beast had time to lift Aerö off the ground and take him to the furnace, blood-coloured flames burst from between the creature's fingers. They licked and leapt to the Skrímsli's hand excitedly.

The creature roared in pain so loud, the ground beneath them trembled, then pulled its hand, releasing Aerö where he stood. Although it had been fast, Aerö's flames were faster still. The air inside the city permeated with the acrid stench of charred flesh.

"You have no power here! How dare you raise those retched flames against us? We were ancient when you vermin were still walking on your fours! We are Gods!" Skel shrieked. "Your powers mean nothing here, sorcerer! Millennia, your kind tried to enslave us, yet here we are still, free and rich. Not even your own Gods managed to make us do their bidding!"

"You helped Skeggor Skalidur, and you will aid me too," said Aerö in a calm voice.

The Skrímsli started to grunt and stomp their massive feet onto the ground at the mere mention of the name. Aerö knew that if they all attacked, the three of them stood no chance. He had to make them listen. He had to make them see that if Arnleaf and Valdis were allowed to win the war, not even the world's bowels would be safe from them. Aerö allowed the gem's whole power to take hold of him.

Like a volcano, the crimson flames erupted from him, leaping sideways to the angered Skrímsli and towards the black and starless ceiling of the enormous cavity, the creatures called their home. The beasts stumbled over each other to put some distance between Aer'ös flesh-melting flames and them. The King, himself, retreated to his jarring throne in fright. At Aer'ös left, his friends stared at him, terrified but safe. His father's pendulum would never harm them.

Aerö allowed the tall flames to burn noisily as he opened his mind to all the Hollowers that lived so many miles beneath the Realm's surface. He did not have much time to make them listen. The raging inferno used his strength too fast for him to bear its weight for more than a few moments.

"We have come to ask for help not wage more wars," he sent his thoughts as far and wide as there were specks of light inside the blackness.

"While you have hidden inside this tomb for aeons, vast powers rose to claim the realm that you once controlled. Sorcerers enslaved your ancient brothers and sisters, they preyed on them and have slain them all. All while you buried yourselves in this pit and covered yourselves with gold. Have you forgotten all about the surface? Have you burned into oblivion all those memories?" Aerö pointed at the many furnaces around him.

"As you hide down here and squabble over your priceless gold, the armies that will purge the realm of us all are gathering. Those of us who wish to see us prosper as you once did in your Kingdom of Peace, are readying ourselves for war, but we are few. We need your help, great Hollowers!" Aerö added, mixing his own thoughts with images of the battle that Undirheim had seen but weeks before.

No sounds now drifted from the gathered masses. Aerö had the Skrímsli's unwavering attention. Taking a deep breath, he let the roaring flames die out.

Along with the receding flames, Aerö felt his very life flow slowly out of him as if whatever held it safely inside him now had unseen cracks. Aerö felt nauseous but held himself together so that the Skrímsli would not see his weakness. He knew that if he had to use his flames again, he would not be able to light a single candle.

The Skrímsli did not move one muscle, they all stood motionless and watched, in shock, the young sorcerer before them speak of the world they had long abandoned to his kind.

"No one is safe from the war that will soon swipe the realm clean. The Beast Lords are gathering just as the humans will. We need you to allow us free movement through your galleries unseen. We need you to join the battle that, if won, will gift us the peaceful future we all wish for — or wait for Arnleaf and Valdis's vast armies to find your home. They will not stop this time, until every last one of us is dead." Aerö took a deep breath and steadied himself.

"You speak big words for an insect," spoke Skel in its grumbling tongue.

"We've seen your kind's destruction of the world we cherished for more aeons than time itself can call to mind. And we have tried to stop them, we have given our aid to him. But that deceitful Skeggor tricked us when he no longer needed our help. And rightfully, he died inside the tomb we had created for ourselves, as do his children as we speak. Despite his treachery, Skeggor Skalidur's sorcerers have been dying the slowest of all deaths, the childless end to his great family." Skel returned to his large throne from where he carried on admiring his clad-with-gold fat body.

"And now you come to ask for help and threaten to destroy us? What could you offer us for our aid?"

"Your life as it had been before the sorcerers arrived," said Aerö calmly, although in truth he simply had no strength left in him to act otherwise.

"We have tunnels deep enough that no sorcerer can conquer. We can wait for all of you to die. What is another thousand years more to us who have seen the Wall rise from the earth?"

"No hole, no matter how deep, will save you, King of the Skrímsli."

Skel fell into a deep silence as if in thought, but Aerö knew the creature simply waited.

"What do you think, old one?" Skel asked the Golden Oak at his left.

"Just as my brothers knew it, so do I. The boy speaks the truth."

Skel watched the old stub with a grim expression. Seeing the King of the Skrímsli look at it doubtfully, the Golden Oak added.

"We do not shed our leaves for anybody, yet he possesses one. I would not take his word lightly."

"Then maybe we can come to an understanding," it hissed at Aerö, with the same sparkle in its eyes that would make Mammon proud.

Aerö listened, although the only thing his mind could see was Greindur Gamall's written words of how disloyal and deceitful the Skrímsli were.

"Don't listen to it, Aerö!" hissed Nóór inside his head. Aerö had been so caught in his own game of persuasion, it almost forgot about his friend and Ári.

"We wish not to go to war, but we may grant you passage for the riches in the tallest tower." Aerö let the King finish his laced-with-greed demands, but knew his answer long before the creature even uttered them.

"I cannot promise you anything else, but what is yours to have. The Ivory Tower is not one of them," he said confidently and watched Skel's waves of fat tremble in anger.

"Then maybe the knowledge you don't have will change your mind," it hissed, smiling at Aerö.

"While I am sure you gathered vast amounts of knowledge in the many years you have lived, King of the Hollowers, unless you know a way to have Arnleaf and Valdis stopped without war, no wisdom will grant you more than what I have already promised you."

Skel choked with laughter. Aerö felt the beast's deceptions crawl their way to him.

"Oh! But I am not talking about a way to end the war. I merely wish to share some knowledge." It smiled again so full of venom, if it but bit its tongue it would be dead. Aerö waited for the King of the underworld to continue.

"We have many ears scattered at the surface. If you are who you claim to be, then your own Queen has captured the leader of the northern humans and two of her aids. Valdis is growing restless."

Aerö felt the little power he had left bubble towards the surface and towards the pendulum which quivered excited on his chest.

"You cannot possibly know…" Aerö hissed.

"Do we have an agreement?" Skel beamed at him.

Aerö did not wait for the creature to mock him any further. He poured his last drops of strength into the stone and let it rage.

"Lie to me, and I will melt that gold you hold so dear through your very flesh!" he roared enveloped in crimson flames.

"I do not fear for my life. I've lived too long already. But if you do not give me all that precious gold, the humans are as good as dead!"

Before Aerö could even blink and melt Skel's tons of flesh straight of its bones, the Golden Oak began to sing, a raspy voice above the cracking of his flames.

The truth about what happened far above,

Is deeply woven in the substance of the war at hand.

Far you must travel to the edges of the sea of sand,

Either to end the war or save the one you love.

The place you seek is where the Healers dwell,

Where those who worship Death have taken her,

But know that if you go there, you will lose your father.

Do what you must, but please choose well.

The old voice drifted hazily above the deafening silence all around the gathered Skrímsli, Nóór and Ári. Aerö's flames, too, choked and died under the silence's suffocating weight. Aerö swayed gently from left to right as he had funnelled all his strength into his bluffing last attack.

From where he stood, Skel, the King of the Skrímsli looked with rage at the Golden Oak.

"Why did you tell him, ancient one?" it grumbled at the talking stub.

"We all must do what Narrū planned for us. You too will have to play your part, Skel."

The King of the Hollowers grunted again, then turned its beady eyes on Aerö.

"You promise to give me what is mine?" it asked, displeased with what the ancient Oak had done.

"That, I promise." Aerö nodded.

Skel nodded as well.

"But I have one more thing to ask of you." A shadow crossed the King of the Skrímsli's face. "I want you to take my friends back home. Promise me they won't be harmed, and once the war is over, you shall have what I have promised you."

Nóór's thoughts exploded inside Aerö's mind the second he had voiced his request to Skel. But after weeks of drifting aimlessly, Aerö knew finally where he needed to be. He would not drag his two friends into more danger than he already had. Nóór's yells rippled through Aer'ös weakened body, but he had made his mind.

"I need you to tell Estrelle and Hïldúúr of what we discovered here. They need to know." Aerö sent his thoughts only to Nóór and Ári. His friends did not agree, they wanted to help Aerö fight the war.

"Go back to Undirheim, Nóór," Aerö whispered audibly this time and closed his thoughts to him.

Skel hissed above the racket that the young Beast Lord now made. A hand extended roughly and seized Nóór, its fat fingers wrapping around his whole body, trapping him once more. But unlike earlier, the brute handled him with care. Another Skrímsli scooped Ári in its giant fist before the Beast could bolt. So far, Skel seemed to keep his side of the bargain.

"Let me go!" Nóór's muffled voice escaped the hand that held him.

Aerö felt sorry and ashamed for betraying his two friends, but he knew that nothing but pain and death could come of what he was about to do.

"I will make you keep your promise, heir of Skeggor! And this time I will make sure that you will not trick us like he did," Skel bellowed over the many gathered Skrímsli.

The creatures grunted, dissatisfied. They had all imagined roasting, boiling, eating raw the three intruders, all of which Aerö had seen inside their minds, yet now they had been ordered to escort them; Aerö through the western tunnels while the other two were to be taken to the East and to their home.

Aerö closed his eyes and prayed that he would not collapse. His Petra had been captured by Valdis and held imprisoned in Ophidia. Naively, he had believed that she was safe. He'd nurtured that hope ever since he had been taken from their home in Bells too many weeks before to count. Aerö felt his chest tear open from the guilt he bore for what had happened to his Petra and his friends ever since he melted Woods and set in motion the terrible wheels of fate.

To some extent, he was the one who made the humans lose their homes, and many their own lives. While they walked for weeks across the desert in search of a new place they could settle in, he enjoyed the safety of the lone mountain wrapped around him, protecting him from harm's way. It was he who brought such suffering upon them, and by some sick game of fate, it was also because of him that Petra was now being tortured or was lying dead.

Aerö knew he had to find her despite the Golden Oak's forewarning words. The war will have to wait. The King and Queen will have to wait for him to end them. Aer'ös thoughts emerged from the tempestuous waters of his mind, drawn by Skel's rumbling voice.

"Remember your promise, heir of Skeggor!" Skel's thoughts roared behind him as two large Skrímsli lead the way towards the western edges of their city and beyond.

Aerö tried to think of other things than what was waiting for him at the far end of the tunnel he now walked. He failed painfully.

They had been walking for but a few hours, the two Skrímsli up ahead bearing bright fires, Aerö at the rear, his mind troubled by guilt-ridden thoughts. Every so often, he glanced back at the vanishing tunnel behind him, his eyes unable to see further than a few paces; his ears, however, heard muffled sounds of footsteps. *There must be more Hollowers roaming the dark passages*, Aerö thought.

But as hours passed the small footsteps never failed to follow. Aerö opened his exhausted mind to whatever sneaked behind them.

"We need to stop for a second," he told the two leading Skrímsli. The creatures stopped and stared at Aerö with their beady eyes, their large bodies barely able to walk in tandem through the gallery.

"I know you're there. Come out!" Aerö projected his thoughts into the deep blackness that enveloped all. Louder and louder, the footsteps echoed until they were beside him. The two Skrímsli turned and watched, their free arms ready to grab and squash whatever made the sounds.

A second later, two small shapes walked into the globe of amber light of the two torches. Nóór and Ári smiled and yapped at him.

Before Aerö could ask them why they were not on their way to Undirheim, one of the Skrímsli stretched its giant arm to seize the young Beast Lord.

"Leave him. It's far too late to turn back now," Aerö instructed, and the creature let its heavy arm fall down next to its monstrous body.

"You shouldn't be here, Nóór!"

"Of course I should," said Nóór, defiantly, still with a grin upon his face.

"You should be on your way to Hïldúúr and your mother! They need to know!"

"And they will. We'll figure something once we save your grandmother."

Aerö's heart expanded in his chest. Nóór had proven to be the most genuine of friends. Still, sometimes Aerö wished the Beast Lord would stop and think. They had two heads, Ári and Nóór, yet they repeatedly failed to use them. Deep down, however, Aerö beamed to have them at his side.

The Heart of Men

"Let's start again," came the voice Syll and Erlend associated now with death. Nephthys walked between the black stone altars her three prisoners were chained to. Their naked bodies shivered violently on the ice-cold slabs beneath them. Their very flesh tried to jump off their bones and run from what was about to happen to them again.

For the tenth time in just as many days, the High Priestess, joined by her five followers, materialised inside the room to perform their flesh-tearing, soul-shattering ritual.

"No…not again!" Syll whimpered painfully. She could still feel the unseen wounds Nephthys' blade had cut into her flesh.

Beside her, Erlend shook feebly at the unbreakable chains that held his arms and legs.

Petra lay motionless, awaiting death to take her. But the Priestesses would not allow such a thing. They needed her to draw her grandson out of the Beasts' mountain.

Petra watched Nephthys approach her. The High Priestess' face peered over Petra, her black-inked face gleaming at her from above.

"We'll start with you." Petra's body arched as she tried to raise her head and spit at her old teacher, but they had not had water in days.

"Now, now," said Nephthys, motherly, putting a hand onto Petra's snowy brow. Petra slumped back onto the flat table, defeated. Another day had come and brought with it unspeakable suffering. The three captives shook in fear of the terrible things that were about to happen to them.

"Still no sign of him High Priestess. Are you sure he'll come?" asked one of the black-clad worshipers of Izanami - the Death Goddess.

"I am," said Nephthys in a clear voice. "He should be on his way to save his friends. The Beasts have surely told him. And when he does arrive, full of courage and hope, I shall take him apart bone by bone. The Queen will be so proud!"

The Priestesses widened their cracked lips into grins that looked more terrifying then cheerful. Nephthys lowered her skeletal hand into her robe and produced her soul-severing dagger. Petra closed her eyes.

The blade danced swiftly on her skin. From hands to feet it moved as lightly as a feather, but Petra felt its sting and her own blood flow free onto the altar. Her two companions in death winced and looked away.

For the tenth time her skin and flesh was being peeled away from what was left of her. Ten days and nights in which Petra prayed to Narrū, not for herself, but to keep her Aerö away. She begged to keep her grandson safely beneath the Beasts' mountain until he learned his strength and was ready to fight. But little did she know that all her prayers had been left unanswered and that Aerö was right then somewhere beneath the sea of sand, moving ever closer to Ophidia and her.

Nephthys once again exposed her bones to the flickering light of the few gasping torches. Her arms and legs drained of the blood that, just as the rest of her, wished to escape the Priestesses' macabre rite. On each side of her, the Priestesses performed their skill onto Erlend and Syll. Diligently, Freyja worked her way down Erlend's arms towards his chest and bowels, her swift hand wielding her blade with absolute precision. His flesh split away from the bones that for thirty years had held it anchored in place. He groaned as she stopped above his chest. Just as Petra, Erlend too was being betrayed by his own crimson fluid. It bubbled and poured out of him as if on its accord, sloshing haphazardly away from him and towards the dimple in the ground where it joined Petra and Syll's. Just like ten times before, the Priestesses shook with excitement at the mere thought of bathing in it.

Petra, Erlend, and Syll felt sick from the sole thought of it. It was something unnaturally filthy to collect the blood of living things, worse humans, and bathe in it. But the one thing that made the three gag on their own innards was what happened next. Nephthys would clap her hands and the same blood they washed their naked bodies in, rushed back into their sickeningly shattered frames. Syll even tried to cut her own arm off after the first time that had happened by rubbing it against the edge of the stone slab, but all she managed was to hurt herself without a drop of blood to leave her body. The bitter potion Nephthys poured down their throats was keeping them alive no matter what.

The Priestesses' room echoed with the music of the three captives' shrieks. The eyes of the five black-robed worshipers of Death and Nephthys gleamed brighter and brighter, the more damage they inflicted. They were enjoying it.

Petra, just like Syll and Erlend, could sense the last of her draining onto the black rock altar she was chained on, and with it, the end of the gruesome ritual. Every day when almost no blood was left in them, Nephthys called the rite to an end and bathed with her Priestesses in their warm blood. Then the thunderous clap would come, and everything would end, just not their lives. Again and again, Petra, Syll, and Erlend had to bear the Priestesses' daggers cut them in the most inhuman ways, and every time they would be put together so that the next day they could start once more.

Petra fought her lungs' desire to breathe in more air. She tried with everything she still had in her that had not yet been taken away, to stop herself from living. But nothing could be done against the Dreki's venom. In the chaos of fading screams, Petra could hear Syll and Erlend take deep painful breaths. With her last strength, she turned her eyes on Syll.

The young warrior from Bells stared into the ceiling, gazing absentmindedly at the many chains and fetters above her, her whole broken being waiting either for that loud clap or for death to come. Neither did.

Moments passed with nothing but the three prisoners' grunts to break the eerie silence that had settled in. Petra winced and looked away when the Priestess that had been cutting Syll, peeled away the pink flesh of her chest. Syll's ribs glistened in the flames' flickering light. She groaned like an animal whose body can no longer understand more pain. Petra's eyes stopped briefly on Nephthys who was still working her way up her legs, then turned her head the other way and stared at Erlend. The little blood she had in her, froze in her veins at the gruesome sight.

Freyja was moving the fastest of them all. Having fully exposed Erlend's limbs and his chest, she was now searching elbow-deep through his innards. Erlend roared, as pain worse than anything he had ever felt, tore through his body. He shook and shivered yet the Priestess was not to be dispirited.

Petra begged for the thunderous clap to come and spare her friend. But as Freyja rummaged through his innards, instead of the wished sound, came Nephthys' intoxicated voice.

"Well done, Freyja!" she beamed at her Priestess. "Well done!"

"Is it time, High Priestess?" Freyja asked, pulling herself away from Erlend, her hand emerging from his guts with a guzzling sound. Erlend's body shook violently on the wet stone beneath him.

"Kill me…" he choked on his own words.
"…Please!" Nephthys moved away from Petra and joined Erlend's altar. She smiled at him and placed a hand onto his brow.

"Almost…" she hissed, caressing Erlend's dead-white skin. "We have been learning from them every day, yet we still do not know what makes them…them," she gestured disgusted at Erlend's peeled away, naked body.

"I think it's time we looked a little deeper. Freyja, open up his chest and show me his weak heart!"

"You are too kind, High Priestess!" Freyja hissed and began to cut at Erlend's exposed ribs.

* * *

Two large ships, each with five fully-rigged masts, sailed across an invisible sea. Their taught sails whistled as they cut the night's absolute blackness. Their hulls sent ripples through the star-prickled surface of the waveless waters beneath.

Sara found herself watching them ride in tandem from the bow of one of them. To her eyes, the large vessels appeared to be gliding between the many stars that shone all around them, from above and from below. This was the most surreal of things Sara had ever witnessed. She peeled her eyes away from the mind-stretching view to the ship she stood on. For someone who had lived most of a life at sea, the masted vessels would have seemed the finest. But to Sara, who had never seen enough water to have the need for boats to rule them, least unending seas, the ships were nothing less than a challenge for the mind to comprehend.

The one Sara found herself on, stretched behind her for what looked like a few hundred feet and was wide enough for fifty men to stand abreast. All around her, large square sails flapped and creaked as they worked hard to catch the winds that pushed them. The amount of cloth that dressed the masts enough to keep the Turmenn warm for years. Sara could not but marvel at the gigantic structure she rode into the skies. Everything was still and quiet, with not a soul in sight, and Sara wondered where were all her friends; what happened to the Turmenn?

Finally, after long moments of staring mesmerised at the two vessels, Sara tried to find some answers to where her friends had vanished or how she had come to be on such a ship at sea. No answers came, no matter how hard she searched for them.

She took a deep breath, acknowledging defeat. To her surprise, she found herself wrapped in her own arms. She felt as if her body was about to swell up and explode with a mixture of happiness and heart-wrenching sadness she could not explain. She was alone on a giant ship at sea, sailing among uncountable clusters of stars.

Sara closed her eyes and listened to the wind caress the many sails, until she heard a sound. She turned around, but there was nothing anywhere in sight. She was alone on a ship that did not seem to cover any distance. She closed her eyes again. Once more, the noises came, muffled at first but growing clearer. Sara snapped awake and turned towards the other ship. There, in the distance, through the obscuring cover of the night, Sara could see two shapes move stealthily about the other ship. She forced her eyes to pierce the veil of darkness. Curiously, and guilt riddled, Sara made out Adriana's shape, her bronze-coloured skin almost invisible against the lack of light. Her friend was being chased by someone else, completely shielded from her sight, their joyful play and laughter making Sara's thoughts travel to Erlend, to her love. Then, when she told herself that she had seen enough of their dance, laugh, and whisper, the unknown shape produced a blade and pointed it at Adriana. Sara yelled and waved to save her friend when the glistening blade came down and buried itself deeply into Adriana. Sara watched helplessly as her friend collapsed and died.

Tears swelled in Sara's eyes too fast for her to blink away. She cupped her face into her palms and sobbed. She cried and yelled for anyone to answer, but no one came. Then a shadow moved behind her, and she knew that she would die just as her friend had, stabbed onto the deck of a ship sailing through the stars.

Sara woke up, covered in cold sweat. Her hands moved instinctively to her back to feel the wound the unseen figure had given her. Sara shivered with relief that it had all been just a dream. She pushed herself onto one elbow and peered into the night; no further than two other sleeping bodies. Adriana's olive face shone in the pale light of the moon above. Sara lowered herself back onto her blanket. Her friend was still alive, and so was she, but Sara knew by now, that dreams like those were always more than just her mind's imagination. Just as she had dreamt of Woods and then of the High Counsellor, weeks before they had come true, Sara knew that what she saw was yet to happen. She wrapped her hands around her shivering body, much like she was in her dream before, and cuddled herself to sleep.

For ten long days, the Turmenn had been walking, the desolated, snow-capped Kórr Mountains at their right. They walked in silence with their heads bowed low, their eyes shielded from the sun's bright light, and from each other. The ones that still had families marched in small groups, their hands not once leaving their loved ones, while those who had lost everything wandered alone. No one talked, as none had anything to say. They had lost their homes, fought for their lives, then starved to death, only to find themselves killed by their very own fallen friends and families. They had all lost too much to care, too much to keep on going. Had it not been for Petra, Sara, and the rest of their group, the Turmenn would have long abandoned their dangerous search for a safe heaven. Despite their immeasurable losses and the war that promised to slaughter all of them, the Turmenn stayed together, lead by Sara.

Hopeless and defeated, the Turmenn marched along the sky-high cliffs of the Kórr Mountains, their thoughts sinking into the deepest recesses their minds could muster as their eyes caught glimpses of the gleaming city to their left. There, beyond miles of dunes of golden sand, the Healers' city, Ophidia, shone brighter than the sun above. Their hearts trembled, terrified of those who dwelt inside that city. The Turmenn had the fortune, or the curse, to meet but one of its inhabitants, the very sorcerers they were at war with, inside their makeshift camp; and just a single one of them had almost killed them all. The power they possessed was something the

Turmenn could not even hope to match in battle. All they could do was pray that they would reach the sea unseen.

To make things worse, The Turmenn were now advancing slowly towards Caraa, the only city in Urukk that planted terror in the hearts of those who heard its name regardless if they were of magical blood or not.

"Are you sure this is a good idea?" came Trevor's broken voice.

Sara jumped, startled. Her mind had been lured to her strange dream all day, she tried to remember all the details she could, in the hope that she could make some sense of it. She helplessly relived her own and Adriana's death the hundredth time, and still, she could not see the bearers of the blades. She felt her frustration taking hold of her.

"Oh…" Sara exclaimed, shaking her head and shaking off the black shadows she'd obsessed over since dawn. "What?"

"Going to Caraa — are, you sure this is a good idea?" Trevor repeated, eyeing Sara curiously. She had changed so much since they abandoned Bells that if he had not seen her lead the Turmenn with his own eyes, he would have never believed a word of it.

"You know what they say about the place, right?" he went on, seeing that Sara took her time to gather her scattered thoughts. Little did he know that hers were spread across vast distances, over black seas and in the emptiness between the stars.

Sara took her time to answer. "No, I do not," she said, matter-of-factly, looking into Trevor's face without a hint of her old shyness. With Petra and Erlend's disappearance, something changed inside her. Things that would have made her hide her face and blush, now merely made her smile. While other things that would have made her whole skin crawl, now barely managed to arouse the faintest of emotions. Sara felt as if the shock that came from seeing the old Priestess take with her, so easily, her friends and loved ones, somehow raised a wall around her heart. She felt stronger, yet somehow less than she had been before; she felt as if some crucial part of her was missing.

"None of us has been to Caraa to know what it's like, but if we are to listen to what the Turmenn say about the place, I would not go there."

"Then, why are we? If there is no sanctuary we can find in Caraa, then why kill us marching to that damned place? Petra was wrong about a lot of things…" Sara took her eyes off Trevor and stared in the distance at the sparkling city at their left. She knew too well where he was steering the discussion.

"We are going to Caraa, not because of what Petra believed. We are going there not even because of what I might believe. We are going to Caraa because we have no other place to go. Despite the things the Turmenn say about it, I'd rather try my luck there, than wait for the sorcerers to find us yet again. If one managed to tear us apart, what can an army of them do to us?"

"Maybe we should not run but go back home," said Trevor just as Sara expected. This was not the first time he tried to make her lead the Turmenn back to Bells.

"Trevor! We are not safe in Urukk until there is no war. The only reason we were allowed to live in Bells and Brim and Woods, was because they had other better things to do. But now the time has come for war, and they will search under each rock for every one of us to kill. Caraa is our only hope. I know it, your brothers know it, even Adriana knows it!" Sara added, pointing at the thread of walking Turmenn behind her. The ribbon of slowly moving feet spread for a few miles. Every guardian who still could carry their own weight and that of their rust-eaten swords, were now patrolling the length of the marching Turmenn. All but Sara and Trevor who insisted on walking with her at the front and making sure she was safe. Sara, however, began to think that all he cared and wanted was to change her mind and turn the Turmenn around to their abandoned Bells.

"Leave my brothers out of it," he said coldly. "They have risked their lives too many times for Petra's maddened plan. They're young and blind."

Sara shook her head, determined not to hear another word of it and return to her dream of ships and death. That at least she knew would do its duty and come true as promised. Trevor spent his energy trying to persuade her to abandon their purposeful march instead of helping the terrified Turmenn or his exhausted brothers. Sara blocked him out of her thoughts and returned to her macabre dream.

"As for that Adriana, that filthy-skinned kynlï…" Sara's thoughts returned to Trevor, who was vomiting words faster than she could understand.

"…you better not take us to our deaths because of what she thinks she knows of Caraa!" Trevor hissed and spat onto the dusty road before him.

Sara stared at him, his hateful words registering slowly in her mind. *What a waste,* she thought of Trevor spitting. There were so many who would soon die of thirst, and he wasted the little he had on the road beneath their feet. As things had changed inside her with the losing of Erlend, so had something changed in Trevor with the vanishing of Syll. He, however, had turned weak and somewhat of a fool.

Then all his words finally clicked in place in Sara's mind, and she could feel her blood begin to boil. Was it really his place to judge how others lived their lives? Was it in his power as a man to order how a woman should behave? Had he truly changed so much that he now failed to see the leader and friend Adriana turned out to be? Sara held her breath to smother the tempestuous anger rising from her guts.

"I know how helpless you feel for what happened to Syll, I feel it too, for Erlend and for Petra. I also know that you believe our safety is in Bells and not as far away from it as our legs can take us…" she said stopping before him, her large black eyes staring at him with something Trevor had never seen before.

…"But you have no right to talk like that about the very people who have risked their lives for you! You blame Petra for everything bad that has happened, while you fail to see your own mistakes. You have enough on your mind to keep you up at night without making more enemies out of the ones who kept you safe while you wasted away."

"Still, it's true." Said Trevor calmly. "And you would better stay away from her if you want the Turmenn to respect you! Think of what they're saying about you fraternising with a damned kynlï."

"I don't want to hear another word of it, Trevor! As long as I am to lead these poor people to safety, I shall decide who I trust and who I want to keep close to my side. You, however, are not one of them. Go help your brothers, Trevor, keep an eye on those you so blatantly want to drive back to Bells and certain death. Go weep and think of Syll and everything she stood for." Sara barked and resumed her walk, breathless but proud; pleased that Trevor did not attempt to follow her. He had walked the line too many times, but now he'd stepped well over it.

Adriana turned out to be the most genuine of friends Sara had ever had. Her bravery and wisdom, her humour was what made her who she was, not that she was or was not a kynlï.

Sara took a few deep breaths and forced her thoughts to once again resume their pursuit of answers. Their sole purpose was to make some sense out of her foretelling dream.

"What was that about?" said a voice from behind, which made Sara jump — startled. Again, she had to pause her restless mission to find who the envisioned killers were. Adriana stared at her with a wide grin upon her olive face. Sara could not help but smile back at her.

"Well? What did he want?"

"You know what he always wants," said Sara shaking her head, exhausted. Trevor had made her burn with such a fierce passion, she now felt lightheaded and upset.

"How are the Turmenn? And are your warriors coping?"

"A few still try to leave the groups and head back to their homes, but most are too hungry and too broken to even raise their heads. They will be useless if we are found again," Adriana said slowly, wiping her sweaty brow with the back of her hand.

"There's something I must ask you and something I need you to promise me, Adriana," said Sara after a few moments in which they walked in silence, their eyes set as they had been for hours, on the gleaming city of the Healers at their left.

"Of course…anything!" said Adriana quickly, but in her voice, a shadow could be felt. She wondered if her friend had finally gathered her strength to ask her what she was.

"I need to know you trust me and my decision to continue our march to Caraa."

"Absolutely!" snapped Adriana, taking offence at Sara's words, but also feeling a pang of relief at her question. It was not what she had feared, but also wished to share with Sara.

"I trust you wholly! As for Caraa, that place is vile and a good deal dangerous, but if we camp outside its walls and only a few of us go inside for food and ask of shelter, the Turmenn should be safe. I know they are nervous heading there, I hear them talk with terror in their voices, but I agree with you as I did with Petra. There's no other place we can go to and ask for help." Sara thought about it for a few moments, glad the trust she placed in her was mutual.

"I need you to promise me something," she added gazing into Adriana's eyes.

"Anything."

"The time will come when I will ask of you to do something for me without you seeing why. When that time comes, I need you to do it unquestioningly. Promise me, Adriana."

Tarn's daughter thought about the leap of faith Sara was asking her to take, then answered plainly.

"I promise. But you must promise me something as well. When you will feel you can no longer bear all this responsibility and worry, you will let me help you carry them."

Sara nodded but did not say another word. Although she fully trusted Adriana, she was not yet ready to tell the world about her visions of the gruesome things that would most certainly turn true. Not yet.

"What do you think awaits us in Caraa?" Sara said finally, desperately wanting to cast away the silence that had fallen over them.

"The Turmenn say a lot of things, but half of them simply cannot be true. We all grew up with frightening stories of bad children being sold in Caraa. Or of how if you have gold, anything can be acquired. Some even say that sorcerers live at the mercy of their wealthy human masters in the city. And that cannot be true." Adriana said, smiling at the many ridiculous things the Turmenn said they knew about Caraa.

"I see one problem then." And Adriana turned her dark eyes to her friend who looked as if she was trying to remember something long forgotten. "We do not have much gold."

"That would have been a problem anywhere we might have gone. Gold is the only thing that can guarantee your safety. But we will manage something. We still have plenty of able hands we can offer in Caraa as payment." Sara did not look convinced.

"I hope so, Adriana, I hope so, or we…" Sara said softly, choking on her breath as her eyes caught sight of something shimmering far in the distance.

Adriana stared at the same spot as well, her face painted with worry and excitement. From the small hill the two had conquered, they could now make out the outline of the Taðr Sea ahead, and on its shore, upon the tongue of land they had been following, Caraa twinkled in the distance, a black mark upon the shiny surface of the endless sea.

"That must be it," said Sara voicelessly, measuring the distance that still stood between them and the source of food and temporary shelter they had been pursuing for many weeks.

"Wow!" was all that Adriana managed to utter. "I cannot wait to have my fill of fish!" she added grinning, her tongue already licking at the imagined taste upon her lips.

"How long do you think it'll take us to reach it at our current pace?"

"Under a week I reckon…" said Adriana thoughtfully.

"I hope they'll last that long." Adriana followed Sara's gaze behind them at the hopeless Turmenn walking in their wake.

"We will," said Adriana with newfound vigour. The taste of food, be it imagined, was enough to make her twice as determined.

* * *

"Please stop! Please!" Syll howled at the Priestesses who now all gathered around Erlend's table. They were about to witness the revealing of what made the humans tick. Freyja wielded her black dagger with such skill, her hand seemed to dance above Erlend's cut open chest.

"Freyja! I beg of you! We used to be friends! Please stop!" croaked Petra at the sorceress, her own gruesome wounds forgotten. She tried to lift herself in order to see better, but her body disobeyed her entirely. All her flesh and muscles had been severed from her bones by Nephthys. All Petra could do was sit and watch, a husk of her former self, a discarded emptied container of everything that made her, her. Freyja did not as much as lift her eyes from Erlend's unravelling white ribs.

Gasps and hisses echoed through the nightmare-inducing room of the Priestesses. Four of them and Nephthys watched with unwavering concentration at Freyja skilfully present Erlend's most inner parts to the world.

Syll and Petra sobbed, unrestrained at the helplessness that clawed at the only thing that had been left intact — for now. Their minds.

"Don't worry, Petra…" said Nephthys without taking her eyes off Erlend's opened body, "…if I fail to find the thing that makes these apes believe they rule these lands inside his heart, I will crack open their filthy skulls and find my answers there."

Petra and Syll cried in silence at the horror of the High Priestess' words.

Erlend stared into the fading ceiling far above him, the tendrils of chains that stretched towards him morphing into helping hands before his failing eyes. He tried, fruitlessly, to raise his own to meet them and accept their aid. Just like Petra's, the flesh that used to grant him movement now spread all around him motionless. He stared and stared and stared absentmindedly towards the waving hands descending from the ceiling, his mind no longer capable of feeling pain or cold. Erlend was slowly falling into death's welcoming embrace, and he welcomed it too. The last thing that formed inside his mind before Freyja put her hands inside his chest and lifted the beating organ, was Sara's beautiful face. He thought of her longingly and hoped that his memories would not follow him in death for if they did, it would be worse than hell to be away from her until she joined him many years later. Or so he hoped.

Another wave of gasps emerged from the five Priestesses as Freyja presented them the beating heart of men. As if mesmerised by its rhythmic throbs, they all stretched their skeletal hands to touch it, to feel the life that flowed through it.

Syll and Petra choked on their guts as they pushed with their last forces to escape the Priestesses' prison on their own as their sentient custodians proved unwilling to allow. The two captives clenched their jaws and waited for their innards to give up.

A second passed, a minute, then what felt like hours, while the sorceresses touched in awe at the pale organ. Erlend drifted peacefully into a welcomed sleep.

When Petra and Syll gave up their hope to see their friend ever come back, to walk among the living, Nephthys' thunderous clap boomed.

Ecstatic, the Priestesses undid their robes and let them fall off their old naked bodies as they let themselves be kissed by the three prisoners' blood. They moaned and hissed with pleasure as the crimson fluid covered their whole frames.

Another clap reverberated through the chamber, and the blood began its slow return to their broken vessels, gurgling, bubbling as it did so. Then the third and final clap came, and Petra, Syll, and Erlend's bodies sealed again to hold it all inside. The prisoners felt nauseous from having their soiled blood back in their frames. Petra had hoped, as did Syll, that the Priestesses would let them die this time and end the sickening cycle their existence had been reduced to. Erlend, at least, had been spared from coming back to the life none of them wished to live. Or so Petra and Syll hoped.

On the other side of Petra, Erlend coughed and stirred. His sacrifice was not yet deemed sufficient. The three of them cried in silence, not from pain, but from the thought of a new day that promised to come with renewed strength and unfathomable horrors. They would sooner lose their minds than their no longer wanted lives.

In their last moments of consciousness, Erlend thought of Sara, Syll, and Trevor while Petra prayed once more to Narrū to keep her grandson safely away from her.

Aerö, however, was closer to her than she even imagined.

Wings of Doom

Do not worry for the wars of men,

Panic when the Gods decide to join the fray.

-Anonymous

The muffled noises of the gathering armies hundreds of feet below drifted eerily into the King and Queen's throne room. Arnleaf Uriel sat on his velvet seat pleased with the speed with which his many sorcerers answered his call to arms. His right hand caressed, lovingly, the purple stone that hung heavily from his neck. Arnleaf dropped his gaze upon his hand and winced in pure disgust. Where once was smooth skin adorned with rings and bracelets of the brightest gold and gems, now loose flesh hung on his ancient bones. He turned his free hand over and peered at it, sickened. He missed the times when his beloved Valdis held, trapped inside her body, countless souls of humans and of Beasts, and wondered how many days or weeks would his eyes have to bear the gruesome image of his decaying self. Should she restore their youth with that of sorcerers, of his own subjects, he pondered, revolving his bright gem inside his palm. *Could it be done?* He asked himself with no trace of guilt, but curiosity inside his heart.

Like the fairest music sung by Sirens, the roaring masses far below tickled his senses. Their rhythmic cries lulled his troubled mind in and out of sleep. The time to purge the realm of humans and Beasts had finally come, and once their slaughtered bodies turned to ash, his millennia-long plan would be at last complete. Arnleaf dreamed of the moment his unstoppable army would roar with satisfaction for their victory; their voices singing in his ears the sweetest music known to him. Arnleaf closed his eyes pleased with his plan.

As the world distanced itself from him, moving ever further from his throne, all its sounds of marching feet and clashing swords and cries for battle fled with it. The King drowned into an endless sea of perfect silence; the lack of all the things the world was made of moments earlier, soothing his flesh and mind. Dreams soon raised their bleached-white sails and took their hulls filled with wonders to him. They came and went as silent as the sea they sailed on, delivering their crates of victory and praise. Arnleaf smiled and revelled in the overflowing contents of the coffers.

But once he had his most desired wishes stacked around him like a fort, ready for him to pry them open and then eat and drink their glorious contents, a woman's voice sent ripples through the endless sea of peaceful nothingness, casting away the ships and all their cherished loads. Arnleaf Uriel opened his eyes with the pain of losing his whole kingdom.

Before him, Valdis' translucent figure shimmered as she approached his throne. Arnleaf yawned saddened at his loss.

"My love!" she cried, dancing towards him, her green dress billowing around her visible pale frame. Old as she was, she still held an iron grip around her timeless beauty.

"My Queen…" Arnleaf responded, shaking his head and all the joyful dreams with it.

"I have great news!" she shrieked happily, moving towards the arched window that welcomed the muffled cries of their training armies far below.

"Come join me," she commanded, laughing girlishly.

Arnleaf ordered his body to obey his Queen's request. He moved slowly from his seat to the tall window Valdis peered through. Only once he was beside her, he noticed the white crow perched on her shoulder. His eyes instantly flared with curiosity.

"Has the boy answered your trap, my love?" Arnleaf wrapped his arms around his Queen, which made the soulless bird flap its bleached wings at him, then settled onto the window ledge in front of them.

Valdis smiled broadly at the golden forest of towers before her.

"They have her. My Priestesses have taken Eldur's mother to Ophidia!" she sang, wiggling herself to face her King. Their eyes stared happily into each other's as an unvoiced euphoria bound them together.

"Soon, my love, the wretched boy will try to save her and I shall have my sweet revenge for what he did to us," she said softly. "I will feast on his filthy little soul!"

"The time to send the armies to scour our lands is almost upon us. Once they are unleashed, nothing will stop them." Arnleaf smiled and kissed his Queen lovingly. Their jewelled brows remained in contact for what felt like years, their hands entwined, their hearts throbbing against one another's. The two delighted in their shared exuberance, their tongues flickered between their lips for the sweet victory they could already taste.

* * *

The days crawled by for Aerö, Nóór, and Ári as they followed the two Skrímsli through the bowels of the world. It became increasingly more difficult for the three to measure how many days and nights they had been walking down the smooth tunnels the Skrímsli dug during the aeons they had lived beneath the surface. Still, they tried, counting their meals and their periods of sleep and asking their two guides.

But for the Hollowers who lived millennia, time had lost its usefulness, so their vague answers proved more confusing than of help. Repeatedly, they claimed that the great veins of burning amber would not have grown at all since they began their journey, or that but one *hnefi* of gold would have been smelted since.

To Aerö, Nóór, and Ári, none of it made any sense, so they kept keeping track of all their meals and how often they were allowed to sleep.

Every now and then, Aerö adventured to ask the two Skrímsli other questions that could give him the barest understanding of the amount of time that flowed unnoticed by them, but the more meals and sleeps they had, the creatures' answers also grew in woolliness. Their latest answer to his relentless questions of time had left him with more questions than facts.

"Half as much as from Dragnar to Sragnar and twice from Gruhr to Rruhr!" one of the Skrímsli roared at Aerö, clearly annoyed by his continuous prodding at their minds.

Aerö backed away and sat next to his friends, who wolfishly devoured the little food they had. Many days had died above the surface, Aerö thought, by counting on his fingers how many sleeps they had, since the food they had filled their pockets inside the Beasts' Lair was finished. Long gone were the many different types of nuts and fruit they took with them when they fled Undirheim. Long gone were the tasteless but filling mushrooms Aerö used to leave on his plate to spoil. As were the fresh berries. He had almost forgotten their taste. During their endless walk through the galleries that time forgot, all they had to eat after their own pilfered supplies had finished were the lichens that grew from the tunnels' ceiling in great beards. The boys forced the dry stuff down their throats and winced in pain as the lichens clawed at their insides unhappy to be swallowed. At least they had plenty of water to drink and wash.

Worse it was for Ári, whose rumbling stomach craved the taste of meat. Yet all he had to nibble on were the same dry and bitter-tasting lichens Nóór and Aerö struggled to consume.

The Skrímsli however feasted on the grey stuff with great relish. From what Aerö could tell from listening to the two Skrímsli's thoughts and feelings, they relied on this monotonous diet.

Another cycle of struggling to eat grey lichens and then rest, washed over Aerö, Nóór, and Ári, and with it the day they marked. By Aerö's reckoning, the three of them, lead by the two Hollowers, had been navigating through the endless Skrímsli dug tunnels for about ten days. Aerö could only imagine the days and nights of worry Estrelle must have had thinking of her only son outside the home she had hoped would protect him. But at least she knew of his wild plans to find the Skrímsli and ask them for help. Just as Skeggor Skalidur had done four thousand years prior. Now Aerö wished to bring together all those who had lived in fear or forgotten by the outside world, to fight alongside him against the King and Queen's gathering armies.

Nóór's parents, however, had been taken by surprise by their son's decision to abandon them and their kind for Aerö. Finndôra must have clawed at the small gap her son had vanished through with her bare hands while Har-úgur, her Feond, struck the cavern's smooth, black walls with all its might. But Aerö knew, from the sheer thickness of the wall they had to cross to reach the caves behind, that neither Finndôra nor Har-úgur stood a chance of breaking through the gap.

Another cycle came and went without a change in what the boys saw, ate or felt about their ever dark and gloomy surroundings. For what they knew, they could be right outside Ophidia or still an immeasurable distance from it.

* * *

Sara woke up in the dead of night, drenched to the skin with sweat. She had yet again cried herself awake. The often gruesome and always terrifying dreams haunted her every night like a famished animal of prey. She wiped her brow and forced her shivering body to sit up.

Bitten by cold, she wrapped her only blanket higher around her sodden frame and stared over the spread of sleeping bodies around her. She watched them stir, and listened to their peaceful breathing. The rhythmic rise and fall of their chests soothed her. A large moon moved lazily across the inky sky, its silvery glow offering Sara just enough light to see about her. She cupped her face in her cold hands and thought about the dream that never failed to awake her.

As always, the first to trouble her had been the waves of puppets, dead bodies summoned to fight for their Masters, that blackened the desert's sands for as far as she could see. The wall of death their decomposing bodies formed, encroached upon the Turmenn from all sides. An island of golden sands was all there was in the middle of the swelling sea of putrefied flesh and bones, of ragged clothes and swords. Defenceless and hopeless the Turmenn awaited their end at the hands of those they'd lost in the battles they but luckily survived. Their brothers and lovers, their fathers and sons, gathered around the crying Turmenn, their hands outstretched not in a gesture of help but bearing swords ready to claim their lives. Sara saw from where she stood at the centre of

the Turmenn, the advancing slaughtered bodies of
Alistair and Taro, but also Petra, Syll and Erlend's
coming for her. She tried to cry, to call their names, but
nothing could be heard but the rumbling of the world
tearing itself to pieces.

The very daylight seemed to flee from what was
coming for the Turmenn. The skies darkened, the very air
thickened and buzzed. And then they came.

From immeasurable heights, the clouds began to swirl
and tangle as they plummeted towards the ground and
the frightened Turmenn far beneath them. They sped
towards their victims like two pitch-black arrows, rotating
against each other as they fell, dragging the very
blackened clouds after them.

The armies on the ground never stopped moving, the
Turmenn's dead friends and families were now but feet
away from them. Another moment and their swords
would eat their way through their terror-stricken flesh.

Further and faster the two bringers of death fell, the
noise of their descent reverberating through the very
fabric of the world. Sara stared at the falling skies above
her with heart-wrenching fear. Within seconds the sea of
dead bodies, many of whom she recognised, and the
falling angels would converge, and all the Turmenn
would be decimated in one great massacre. Sara could not
take her eyes from the sky, tearing itself. When they were
but feet above the gathered Turmenn, the two angels

unwrapped their long black wings and blocked the little light that still dared to fall upon the ground. Death came swift and painless.

A cold hand rested on Sara's shoulder, the unexpected touch pulling so forcefully on her thoughts, they almost snapped. She turned around in horror to what had crept behind her while her mind relived the dreadful dreams that chased her every moment. Sara let go of the blanket her hands held and turned to face whoever preyed upon her.

"What's wrong?" said Adriana in a mere whisper, and Sara felt her body melt with welcomed relief.

"You've been staring at the sky as if afraid it might come down upon us. Is everything alright?" Sara pulled together her scattered thoughts and nodded.

"It's nothing…" she lied, "…couldn't sleep." Adriana raised one eyebrow, and Sara knew her friend did not believe her.

"I hear you wake up every night, Sara. You scream and fight in your sleep, then you stare into the distance, troubled. What is happening?"

Sara dropped her eyes onto the ground and clenched her jaw. She was afraid her body would give up and blurt it all.

"It's nothing, really," she lied again, then turned her back to Adriana and stared at the bright orange light of fires radiating from Caraa. The city Petra, and now Sara, lead the Turmenn to, was but a few days away. Adriana tightened her grip around Sara's shoulder.

"Try and get some rest, Sara. We'll soon arrive at Caraa. A place like that, even if it proves to be but half as dangerous as the Turmenn believe, will require all our strength."

Sara lowered herself back onto the cold ground and cuddled herself to sleep. Her mind exploded with a thousand thoughts, the second Adriana returned to her own blanket. She thought of Petra and of Syll, but once her mind decided, unwavering, to pour itself over the memory of Erlend, Sara could not contain her tears any longer. She sobbed and sobbed until she shed all the tears she had. Pained, cold and terrified of what her dreams foretold, Sara let her mind be pulled into a restless sleep, flooded with the dreams she could not stop from having. She bit her lip and dived into nightmares laced with death.

In but two days, the Turmenn would reach Caraa, and her dreams would frighteningly start to come true. The Turmenn's troubles were just about to begin.

Sin City

Estrelle prowled through the winding tunnels that lead from her chambers to the lower levels and the training grounds. In her Wolf form, she moved like a wisp of smoke through the deserted hallways, the white of her fur barely visible against the dark, unlit walls. Since Aerö ran away from Undirheim, all the lamps that had dotted the insides of the Beasts' Lair were now gone. The Beasts Lords and their Beasts did not need them to navigate through the maze of pitch-black passageways. Estrelle's mind ran through a dark labyrinth of its own making, chasing thoughts and answers, thinking of Aerö and of Nóór and their dangerous decision to go find the Skrímsli.

But the Queen of the Beast Lords knew that her people would not have agreed with her son's plan. They feared those very beings just as much as they feared Arnleaf and Valdis. None but Finndôra wished to ask the Hollowers for their help, and even if she had known that her own son wished to follow Aerö, she would have squashed his plan most brutally. Estrelle growled as she thought of Aerö. Many days had passed since they'd escaped Undirheim and by now the boys would have either found the Skrímsli or died in the labyrinth of unknown tunnels. Estrelle relived the chase after Nóór and Aerö, and how she tried to stop them. She had agreed to allow Aerö to look for the creatures, but she did not think Nóór would dare to follow him. She was wrong in thinking that the young Beast Lord would let his friend take on such a dangerous task all by himself.

Now, because she'd failed to stop Nóór from leaving Undirheim, the Beast Lords questioned her leadership with renewed vigour; most of them, led by Finndôra, demanded she give her crown to Hïldúúr.

Estrelle sped down tunnels devoured by darkness, towards the training grounds where her people had gathered, she knew, to plan her removal from the throne. She had ruled them well, for many centuries, and was determined not to allow them to fool themselves that by appointing Hïldúúr as their King, the real danger they all faced would vanish. They were at war, and soon Arnleaf and Valdis would hit them with the might of their unstoppable armies. They stood no chance against such an enemy. Their only option was to train and hope that Aerö would succeed in finding help. Without him, they would not survive the first day of the Great War.

Estrelle plunged into the thickening air that gathered, the deeper she went. Hot and stuffy, the darkness before her grew like an invisible wall, determined to slow her, to stop her. Estrelle growled as the mountain itself appeared to have sided with Finndôra. She ran faster.

Inside the training grounds, away from their Queen, the Beast Lords argued angrily about their future. Half agreed with Finndôra and her plan to have a new King to rule them, while the other half still gave Estelle their full support. The training grounds reverberated with their thunderous voices.

"She cares more about her son than for our future!" boomed Finndôra at the gathered few dozen Beast Lords.

"She failed to protect our precious young ones! We are few already. If we are to survive, we mustn't lose them!"

"Weren't you, too, in Nóór's pursuit?" asked a female Beast Lord from the opposing group.

"He was your son, after all! Shouldn't you be just as guilty?"

"How dare you?" Finndôra hissed, and her large Feond behind her stomped its massive feet. "That boy of hers tricked our son into following him. He must have used his skill on our Nóór."

The gathered Beast Lords and their Beasts hissed and growled.

"And weren't you the one to suggest that we ask for help?" Finndôra darkened with rage.

"This is not helping," said Hïldúúr, calmly, from among those who still put their trust in Estrelle.

"Have we gathered here like vermin, hiding from the same Queen who kept you safe for centuries and who is The First's daughter, to point fingers and pass blame? Yes, our Nóór is gone, and partly the Queen is to be blamed, but we all share that guilt. This…" he added, pointing at the Beast Lords and their Beasts, "…is not about our son. Neither is it about who should have stopped the young ones from leaving our home. This is about our future and the war that promises to end us all. If Estrelle threatens our survival, then we must choose a new leader, but I will not agree to put another on that throne because Nóór chose to follow Aerö." He boomed angrily.

"He did not choose!" Finndôra roared. "He used his skill on our Nóór! He made him follow him!"

"That is not true, Finndôra," came Estrelle's rough voice as she entered the large chamber in her White Wolf form.

The Beast Lords turned in shock to face the Queen they were so ready, moments prior, to betray. Half of them, including Hïldúúr, bowed their heads at her. She lowered hers.

"Had you been listening to your own son, Finndôra, you would understand that Nóór would have fought his way out of this mountain if he had to."

"Why…why are you here?!" Finndôra spat.

"I am still your Queen, Finndôra! Know your place!" the White Wolf growled, the red cross scar upon Estrelle's forehead glistened in the orange light of the great veins.

"You…" Finndôra began.

But Estrelle had heard enough of Nóór's mother.

"You should be training, all of you! Not fighting for power. We have a war to fight and if the Gods allow, survive. But if my throne is what you all desire, then once the war is over, you shall have it. Until then, prepare for war, sharpen your skills, and worry not about who sits upon that seat."

"You will kill us all!" hissed Finndôra determined to show she no longer regarded Estrelle as her Queen.

"You are wrong again. The sorcerers will hunt us down and kill us all. They are the ones you should be fearing."

Finndôra took a step closer to Estrelle and Har-úgur threateningly followed, but this time Hïldúúr intervened. He wrapped his hand around her arm and held her put.

"Enough! The Queen is right. We should be training for what lies ahead. If we survive this war, then we shall choose another leader, but until then, she is our Queen! Show your respect!"

And the Beast Lords bowed their heads, including Finndôra, who mockingly lowered hers. She might have lost today, but when the war was but a bad memory, she would make Estrelle give her throne to Hïldúúr. If not sooner.

* * *

Exhausted, the Turmenn followed the long tongue of land that stretched into the Taðr Sea. They had been marching with their eyes glued to the large city before them for two long days, excited to have reached its walls, but also anxious of what lay behind them.

Sara walked ahead of the fear-stricken Turmenn, along with Adriana, Ishim, and Ezkiel. The four women let their skin be kissed by the sun's warm rays while fragrant winds caressed their faces. They enjoyed the change in scenery. The tall, barren mountains were far behind, replaced by endless spans of bluest water.

They stared at it in awe. None of the Turmenn had ever seen so much water rise and fall in waves, the sea's gentle murmur soothing their strained frames and senses.

"There's so much of it," said Adriana, mesmerised by the movement of water sparkling in her eyes. "Does it ever end?"

"I…I do not know," said Sara, thinking of the maps she had seen in Petra's forbidden basement. None of them showed any land other than Urukk. Her eyes searched the vast glinting distances for land. All Sara saw, like Adriana and the two sisters, was more blue water but also the likes of something she had dreamt. Sara felt a shudder travel through her body as she remembered the gut-churning nightmare. Nauseous, she peeled her eyes away from the Taðr Sea's infinite span and stared at the narrow stretch of land before her.

In front of them, Caraa's walls rose short and broken, an unwelcoming sight for the few hundred souls that hoped they would bless them with safety. They advanced, blistered and broken, towards the city that slowly revealed itself to be more dangerous than their promised salvation.

"What do we do?" came Daniel and Sam's rough voices. They had been herding the Turmenn for weeks, keeping them moving together at the same pace, chasing the few who tried to run away and even carrying the few who simply could not bear their own weight any longer. Sara smiled at them and welcomed them next to her.

"Have some food and rest, boys," she said, putting her hands on the boys' shoulders. "We still have a few hours of walking before we camp."

"We're fine!" said the boys, shrugging, but their bloodshot eyes and heavy shoulders told a different story. They were exhausted.

"We need a plan," Sam said, and Daniel nodded knowingly.

"We can't just walk in there, all hundreds of us. Sam is right, we need a plan."

"For once, I agree with the boys," said Adriana, smiling at them. Her awe-inspiring beauty radiated in the bright sun.

Sam felt his blood rise from his feet towards his torso.

Daniel shifted his gaze from his brother's stupefied look, to the labyrinthian collection of derelict buildings before them.

"Fine…" Sara caved in, smiling at the boys, yet her eyes betrayed the pity her heart felt for Sam. "…I will tell you what we plan to do, but after that, you will take it easy and replenish your strength. Agreed?"

The boys nodded sheepishly.

"We will camp outside the city's walls, close enough to be able to take refuge behind them if anything happens. While the Turmenn eat and rest and tend to their worn bodies, a few of us will go into Caraa to find more food and water, but also transport to the southern plains."

The boys and Adriana turned their eyes to her.

Ishim and Ezkiel looked at each other with something that resembled worry in their eyes.

None of them knew Petra's whole plan, but Sara.

"If you look across the sea, you can sometimes see large ships with many masts bobbing purposefully across the waves. By their size, I say we need no more than two."

Sam and Daniel stared at her, unable to speak.

Adriana raised her eyebrow at her, the very gesture Sara had grown to recognise as suspicion.

"How do you intend to pay for them?" came Trevor's voice from behind and all five of them tensed.

"We must have something they need. Those ships are our safest, fastest way to reach true safety. We will have them take us to Stórvatn even if it means giving their owners all our possessions."

"And if all our possessions are not enough? Then what?" Trevor asked, his words seething with venom for Sara's refusal to agree with him and take the Turmenn back to Bells. If she could not see sense, then he would do everything within his power to prove just how wrong she was. The Turmenn deserved to know, and they earned a life away from war and death and everything that Petra, and now Sara, had brought upon them.

"We will find a way, Trevor," Sara spoke softly and moved closer to Adriana so that he could join between her and his younger brothers.

Trevor accepted her offer.

"We should try and sell some of the things we have no need for, to begin with."

"We have their swords…they ought to be worth something," said Sam and Daniel, completing each other's thoughts.

"We also have many good skills, we might be able to get paid for them." Came another voice from behind the line Sara and the others formed at the forefront of the marching Turmenn.

They all turned to find Grov hauling his large body towards them. Sam and Daniel welcomed their friend between them. They all nodded, but did not say another word. They feared Grov might actually be right and that they may need to consider living in Caraa for a few days or weeks until they had enough to pay for the two ships Sara told them about.

"You seem to know a lot about these ships even though you have never seen the sea before," Adriana whispered in Sara's right ear.

Sara felt her blood freeze inside her veins. How long will she be able to conceal her unexplainable, surreal dreams? She would only tell them if she had no other way of keeping the Turmenn safe. If she was what she thought she was, even if only partly, the Turmenn would not follow her, and everything Petra had done, and Erlend, and now her, would be in vain.

The group's voices died away, and they walked in silence. Their eyes moved left and right, and up and down across the widening city before them, their bodies bruised and broken, their minds racing at what lay ahead, and at the ones they'd lost to get there. Erlend, Syll, Petra and Tarn were all summoned in the memories of their loved ones, as were Alistair and Taro.

Good people, loved leaders, husbands and fathers, cherished friends; all had made the final sacrifice so that the rest of them could find safety. To everyone who did as much as gaze towards the city, it was clear that Caraa was not the place they sought.

A few hours later, Sara and Adriana gazed doubtfully at the span of walls before them; old and ill-cared for; worse, collapsing in many places. Caraa was not a place that relied on its fences to keep the myriad of souls that lived within them safe.

"At least they do not seem to need to be defended," said Adriana wearily.

Sara nodded, uncertain. "I hope you're right…"

"We'll have everyone gathered in a few more hours. Ishim and her sister, the boys too, are bringing everybody here."

"Good. Once they all have a place to stretch their legs and eat the food they still have left, you and the boys will come with me inside. Ishim and Ezkiel and the rest of the warriors will stay behind and make sure the Turmenn are safe."

Adriana nodded, her eyes fixed on the shabby-looking Caraa before her.

"Are you sure we will find what we need in here?" asked Adriana softly, and for the first time, Sara noticed doubt in her voice.

"I am. We will manage to get those ships and sail to Stórvatn, I am sure of it."

"Alright, then."

A sea of shallow, decrepit houses stretched before them, none looking strong enough to invite someone in. All teemed with beggars, whores, and dealers of raaf, a black powder that promised to take away the hunger and enhance the senses. The more Sara saw as she walked towards the harbour, the more she realised that Caraa was worse than the Turmenn had feared.

The night was fast approaching, quiet and cunning, seeping into the city from behind the walls, encroaching onto the defenceless souls that resided within. Sara, joined by Adriana, Sam, and Daniel, moved between the abandoned-looking houses, watching as they came to life one by one, the moment night engulfed them. Lights flickered behind their boarded windows; candles, red and bright, spewed their light and called for those who waited for their rebirth to move towards them from the shadows like blind moths.

"What is this place?" asked Daniel, tightening his grip around the hilt of his sword.

Adriana looked sideways to Sara who did not flinch,

"They're brothels, whorehouses," she announced plainly.

Daniel could see Sam's face ignite.

The city spread for miles in all directions, filthy streets upon filthy streets swarming with insects and murky people, the kind with which the Turmenn's leaders did not wish to deal.

"We'll never find anything like this. We need to separate. Sam and Daniel, you go and find more about this place, and if possible, find food. Sara and I will make our way towards the harbour. We'll meet back at the camp by dawn."

"Are you sure splitting is a good idea?"

"As long as you stay out of trouble and don't promise anything to anyone, you should be fine," said Adriana, putting a hand onto Daniel's shoulder. "Remember, boys, this is not Bells. Do not interfere with the ways the locals deal with things, and absolutely do not pick fights with them. Understood?"

"Of course," replied both Sam and Daniel.

"We'll see you back at the camp."

The boys nodded and turned left onto a wide street that seemed to lead to better lit, better-populated places. Sara and Adriana continued their brisk walk towards the harbour and its many ships moored for the night.

"What should we do?" asked Daniel, looking around at the desolate, dark streets that led away from the one they walked on.

"We should find an inn. That would be the best place to find people to talk to."

Ahead, shined bright, taller buildings. Moments later, the streets began to fill with people, slowly at first with hooded figures in dark alleyways snarling at them, then with white-haired people that dared to walk within the light.

Sam and Daniel quickened their pace towards them. Hordes of people moved about, in and out of bright-lit places up ahead. The two brothers were now close enough to see, among others, the white-haired people enter one of the larger buildings they had seen in Caraa. Sam and Daniel followed.

Faces stared and pointed at them as they walked towards the busy inn. Women dressed in nothing but loose shirts that did not manage to conceal one thing, waved at them invitingly. Daniel pulled on his brother's arm as he failed to unglue his gaze from them.

The large inn spewed bright orange light from lamps fixed onto its peeling walls, and through large windows that allowed the boys to see inside. Above, tens of smaller windows glowed bright red.

"Are you old enough to come in here, boys?" barked a voice, and the two boys turned to see a large man staring at them scrutinisingly.

Sam opened his mouth to speak, but his voice failed to answer his summoning.

"Of course you are, lads!" the man boomed and slapped the two boys on the shoulders. "Come in! Come in!" The boys followed reluctantly, and stepped inside the brightly-lit inn. Sam and Daniel instantly felt their bodies freeze in place at the sight before them.

What shocked them was not the vast space that revealed itself to them the moment they entered the inn, nor the large tables sunken in the ground so that the paths that webbed between them and the bar were almost at the same level as them. Nor were the young boys and girls that carried plates and mugs around the tables, some too young for Sam and Daniel to be comfortable seeing working in a place like this. What made the boys fight the urge to turn around and run were the hundreds of Healers, Elementals, and humans that occupied the many seats. To their horror, the two realised that those they had followed inside, the old, white-haired figures they had seen roaming the streets, were in fact Sorcerers. Sam and Daniel looked around, waiting to be noticed. Their hands were clamped around their swords' hilts with such force, they turned dark purple. No one did as much as glance at them.

"Please follow me," called a young woman dressed from head to toe in sparkling, beaded golden chains.

Daniel turned around to face the girl. Sam stared at her stupefied. She might have been the most beautiful girl Sam had ever laid his eyes on despite the sheer number of striking young women that worked there. The two boys quickly followed her to their table, sunken like the rest of them, cleared of plates and mugs but ready to be filled again.

"The main attraction will be presented soon. Would you like something to eat or drink perhaps?" the girl added, casting a smile that would have crumbled the bravest of men.

"Two mugs of mead…please," Sam stammered nervously. Daniel looked at his brother, dumbstruck.

"We have no coins, brother!" he hissed, coughing into his fist. An extra measure to make sure that no one heard him. "What are you thinking?"

"Well, we are here now. We might enjoy ourselves a little," Sam added, smiling mindlessly at the shimmering figure of the black-haired, olive-skinned girl.

To Daniel, the girl resembled Adriana; slim and strong, dark-skinned, and incredibly beautiful.

Sam seemed not to notice, or even to remember Adriana for that matter. He gazed mesmerised at the girl who took their order and his heart, and left with them across the room.

Only when a party of three other people joined their table was Sam able to break the spell. Tall and white-haired, the three must not have been older than their brother Trevor. The boys' hands searched urgently below the table for their swords.

The sorcerers did not look twice at them. Just as Sam had been but moments prior, they too seemed bewitched by the beautiful boys and girls that wore nothing but beads and golden chains.

Unlike the rest of Urukk, Caraa had assured its people's safety, not by building thick, high walls, or training vast armies, but by making itself known as the only place in the whole realm that one could buy whatever they desired had they the coins to pay for it. Raaf, slaves, and whores were all up for sale in this place.

Sam and Daniel shuddered as they watched the three men's eyes undress, bead by bead, the thin bodies of the young boys and girls.

"This is wrong," muttered Daniel under his breath.

Sam nodded, turning, searching the room for the girl he felt his whole body sing for.

From the far end of the brightly lit room, the young woman approached them with their mugs of mead. She carried herself with grace and pride.

"Here you are," she said, smiling at Sam. "Main attraction is about to start…" she repeated, "I'll come back after if you need more mead or food."

Sam thanked her sheepishly, taking the mugs from her hands. Their fingers touched, and Sam almost collapsed under the weight of his emotions.

Daniel smirked at his brother, amused.

"What?" Sam hissed, feeling his brother's eyes burn through the back of his head.

"Nothing! Nothing!" Daniel roared, but his words died out in the loud gong that announced the beginning of the performance the girl told them about.

The light dimmed, the constant chatter died, and from behind the bar, the few dozen boys and girls, all dressed in beads and gold, began to dance before the melting eyes of their much older public. They moved on nimble feet and with mind-ensnaring grace. Their bodies shimmered as their garments caught the flicker of dimmed flames. They swayed and turned in perfect harmony with the rhythmic gongs, slowly, inch by inch, revealing their whole bodies to the glaring masses. They smiled and sang, and to Sam's surprise, among them was the very girl he'd given his heart to. She, too, unfurled her chains and showed her naked body to the room.

Daniel's smile vanished from his face as Sam tightened his grip around his mug so strongly it began to tremble.

Daniel placed a hand over his to calm him down, or at least make him quiet.

The music quickened as the room danced in the music of the falling beads and chains. All eyes were on the swaying, naked bodies of the inn's servants. Some young boys and girls vanished from the room, taken by men or women up the stairs while others perched themselves onto the laps of older, richer men, some even landed kisses on the battered cheeks of ancient sorcerers.

Sam and Daniel became painfully aware of the red lights that glowed from the high windows they had seen from the outside. This was not an inn that served delicious food and mead, but rather, shockingly, the boys and girls, all beautiful and gracious, were the items sold. The two brothers felt their hearts throb in their throats as they observed helplessly, old men and women take upstairs, the reason they had come here for.

The music stopped, and all those who were left untaken, covered their fair bodies with their beads and resumed serving at the tables. Sam stared with a mixture of relief and nausea as the girl he liked was clearing tables.

"We cannot stay here," Daniel announced pushing away the half-empty mug he could no longer finish.

"I need to talk to her," said Sam in the quietest of voices.

"Are you mad?"

"You don't understand, brother! I cannot sit and watch her work in such a place. This is not right!"

"Brother! Sam! We cannot get involved! We have already risked enough by drinking these mugs! We cannot stay, and you cannot talk to that girl!"

Sam simply ignored his younger brother.

"Maybe if you weren't so damned picky with girls, you would understand!"

"This has nothing to do with me, brother! Please, Sam, let's go!" Daniel pleaded, but his brother had already drunk all of his mead, and his thoughts were now murky.

"But maybe you're a kynlï," Sam blurted into his drained mug.

Daniel's face exploded in a thousand shades of red. He grabbed his sword, climbed out of his sunken seat, and strolled out of the brothel they'd mistakenly taken for an inn.

Sam stood too, ready to follow his brother, but the girl that served their mead rushed towards him to collect her coins. Sam looked around for an escape.

"You're leaving so soon?" she asked, smiling, "I hope it's not because of our main attraction. We have everything," the girl said invitingly.

"No, it's not that," stammered Sam rummaging through his empty pockets for the coins he knew he did not have.

"How much for you?" asked one of the three sorcerers who were still at Sam's table. One of them placed his hand onto her leg, caressing it.

"I'm afraid I'm not available now. Please wait until the next performance." She smiled brightly.

"You don't have to do this," Sam whispered to the girl, who turned her dark eyes on him and stared, unwavering.

"You can come with me, with us, away from this place. I can help you get away."

The girl did not as much as blink.

"Ha!" the three sorcerers howled with laughter.

"You want to save this whore, boy?" they roared, banging their mugs on the table. One of the sorcerers grabbed the girl's hanging beaded chains and pulled on them so forcefully, the girl crumbled on the table over mugs and plates, right next to Sam.

Sam stood and looked around alarmed, but no one turned their eyes on them. This, sickening as it was, was normal in such places.

"Leave her!" said Sam.

"You don't get it, boy, do you?" the three white-haired men laughed. The one who had pulled on the girl's clothing was now moving his hand slowly up her leg.

Sam felt his guts ready to give up and burst through his clenched jaws.

"This is not just a whore! She is a Fölur-Blöö! A filthy pale-blood! A powerless whore whose sorcerer parents sold their disgusting offspring and buried their shame."

"She is worse than those raaf eaters in the alleyways!" the sorcerers howled at Sam who felt his whole body shake with rage.

"Do not talk like that!" Sam hissed.

"It's alright!" the girl smiled brightly, trying to regain her balance.

But she was too late, Sam had already drawn his sword and pointed it at the sorcerer who still held her by the leg.

"You will die, boy!" the sorcerers boomed and released the girl so that they could offer their undivided attention to Sam.

"Please don't!" the girl pleaded, getting back to her feet. "Please don't fight. It scares the other guests."

The sorcerer who had her pinned to the table swung his arm and slapped the girl pitilessly.

"We no longer want you, whore." They grabbed Sam roughly by the hair and arms and dragged him through the happy-cheering room and out through the back door.

* * *

Sara and Adriana walked in silence through the mostly abandoned streets of Caraa. With quiet steps, they inched towards the crashing sea and the harbour beyond it.

Faces peered at them from dark alleys, hooded, obscured faces stared at the two women who dared to venture through the dark streets of the city. They licked their raaf-black lips at them, but did not leave the safety of their concealed places.

Sara and Adriana acted as if they knew where they were going and that they belonged on those affrighting streets. They did not, and they knew it. They felt it with every bit that made them, them.

The hidden faces also seemed to know it.

From time to time they crossed streets flooded with light; some orange and inviting, some of the brightest red that made them quicken their purposeful walk. Many weeks had passed since they'd abandoned their loved homes and summer was about to end. Cold winds, chilled by the restless sea, battered at their faces. They were getting cold, they were hungry, but above all, they were tired.

"I really do not like this place," said Sara quietly, as they crossed another street painted in red. In Caraa there were plenty of them.

"Neither do I," whispered Adriana, slowing her pace to better see the masses that queued outside red windows.

"No wonder they don't need any walls," she added. "They have every soul imprisoned either with that ash they eat, or with fleshy pleasures. This is no safety."

Sara nodded, deep in thought. Despite her dreams, she wondered if they really could arrange for ships to take them south into the land of humans.

Sara and Adriana walked in silence, only rarely talking and that only when they crossed yet another street that glowed bright red. Inside their minds, however, thousands of thoughts fought for the chance of being listened to. Their journey to Caraa flashed before their eyes, an avalanche of deaths and hardship misting their eyes and poisoning their hearts. They saw blood gushing from the bodies of their loved ones. They saw the Beasts, the riders, they saw death. They thought of Sam and Daniel somewhere inside this blighted city. Exhausted, their minds flew from place to place, from face to face until it finally settled on the reason they were walking in the dead of night towards the harbour.

This would be the final deed she would do for the Turmenn, Sara thought. And once the ships took them to safety, she would lead a simple life, much like the one she once had up in Bells. She craved peacefulness, she yearned for Erlend and his love for her.

Adriana hoped that they would somehow manage to acquire the much needed ships and sail safely to Stórvatn and the land the humans still inhabited in peace.

A cold breeze whistled as it squeezed itself to pass through Caraa's narrow streets. Sara and Adriana's thoughts returned, hurriedly, to their surroundings. The street was empty, the night was thick and cold, the harbour was within their reach.

The road they followed slowly bent away from the thunderous sea they could now hear. The two women strained their eyes to pierce the piling darkness up ahead, yet there was nothing they could see but blackness.

"Let's go this way," called Sara, pointing at an alley at their right that promised to take them to the harbour.

Adriana nodded slowly. She did not want to leave the road they had been walking on in apparent safety, and enter the tenebrous alleys of the raaf-eaters. Still, the sooner they found what they were looking for, the quicker they could return to Turmenn's makeshift camp outside the city's walls.

Shuffling sounds and whispers reached their ears as they walked between derelict buildings and heaps of long discarded things that rose like mountains all the way to the first floors of the constructions. They quickened their pace until their feet burned with the effort of their march.

Taller buildings rose ahead of them, multi-storied giants behind which the Taðr Sea crashed and hissed annoyed at the large obstacles that stubbornly stood in its way.

Sara tried to measure the ridiculous construction.

Adriana, however, kept her eyes ahead of them where hooded figures moved about in packs. Her hand instinctively nested around the hilt of her sword.

More figures gathered up ahead, some moving crates, others observing, some hooded, some bare-headed; their long manes of silver-white whipping at the night. With some relief, the two women approached the standing figures, happy to emerge from the dark alley into the vast harbour.

Sara's eyes never left the large constructions before them. The closer they got, the more incredible they appeared. Wide and tall the building blocked the sea from view, its surface smooth and dark, with many windows cut into its face. Sara stared at it in wonder. Against its colossal size, the contours of people moving to and fro with crates, appeared but ants.

"Hey! Who's there?" a rumbling voice boomed from ahead, its owner's hand pointed at them. "What are you doing here at this hour?" the white-haired man asked, gruffly.

Sara and Adriana made their way to the group of men now staring at them.

"Don't stop!" the man boomed at the workers, whom he seemed to be in charge of. The moving of crates from the gigantic building quickly resumed.

The old figure approached the two women walking on their own under the cover of the night. Just as Adriana, whose hand petted her blade's pommel, his hand lingered on his chest.

"Well?" he demanded in surprise, as Sara and Adriana exposed themselves into the orange light of torches that surrounded the many working men.

"If you're looking for coins or raaf, come later, once the men are finished, but they might be too tired to enjoy your services," he laughed, measuring the two women from head to toe while nodding.

"You're not the usual that come around here to take advantage of my men," the white-haired man added, stepping closer to Adriana. His right hand stretched to grab her by the arm, while his other held something protectively onto his chest.

Sara and Adriana gasped as they realised what they had walked upon.

The sorcerer regarded them with a mixture of curiosity and amusement.

"We are not here for the pleasure of your men." Adriana slapped his hand away from her and pulled her sword free from the scabbard that held it concealed.

"Ha! That won't do you any good!" the Elemental boomed and opened his fist to show them his green gem. The polished rock glimmered in the flickering light of the many flames around them.

"Put it away before you hurt yourself, woman. Or before I burn your hands straight off it!" he said, smiling. He was broad and confident; two humans were no threat to him.

Adriana held her stance. Despite the heart-stopping terror that now ruled her flesh, she spoke without a hint of fear.

"Try me."

"You cannot kill me with that!" he boomed.

"Maybe not, but it can still cut you pretty badly," Adriana said calmly, and the sorcerer almost collapsed with laughter. His gem flickered alive.

"Are you in charge of the harbour?" Sara spoke for the first time, her voice calmer, crisper than the night.

The man smiled and bowed mockingly before her.

"Then we are interested in your ships."

"My ships?" the sorcerer asked surprised and looked over his shoulder at his men and the enormous building they feverishly emptied.

Sara and Adriana followed his gaze towards its upper storeys and felt faint. This was no building like they had seen before, or truly not a building at all. It rose high towards the skies, giant and black, its upper parts melting into the starless heavens, but now that they stood next to it, they could see its stupendous masts glow faintly in the torches' light. Five masts with furled white sails held the skies in place, their size too great for Sara's mind to grasp. She had seen them before and knew her dreams were once again becoming true, yet she stared at them in awe, as did Adriana, their shadow falling heavily on them.

"What do you need to be brought here?" he added, smiling.

"How many of them moor inside the harbour?" asked Adriana already running numbers in her head.

"If you have coins we can bring anything. If slaves are what you wish to haul to Caraa, then I'll keep some for myself."

"We wish to take five hundred souls across the sea to Stórvatn," Sara said slowly. "We'll need two ships like this one," she added, pointing behind the broad sorcerer.

The smile drained from the Elemental's face hearing her words.

"You wish to take slaves to Stórvatn?" he asked incredulously.

"Not slaves. My people."

The sorcerer stared at them, amazed.

"You would make much more by selling them in Caraa, but if you wish to take them all to ol' Stórvatn, you will need many a coin! Ships come heavy and go empty to Stórvatn every day. Bring your people here, and you'll find the ships you need. But don't forget the coins!"

Sara nodded slowly.

"We won'y," and with that, she turned around towards the uninviting darkness of the streets beyond the torches' warmth.

"How will we pay for them?" asked Adriana, once they had found again the road that led back to the broken walls and to the frightened Turmenn.

"I don't know yet, but we will manage somehow."

Adriana raised again an eyebrow at her and Sara knew she suspected her of knowing more than she was telling.

"Let's see if the boys found anything. We'll tell the Turmenn at dawn. If we are lucky, we'll leave this damned city behind before the week is gone."

The two made their way through Caraa, past dark alleys occupied by hooded figures with black lips and beneath tall windows that vomited red light. The city they had hoped to offer the Turmenn safety, proved to be more dangerous than marching back to Bells.

* * *

Daniel waited outside the thought-to-be inn for his brother to come after him. He waited and waited, but no one left the place save white-haired sorcerers and women whose ways of living he preferred not to think of. Sam was nowhere to be seen. After a while, the anger that had put his frame in motion and commanded it to leave the inn, finally subsided and Daniel was once again in full control of his own legs. He could not believe his brother would not come for him. He walked, disappointed, back towards the entrance of the inn.

"Back so soon!" The same large figure that had invited him and Sam inside, approached him. Daniel smiled feebly and walked passed him into the bright innards of the sinful room. The table Sam and he had shared with the three sorcerers was being cleaned by one of the young boys in beads and golden chains. He looked around, Sam was not there. Annoyed, but also worried, he searched the room, his eyes moving over the many heads, some white some not, for Sam. Hoping that his brother was not stupid enough to follow the girl he liked up in the red-flooded rooms, Daniel decided to look for Sam outside.

Hordes of people moved about from door to door and inn to inn - as he still liked to think of them. Maybe Sam had left the place through some back door. Daniel made his way around the building.

The alleyway that separated the inn from the rest of the buildings was dark and narrow, and Daniel wondered for a moment if he should let himself be swallowed by the dark. Who knew what things lurked in its depths, beyond the short distance still illuminated by the orange lights behind. His sword cried as he unleashed it.

Daniel walked slowly between the rickety buildings, squinting to see into the dark. After a few moments, he reached a door that stood ajar and let light spill out. In the cone of light, a figure lay collapsed and motionless. Daniel rushed apprehensive to the fallen figure.

He caught his breath as he saw the state his brother was in. He knelt next to him, his sword clattering painfully onto the paved ground.

"Sam! Sam!" he called, lifting his brother's head off the cold stone. Daniel gasped at the gashing wounds on Sam's face. He had been beaten raw.

"Sam!" The door creaked as it opened fully. The light that barely escaped the gap, widened and fell onto the two brothers mercilessly. Daniel squinted as a shape, walked through the light towards him. He touched the ground beside him for his sword.

"You're not from here, are you?" a woman's voice came, calm and hollow.

Daniel squinted at her.

"Who are you? What happened to my brother?"

But the shape was already next to him, pulling on Sam's shoulder.

"We need to take him from here. He's not safe. You're not safe," she added.

"Who are you?" Daniel insisted. His eyes were slowly getting used to the flooding light. The girl beside him looked much like the hooded creatures that lived within the darkest alleys. Ash-faced and gaunt, her face spoke loudly of the hardship of life in Caraa. It took Daniel a few more moments to recognise the girl. Without the beads and golden chains, she was unrecognisable.

Sam grunted as the two hauled him away from the inn and into another street that opened at their right.

"It's you!" mumbled Sam. His swollen lips tried fruitlessly to form the words.

"Be quiet, Sam!"

"You came for me," he muttered, ignoring Daniel.

"You owe me two coins!" the girl said coldly. "I would very much like to have them."

Sam chuckled choking on his blood.

Beneath the Serpent City

While Daniel and the girl hauled Sam through Caraa towards the Turmenn's camp, beneath Undirheim, the Beast Lords gathered around Estrelle's throne.

The Queen of the Beast Lords waited patiently in her Wolf form on her monstrous seat. With her head on her paws, she seemed to be asleep.

Her subjects entered the enormous chamber in small groups. None of them knew why their Queen had summoned them. Hïldúúr and Finndôra were among the last to join the few dozen waiting anxiously around the throne of bones.

"You asked to see us," said Hïldúúr in his rough voice, unsure if Estrelle was truly deep asleep or merely resting.

The Queen of the Beast Lords cracked open one eye and gazed at the awaiting ring of men, women, and Beasts.

"That, I did," growled the White Wolf.

The gathered Masters and their Beasts waited, annoyed, for Estrelle to tell them why she had asked for them at such an early hour.

"Well?" asked Finndôra crossing her arms before her Queen. "Why are we all here?"

"I need you to ask your Beasts, especially those of you who are in charge of guarding our borders, to spread a message to their kind across Urukk," said the White Wolf slowly. Her massive jaws had been designed to tear and kill rather than speak.

The Beast Lords looked doubtfully at each other.

"It's been more than a fortnight since the boys left Undirheim, and the creatures of the realm need to be prepared. I have studied Skeggor's journal, and by now, Aerö and Nóór ought to have reached Ophidia or are about to do so. The Beasts of Urukk will be asked to join the war and fulfil the promise they have made to Skeggor. They will be called upon. They must be ready."

"Have you really lost your mind?" spat Finndôra throwing her arms in angered disbelief.

"You have no way of knowing if my boy is still alive or if your son dragged him to his death!" The White Wolf blinked slowly at the female Beast Lord who defied her with every given chance.

"No one will listen to you, Estrelle! You've lost your son, and you're about to lose your people. Ask the Beasts of Urukk for their help. Tell them to join our war! Ha!" Finndôra boomed mockingly.

"You continuously fail to control but a mere handful, yet you ask of us to somehow make all Beasts obey your words?"

"Finndôra listen…—"

" I am done listening to you! You are no longer Queen to us!"

"Finndôra!" Hïldúúr hissed at his beloved wife.

Estrelle growled quietly, still seemingly asleep upon her throne.

"Hïldúúr will be our King, we all agree. You are too weak to rule!" Finndôra vomited the words breathlessly.

But this time Estrelle had had enough.

Before anyone else could notice, the White Wolf dug its terrifying claws into the throne and leapt into the air. With the speed of a lightning bolt, and as invisible as a gust of wind, Estrelle charged at Finndôra. A split second was all it took her to cover the distance and collide with Nóór's mother, who much like the rest of the Beast Lords was utterly taken by surprise.

Finndôra collapsed with the White Wolf atop of her, snarling murderously at her. In her Wolf form, Estrelle was twice the size of Hïldúúr's Ashäël, and at least five times that of the woman beneath her.

Finndôra grasped at the floor trying to escape the enraged Queen.

"Estrelle!" yelled Hïldúúr along with the other Beast Lords who now encircled her and Finndôra; their Beasts all growling and stomping in fear.

Their voices, however, were not being heard by the two they watched and dared not to intervene.

"I've had enough of your continuous complaints and threats, Finndôra! If you refuse to bow before your Queen and think I'm weak, I'll show you what I'm capable of!" the White Wolf growled but inches from her face.

Finndôra turned her head and shrieked in the most disobedient of voices.

"Har-úgur! Kill her!" But the Feond was already moving its massive bulk towards Estrelle. It lifted one giant fist above its head, ready to squash her.

The White Wolf's eyes flared with rage as the pinned down Beast Lord under her dared to order her Beast to attack. Estrelle leapt away and ducked the blow with ease. She glared at Finndôra as she stumbled to stand up.

Estrelle was not going to allow her that. She charged again, moving like a cloud between the Feond's blows, who despite its size and strength, was no match for the White Wolf's impossible speed.

Estrelle reached Finndôra just as the Beast Lord managed to regain her footing. With a bark and another leap, she was again upon her. Estrelle dug her dagger-like fangs into Finndôra's robes and pulled her to the ground then shook her mercilessly, like a worthless rag.

"Estrelle, please!" yelled Hïldúúr, terrified of what might happen to his wife if the Queen failed to stop herself.

Har-úgur charged again, pommelling the ground as it tried fruitlessly to strike Estrelle.

The White Wolf evaded him, pulling Finndôra in her jaws. She shook again at the helpless Beast Lord, tearing her robes, slamming her against the ground. Then when she had enough, she spread her paws for balance and flung Finndôra through the air. The female Beast Lord's body slammed into the throne she so determinedly wished to take from Estrelle.

A gut-wrenching thud echoed through the chamber as Finndôra helplessly crashed into the giant seat of bones.

Hïldúúr rushed to aid her, not caring if the Queen would turn her rage upon him.

Estrelle had no lesson to teach her most trusted Beast Lord.

Har-úgur, however, was not going to allow the one who sent its Master fly across the room, be it the Queen herself, to leave unpunished. It dropped its colossal body on all fours.

Instantly the ring of Beast Lords and their Beasts stepped backwards a few steps as they all knew what the Feond was about to do.

Estrelle snarled at the Beast untroubled.

A crack split from side to side on Har-úgur's mouthless face, a gap that tore its face in half. The Feond moaned in pain as its featureless mug morphed into one that screamed of mindless rage. Within moments, a mouth that could devour Estrelle whole gaped at the White Wolf before it.

"You dare…" said Estrelle forming the words with great difficulty, "…to challenge me, Har-úgur? I am your Queen! You will obey me, or I'll break you as I broke your Master!"

Har-úgur inhaled deeply, then released a thundering roar. Its Master might have been defeated, but it would not back off.

A ridge rose on the White Wolf's back as Estrelle bared her fangs. Without taking her eyes off Har-úgur,

Estrelle lowered her body to the floor, panting. When she released her roar, even the incapable-of-feeling-fear Verndari trembled in the pits of Undirheim.

The Feond's whisper, by comparison, died away the second the White Wolf opened her jaws.

"Bow before your Queen, Har-úgur!" growled Estrelle.

But the Feond was beyond the reach of words or reason. It expanded its wide chest and charged, maddened.

Estrelle dodged and leapt away from the Feond's mindless blows, toying with the creature. She enjoyed fighting again. Too many weeks had passed since she dared to leave the safety of the Lair to go hunting. The white beast inside her craved the taste of blood. But good as it felt to fight again, Estrelle kept her distance from the Feond for she knew that one aimed blow would cripple her.

Frustrated, as none of its fists met their intended target, Har-úgur turned its rage upon one of the spiralling columns that held the throne room's ceiling in its place. The Feond threw itself against it with all its weight and force. The throne room shook with the ripples of its witless attack. Once, twice, three times Har-úgur hit the old-as-the-mountain pillar before sending it crumbling to the ground.

The ring of Beasts and Beast Lords jumped aside as the mile-long column collapsed upon itself.

The Feond did not wait for the White Wolf to realise its plan. It moved into the shattered body of the column and began to throw enormous chunks at Estrelle.

The White Wolf dashed and dodged a dozen flying boulders, some of which hurled terrifyingly past the gathered Beast Lords. She could keep up with the Feond, she knew that, but how long until some of the Beast Lords or their Beasts got squashed to death by Har-úgur's haphazard attacks she did not know. The White Wolf roared again as another giant chunk of rock whistled passed her.

"You're just as wilful as your Master," Estrelle growled, then darted between the flying torrent of debris towards the Beast. She roared again, the power of her lungs dispersing the cloud of dust that billowed around her. Like a white shadow, she rushed towards her enraged prey. Estrelle evaded another hurling boulder then leapt onto Har-úgur.

But the Beast was waiting for her. Its right fist went for her relentlessly. Then when the White Wolf dodged its blows again, the Feond turned its massive body away from her and with his other hand grabbed her. The White Wolf growled as it felt Har-úgur's giant hand hold her. Her body was too large in this form for the Beast to wrap its fist around her. She shook and turned, hoping to make the Beast let go of her. She did not have much time before Har-úgur would realise it had no chance of killing her like this and then it would, undoubtedly, bring its free fist upon her.

There, suspended in midair, held by the strongest creature in Urukk, Estrelle understood the depth of the Beast Lords' disloyalty to her. None of them did as much as twitch to come to her aid.

Har-úgur roared, frustrated, at the white mass of fur trapped in its fist. The time had come to finish this. With effort, it lifted its massive limb above its head. Its sheer weight alone would crush the life out of Estrelle.

Painfully, Estrelle turned inside her own skin and dug her claws into the Feond's chest. The attack offered Estrelle the opportunity she had been waiting for. Har-úgur lowered its hanging hand to grab the snarling wolf securely. Estrelle did not wait for the Beast to pin her down in both its fists. The moment the Feond slacked its hold on her, she turned her jaws upon the hand that held her.

The spray of blood painted her fur bright red.

Har-úgur dropped her, howling, thick blood pouring from the wound in rivers. To the Feond's horror, as much as to the other Beasts and Beast Lords, the White Wolf stood panting on the ground with the Feond's hand trapped in her jaws. She had torn the limb straight off Har-úgur's body.

Finndôra's Beast grabbed the bleeding stump with its other hand and howled as it moved away from her. It took with it the shame of the defeat and left behind the severed hand.

A fair exchange, thought Estrelle as she dropped the bleeding limb in the already spreading pool of blood beneath her. Unable to contain her thirst, the White Wolf licked a few times at the wasted blood. Covered entirely in blood, Estrelle returned to her preferred form, that of a human. She licked her hands clean.

If the Beast Lords and their Beasts had held to their wits with iron fists, their resolve now faltered. They looked at their Queen in horror, terrified for their own lives. The moment she regained her form, they were already running for the entrance and the dark tunnels beyond it.

"Do not run from me!" Estrelle called after them. "Go and do your duties to this Lair! Go and spread the word that war is coming!" The Beast Lords did not stop but ran as fast as they could away from their enraged Queen.

Hïldúúr was the only one to stay behind with Finndôra safely cradled in his arms. He looked at the painted-in-red Estrelle with sadness, but also devotion. Unlike the rest of the Beast Lords, he knew his wife had crossed the line this time and understood his Queen's horrific actions. The Beast Lords had no time for quarrels for the throne. War had begun, they would soon be hunted by the

Order's armies, and Estrelle had made sure the Beast Lords will obey all her commands. *At least for now.* She would give her life for them, but for that, she needed them to give theirs for her. To be united. To fight as one against an enemy that will soon prove to be vastly superior to them.

"How is she?" asked Estrelle with genuine concern. They could not afford to lose a single Beast Lord regardless of how difficult they were.

"She's just unconscious," Hïldúúr answered, kissing Finndôra's brow. "Thank you for not harming her beyond needed."

"I would never kill one of us, Hïldúúr!" said Estrelle licking the rest of her skin clean.

"I know…but for a second, and I'm ashamed to even think it, I thought you really went berserk."

Estrelle smiled and placed a hand on Hïldúúr's shoulder, while the other she offered to Ashäël to clean for her.

The Hound licked it with pleasure.

"Thank you!" she said with finality. "Thank you for yet again proving what a great friend and leader you are. Once the war is over, if we are blessed to survive it, you may have the throne."

"We both know that that is not something I want nor that will happen."

Estrelle smiled again.

Together they took Finndôra to the chambers she shared with Hïldúúr, then she retreated to her own. She had harmed a Beast Lord and a Beast today, both acts unforgivable by the Beast Lords' laws. She will have to pay for them, she knew. But for now, she hoped that was enough to make the Beast Lords survive the war. If they would not be ruled by reason, then they will be by fear.

Deep in her chambers, Estrelle washed Har-úgur's blood with the water that had filtered through sand and rock and finally weeks later reached the Beast Lords' Lair. But despite the precious things it gathered on its travels from the surface, no amount of it could ever wash the guilt she felt for what she did.

* * *

Sara and Adriana rarely talked on their way back to the Turmenn's camp. The night was quiet, and they feared they could easily be overheard. They felt pleased with the outcome of their search for Caraa's harbour and its ships. All they had to do was figure out how to convince the captains of the ships to take them to Stórvatn. The Turmenn had no coins.

"How are we to pay for them?" asked Adriana clearly concerned. Despite Sara's unwavering belief that they will manage to secure the ships, she needed more than her ambiguous words.

"We'll sell whatever can be sold." *I'm sure the sorcerer would find them worth his ships and time...*

"And if it's not enough?" asked Adriana seriously.

Sara chuckled happily. "You sound just like Trevor!" she giggled girlishly.

Adriana pursed her lips, annoyed at Sara's solid resolution that they will have those ships. Without the coins to pay for them, they simply had no chance of reaching Stórvatn by the sea.

Sara beamed at her, with the full, genuine smile of an innocent.

Adriana felt instantly unsuited to defend herself against such spells. Deep down, she had to agree with Sara, she did sound just like Trevor.

"I know I have not given you the answers that you seek, Adriana, but my question has not changed. Do you trust me?" Adriana felt Sara's dark eyes see through her.

"Of course I do!" she replied at once. "But I do wish you trusted me enough to tell me more."

Adriana was right, of course. Sara had asked her to blindingly follow her command, while she refused to give her friend the simplest of explanations.

Why was she so terrified of telling Adriana that she dreamt of things that had yet to happen? Was she afraid of Adriana questioning her heirdom, or was it because she did not know the answer herself?

The two walked in silence.

"Remember when I asked you to promise me that you will listen to me without asking questions?" said Sara after a few moments.

Adriana said nothing, her silence marked the seal of their agreement.

"Then listen to me now. We will have those ships and sail to Stórvatn, trust me on that. One I shall lead myself, while the other will be under your command. But please be careful!" she added, stopping in the middle of the road.

Adriana turned to face her.

"Once at sea, no one can help but those you're sailing with. And when those we're trapped with are both friends and foes, terrible things tend to happen. Before we reach Stórvatn, someone will try to kill you, Adriana, someone you trust. I beg of you to never lower your guard."

Adriana stared at Sara astonished.

"Who?"

"That I do not know."

"How do you know this?"

"I simply know. I trust you to lead half of the Turmenn. Please don't stop trusting me now, Adriana!"

Adriana nodded. "I promise! But if we reach Stórvatn and someone did try to kill me on our journey there, you'll tell me everything."

It was Sara's turn to nod.

Just as they had done on the way to the harbour, Sara and Adriana crossed, every now and then, the streets flooded with light and filled with people wishing to buy their pinch of raaf or short-lived happiness. The mix of orange-crimson lights caught in their misty breaths as the two quickened their pace towards Caraa's forsaken walls and their camp beyond.

"I hope the boys have not done something stupid," came Adriana's smothered voice as she cupped her hands to her mouth to warm them.

Sara looked with doubt at her. Knowing them, that was precisely what they did — cause trouble.

"They may be completely mad…" said Sara wrapping her red dress tighter around her frame, "…but I do trust them wholly. But I do hope they are safe back in the camp."

"Isn't it too late for two young women to be walking on their own?" called a voice from their right. Both Sara and Adriana turned their heads, alarmed, into one of those streets painted in red. Walking towards them, fast and purposeful, were three men in black coats and with swords in their hands.

"You don't look like you're after raaf either. Where have you two been?" said another, moving close enough to Sara and Adriana that the two could see his face. He was younger than they were, thin and tall, yet his eyes gave more away. They had that noticeable glow of meanness.

"Well?" he asked, brandishing his sword at them.

"Our husbands work in the harbour," said Sara calmly.

"They are unloading those large ships," added Adriana building on Sara's lie. "We brought them food."

"Is that so?" asked the third of the men as he exposed his white head to the red light raining from the windows.

He spoke with the authority of someone who actually had it.

"Of course!" responded Sara bowing slightly.

"Then you may go back to your families," said the sorcerer. "But before you go, tell us, have you seen two boys and a girl on your way from the harbour?"

"No…" Adriana said, shaking her head, "…no we have not." The sorcerer nodded then turned around towards the other two.

"They could not have made it further. One is injured, and one is a girl." The men turned their backs to Sara and Adriana and walked back into the painfully bright-lit street they had come from.

"If you see them, the two boys and the girl, stay away from them. They are dangerous."

Sara and Adriana nodded, bowed their heads, then turned around and walked as quickly as they could without breaking into a full run.

"What was that about?" said Adriana more to herself than to Sara.

"Whatever it is, I do not like it," said Sara after a few long moments.

The two were but a few streets away from Caraa's broken gate and the Turmenn's makeshift camp, when three shapes formed again before them. Sara and Adriana could feel their blood slow down inside their veins. Adriana, who had been walking with her hand on the pommel of her sword, drew her blade.

The three dark shapes ahead seemed to be waiting for them. Sara and Adriana slowed their pace as well. They did not know what the three wanted from them, but it could not be good. One of the figures seemed to wave at them. It suddenly dawned on them that there, ahead of them, were not the two humans and the sorcerer they had encountered earlier, but Sam and Daniel and someone else. Sara and Adriana rushed to them in alarm.

"What happened to him?" hissed Sara as she caught sight of Sam's face. Adriana rushed and took the weight off the girl who'd helped Daniel carry his brother through Caraa.

"Please tell me you're not the ones they're looking for!" Adriana snapped at Daniel. She had been charged with the command of all the Turmenn's guardians, and Sam and Daniel were always the ones who gave her constant grief.

"What?" yapped the girl neither Sara nor Adriana recognised. "Who's looking for me?"

"A sorcerer and two other men…" said Sara calmly, observing the girl's reaction closely. Her skin, if possible, turned translucent with fright.

"We need to go, now!" the girl barked, pulling on Daniel's arm.

"Thank you for helping our friends," said Adriana patronisingly. "We'll make sure they're well looked after. You can go back now."

"She's coming with us," came Sam's gurgling voice. His head lolled from side to side, swollen and raw.

"I'll be damned if she is!" hissed Adriana, who felt she had reached the end of her patience with the two.

"She's coming with us!" Sam repeated, coughing a mouthful of blood onto the paved road beneath him.

Both Adriana and Sara looked at Daniel, who nodded in agreement with his brother. He may disapprove of her, but she had helped him carry Sam across the city. They ought to at least listen to the girl if they were not willing to help.

"If those wounds won't kill you, Sam…" Adriana growled in defeat, "…I will!". The four of them hauled Sam's body in pairs through Caraa's unlit streets and alleys.

By the time the city's gate greeted them, leaning sickeningly on itself, ready to crumble, a new day was being born beyond the distant horizon. The five of them, Sam and Daniel, Sara and Adriana, and the girl, were happy to have escaped Caraa and those who looked for them. At least for now.

Although dawn's purple cracks could be barely seen across the eastern skies, tearing the night away, the camp was already buzzing with movement. The Turmenn, who had disliked the idea of travelling to Caraa from the very start, found it impossible to sleep now that they were outside its walls. All they could do, was sit in warmth around large fires and observe the sinful city before them; its naked windows bleeding crimson light and sending chills throughout their worn bodies.

It became apparent to Sara that the five of them would not manage to enter the Turmenn's camp without being noticed. But out of all the people in the camp, Sara prayed her path would not cross that of Sam and Daniel's older brother.

But as chance had it, or truly the distrust he felt for her, Trevor awaited in the pitch-black shadow of the gate for Sara to walk through.

"What have you done to him?" he demanded, pushing Adriana roughly away so that he could bear his brother.

"Brother…" came Daniel's breathless voice. Trevor, still hauling Sam's weight, drew his sword at Sara.

"What have you done?" he boomed.

Adriana quickly released hers as did the two sisters who came running to the gate. Ishim and Ezkiel looked as if they had not slept in days. Still, they drew their swords and pointed them at Trevor.

"What happened?" Ishim asked Adriana.

"It wasn't their fault," moaned Daniel, trying to raise his voice over the tumult of shouting.

"Who did this to him?"

"Who is she?"

They all threw questions, nodded, shouted, and brandished their swords. Soon the whole camp joined the commotion at the gate, some curious, but most scared. They had enough of running from death, enough of hunger, enough of losing their loved ones.

"Listen to me!" Sara barked from the top of her voice, and all voices fell silent. None of the Turmenn had heard her shout before.

"We have made it so far! We have lost so much! Now is not the time to throw all that away. We have found the harbour and its ships! Tomorrow we can all leave for

Stórvatn!" Sara boomed, and the Turmenn seemed to feast on her words.

Adriana however looked unsure. Without a plan, they stood no chance of paying for those ships.

"Adriana! Trevor, Daniel, and I will take care of Sam and find out who did this to him, but now I need you to gather the Turmenn's few possessions. We cannot linger here, now that they are looking for them. Gather everything that we can sell. We must all be in the harbour by dawn tomorrow."

Adriana nodded. Although deep down, she knew the plan made little sense, she chose to unquestioningly have faith in Sara.

In her absence, the Turmenn's shepherds erected a small tent in which Sara could tend to the wounded.

Trevor and Daniel lowered their brother onto the rough ground. Sam looked worse in the growing light.

"Who did this to him? And who are you?" asked Sara as she rummaged through her belongings for bandages and water. The girl did not speak up.

"Daniel!" Trevor snapped, but his young brother did not know how he should tell them where they went and who she was.

"Sam and I went inside one of their inns…or so we thought, to see if we could find anything about this place," he said looking away embarrassed.

"It turned out to be one of those places people buy…" his voice faltered.

"Daniel!" Sara barked at him. "I told you not to do anything stupid!"

"We went inside. The place was filled with sorcerers, throwing their coins on boys and girls they then took… This place is wrong!"

"Who is she then?" Sara asked, nodding at the girl who sat sulking away from them.

"She's…" Daniel's voice hung inside the tent. The girl had not told him her name.

"I'm Maya," she said in a cold voice. "And that stupid friend of yours owes me two coins." Sara and Trevor looked at her in astonishment.

"He also got himself beaten up by three customers who were a little rowdy. He tried to help me — as if I needed help," she scowled.

"Now I am being sought by Kann and his men!" she emphasised.

"You cannot stay here, girl," said Trevor in a tone so cold it made the others shudder.

"She has nowhere to go," moaned Sam who slipped in and out of consciousness.

"Sam! We have enough problems as it is!"

"She was sold by her own parents, brother!"

"Shut up, you idiot!" snapped the girl. "Mind your goddamned business!"

"Just because she has no powers, her sorcerer parents sold her to that whorehouse!"

Maya stood up. For a second Sara, Trevor and Daniel did not know if she was about to run or beat Sam to death. She did not seem to know either. She sat back down.

"I may not have had much, but I did earn my coin! Now I cannot do that because of you! Kann will skin me for running away."

"She stays," concluded Sam giving the girl an awkward smile.

She scowled.

"If you know the city and can help us get those ships, then you may come with us," said Sara after a few moments.

"When we leave this place we'll shed our past and head for a new future."

Maya seemed most uninterested.

"I'll help you get to the ships. But if you have no coins, I wonder, how far are you willing to go to get your people on them."

Sara could feel Trevor's stare glued to her, waiting for her answer.

Her answer never came.

The morning passed quickly in the camp that fermented with movement. Bundles were piled near the gate, things were being hauled, the Turmenn gave their guardians the very few things they still owned. No one opposed the plan, for they had lost all of their riches long ago.

Sara tended to Sam's wounds while all the other guardians gathered the goods and prepared the Turmenn for their last march. The tension was so high, one could almost see it. After so many weeks of walking across the realm, tonight the Turmenn would reach, at last, the sea. From there, down to Stórvatn, they would rest and heal. War would be behind them.

"Is that all?" Sara asked Grov as she approached him near the gate. The boy nodded.

"They left behind most of their things when we abandoned the last camp."

Sara nodded. She had been the one to order them to leave behind everything that was not needed for survival. She now felt a pang of guilt clawing at her innards.

"Then we'll be ready to leave at nightfall. We must make sure we reach the harbour before the ships sail to Stórvatn at first light."

"They all are ready to start fresh on the Great Plains."

"And so they will."

"Daniel! Let the Turmenn help your brother. I need you to be able to fight if we find trouble. Stay by Grov. Trevor, walk behind with Ishim and Ezkiel, and make sure no one is left behind! Adriana, you walk with Maya and me ahead of the Turmenn."

"Turmenn! Please walk in silence. Do not speak or stop or stare at anyone! Walk with the pairs you've been signed to. Do not leave your groups!"

The Turmenn nodded, terrified at Sara's words. Half of them would have rather stayed out in the open for the sorcerers to find them than walk through Caraa after nightfall.

Maya walked with Sara and Adriana a short distance ahead of the bulk of their people. Daniel and Grov a few paces behind them. They all carried small bundles in their hands or on their backs. Sara carried with her their most precious of belongings.

"How will we go all the way to the harbour without being seen?" asked Adriana, who was still sceptical, at best, about Sara's plan and wished at least to know as much as possible about their means to get there.

"I know the city well." Maya turned to face her. "There are alleys no one uses this late at night. It takes longer than walking through the city as you did last night, but this is safer."

"You have a lot of people you don't want to be seen by, this is the only way," Maya added reading Adriana's thoughts.

"Alright then! Lead the way." Sara smiled at Ariana, who shook her head. How could she be smiling at a time like this?

But Sara knew already that somehow, they would manage to sail on those ships. How they will manage that, she had yet to figure out.

Maya navigated a series of narrow alleys, cramped spaces and canals, before Sara had to call the march to a halt. The Turmenn were lagging behind. With every turn or obstacle, they found, more and more stopped to catch their breaths. Guiding a handful of people through those places would have been hard, but five hundred souls seemed almost impossible. The Turmenn now stretched into a long, thin ribbon of anxiety and hopelessness. If but one warrior showed his face to them, their guardians would find it difficult to even draw their blades. They were trapped.

"Keep the Turmenn together!" hissed Sara at the guardians who themselves could barely fit down the small passages.

"We mustn't stop!" called Maya. Her dark skin beaded with sweat despite the chill that settled in Caraa.

"The girl is right!" said Adriana, signalling for the Turmenn to come through.

"We're almost there!" Sara could already hear the Taðr Sea's crashing waves.

They made progress, painfully slow. At every turn, they had to wait for the Turmenn to squeeze through. At every canal, their guardians had to form human chains so that the Turmenn would not drown. They were cold and wet and tired.

But the closer they got, the more energy the Turmenn seemed to have. The crashing waves, the salty mist that settled on their skin, the shouts of men ahead, made them quicken their pace. Salvation was but a few streets away.

With difficulty, the Turmenn extricated themselves from the narrow confines of the alleys Maya had taken them through, but one by one they emerged unseen and unharmed into the wide harbour. Before them, the ships that would take them to safety bobbed heavily as armies of men unloaded crates from them. Sara and Adriana spotted the sorcerer they had met the night before and walked slowly towards him.

"Maya, you should stay back with the others. If the men who are looking for you are here, they won't be able to find you."

The girl nodded and let herself be swallowed by the surge of men and women funnelling into the open space. Without realising, she stopped next to Sam and Trevor.

"It's you!" he said, smiling at her. Maya shook her head in annoyance.

"When this is done…" she said coldly, "…I still want my coins!"

Sam laughed painfully beneath his older brother's stare.

"If we escape this, I'll be happy to pay all my debt to you."

This time, Maya smiled back at him. Sam felt his knees give way.

"So, you're back!" boomed the sorcerer, looking behind them at the sea of heads. "And you've brought your people with you. Good…Good!" Sara looked past him at the regurgitating ships.

"Yes, these two are going to Stórvatn empty. Show me the coins, and you can take them."

"We have no coins," said Sara unfazed. "But we have some things we gathered in our journeys that might be of interest to you." The sorcerer looked at her doubtfully.

"No coins, no ships!" he said, turning his back to her.

"So, you would rather send your ships empty across the sea than have these?" Sara said, unfastening from the bundle she carried the two black swords they took from the two Draugur they had fought and killed. The sorcerer's expression changed from defiant, if not bored, to utterly shocked.

"Where did you get those?" he hissed tentatively stretching a bleached hand to touch them.

"Those are Draugur swords! Where did you find them?"

"Find them?" asked Adriana, mockingly. "We killed for them!" and she released her own sword to punctuate her words.

The sorcerer was visibly fighting between believing them and laughing. He chose to smile and stare in Sara's face.

"If you have truly killed two of the Queen's beloved Shadows, then I do not want to have anything to do with you," he said calmly. "But, I do want those swords."

"Then have them and take us to Stórvatn. We have no use for them."

"Then again, I could just give you to the Order to be killed for what you've done. And still keep those blades."

"You can try," said Adriana coolly, pointing her sword at his throat. "Had you been your Queen's devoted subject, you wouldn't be profiteering from trading slaves and raaf."

"I like you, woman!" the sorcerer boomed. "I'll take you to Stórvatn for those swords." And he pointed at the two large ships, each with five rigged masts. "These are my girls! Heimdóðr and Hermóður, goddesses over this sea."

Sara and Adriana looked at two gigantic ships and wondered how the waters bore them on their waves. They seemed too large and too heavy, not to sink.

"They are almost unloaded, but I can take you on them. We shall leave at dawn. But first, may I have the payment?" he added, stretching his hands to Sara ready to receive the Draugur's swords.

"You'll have them once we are onto your ships."

The sorcerer seemed displeased, but nodded in agreement.

"Follow me then." *I'll find out how you got your hands on those swords, and then I'll decide how devoted I really am.*

The Turmenn crossed the harbour in the groups the guardians assigned them to. They marched with new hope in their hearts that they would soon forget their pains and leave behind the land that tried so eagerly to smother them. The memories of those they lost, however, would never go away. Because of them and their absolute sacrifice, they had survived.

"Guardians!" Sara called over the creaking of crates. "Stay with the groups you've been assigned to. Keep them safe. Once we are at sea, you will be the ones responsible for taking them to Stórvatn."

"I will take Heimdóðr and Adriana, Hermóður. Sam, Daniel, and Ezkiel lead your groups on Heimdóðr. Trevor, Grov, and Ishim follow Adriana on the other ship. From now onwards, Adriana is your leader. Obey her, trust her to take you safely to Stórvatn."

Trevor turned his back to Sara. "I have no plans to follow you in this mad search for safety," he said, moving away from the gathered guardians.

"Trevor, you can't possibly..." Adriana tried to reason with him, but he had already chosen to leave his only friends and family.

"We need you to reach the safe shores of Stórvatn! You cannot abandon us now!" snapped Sara.

"Safety? Safety? As long as there are Beasts and sorcerers, none of us will ever know such a thing! We are but ants before their strength. We have no hope in finding shelter anywhere in Urukk! Open your eyes and see just how ridiculous your journey is!" Trevor hissed, stepping away from Sara.

"Brother!" barked his two younger siblings together, rushing after him to make him change his mind, to make him stop. Or if they failed, join him. After all, the same blood bonded all three of them.

"Boys, you mustn't!" said Sara calmly, stepping before Sam and Daniel.

"Trevor! Wait!"

"Listen to me!" she urged. "We are so close to reaching our destination. We need your help!"

"Step away." Sam hissed at Sara, and Daniel was already darting passed her.

It was Adriana who managed to stop them. She nimbly moved after them and slapped both Sam and Daniel on their faces. Her hands touched their cheeks with the force of thunder.

The boys stopped, taken aback.

"He has made his choice long ago! Do not pledge your life for his now, when so many are already in great need of you. Trevor has selfishly decided to abandon our quest for a new home after the battle of the Korr Mountains. Where was he when the Greeds revealed their plot? Where was he when the Priestess attacked us? His only care has been for his own skin and Syll's. Let him stay behind and rot in guilt!"

"He is our brother!"

"Then help us reach Stórvatn and return to him. If the southern plains are truly what we hope them to be, then we will no longer need protectors."

Sam and Daniel looked furiously at Adriana.

"Go with them, young brothers…" came Trevor's rough voice, "…and see with your own eyes the fallacy of Petra's words of safety. Come back when you are older. This place is not for children." And with that, he moved away from the gathered Turmenn and their guardians, and vanished through the maze of buildings that surrounded the vast harbour.

Sam and Daniel yelled after him, but only their own echoes answered back.

For the first time since she knew them, Sara realised, the two brothers cried their hearts out. Sara felt their pain as if it were her own and cried with them. Slowly, insidiously, but without doubt, the Turmenn dwindled on the verge of dying out. If they were to start a new life, build a prosperous village in the southern plains, then not a single Turmenn could be allowed to stray. However, a few more will lose their lives before their wish for safety would be granted. The Gods' ambition to punish the humans living in the northern parts of Urukk was not yet fulfilled.

The men that hauled the heavy crates the two ships carried from Stórvatn, moved aside to let the hordes of Turmenn pass. They watched them as they climbed the steep ramp up to the decks. They whistled and shouted at the young girls and women as they squeezed past them. Some even tried to grab the ones closest to them.

Maya could feel the men watch her intently. Every time she turned, they stared at her with the only thing that truly scared her: dawning recognition.

"Aren't you a pretty one!" barked one of the workers grabbing her by the arm as she began to climb the wooden slope. Maya pulled her arm away from him. The man grabbed her more forcefully.

Sara and Adriana watched the stream of Turmenn split in half as they advanced towards the ship they had been told to board. Still in the harbour, the guardians wished each other good luck. This would be the first time since they all joined under the Turmenn banner that they would be separated. Once the ships left the harbour, they would be confined with those they shared their ship with and no one else.

"Hey! Take your hands off her!" boomed Adriana, noticing the man manhandling Maya.

"Boys! I'm keeping this one!" the man roared as he pulled Maya after him. The other workers roared with laughter. All the men seemed to search the procession like animals of prey.

Adriana rushed towards Heimdóðr where Maya was being dragged against the stream of people, off the ship. Half way down the ramp, she met the men.

Sara, Daniel and the sorcerer whose ships they were on, followed.

"I'm keeping this one!" shouted another, moving down the ramp with Robin under his arm. The girl from

Bells, whom Sara recognised, kicked and screamed at the man.

Adriana did not even try to reason with the men. She drew her sword quicker than their eyes could see and pointed it at the one holding Maya. The tip of the sword pierced the man's throat just enough to draw blood.

"How dare you, whore?" the man shrieked, enraged.

It took Adriana a few moments to register the man's words. She tightened the grip on her sword and pushed it a little deeper.

The man howled, but did not let Maya go. The other one carrying Robin, stopped, and with his free hand, drew his blade.

In a blink of an eye, ten more swords were drawn, some of the guardians some of the workers on the ship. The Turmenn had barely got on the ship's deck that fights had already broken out. This was going to be a long journey.

"Release the girls or die," said Adriana calmly, her dark skin shining in the morning light.

"Are they yours?" the old sorcerer asked Adriana.

"Mine?"

"Are they your slaves?" the sorcerer asked again trying to appease the masses. Dawn was upon them, and the ships would have to leave the harbour on its tide or wait another day.

"I am sure you know the customs here," he added amused. "The sailors must be paid as well. They take coins, but love girls more."

Sara and Adriana felt horrified by the sorcerer's words.

"Take your hands off them!" Adriana repeated, turning the blade slightly. The man howled, but his voice was drowned by even louder cries.

From the other side of the harbour, three shapes ran as fast as they could, shouting and cursing.

Adriana turned to look at Maya who trembled with fright. Kann had found her.

"Stop those ships!" his voice boomed louder than thunder.

On the other ship, fights were brewing too. Some of the men took hold of girls as well. One even had the poor choice of landing his hand on Ezkiel.

Ishim's sister instantly drew her blade and cut the man's hand off.

Swords were drawn on Heimdóðr too.

Sara had to do something, or they would be found harbouring fugitives, and none of them would ever leave Caraa. She pulled out of the bundle she carried, one of the black swords the Shadows had used to slay so many of her friends and pointed it at the sorcerer's chest. The Elemental's gem clinked against the blade.

"Take the ships to sea, or you shall feel the power of these swords!"

The sorcerer stared at her stupefied, then laughed; a full, healthy chuckle.

"I do not know what you have done, but I do like you girls!" He grabbed Sara's hand and pulled her after him across the ramp and to the other ship.

"Cut the ropes!" he boomed at the men who waited for his command.

Heimdóðr and Hermóður bobbed and creaked as the thick ropes that held them secured inside the harbour were cut free. Each of the five tall masts unfurled their sails, and before Kann and his men could reach them, they were already being pulled by the rising sea.

At last, the Turmenn left behind the northern lands, months after they began their journey. But they were not yet safe. They needed to reach Stórvatn and the southern plains.

Sara and Adriana watched their groups of Turmenn cry as the ships swayed gently away from Caraa. They had escaped it, mostly unharmed.

* * *

Deep beneath the surface, Aerö, Nóór, and Ári followed the two Skrímsli through the endless labyrinth of tunnels the Hollowers dug in the aeons they'd lived in Urukk's darkest pits. They had been walking for countless days. They were tired and weak from their sole diet of lichens and water, and felt confused from the lack of time. They could no longer bear the weight of the world above them.

"Is it much further?" asked Aerö of the two Skrímsli ahead.

But the creatures had long stopped answering his only question.

They walked and ate and slept, they walked and ate and slept. No change in their surroundings, no change in their guides' silence, no change in what they ate. Aerö could feel his mind ready to leave him if it took much longer. Nóór had also stopped talking. The long journey through the entwined bowels of the world proved to cost them more than Aerö had initially thought.

Then, as they reached another cavern, large and wet, just like the other few dozen they had already seen, the Skrímsli stopped and grunted at each other. For a second Aerö wondered why his powers did not work for all he heard were the beasts' grunts, but then he realised they were not saying anything. Instead, they stood and pointed at a tunnel that opened to their right.

"There…Up…city." Aerö stared at the two, stupidly. After all the winding tunnels filled with darkness, his mind seemed unable to grasp what the Skrímsli were saying.

"What did they say?" asked Nóór with hope in his voice.

"I think we're finally there. We are beneath Ophidia!"

"Up…city," the two Hollowers grunted again then turned around and started the long journey back to their golden citadel beneath the vastness of Urukk.

Aerö called upon his father's flames to burn the place with light.

"Nóór, there is still time to stay behind. Where I am going, no Beast Lord has set foot in four millennia. They will try to stop us. They will try to kill us. Do not follow me." Ári yapped, and Nóór scooped him up. He was still small enough for Nóór to do that.

"Ári is right. We did not come all this way to sit behind and watch you get yourself killed. We are coming."

"Then what are we waiting for?" Aerö said, smiling at them.

I'm coming, Petra! He roared inside his mind for only him to hear. *I'm coming.*

The Battle of Ophidia

Oh, Goddess of Death, let this blood bless our flesh,

As you bless our souls with power.

Izanami, Queen over Oblivion, hear my prayer.

Take these souls and grant us everlasting youth, in your Kingdom of Ruin.

Nephthys, High Priestess of Death

Petra woke up to the rhythmic grunts of pain and the chime of chains coming from her right. For a few moments, she refused to open her eyes to the world that had somehow compressed itself into the dungeon they had found themselves in many days before, and from which, she felt, they had no hope to escape. Petra opened her eyes and let the cold dungeon pour into her with its chains and cages and black altars. Much like Syll and Erlend, she had grown accustomed to the lifeless bodies rotting in the many cages piled against the walls, and to the severed limbs still hanging from their shackles. Not even the black altars the three of them were chained on, managed to make Petra shudder with revulsion. The stone tables waited patiently for the captives' naked bodies to be cut so they could drink their blood. The Priestesses would enter the large room and meticulously start to peel away layer after layer of their three prisoners' skin and muscles. Every day, Petra, Erlend, and Syll woke up knowing that the Priestesses would yet again unmake them.

At Petra's right, Erlend pulled at the manacles that held his hands and legs sprawled on the black stone altar. He did this every morning without fail, his resolution to escape the place and return to his Sara was unbreakable. He pulled and shook the metal chains that held his wrists until his flesh gave way to bones. Blood gushed and splattered, but to no avail. Like every morning before this, his bones crumbled without managing to make a single scratch on his restraints. He slumped his hands, acknowledging defeat and waited for the Priestesses to come and take him apart then put him back together. With his mended wrists, he would try again the next day.

"It's pointless," said Petra, wincing at the wet thuds as his arms hit the altar. "These chains are forged with spells by sorcerers, not by humans and fire. No matter how hard you pull on them they'll never come undone."

Erlend said nothing. He would not give up his hope to see Sara again.

Syll waited patiently for Nephthys and her followers to return and perform their ritual again. She did not even bother to look at the ugly room around her. She did not know for how long Nephthys planned to use their blood, but the longer they postponed their killing, the longer she had to come up with a plan to return to the Turmenn and her Trevor.

But little did she know, that while she lay there on the black rock table thinking of him, Trevor only thought about himself. He had just abandoned his two brothers and the ones who desperately needed his help.

Petra, Erlend, and Syll waited in their own way for the Priestesses to materialise among the altars with their white skeletal hands wrapped around black blades.

* * *

Not far from Ophidia's impeccable white walls, beneath Naga's Forest, Aerö, Nóór, and Ári were already half way through the slow ascent towards the surface.

Aerö trembled with excitement at the thought of feeling the sun's warmth upon his skin. His eyes craved the uncountable colours he had been deprived of, just as much as his stomach desired food. He had been away from light and wind and rain and everything that made living above the surface so different from the Beasts' dark cave.

For Nóór and Ári, however, this would be the first time they would look upon the world from its bright outside, rather than the gloomy insides they had been born in. They, too, trembled at the mere thought of gazing upon Urukk's immeasurable vastness. But unlike Aerö, they shivered with fright.

"It will be alright," said Aerö feeling his two friends' emotions grow with every step they took. He understood their fears. He remembered the darkness that made its way into his heart the moment he was sealed into the Beasts' dark Lair. How he'd felt his mind and body crushed by the weight of the lone mountain as it hung above his head. He knew how different the Beast Lords' world was from that of the rest of Urukk. Nóór and Ári will be soon experiencing the very opposite of all he felt that day.

Nóór said nothing, but thought of the reason why they were about to leave the safety of the caves for the inescapable dangers at the surface. He dreaded the sole thought of so much openness and the perils it most certainly contained.

Aerö, too, thought of what lay before them. He put his hand beneath his shirt and cradled the red gem. Its warmth and quiver reassured him that he had made the right decision coming to Ophidia to save his grandmother. His heart filled with an intoxicating mixture of fright and excitement, of dread and longing. So long had passed since that icy night the Hound took him from Petra, that she might not remember how he looked. She probably believed that he had died those many months ago.

The two boys' thoughts wandered aimlessly as their legs did all the work of climbing. Every now and then, they stopped and looked behind at the receding darkness. Ahead of them, the tunnel slowly narrowed. There was also something else that pulled their thoughts back to their bodies and their changing surroundings — wind. Warm and dry, it carried scents of leaves and flowers, of moss and mushrooms. Aerö recognised the sweet smell of the forest immediately. Nóór did not know what his nose tried so frantically to tell him, but he liked it. Aerö could feel his skin prickle with excitement.

Another step, another gust of air rushed passed them. Another step and richer scents ensnared their senses. The two boys and the young Hound dragged their feet towards the end of the tunnel, pulled by invisible yet inescapable forces. They had no say in what their bodies did. All they could do was follow them and see where their feet took them.

At last, they seemed to see the end of the narrowing tunnel. A wall of rock filled their passage up ahead, and for a moment, Aerö's heart trembled with fright that wherever the two Skrímsli took them was not the path to the outside they hoped to find, but a dead end. But then, a sliver of bright light cut the stone in half, a crack much like the one they squeezed through to escape Undirheim. Through it, the sun's bright light poured like molten gold into the tunnel. Aerö stepped right into the raining brilliance, welcoming its warmth. Nóór, however, lingered in the darkness, too afraid of it.

"I think we can squeeze through it!" called Aerö from the swirling clouds of dust that sparkled all around him. His hands felt the width of the crevice.

"Come!" he urged his friends to join him.

Nóór and Ári reluctantly stepped into the spilling light, testing its warmth, as if afraid it might burn them.

"Are you sure you want to come?" Aerö sniggered.

"Of course," Nóór boomed, determined, after a few long moments, but his voice quivered under the weight of his fright. Then, one by one, the three of them stepped through the raining light into the thin opening inside the rock through which they could already see the bright outside.

* * *

Nephthys paced her ill-lit room, nervous and angry. Her chambers were a hallway away from where her three prisoners were being kept for her priestesses' enjoyment and delight. But despite the many days they had been offering their captives' blood to Izanami, the Death Goddess they'd sold their souls to, the boy refused to come. Valdis' command to have the Gudmaour killed before he learned his strength was not going as planned. How long would she have to wait to feel her blade slide quietly between young Aerö's ribs? How long until she could assert her right to be the Queen and King's High Counsellor?

"Not long," she hissed, admiring the many mouldy jars she had been collecting for centuries.

"Not long," she repeated, peering into the one right by the only torch inside the room. Its cloudy contents glimmered as light passed straight through. A small hand seemed to wave at her from within the thick glass prison, then a single eye and a single foot. The poor creature, whose half had been placed inside the jar for all eternity, blinked at her alive. Nephthys smiled and caressed the glass most lovingly.

"Maybe that's what I should do to Petra." Her thoughts turned to the many severed creatures still alive inside her countless jars.

But today was not that day. Today she planned to finally crack open the humans' skulls and peer inside their brains. She had long suspected that whatever made the human act as if the world was theirs, lived inside their skulls. And now, after days and days of prying open their disgusting bodies, after peeling away inch after inch of their filthy flesh without a trace of what she wished to find, Nephthys knew their heads would hold her answers.

Today, she would allow the two humans, who happened to be inside the tent when she took Petra, to die. They will show their most intimate of secrets to her and her Priestesses, and then they will be left to die. After all, Petra was the only one they truly needed to fulfil the Queen's feverish wish.

Nephthys could feel her anger morph into something far more dangerous for those who waited hopelessly for her return. Eagerness to see inside their heads and find her answers.

* * *

Aerö, Nóór, and Ári crammed themselves into the narrow slit into the wall. They pushed with everything they had, but when their feet failed to take them upwards through the shaft, they pulled themselves with their bare hands until they thought they had gone blind. A whiteness brighter than the brightest light burnt their eyes as they crossed from the dark world beneath the surface into the one ruled by the almighty sun.

The narrow shaft they had been climbing opened inside a hollow tree, but once outside its wrapping bark, the boys and Ári had no place to hide from the ball of fire blazing in the sky. They had emerged right on the edge of Naga's Forest, but a short distance from Ophidia.

Aerö let the sun's warm rays kiss his whole body before he turned to see his two companions' reaction to the outside world.

If Aerö's return to the surface matched that of his expectations and memories of it, for Nóór and Ári the whole thing was far far worse than they had dreaded as they climbed towards it.

Aerö almost burst out laughing.

Nóór held his hands pressed to his nose and mouth, choking himself to death. Aerö stared at him with a wide grin stretched across his face as his friend fought to hold himself together. Aerö knew exactly how Nóór felt, for he could hear his mind. The young Beast Lord had never seen such vastness in his life, and felt — just as Aerö did after being confined inside the narrow galleries of Undirheim — that his whole being was about to break and drift away.

Ári did not last out in the open more than a few moments. He dashed passed the two boys and back inside the hollow tree they had emerged from.

"I knew it would be large, but not even the most descriptive books come close to its vastness," Nóór gasped through his clamped fingers.

"This is just a small part of it, Nóór." Aerö grinned at his friend, enjoying his astonished reactions to everything he said.

"Then how can anybody find anything when they can't even see the edges of their world?" Ári yapped from his hiding place, and Aerö smiled even broader.

"Or smell them!" Nóór corrected himself, repeating Ári's thoughts.

"No one smells each other at the surface," Aerö felt like saying, but thought it would confuse the two who had never seen the light of day before. Instead, he led the way out of the forest and into open land.

Before them, a sea of golden sand stretched far beyond the eastern borders of their realm. Far ahead and to their right, walls of barren rock rose towards the heavens menacingly. To their left, the Taðr Sea rose and fell in the rhythm of its crashing waves. But none of Urukk's unquestionable beauties made the three, who watched the realm reveal itself, gaze at them in awe. Their full attention poured onto the city but a few hours away from them. Sheltered in the last patch of shade before their march across the stretch of desert to Ophidia, Aerö waited for Nóór and Ári to join him. Something was nagging in the back of his mind, something he ought to have remembered, but could not put his finger on. There was something about this forest that itched at the fringes of his mind. Aerö searched his thoughts for the elusive memory but failed, miserably, to retrieve it.

"So that is the place," said Nóór as he passed the last row of trees carrying Ári in his arms.

The young Beast twisted and turned to escape his Master's grip. The Hound would not be so easily convinced to walk across the desert.

"That is Ophidia, the Serpent City. Home to the Healers and birthplace of their Queen."

"And where your grandmother is being kept."

Aerö nodded solemnly. He never questioned his decision to rush to save Petra, but now, as he stood before the Healers' city, Aerö wondered how they would be able to fight a whole army. After all, they were nothing more than three impetuous and daring, but most of all, inexperienced young ones.

* * *

Heimdóðr and Hermóður sailed in tandem across a nervous sea. The Turmenn watched as the giant ships left Caraa behind and headed for Urukk's breathtaking shores south of the Wall. They creaked and swayed as they slowly conquered wave after wave.

The Turmenn had boarded the two ships in such mayhem and haste that hours after they escaped Kann and his men, they had yet to settle. Mothers searched frantically for their young ones, friends and families cried for their loved ones. The few hundred humans were on the verge of uproar.

Both Sara and Adriana, each with their group of trusted fighters, tried their best to calm the masses on their ships. Daniel, Ishim, and Ezkiel; Grov too, soon realised that, unlike the times the Turmenn rebelled against their leaders during their long march along the sea of sand, none of them had anywhere to go to cool their heads. Tempers seethed on both ships, and if not stopped, the Turmenn's burning rage would take them both apart. Sara and Adriana watched helplessly as the sea had somehow turned their friends in savage brutes ready to tear each other.

To make things worse, the Turmenn also chose to fight those who steered the wood and iron monsters they all rode across the Taðr Sea. It did not help that they still tried to take the Turmenn' girls down on the lower decks.

Even the one whom had his hand chopped by Ezkiel, grinned at her from the nest of ropes he had collapsed on, where he was now being treated by the old sorcerer. It soon became an all-inclusive brawl. Sara could not sit and watch the Turmenn fight for any longer.

"You are not a Healer," she said to the sorcerer who was in charge of all their lives until they reached Stórvatn.

"Of course I am not," he boomed looking down at his large gem swaying back and forth with the ship's rocking.

Sara did not need to follow his gaze to see the sparkling stone.

"Then allow me," she interrupted, kneeling beside the wounded man. He might be just like all the other sailors on the Elemental's ships, thinking of women as nothing more than crates they hauled across the sea, but no life, no matter how vile, should be left to die.

"Have you done this before, human?" the Elemental asked.

But Sara's eyes were focused on the one who needed her attention. The man simply lay on the coils of ropes, his body almost drained of blood, yet his eyes still followed Ezkiel.

"My name is Sara, and I need some water, a red hot iron, and some clean cloth."

The sorcerer looked at her intrigued, then nodded.

Within minutes, water and cloth was provided with which Sara skilfully cleaned the young man's wound, but when it came time to close the bleeding gash left behind by Ishim's sister, she looked around for the hot metal she had asked for.

It was the Elemental's time to show his skills. He took the sailor's arm from Sara and gently pressed his hand against his throbbing flesh.

Sara knew exactly what she had to do. She took a length of rope and placed it in the sailor's mouth. "Bite this!" she urged the man.

The Elemental then released his flames. Bright orange tongues of fire lashed between his fingers and the stub he held for no more than a second. If the screams were not enough to make the other sailors and the Turmenn sick, then the stench of sizzling human flesh took care of that. Still, the Turmenn and the seamen would not stop from fighting.

"My name is Eyþór. Thank you!" he said, staring into Sara's eyes. Then he stood up and walked towards the middle of the brawling men. None paid him much attention. But when he raised his gem above his head and let it spew its flames, they all dropped to the floor as one.

Funny, thought Eyþór as he watched his men and Sara's people clutch each other beneath his roaring flames. Before death, they were all equal.

* * *

The City of Serpents shone brightly in the sun's strong rays. Aerö, Nóór, and Ári walked towards the white-walled marvel, shielding their eyes. Ophidia was larger, taller, thicker walled than the boys imagined it to be.

"How will we get inside and find your grandmother unnoticed?" said Nóór inside his head so that both Ári and Aerö heard. The closer they got to the Healers' city, the less they dared to speak out loud.

"The truth is…" answered Aerö, shifting his gaze upon his friend, "…I don't know where she is or how to find her."

Neither Nóór nor Aerö liked how hopeless and scared his thoughts sounded.

But despite the boys' lessening courage, the Serpent City grew before them, white and bright, a diamond on the shore of the Taðr Sea. Towers pierced the heavens, bridges leapt from dome to dome, while the ring of walls that enclosed them all securely sparkled preciously. The

617

whole city seemed to have been made of the whitest, purest stone. The three young friends could simply not take their eyes away from it.

To Aerö, Ophidia resembled, somewhat, Seribu Menara with its slender towers and cobweb of roads. To Nóór it simply did not look like anything he had ever seen or dreamt of before.

"I don't think we can climb over these walls, Aerö." Nóór's thoughts drifted through the empty space. Their conscious minds burned like lamps that only Aerö was able to see. "We must use the gates," he added, pointing at a gap into the seamless ring that hugged Ophidia.

"I do not like this," whispered Aerö, looking around. Besides the Naga's Forest behind them, all his eyes could see was sand.

"Nowhere to run, nowhere to hide, and worst of all it seems too easy."

"Maybe they do not need to close the gates if they are not at war."

"But they are. And even the City of Sands had its gates closed shut despite having much stronger sorcerers within."

"Do you think this is a trap?" asked Nóór, concerned but not overly scared. He had already understood the danger they were in. To think that they could enter the

Healer's City, free their prisoner, then leave unnoticed, least of all unharmed, was naive and foolish. The chances were, they would not manage to return to Undirheim and their worried parents.

"Do you think Skel and that golden tree deceived us?" Nóór went on, but Aerö shook his head.

"While I have no doubt that Skel would happily betray us for a hand of gold, the Oak would not. I have met its kind before, and they are to be trusted. They are the last to still live by the vow they made to Skeggor." Aerö's thoughts boomed like thunder inside Nóór and Ári's heads.

"However, I do think that we are expected," he added as the three stopped before the narrow slit in the perfect wall before them. Through it, Ophidia glowed invitingly.

"Then we don't have much choice but to fight to find her."

Aerö nodded, realising the mistake he had made in bringing Nóór and Ári with him. They were doomed to die.

* * *

On Hermóður, just as on its sister ship, the Turmenn and the men who sailed the ships across the sea instantly stopped fighting at the sight of the sorcerer's flames. Despite being a hundred feet away on a completely different ship, they knew better than to anger the one who could easily kill all of them, or worse set his two ships ablaze and simply watch them burn or drown whichever they preferred.

Adriana was the only one who seemed to welcome the Elemental's orange flames. She looked around the deck for the one who shared her responsibility, and hopefully, also her life beliefs.

From across the giant ship, Ishim stared at her. They held their gaze and smiled widely at each other.

"Adriana!" came Grov's high voice. The young warrior moved through the packed deck below, his large body advancing on the path that quickly formed before him. The Turmenn knew better than to stay put and be crushed under his weight.

"There is food below and shelter, blankets too!" he said, excitedly. None of them remembered the last time they had all three.

"Very good!" she smiled at Grov, but immediately lifted her gaze to see Ishim. The young woman was no longer there.

"Make sure they do not fight for food or blankets."

Grov nodded ready to return below the deck and find himself a blanket to crash on.

"And also tell the others that, unless they have business with me or feel the need for air, they all must stay beneath the deck and rest. There have been enough adventures for us all. Let's rest before we reach the shore."

Grov smiled broadly, something he had not done in many days, not since his good friend, Taro, died, poisoned by the Greeds.

Adriana smiled back at him and thanked him for his help. With a little luck, the Turmenn would use the few days of peace they had been granted by Narrū to rest and eat and not to start fights with those who steered the ship, or with each other. Stórvatn was but a few days away, and all they had to do was wait. Ahead of them, just over the horizon, was the safety and the new home the Turmenn had been dreaming of for months.

Adriana's wandering thoughts rushed back to her as someone moved behind her. Startled, she turned around ready to pull her sword and slay whoever wished to harm her. Her hand however met Ishim's.

* * *

"Are you ready?" Aerö asked Ári and Nóór, before the three entered the Serpent City through the narrow gap into the wall.

The two sent their approving thoughts to him.

"I don't know what trap they set for us, so please be careful. We are waited for, they will be watching, and we have nowhere we can hide. We look nothing like them." Aerö added examining his ragged clothes, then Nóór's. In Undirheim's perpetual umbra, no one paid much attention to one's appearance, but at the surface beneath the flood of light, Aerö could see the truth about their mien. They looked nothing like the fighters they thought they were. They looked worse than beggars.

In any other place than this, Aerö thought, they could have played the beggar's role and walked about untroubled; anywhere, but here. Ophidia revealed itself through the slender gap before them. The city shone so brightly, their eyes hurt. Its streets fluid and clean, and filled with sorcerers dressed in the finest robes. Healers mostly, but also Elementals, funnelled through the web of streets into the many squares dotted about. Ophidia was gathering is forces.

The two of them could never pass unnoticed. And then there was Ári. A Beast inside the Healers' city would be killed the moment it dared enter. Not one of Ári's kind had put one paw inside a sorcerer city in almost four millennia.

When there was nothing else to be done but to put their feet in motion, Aerö thought to try one final thing. Without a real plan to save Petra, and on their own, they had nothing to lose. He braced himself against the bright white wall and closed his eyes.

Both Nóór and Ári looked at him closely as they felt his mind pull away from theirs.

Aerö opened his mind to the endless sea of nothingness that contained all the minds his skill could touch. He let his mind drift aimlessly on unseen waves, until he felt something inside him tremble. He took a deep breath and held it in as he imagined his thoughts morph into the shape of a spear. He pushed it through the shimmering darkness.

A crack, a tear, a cry, was all Aerö had time to notice before the obscuring veil broke, and from behind, a universe of bright-lit dots exploded. The rush of thoughts and feelings almost swept him off his feet, had it not been for Nóór to grab his arm and steady him. Aerö's thoughts were no longer drifting, but being carried by the torrent of minds. He could not focus on one, there were too many, but the same emotion burst through him: anxiousness and disbelief. The sorcerers' excitement and doubt that a rogue Elemental and a Beast Lord were about to walk straight in their midst could not be clearer. Aerö had been right. They were expected.

The sea minds pouring inside Aerö were so overwhelming, that Eldur's pendulum was ready to awake and lend its aid. Aerö could feel the gem heat up beneath his shirt. He had to make it stop, or the stone would flare once more as it had done in Woods.

With everything he had, Aerö tried to put back together the black veil that held the many minds away from his, and which himself had torn.

"Run!" he hissed between clenched jaws at Nóór and Ári. They were so close to him that the moment his father's flames would burst, they would be dead.

But then, as he prepared to feel the roaring crimson fire leap from him and char the world around him, he felt them, heard them. At first, he thought his mind and ears were mistaken, but then he saw them with his mind and knew where they were being kept. It was not only Petra's thoughts and prayers he had heard, but also Syll and Erlend's. His insides were ready to crumble at the pain they shared.

Everything collapsed back into nothingness as Aerö opened his eyes and regained his balance, only to find Nóór still holding him upright.

"What happened?" the young Beast Lord asked, concerned, but mostly excited. Nóór's hand pulled on Aerö's shoulder, shaking him like a leaf.

"I found them. I know where they are!"

"Them? Who? How?" Nóór's mind roared all the questions it could muster.

"I can hear their thoughts, just as I can hear yours. They are being kept somewhere beneath the city. I can find them!" Then without allowing Nóór the chance to shout more questions, he added "They have Petra and two others from my village. Come on!" he called as he vanished through the narrow gap and into the city beyond.

* * *

Up in their stolen tower, Arnleaf Uriel waited eagerly for his beloved Queen to return with news of the Gudmaour's whereabouts. Weeks had passed since they set in motion their terrible plans. The Queen's plan to capture Petra so that Aerö would leave Undirheim to save her, but instead be killed; and Arnleaf's to expunge the humans before they could take the news of war beyond the Wall and into the lands inhabited by men. The two were growing restless with every passing day.

In the middle of the throne room, upon the mirror-like surface, Valdis Ezelle materialised, belched out by a cloud of blackest smoke. She moved barefooted towards her impatient King.

"My Queen? What news have your spies brought from beyond the borders of our tower?" he said, standing up to meet his Queen before their velvet seats. She took his hand and sat beside him.

"Good news, my love. Good news!" she sang, delighted.

"That blasted child is on his way to meet his death! The Beasts throughout Urukk speak of his departure from Undirheim."

The King beamed at her.

"The Wolf, however, has been also hard at work. She has sent her minions from Wündalær to the Taðr Sea and all the way across the desert to the Wall. She is spreading news of war and asks all those who had answered Skeggor's call all those millennia ago, to stand by their oath and fight under her banner." Valdis spat, disgusted, the last words.

The King stared into the painted faces of their many younger selves, then turned and kissed his Queen. Her anger vanished as his lips made contact with her shrivelled skin.

"She is naive to think that anyone will follow her in the war against us! They will all scatter before our armies' might just as they did the day we banished Skeggor and his filthy kind. She stands no chance. The White Wolf will lose her throne and then her life, but before that, she will lose her son," he whispered, lovingly, in Valdis' ear.

She felt her body shiver in the rhythm of Arnleaf's calm words.

"With our armies growing every day, but one small thing remains to be decided before we send them forth," said the King, pushing away from Valdis just enough to lose himself in her dark eyes.

"We have still to find a leader for our armies, my love."

"To that, I might just have an answer," smiled Valdis at her King.

Arnleaf looked at her, intrigued.

"If Nephthys manages to kill the boy and Petra, I will grant her, her wish. She will become my High Counsellor and prove herself by leading our armies. She will claim back our lands from all those filthy Beasts and humans we allowed too long to live."

The King smiled and kissed her brow again. "So you have changed your mind about bringing him back," he asked curiously.

Valdis' eyes darkened. "I will not grant him the pleasure to walk upon the land of the living unless I have no other choice. For what he did, not even the punishment of eternal entrapment between this world and that of the dead will absolve him of his sins. He shall remain in limbo until the end of time." The Queen hissed at her King, but allowed herself to be kissed again and again.

* * *

Aerö and Nóór dashed through the narrow cut into the seamless wall and hid behind the closest building at their right. The city buzzed like a hive with the many sorcerers that moved about the city.

Much like Seribu Menara, Ophidia had been built in a circular shape with the tallest buildings gathered at the centre while towards the edges they slowly tapered off. White squarish buildings no taller than the wall they merged with, offered the needed protection to the two, who desperately tried to move unseen.

Nóór even carried Ári beneath his shirt so that the Hound would not be seen even if they were. Two boys, ragged and dirty as they were, could still be overlooked, but a free Beast inside Ophidia would not. So Nóór held a squirming Ári beneath his shirt, trying not to be seen while fighting the small creature that bit and clawed at his skin.

The boys ran as fast as they dared through the shadows that clung between the rising buildings. The further they went, the taller the buildings grew, and the clearer it became that the sun never managed to shine upon those alleyways. The two boys and the unhappy Hound, navigated through the growing dark maze of streets and passageways without a map, but instead, drawn by Petra's thoughts as to a beacon. Aerö refused to search for her again unless he had to. He had been lucky to pull the veil around the spilling minds before Eldur's pendulum stopped them for him, the way it stopped the Beasts in Woods.

"A little further and to the left," Aerö told Nóór and Ári before they even formed their thoughts.

Finding their way inside the darkening labyrinth at the foot of Ophidia's leaping towers quickly became too difficult. Nóór released the young Hound when it became clear that no sorcerers ever adventured beyond the clean and bright-lit roads and white-paved squares.

Above the three, the hundreds and hundreds of feet of bleached stone rained their heavy shadows, hiding them from view. The Healers were indeed expecting them, Aerö had heard their thoughts, but none of them seemed to know when they would appear. That was Aerö's only chance to find and save Petra, Syll, and Erlend without being seen.

At the end of another alley, Aerö had to find his bearings. Nóór and Ári watched his back as Aerö peered around the corner and along the busy street that bathed in the sun's glory. Careful so he would not be noticed, he measured how much they had already covered and how much was still left before them to the very heart of the Healers' city.

"Not far," Aerö whispered as he rejoined his friends inside the perpetual darkness that reigned in the narrow alleys the three used to cross Ophidia unseen. But no joy came from the three. They knew that the closer they were to Petra, the deeper they were inside the Serpent City and further from safety.

Looking like nothing else around it, an odd structure rose amongst sky-piercing towers resembling none of them. Its size, at least several storeys high, was negated by its rather unusual shape. A dome, a perfect half-buried sphere, occupied the place where the greatest of towers could have been built. It stood out like a blemish against the city's other shapes. Aerö knew the moment his eyes saw it; that was the place Petra, Erlend, and Syll were being kept by the Queen's Healers.

The three approached the bulbous building, careful not to be seen, pitilessly relinquishing the shadows that had kept them safe. Ahead of them, stretching down onto the dome's face like a black sliver, gaped at them, the only entrance they could see. Their only problem: that between them and the crack in the otherwise seamless structure, were the few dozen feet of bright-lit pavement and the hordes of sorcerers roaming about.

"What now?" asked Nóór peering from their last island of shade.

"We must go in somehow. They are down there, I'm sure."

"Can't you open your mind to see at least how many of them are in there with them? What if that is the trap? I think we're safer here out in the open than inside that tomb."

Aerö smiled at him, amused. "For someone who has lived all their life under a mountain, you seem very fond of the outside," Aerö sent his thoughts to both Ári and Nóór.

"I can't open my mind to all these people, Nóór. I don't trust myself to have the strength to stop it once I let them in. If my father's pendulum ignites, you two would be the first to die."

"Then what?"

"Grab Ári. We'll walk in."

* * *

Several dozen storeys beneath Aerö's feet, Nephthys was preparing to leave the comforting darkness of her room to meet her prisoners. For days she had been studying them in great detail, searching in their repulsive bodies for the thing that made them tick. Today, thought Nephthys, was the day she would finally find the answers she so ardently wished to have. Today, she would gain knowledge, not even the Healers of old had possessed. That, however, also meant that she would finally allow the two apes that accompanied Petra to die. After all, her answers lay hidden in their heads. It was time.

Nephthys' old bones trembled with excitement as she moved from her small room, down a winding corridor, and into the round chamber built specifically for Izanami's demanded sacrifices. There, upon three of the ten black altars, lay her captives. The High Priestess licked her lips as she imagined her black blade sliding smoothly into their flesh and their hot blood wash over her. She closed her eyes and cherished the sweet smell of death, soon to be exuding from their broken frames, letting herself be carried by it to her Goddess herself. But the answers she wondered about for decades, planned for months, and searched for days, were not about to be revealed to her as she had fantasised.

As she opened her eyes to revel in the terror her presence instilled in her three captives, her hand already stretched to feel their shaking frames, the alarm she had been waiting to hear for days bleared throughout the vast city above. Nephthys hissed as the ear-piercing cry announced the boy's arrival. She would see to his death and then find her answers. The two apes were going to live a little longer than she initially intended to allow them to.

The moment the alarm was sounded, Petra knew that none of her prayers made it further than the altar she was chained to. Despite her pleads and promises to Narrū, Aerö answered Nephthys' lure to come and save her. How could he believe he had the power to save her when he lacked that to even save himself? Petra shook the chains that held her put and cursed at the High Priestess.

Erlend and Syll began to rattle at their chains as well.

Despite the pounding noise and the urgency to reach the surface, Nephthys found the time to smile at Petra mockingly. Everything was unfolding just as the High Priestess and her Queen had planned.

Within moments, before Nephthys had time to reach the stairs that led above, Freyja burst inside the room, her hand already busy wielding her black blade. She stopped before her Mistress.

"High Priestess! The alarm! The boy has come!" she hissed, putting the dagger beneath her robes.

Nephthys smiled at her, excited to fulfil her Queen's most fervid wish.

Behind her, the other four Priestesses soon followed. Like pockets of darkness, they darted between the altars after their Mistress, none paying any attention to the three who seemed to have found the will to live.

Freyja stopped and looked behind at the three thrashing and yelling as hard as they could.

"I was just thinking the same…" came Nephthys' voice over the tumult of chains and yells, and the blaring alarm.

Freyja turned around to face her Master. Whatever Nephthys was thinking about, Freyja was certain that was not what she had in mind.

"I do not trust to leave them alone now that we are so close to fulfilling the Queen's request. Stay behind and make sure that traitor Petra does not manage to escape. Her punishment is mine to give," hissed Nephthys as she turned around and vanished through the room's arched doorway.

Without a chance to reply, Freyja was left behind by her Master and fellow Priestesses to childmind the three she had been dissecting every day.

"Keep quiet!" she hissed, the moment the High Priestess, and her disciples began their climb back to the surface.

Petra, Syll and Erlend shook the chains that tied their wrists and ankles even harder.

Freyja searched her robes for the blade that would comfort her nerves. "Quiet!"

But nothing could make Petra and her two companions stop from their convulsions. Freyja moved towards them with her blade in hand.

"Freyja!" Petra bellowed as the Priestess approached her.

"I said, keep quiet!" she hissed, brandishing her blade above Petra's naked body. The look upon her face of pure torment.

Seeing the Priestess place her blade upon Petra's white arms, Syll and Erlend rubbed their wrists inside their manacles until their veins got severed. No matter how hard they pulled, the chains would just not give.

Freyja placed her free hand onto Petra's brow and pushed her damp hair away from her face. The two women stared into each other's eyes for what felt like hours. Then Freyja tightened her grip around her blade and cut.

Petra's shackles came undone faster than she, or her two friends, had time to realise what had just happened. Petra stared taken aback at Freyja who was already moving to unfetter her ankles.

"You were right," said the Priestess in a low voice now that all the chain-shaking had died.

Syll and Erlend watched her just as shocked as Petra.

"We were once friends." Petra stared at her, unable to speak.

"If the boy had not shown himself today, Nephthys was determined to kill your friends and torture you until the end of days," added Freyja, undoing the last manacle.

Petra slid off the cold slab of rock, her legs too weak to bear her. The Priestess made her way to Syll.

"But now that the boy is here and the Queen's request will be fulfilled, there is no need for you to die. At least not right away. Once the Gudmaour is no longer, Arnleaf and Valdis' armies will burn Urukk to the ground. And with it every human, Beast and Beast Lord."

Every few moments, Freyja's eyes darted towards the doorway to the surface like an animal whose whole existence had been spent running away from fangs.

Within moments, Syll was freed, and her wrists healed. She too tried to stand but miserably failed just like Petra.

Erlend had stopped pulling on his chains the moment Petra's shackles came undone. All his energy was now used to pull away from Freyja's ancient claws. To him, those hands were Death's. She was the one who always cut him, peeled him, pried inside his very heart. Those hands did all the work and damage. The Priestess grabbed Erlend's feet and freed them one by one. He shook and wriggled weakly in her grip.

"Hold still!" she hissed at him as she fought to unchain his right hand. Once freed, she healed his severed wrist and set out to undo the last manacle.

Syll and Petra pulled themselves back on the altars, their legs needed more time to find their courage.

Freyja worked as fast as she could to release Erlend's last chains.

A click echoed through the room as the shackle finally came loose, quickly followed by the sound of shattered bones. The moment his left hand was free, he swung his fist and planted it squarely on Freyja's jaw.

The old Healer stumbled backwards and fell in the dimple in the ground she and her fellow Priestesses used to collect their captives' blood and bathe in.

Erlend panted as he cradled his own broken bones. "You devil!" he boomed.

"I deserved that," the Priestess croaked almost incomprehensibly with her grotesquely broken jaw. The lower part of her face hung loosely from one corner.

Both Petra and Sara winced as she stood.

"But you must keep quiet if you want to live."

Erlend was ready to show her the strength in his right fist, but Petra intervened. Freyja walked back to him and mended his broken arm.

"We don't have time for this, Erlend. She's right. If you two are to escape this place, you must leave now!"

"We? What about you?" asked Syll, staring disgustedly at the Priestess as she put her face in order in front of her.

"If the Gods have truly brought Aerö here, he'll need my help."

"You'll be killed!"

"He must survive, I must make sure of it."

"I shouldn't have freed you…" said Freyja calmly, "…but if death is what you crave, Izanami will offer it to you."

Petra tried again to stand, and for the first time in a fortnight, she succeeded.

* * *

By the time Nephthys emerged from the half-buried dome into the light-bathed streets of Ophidia, the alarm that had interfered with her search for answers was no longer needed. A restless silence fell over the bleached city of the Healers. She did not have to search the gathered masses for the one she was eager to slay. Right before the narrow slit that marked the dome's sole entrance, not one, but two boys and what it looked like a young Hound had been surrounded by a sea of men and women in black robes.

"If we don't run now, we're dead." Nóór sent his thoughts to Aerö who had been trying to measure the shimmering sea of white manes compacting around them. The sorcerers were beyond countable.

"Not yet, not until I know she's safe."

Ári, who had been guarding their backs, yapped. The boys turned just in time to see Nephthys and four other shadowed shapes emerge from the strange structure Petra, Erlend, and Syll were being held captive in. The leader smiled broadly at them.

"The Queen was right," she said to her four disciples. "The boy would not come out of Undirheim unless his loved ones are in danger." She stepped forward, closer to Aerö and Nóór, then looked intently at them both as if unsure who was the one Valdis and Arnleaf wanted dead so dearly.

"So, you must be mighty Skeggor Skalidur's heir," she hissed at Aerö after a few moments, having made her decision. "I was expecting something…well…something more. The King and Queen seem to believe you wield some unimaginable power."

The four Priestesses behind her croaked with laughter; their tattooed faces splitting with amusement.

"I've dreamt of this moment in great detail, but even in my fantasies, I did not expect this! The Gudmaour and a Beast Lord in Ophidia. We have not seen your kind in here in millennia. None of us remember the old days when you were part of the great Order, boy!" she hissed at Nóór.

"How does it feel to belong to the dying house of Skeggor? How many of you are still left? Ten? Twenty? Ha!" Nephthys roared with pleasure at the torment her tongue was inflicting.

Nóór trembled with anger.

"Do not let her cloud your thoughts, Nóór!" Aerö's mind boomed over the rumbling voices of the many gathered sorcerers around them.

There were by now, at least a thousand pairs of eyes following their every breath, their every twitch. Aerö slowly put his hand onto his chest and held his father's pendulum for comfort. Aerö knew that soon he'd call upon the gem's red flames and they would answer.

"None of it matters, however," croaked the High Priestess. "You will both be dead as will be your dear Petra. And once your heads will decorate my chambers, the King and Queen will slaughter every single human, Beast, and Beast Lord in the realm."

"Where is Petra? What have you done to them?" asked Aerö without paying much attention to the Priestess' venomous words.

"She is still alive. She has sins she must atone for before I allow her to take refuge in the world beyond. Izanami won't have her just yet." Nephthys grinned at him with pleasure, then moved closer to him, close enough to stretch her arm and grab him.

The hordes of sorcerers watched enthused at the two young boys and their Hound pet about to get slaughtered.

Nephthys outstretched her claws to take hold of the boy that had escaped Seribu Menara's most defended, inner chambers.

Aerö, however, was not about to allow her to put her skeletal hands upon his flesh. They reminded him too much of Velas and his endless lies. The moment her hand brushed against his arm, Aerö called upon his father's gem.

Nephthys howled as her fingers sizzled the moment they touched his skin. She pulled away and took out of her robes the black dagger, so many creatures had lost their lives to.

"How dare you?!" she barked, and every single sorcerer that formed the wall around the boys and Ári rumbled with the sound of produced swords and daggers.

"Great!" moaned Nóór in Aer'ös head. "Now, we cannot run."

"It's not us who should be running," and he let the scarlet flames that licked his skin, reach out for Nephthys and her minions. They stumbled backwards towards the narrow slit they had just emerged from.

Behind them, down the winding stairs, Petra, Syll, and Erlend were being freed from the chains that bound them to the altars.

"Kill them!" she hissed, cradling her wounded hand.

"Kill them!"

The four Priestesses behind their Master moved to show their devotion, but the wall of sorcerers behind the boys were closer. All they had to do was take two steps, and their sharp swords could cut their flesh with ease. And so they did.

Aerö did not need to turn around from Nephthys to the charging sorcerers behind him for the scarlet gem knew all too well what needed to be done. Aerö could feel his body steam with the increasing power the pendulum was ready to release. He closed his eyes and let the gem do all the work.

Flames whipped at the attacking sorcerers, charring their flesh and bones inside their robes. Their eagerness to slay them had been their mistake. The more they pushed to reach him, the more they failed to evade the flames. They were the ones now trapped between Aerö's roaring inferno and their zealous kin.

Nóór moved aside and shielded his face from the heat that almost set his shirt ablaze, but mostly from the smell.

Nephthys glared at them with malice.

"Try as you might you won't escape me, boy!" she croaked as the melting sorcerers behind him reared in terror away from him.

"Kill him, you fools!"

This time her four hooded followers were the ones to charge. They too had daggers in their hands, but unlike their now dead brothers, they planned to use more than their blades to slay them. They instantly began to chant.

Nóór and Ári trembled as their voices echoed from beneath their hoods.

Aerö had seen it all before. Despite Velas' pretended friendship, the old Healer had taught him more about the skills than he should have. He knew that Healers had no powers to strike down their enemies with spells like Elementals. Instead, they used poisons and venoms to cripple them so that they could then slay them with their swords. Aerö could not allow them to get close to them. He must not fall into the same trap his mother fell into when Velas used his Rana to escape the Hounds and almost killed her. Or when he offered her that cross-shaped scar upon her brow fifteen years before.

"Stay next to me!" he commanded his friends as he remembered his few nights of training with Estrelle inside her throne room. She'd told him then, that he could do something that other Elementals could not, a final gift from his dead father.

Aerö asked the pendulum for help. The gem quivered as it always did, like a tiny heart next to his own. And then he saw Eldur's incredible powers come to life through him.

The four Priestesses managed to take but a few steps when they reached a wall invisible to all. They wiped their brows beneath their hoods and looked around confused. Their contours shimmered even though they were feet away from Aerö. Then, one by one, they understood the power that made their very King and Queen, their Gods, so desperate to have him slain.

Shrieks burst through their shrouded frames as bright flames erupted from within them. They had made the grave mistake to walk straight in his trap. The moment they began their chants, the gem sent forth a wall of heat so great, the Priestesses' wet innards steamed and turned to ash. Their robes collapsed upon the ground two seconds later.

Aerö however, knew he would not manage to pull that trick again. He swayed, exhausted, as the spell took its heavy toll.

"NO! You will pay for that filth! Like your mother, like your father, and like your Petra! I will cut your soul, I promise you that!" Nephthys cried mad with rage. "Let me show you what true powers are!"

Aerö knew that whatever she was about to do was not going to be good.

Nephthys held the blade in her right hand and cut her left wrist clean. Her face did not as much as wince when the blade severed her inked flesh. Blood, thick and dark glopped from her veins onto the white stone beneath her feet. Aerö could feel the taste of fear in his mouth, and that of vomit. He had seen the ritual performed before by the High Counsellor on the cliffs of Undirheim before he and his army began their terrible attack.

"Aerö!" Nóór's thoughts flooded Aerö. "Aerö!" Nóór called again, holding Ári in his arms.

Aerö was busy following not only Nephthys' every move, but also that of the countless sorcerers moving away from them. They were scared, and they had good reason to be. If the Priestess before him wielded but half of Vondur's strength, they were all in danger.

"Be ready to fight! Leave Ári alone and find yourself a sword. You'll need it!" Aerö sent his thoughts to the young Beast Lord.

Nóór looked around among the smouldering robes and bones of those less fortunate Healers who found themselves trapped between Aerö's crimson flames and their own kind. Under a pile of smouldering robes, he found what he was after.

Nephthys glowered at them as her lips mumbled the needed chants of her terrible spell.

"Come forth, my dears! Come out into the light!"

Aerö, Nóór, and Ári felt their blood freeze in their veins. Whatever the High Priestess summoned, they were convinced they would not like.

* * *

Holding onto the black altars' edges, Petra moved towards Erlend and Syll. The three of them had been so close to each other, yet so far away, during their unwelcoming stay inside Nephthys' atrocious home.

From the High Priestess' room, Freyja returned with the three freed captives' belongings.

Petra, Syll, and Erlend were happy to finally cover their unclothed bodies. Petra smiled as she felt, inside her returned garments, the only treasure she still had.

From above, Nephthys' shrieks descended through the spiralling stairs and filled the round chamber.

Freyja's face turned whiter than the buildings her fellow Healers loved to build.

"What is happening?" asked Syll and Erlend as both stopped from forcing their shirts to slide over their bodies.

Petra's face went just as white as Freyja's. All around them, cracking, tearing, clinking noises made the four cling to the stone altars for what was to come.

"Do not make a sound!"

The cages piled all around the room began to shake, chains to rattle; then their barred doors opened.

Petra, Syll, and Erlend climbed, without making a sound, onto the black slabs of rock they'd tried so hard to get away from. No one dared to make a sound as the poor creatures that found their death at the Priestess' hand, now crawled and limped on rotten limbs back to their Master.

The three, who had but moments earlier been freed, were suddenly in no hurry to return to the surface.

Syll covered her mouth and nose as a rotten creature walked right past her. It took Syll a few good seconds to realise what the poor creature was. A boar whose spine and skull protruded from its flesh, was not so easily identified. Syll felt her whole body shudder at the smell engulfed them.

A dozen creatures crawled out of their cages and climbed the spiral stairs towards the surface. Their Master needed them.

"We cannot just sit here and do nothing!" Erlend said after a few moments. He had been subjected to so much pain and torture in the past fortnight that the thought of fighting the Priestess who took him from his Sara, was becoming increasingly appealing. He stood up the moment the last creature left the room.

"I was not planning to," said Petra, who was already standing. "But you two should stay behind or run back to the Turmenn. By now they ought to have reached Caraa."

Syll and Erlend turned to face each other, both thinking of the very same thing. Could they leave Petra behind and sentence her to certain death? Could they just walk away from the young boy, their friend, who was but feet above their heads fighting for his life? Could they?

* * *

Nephthys grinned as the voices of her pets rose from the bowels of her home.

"Kill them, my beautiful!" she hissed, as the first rotten maw emerged from deep within the pitch-black entrance of the dome.

"Ready?" Aerö asked his two companions, who now wished they had stayed behind under their lone mountain. Even a life lived in fear was better than no life at all.

Nóór nodded once, before he saw what the thin slither of darkness belched out into the light. It was too late to run now.

Boars and bears and creatures neither Nóór nor Aerö knew existed, answered the High Priestess' call. All snarled and showed their fangs the moment they were face to face with those they were ordered to tear. All looked thin and dirty, but far worse, all looked dead.

Nóór and Ári swayed spinelessly as they realised what the Priestess commanded. Unlike Aerö, who had seen the depth of the Healers' unnatural gifts, the Beast Lord and his Beast could not believe their eyes. The profanity was beyond that of the imagined. Nóór's hand slacked around the sword he had taken moments prior.

"This is against all the laws of nature," Nóór moaned, and Aerö understood the pain his friend felt. The Beast Lords were known to treat their Beasts much better than their own selves.

"We need to kill them if we want to live."

"They are already dead!" Nóór hissed, unable to comprehend the ungodliness of what was happening before him.

Aerö had no choice but to call upon his flames, or they would all be killed right then. Nóór was in no shape to fight dead creatures.

Nephthys moved away from Aerö as his body was once more consumed by flames. Then one by one, a dozen vicious creatures sped towards their prey, their fleshless jaws ready to bite them. Aerö could not defend himself and Nóór without his help.

But as the summoned creatures licked their bare-bone jaws in preparation of the feast they had been promised, Ári turned his fangs upon his lord. Nóór snapped out of the dream-like state his mind took refuge in, the moment his Hound's fangs sank deep into his flesh.

"Thank you, little one." Aerö heard Nóór say before everything was lost in the blur of battle.

Nóór's sword cut at the charging creatures summoned by the Priestess. Ári growled and yapped around his feet, biting, tearing, clawing at the putrid beasts Nephthys controlled. For the first time in their lives, the two fought side by side against opponents other than their kind. There was no more time for training, no more time for learning in the depths of Undirheim. Now they had to fight for their own lives and hope that all the time they spent inside the training grounds beneath their mountain, was enough to save them.

Aerö too, fought with every fibre in his body. Tongues of flames flew in all directions as he fended himself and his two friends from the many brutes that assailed them. Nephthys sat and watched gleefully from the shadow of the dome. Soon the boy would die just as the Queen had asked of her without the need to even lift one finger. Her pets would do it for her. Still, she could not ignore the boys' sheer strength. He had managed before to trick Arnleaf and Valdis, kill Velas and Vondur, even slaughter her four Priestesses. But his luck had run out, Nephthys decided, as she watched him struggle. They should lay down their weapons and give in to death. The quicker they died, the sooner she would return to her three captives and resume her search for knowledge.

Neither Nóór nor Aerö thought of giving up. They slashed and hit and burned away at the invading creatures. Blood soon stained the white cobbles beneath their feet as the boys, and Ári, slowly lost their strength. Cuts and bruises spread onto their skin like the tattoos the Healers had, but red. No matter how much damage they inflicted, the dead creatures refused to die again. Even Aerö's flames proved to be close to useless. Within the first few seconds of the battle, all creatures charged at them ablaze, untroubled by their sizzling flesh.

"Behind!" cried Nóór to Aerö as he drove his sword straight through a boar's exposed skull. The creature crashed into both the Beast Lord and his Beast before finally dying.

Aerö sent a flying orb of flames into the creature that tried to tear him from behind.

"Their heads!" boomed Nóór's thoughts so that the Priestess would not know they knew her demons' weakness before it was too late.

"I need a sword! The fire does nothing to them!"

"Aerö!" cried Nóór, as he threw his sword to him while he dashed at the piles of smouldering robes that once covered the now incinerated Healers. Among them, he picked up another one.

Nephthys watched the battle from her place of shade. Her creatures and the boys moved with such speed, it was difficult to see them in great detail.

"We must kill them all as quickly as we can. Once she knows we can stop them, she'll come straight for us!" Aerö urged his friends.

Ári yapped as he engaged with another beast the like none of them knew where to place. It looked to them as if a pig had somehow grown four wings. Then again, none of the creatures they fought looked much like their living kin.

"Ready?" asked Nóór, brandishing his newfound sword in front of a large deer. Its long neck asked to meet his blade.

"Ready!"

Flames flew from Aerö all around the cobbled square, as he tried to distract the High Priestess and the many Healers watching them from afar. Their swords moved up and down and side to side in a frantic attempt to slay the already dead beasts as quickly as they could. Another two went down struck by the boys' swords, the dear-like creature Nóór decapitated and a bear as Aerö drove his blade through one of its maggoty eyes.

"Kill them!" Nephthys roared as, one by one, her animated puppets collapsed to the ground, beheaded or impaled.

Nóór and Aerö, once they knew what they needed to do to stop them, killed the creatures swiftly.

The High Priestess was becoming increasingly angry at the boys' success. Every time a creature attacked the two or Ári, they sent it crumbling to the ground. Even the small Hound managed to pin one down just enough for Nóór to smash its skull.

Nephthys could not sit any longer and watch Aerö make a fool out of her in front of all the gathered Healers. She would show him why the Queen, the Goddess herself, gave the task to slay the Gudmaour to her. Slowly, she advanced towards her prey. The boys still had four beasts to keep them focused while she crept close enough to deliver her final attack. From her robes, she pulled for the last time her obsidian-black dagger.

Heads rolled, flames flew, and blood splattered on the white stone as Nóór, Aerö, and Ári sent two of the remaining four creatures back to the graves they'd crawled out of. They were exhausted and wounded, but soon there would be no more dead beasts to slaughter.

"What then?" thought Nóór as he stopped a horned creature from charging into Ári. The Priestess would be next for sure, but if they somehow managed to outlive the Healer, would the rest of them descend upon them or flee terrified? Nóór hoped the latter, as he barely had enough strength left in him to lift his sword. Aerö did not look much better either. His flames were weaker, his speed considerably slower, his strength visibly lesser.

Step by step, Nephthys approached the boys while Petra, Syll, and Erlend climbed the spiralling stairs behind her. They would not sit behind and let the High Priestess slaughter a young boy, least Aerö. Petra would make sure of it, even if it meant giving her life so that he could keep his.

Nephthys was following the Gudmaour too intently to notice her freed prisoners behind.

This was the moment, decided Nephthys, as Aerö and Nóór shattered the last two creatures' heads. She tightened her grip around her dagger and broke into a run, blade pointed at the Gudmaour's heart.

Aerö only had time to summon the weakest of flames. Nephthys' robes went ablaze, but that would not stop her. She was not afraid of dying if it meant taking the damned boy with her. Her Queen would bring her back. She put all her strength behind the blade and charged.

Nóór and Ári, who were too far to stop the Priestess reach Aerö, yelled at him, but their friend had no time to escape her spineless attack.

"Now you die!" she croaked as she pushed her dagger to meet the Gudmaour's heart.

Aerö only had a blink of an eye to dodge her killing blow. He failed. Nephthys' blade struck with full force, not in the heart as she had aimed, but in the tiny scarlet gem. Aerö could feel his father's pendulum groan from the force of the Priestess' blow. It quivered gently against his fleshy heart before it finally began to crack.

Nephthys smiled at him madly, thinking that she finally succeeded to fulfil Valdis' wish.

Aerö, however, was far more frightened by the slowly shattering gem. The village of Woods flashed before his mind's eye as he remembered the gem's stored inferno.

Hair-like cracks began to spread throughout the crystal, each hissing, as they claimed another inch of it. Then when the gem was ready to give up and fully shatter, Aerö knew he had to get his friends away from him. He looked around for Nóór and Ári. They were but feet away, rushing to save their friend, pointing their blades and fangs at the cowardly Priestess.

"No, you fools! Run away!" he growled, but his friends were now too close to stop. Aerö's eyes drifted beyond the High Priestess, drawn to the entrance of the dome. There, but moments before his own life would be taken along with that of Nephthys, Nóór, and Ári, and every other Healer in Ophidia, Aerö saw Petra step into the light. His heart stopped the moment their eyes met. After months and months of being on the run, abducted and deceived, trapped under a mountain, Aerö found himself smiling at Petra as she smiled back.

Nóór stopped, terrified, but feet away from Aerö as a globe of crimson light engulfed his friend and Nephthys.

The High Priestess laughed, excited that she would soon see Izanami. They were all going to die.

Aerö might not be able to save them, but he would roam the world beyond devoured by regret if he did not at least try. With his last moments of consciousness, Aerö asked the gem to lend him one more flame before they both departed from this world together. Eldur's pendulum quivered and produced one last tongue of scarlet fire. Aerö put his every bit of strength and will into it, then unleashed it upon Nóór and Ári.

"I am sorry!" Aerö sent his thoughts to his two friends who risked their lives for him and his dangerous quest.

The two broke into a run towards the only cover they could reach, the dark slit into the face of the stone dome. But the flames were faster than their legs. With the force of the hottest, fiercest wind, Aerö's last tongue of flame sent the two half flying, half stumbling, into the standing shapes at the entrance of the dome. Petra, Syll, and Erlend, Freyja too, went falling down the coiling stairs along with Nóór and Ári.

Then the world exploded.

Brighter than a thousand suns and hotter, the scarlet gem released all of its power in the centre of the busy city. The globe of fire that had engulfed Aerö and Nephthys grew in size and strength until it swallowed the whole of Ophidia. The Serpent City sizzled under its unstoppable force.

The world trembled, moaned and cracked above the thick stone that shielded Petra, Syll, Erlend, and the boy that collided into them and saved their lives. Then just as quickly as it started, Ophidia was still again.

The realm of Urukk, however, was just about to start to crack.

Loose Ends

Every End has a Beginning.

On Heimdóðr and Hermóður, every soul watched into the distance at the bright red sun that fell into the Taðr Sea. For most, whatever had happened on the shores they just escaped, was either a bad omen or a good sign. They had made it.

For two, however, the burning city of the Healers was a sign. They knew they had run out of time. For many weeks they lived among the Turmenn, watched them, listened to their selfish hearts; the time they wasted in their midst only enforcing their King's passion to have all of them killed. The time had come to do what they had promised.

While Ophidia burned savagely into the distance, in the bowels of Heimdóðr, a handless sailor tossed and turned in pain. Despite Sara having cleaned his wounds and Eyþór's sealing flames, the man now burned with fever. Apart from him, all others were above onto the deck staring speechless at the strange display of crimson flames.

"You don't deserve to live, filth! Even for an ape, you are revolting," said a voice coldly. The man opened his eyes and stared into the face of death. Had it been a dream induced by fever or had an angel truly came to take him from this world, the man would never know.

Hours later, his body would be found by Sam and Daniel; his heart carved out, his tongue fed to the fish.

"We need to talk," Daniel told Sara when no one seemed around. They had concealed the murder in the hope that they would somehow find out who had done it. Sara nodded as the boys explained. The boys were right; a ship with a few hundred souls housed in its belly was dangerous already, without a murderer amongst them.

As Sara stared out into the endless open, tracing the night's insidious advance, she felt nausea take her. The dream she had those many nights before finally found her. Adriana would be dead by dawn.

Hermóður bobbed alongside its sister across the Taðr Sea. Hours passed since the Turmenn, and the sailors on it witnessed the great fire claim Ophidia, yet only now with night approaching fast, did they return to their blankets in the bowels of the ship. For hours they waited, trampling over each other, for the crimson flames to appear again. None of them understood what had just happened, and none of them cared unless the fires decided to come after them. What they cared was that the Healers were no more.

"Good riddance!" spat the Turmenn as they returned to the lower decks.

"The fewer, the better!"

Adriana sat quietly and listen to the Turmenn who had lost most of the ones they loved, yet still had the energy to curse and hate whole races. Maybe that was what was left behind once everything else got torn out of their hearts. Bitterness.

Slowly, the Turmenn and the sailors returned to their cots and warmth.

Adriana was among the only ones who did not celebrate the fall of the Serpent City. She sat alone and watched the stars reflect their shiny faces in the inky sea beneath. If she but gazed upon the black horizon, she could swear the ship was flying among clouds and stars, and not onto the sea's low waves.

How could they sleep when such breathtaking beauty surrounded them? Adriana thought, as her eyes drifted towards the other ship. That too, seemed empty upon its upper deck, but Sara's figure remained.

A diamond-encrusted veil covered the whole of Urukk. The night had come. The murmur of waves beneath the ship and the whisper of wind in its sails were the only sounds Adriana could hear. All was still. All was quiet. Then Hermóður's wooden deck groaned, disturbed from its slumber under light footsteps. Adriana did not need to turn around to see who walked towards her.

A moment later, the sound of footsteps stopped, and from behind her, Adriana felt her naked neck caressed by a warm breath. Her body blossomed with emotions she never knew she could feel, just as their fingers interlinked. Under the inky cover of darkness, their bodies touched and shared their warmth.

"Come with me," Ishim whispered in her ear. Adriana could simply not resist the beautiful woman's spell. She stood up and followed her to the giant ship's dark side. There, among the stars, and more importantly shielded from any light or eyes, they kissed.

Sara spent all her time and thoughts, trying to think of any other way to catch the unknown killer. But in the end, agreed with Daniel that they could use the Elemental's help. After all, Eyþór was in charge of the two ships and was responsible for both sailors and haul.

"Who would do such a thing?" he asked as they moved furtively towards the lower deck where one of his men had been savagely killed.

Sam, Daniel, and Sara followed him as quietly as they could. They had agreed to keep the sailor's death concealed in the hope that whoever did it would go back to admire their work.

"To slaughter a man like that is cowardly, especially when he was already wounded. What creature would do such a thing?"

"I do not know," said Sara, although she had her hunch.

"Maybe he got in trouble with the other men," said Sam as he remembered how ill-tempered they had been when Sara and Eyþór made it clear that no girls were for sale.

"I am not sure of that," mumbled Sara but refused to say more.

No smell gave yet away the slowly decaying body of the man but feet away from them. Sara surprised herself as she put her hand to her mouth to stop herself from gaging. She had seen worse, but the ship made her feel increasingly nauseous.

Unseen, the four took cover amid the crates of things Heimdóðr worked hard to take across the sea. They would wait for the sly murderer to come.

Hours passed, and one by one, Sara, Eyþór, Sam, and Daniel fell asleep, rocked by the ship's soporific motion. Then, when the floor creaked in the night, they knew they had been right. All four opened their eyes to see the killer smile at the heart-less, tongue-less man. Sara's heart stopped beating as her dream and fears became true.

Before them stood, tall and proud, Ezkiel.

"Who are you?" boomed Eyþór as he flooded the ship's depths with his flames.

Ezkiel stepped backwards, startled by the four who had been waiting for her. *These apes were not as dumb as they looked*, she thought, then smiled at them. She was hoping to set the ship ablaze with every single human soul trapped in its bowels. Now she had to find a different way to carry out Arnleaf's request.

"Put down your gem, Elemental!" she hissed, gesturing vaguely with her dagger. "I am only doing your King's bidding! Lay down your weapon before you hurt yourself." Eyþór could not believe the woman's daring. Did she not know how easily he could kill her?

"Explain yourself," commanded Sara.

Ezkiel's mien morphed from patronising to disgusted. "You do not get to ask me questions, ape!" she barked, but her voice was cut sharply by the two swords that immediately pointed at her throat.

Sam and Daniel stared coldly at the one they had fought with, ate with, laughed with during their march to Caraa.

"I suppose there's no harm telling you the reason why you will be dead within the hour," she laughed, placing a finger on the tip of Sam's sword.

"You'll wish you stayed in Caraa, boy. I wonder— can any of you swim?" she croaked, amused.

"Speak!" boomed Eyþór.

"The King wants all these filthy humans dead before they reach Stórvatn. They mustn't poison more minds with their blasphemies! They must die in the name of your King. That is your God's wish, sorcerer! Keep your oath!"

"Lower your swords," he ordered Sam and Daniel after a few moments. He had an oath to keep.

The boys looked incredulous at the sorcerer. "She killed one of your own!"

"That filth was but a human, do not insult me, boy! Put down your swords or die!" he hissed as he let his flames burn brighter. If the boys did not obey, the sorcerer would burn the whole ship in his madness. They had no choice but throw their swords away.

"Eyþór, no," said Sara.

"Good!" Ezkiel smirked. "Your King will be pleased!"

"That, I somehow doubt," the Elemental said as he set his flames free onto the woman's flesh.

She shrieked in pain as she melted like wax.

"No one kills on my ships," he hissed as his King's seraph died, consumed by his merciless flames.

"Whatever you have done to bring such wrath upon you, I want to know," he told Sara who knew she owed him as much.

She nodded mindlessly, her thoughts, however, were in their entirety turned to Adriana.

On Hermóður, the night seemed to have changed most things for the better, Adriana thought, as she allowed herself to be kissed under the jewelled sky. For the first time in months, the Turmenn slept knowing that no harm would come to them; they were fed and watered. But most of all she thought of the young woman next to her. How much Adriana longed for her soft touch, for her embarrassment-laced kisses, only she knew.

The two young women stared at the vast sky in an entanglement of limbs, ecstatic to have found each other.

"Why didn't you say anything?" Adriana asked, caressing Ishim's naked shoulders. "I dreamt about this moment ever since our eyes met."

"Shhhh…don't speak," Ishim whispered in Adriana's ear.

Tarn's daughter, however, was not so easily dissuaded, or so she thought. With a swift move, Ishim climbed on

666

top of her and kissed her. Adriana had no defences against her spells.

Their lips touched for a long time, but entertaining as it was, the King's order had to be obeyed. Without pulling away from Adriana, Ishim produced the dagger she had hidden under the tarps in preparation for her kill. She had planned to slay the olive woman and then throw her body in the sea. After that, just like her sister would on Heimdóðr, she would set the ship ablaze. Two burning ships riding the sea in tandem.

The women kissed and smiled, Adriana grateful to have found her, Ishim grateful to have had her fun before she would fulfil her promise to the King. The moment had come.

Adriana arched her back so that their eyes met one last time under the jewelled welkin high above them.

"You don't have to do this," she said, full of sorrow.

Ishim stared at her, then smiled knowingly.

"Of course I do," she said brightly kissing her one last time. Curious as she was to know how did Adriana discover her plan; there was no time for words. She was already doing her the favour of a quick death. The rest of her kind would soon die the most painful of deaths. Either burned or drowned or both. Ishim felt generous.

"The very Gods have ordered your demise, but thank you!" Ishim smiled genuinely. "You've made this abominable task a great deal more pleasant. Still, the time has come for you to die." With that, she tightened her grip around the blade and sent it to take the only human life she ever liked.

"I prayed it wouldn't be you," Adriana whispered as she raised her own concealed dagger and planted it into Ishim's cold heart.

Ishim's hand dropped the blade she held, and while still staring into Adriana's tearful eyes, she collapsed on top of her.

Sara had been right, thought Adriana as she threw Ishim's dead body overboard. Someone she trusted, someone she wanted most to trust, had tried to sever her heart and actually succeeded.

Despite still breathing, despite being alive, Adriana no longer had her heart. Ishim took it with her into the unfathomable depths of the Taðr Sea.

* * *

Petra rushed over the broken bodies of her friends, of Freyja's and the boy who sent them tumbling down the stairs and saved them. She had risked so much, sacrificed so many so that her grandson would survive. And yet, despite everything she had done to keep him away from those who wished him dead above all else, Aerö walked straight in their trap, for her.

"Stupid boy!" she growled in pain as she began the long climb out of the dome-shaped tomb the Priestesses had built.

"Petra, don't!" coughed Erlend, trying to extricate himself from the entwined prison of limbs. He groaned in pain as at least one bone inside his body moved the wrong way.

"Aerö!" she cried as she pulled herself towards the smoking slit in the ceiling.

"Petra!"

"Can't you see, you fools? If he is dead, then everything we've done has been in vain. Every single one of our friends that died has been for nothing. He cannot be dead!" she cried from the edge of madness.

"Aerö!"

Petra could not believe her eyes the moment she emerged through the narrow doorway. Where once rose above the Taðr Sea the bright white city of the Healer, now a charred collection of collapsed and smouldering towers clawed at the eyes of those who had survived its transformation. Few buildings stood whole and fewer still, not burning. Petra could not see a single sorcerer alive throughout the vast spans of the once white streets that radiated from the square. She moved reluctantly out of the shade and into the columns of light that pierced the rising clouds of smoke.

Behind her, the boy that saved their lives and Freyja emerged first, then Erlend, helped by Syll. They all stared mindlessly at the utter destruction of Ophidia.

"My city! My friends!" Freyja dropped to the ground, unable to bear the sight of her home smouldering in ruin.

Syll, Erlend, and the boy followed Petra into the descending shard of light. To Petra's surprise, the boy held in his arms, a young Hound. She froze in place as she realised what had saved them from Aerö's unstoppable flames.

"You're a Beast Lord!" she said voicelessly.

"My name is Nóór. You must be Petra."

Petra's heart melted at once. Aerö had not only survived these many months, but also made good friends. She turned her eyes from Nóór and resumed her search among the piles of debris and burning robes and bones.

"Aerö!" she called again, but her voice sounded weaker. Nothing could have survived Ophidia's absolute destruction. Not even Aerö.

With the corner of her eye, she saw the tiny Beast the Beast Lord held, dash into the choking smoke. A yap called for his Master moments later.

A few feet away from them, covered in Nephthys' burning remains, Aerö coughed for air. He did not have the time to realise that he was still alive when Petra crushed his broken frame and hugged him.

"You're alive!" Petra cried and laughed. Her heart did not know what to do, to break or to rejoice.

"Petra!" Aerö mumbled coming back to his senses.

"You truly are your father's son!" she kissed his brow and hugged him dearly.

He could but cry for what had happened in the many months apart, and for what was about to come.

"The Oak was right…" he said between deep breaths of air, but only Nóór knew what he tried to say. "…coming here has caused me to lose my father." He opened his fist, and inside it, Eldur's scarlet gem lay shattered into glittering dust.

The very moment Aerö's hand revealed the dead remains of Eldur's stone, inside her robes, Petra could feel her own hidden treasure tremble for her attention. She had no choice but pull it free into the patch of light that shone between the seven who survived sure death.

"You do know when to show yourself," she mumbled as she placed the Unreadable Book upon the blackened ground.

Freyja's eyes almost jumped out at the sight of what Petra had had with her all this time.

Aerö stretched his empty hand and touched its seamless covers. The Unreadable Book quivered at his touch, then opened.

The huddled together two Humans, one Beast Lord and two Sorcerers gasped as the book's blank pages slowly revealed their message for young Aerö.

Go now, Skeggor's heir and find the home of your forefathers,

Haetta Island and their Lair await for you across the waters.

Epilogue

The serenity that ruled Seribu Menara's Inner City was short-lived. Cries erupted from the Ivory Tower's topmost chambers. The thousands of sorcerers who had been gathering for weeks throughout the Seribu Menara in preparation for war, turned their eyes upon the impossibly tall tower. There, at its top lived the King and Queen that ruled them, their Gods.

Following the angry yells, purple flames burst through arched windows like the breath of a great dragon. The strength of Arnleaf's spell made the thousands of great sorcerers below, tremble at his unleashed might.

"NOOOO!" Boomed the King as he released his flames inside the throne room. The walls covered in paintings and many silver lamps all burned and melted in the swirl of purple flames.

"How could he defeat them all? My Healers, my Priestesses, my home!" Valdis shrieked. Her skeletal hands pulled at her dishevelled hair without mercy.

"How can he make fools of us over and over again? HOW?"

"How is he still alive?" Valdis matched her King's loud roar.

"He will come for us. That damned child will come to avenge his father and claim what we took from his forefather! The boy will not stop until our Order is undone."

"Not if I can help it!" hissed Valdis from the brink of madness. "I shall bring into our service every single soul I have collected the aeons we have ruled this land. I will obliterate the whole of Urukk before I let one of his kind to rule it!"

The King and Queen were not the only ones to notice Aerö's powers flare. Throughout Urukk, eyes that knew what to look for, observed the boy's incredible power. From Undirheim to Rokksvaart to Seribu Menara, eyes turned towards the spot that marked the beginning of the last Great War.

Estrelle and her kind listened as the very mountain trembled under her son's strength.

Looinn, too, realised what had just happened as did Skel.

The whole of Urukk now collectively knew that Skeggor's foretold heir had come and had in him the power to slay Gods.

But the war had not yet started; the summoning had not been done. Until then, the many fragmented armies would need to prepare.

Oblivious to all, the ones who later would decide the outcome of the last Great War between the races of the realm, had journeys of their own to make.

As Aerö, Nóór, and Ári, whom he simply had not been able to convince to go back to their home, crossed the Taðr Sea aboard the oddest of vessels, with nothing else in sight but water and giant birds with wings so large they cast deep shadows as they flew hundreds of feet above them. And as Petra, Syll and Erlend rode the waves towards Caraa, the Turmenn followed Urukk's shores towards their journey's much-desired end.

From her usual spot at Heimdóðr's bow, Sara's eyes stayed glued upon a sparkling gem far into the distance. She had been looking for it since the ships forsook Caraa, and now, days later, Stórvatn was in reach.

"If only Erlend was here with us." She spoke quietly, her words perfused with love and sadness. She hugged herself and allowed her body to be caressed by the sea's fragrant air. So many things made sense now that she found that Erlend left her before he left the group.

"Your father would be so happy to know that you exist," she sang, touching gently, her not yet, but soon to protrude belly.

The End

Book Two

of the God-Slayer Chronicles

Aerö's journey concludes in Book
Three - The Gudmaour. Enjoy!